Blake's Reach

BLAKE'S REACH

A NOVEL BY

Catherine Gaskin

J. B. LIPPINCOTT COMPANY

PHILADELPHIA AND NEW YORK

for Moira Gaskin

PART ONE

CHAPTER ONE

JANE PUSHED HERSELF FORWARD IN THE HAY, CRANING TO GET THE
last glimpse of the coach before it vanished along the road that led
south to London. It was a day of spring unexpectedly dropped into
late February; all morning there had been showers, and the air was
sharp and clean. From the heights of Hampstead Heath the towers
and roofs and steeples of the distant capital were clearly visible—a
glittering city, and for Jane, who had never seen it at closer hand,
one possessed of a devilish, compelling enchantment which gave
her no peace.

It wasn't that life here at The Feathers was dull, or that they
didn't hear enough of London and its doings. A coaching inn on
the road to the North from London, placed strategically at the end
of the long upward pull to the Heights, would never lack business.
They heard the gossip of the capital almost as soon as it reached
the coffee shops in Fleet Street. The excellence of its food and service was well known, and, in its time, The Feathers had served many
important political figures, as well as the men and women who
made up the world of society and the Court. The Feathers was
nothing if not cosmopolitan, carrying out its business, as it did, almost on the fringe of the great city. But the fringe, for Jane Howard, was not enough.

Especially now it was not enough. London seemed to be caught
in a fever of uncertainty and unrest, and the travelers brought it
with them to The Feathers. Now, in the second month of 1792,
the fever was mounting. Its center and starting point was the Revolution in France, carried on in bloody haste and passion in the
strange unfamiliar names of Liberty and Equality. In the minds of
most people who stopped at The Feathers to eat and rest—and, if
the London papers were to be believed, in the minds of most Englishmen—there was no doubt that, sooner or later, they would go
to war with France, and in that thought lay their disturbance. War
was many things—but most of all, war was change.

The English could think back to their own taste of revolution, when the American Colonies had fought and defeated them; its memory was still bitter. But this business in France was another matter, and uncomfortably close to home. It was difficult—no, impossible—to imagine their own King, "Farmer George," stubborn and difficult as he was, with increasing and longer periods of madness upon him, being taken prisoner by his own people, and even threatened with death. Such things did not happen in England. But it was a time when strange ideas were drifting about, and it led to restlessness, and questioning. It wasn't only the travelers who stopped at The Feathers who talked of the disturbances and the new ideas. They were on the tongues of the villagers as they sat over their ale. Now it was possible to hear mention of war and revolution mixed with the peaceful talk of crops and weather and the enjoyable scandals of the countryside.

Jane heard the talk as she refilled tankards, or helped Sally Cooper, the innkeeper's wife, serve an elaborate dinner in one of the private rooms. She listened, and thought back on what she heard, and it served only to increase her own personal restlessness. The times were stirring, or was it simply, she wondered, that spring was upon them unseasonably?

She settled back in the hay, and loosened the shawl she had thrown about her shoulders. It was spring, and yet another coach had continued its journey on to London, and, as always, left her behind. She looked at the black oak beams above her head and sighed—a rebellious sigh that went only halfway to expressing what she felt.

The loft was as still as a church mid-week, but Jane guessed that she wouldn't be left long to enjoy its stillness. Sally frequently turned a blind eye to her absences, forgetting to notice that the key to the outside storeroom was gone from its hook in the kitchen. But within the hour a coach was expected from London, bound for the North, and the usual rush to serve the travelers and get them on their way would begin. Jane knew well she couldn't be spared, and so when Sally's deep voice calling her name came floating across the stable yard, she would descend the ladder reluctantly, and exchange the smell of dust and apples and hay for the stronger smells of brandy sauce and pork slowly roasting on the spit before the fire in the kitchen.

Jane didn't dislike The Feathers, but it irked and frustrated her to be continually on hand to serve and help to speed on the travelers, constantly watch their departures to places she had never been, to have to stay while they moved on. The worst times were when coaches from the North started on the last stage of their journey south to London; her heart followed them with a badly concealed longing and envy, and in the kitchen she would bounce the copper pots on the range, or knead the dough, her arms covered with flour to the elbows, with unnecessary energy. These were the times that Sally's three daughters, Prudence, Charlotte and Mary, had learned that Jane's temper was not to be trusted, and they stayed clear of the sharp side of her tongue.

It wasn't possible to live in a coaching inn, especially one on a road as much traveled as this one, and not share a little in the lives and personalities of the passengers who stumbled wearily from the hard-benched coaches at all hours through the day and the night— the long twilight evenings of the summer or the winter nights when the horses came into the yard caked with mud, and icicles hung inches long from the carriage lanterns. Jane had seen and observed them all . . . the humble ones, the curates in shabby black or the more prosperous parson with tight gaiters, merchants' clerks, governesses—careful of their dignity even when traveling in public coaches—sailors going home on leave. The rich rode in their own carriages, some of them velvet-lined and silk-curtained, the ladies wearing large hats and clutching miniature dogs on their laps, the gentlemen with waistcoats of wonderful colors, and hands that flashed with rings. Jane's eyes were on them ceaselessly as she moved about her tasks, her mind storing up information about worlds she knew only by words dropped carelessly as she poured the wine. Every kind of person came to The Feathers, and The Feathers endeavored to serve them all to suit their needs and the size of their purse. The demands for food and ale, for fresh bed linen and warming pans were endless. Jane's body was as strong and supple as a cat's, but by candle-lighting time, her legs ached dully, and she understood why middle-aged Sally dropped on the kitchen settle with sighs of exhaustion. If you had to work—and Jane wished she didn't

—The Feathers was a good place to be, with abundant and good food, and brisk gossip to go with it. She always enjoyed the gossip— a whispered piece of scandal about the young baronet who sat over his wine in the front room, tart observances on the manners and airs of the lady whose coach had just rolled away. In a sense gossip was information, and Jane had a great curiosity about things that even remotely touched her life.

But there were times when she had thoughts that weren't to be gossiped about—that couldn't be shared with Pru and Lottie, or even with her favorite, Mary . . . thoughts that disturbed her, and made her restless, thoughts that caused her eyes to follow the coach down the road with greater keenness. There was no way of communicating these things to Mary, though she had the feeling, sometimes, that Sally knew them without being told. On these days she waited until the quiet of the afternoon, then she crossed the yard, ignoring the glances of the stable hands, and climbed the ladder to the loft, where the loose hay made a couch for her. Here she felt secure to do as she pleased—free to enjoy the hint of warmth in the breeze that came through the gap in the wall, to kick off her heavy shoes and wriggle her toes against her coarse stockings—free to close her eyes and think aloud the thoughts that couldn't be spoken elsewhere.

Today her mind followed a track which in the last months had become routine—though with the remembrance of last night's angry scene with Sally and Tim Cooper to sharpen it. Yesterday had been the twenty-sixth of February. Sally was too busy to keep close track of passing time, but by her rather loose reckoning of the year Jane had been brought to The Feathers as an infant, February twenty-sixth, 1792, was Jane's eighteenth birthday. Her dark brows knitted sharply over this. At eighteen most other girls had married and already christened their first squawling infant at the parish church. Eighteen was almost on the shelf . . . yet here she was— if not a beauty by the standards of some of the ladies who called at the inn, then at least more than able to draw and hold the glances of the men—with no one she considered worth marrying in sight.

It was over this that Tim had quarreled with her—Sally less violently taking his part. It was well known in the village that Jane could marry Harry Black at a day's notice, if she would have him. The trouble was that she didn't want him—and she didn't know what she wanted in his place.

The thing that puzzled everyone, Jane included, was that Harry Black stood for such treatment as she gave him. It wasn't as if he were of no importance, or had nothing to offer her. Harry was a giant of a man, famed for his strength through all the neighboring villages; he was blond, thick-necked, blue-eyed, with enormous hands which were slow and heavy in their movements. If Harry leaned back in a chair it broke beneath his weight; when he wound a clock it inexplicably came to pieces. He had regular, good-looking features; he bore himself erectly and was proud of his physical appearance. He was also boastfully proud of the success he had with women. Apart from this, Harry was the only son of Thomas Black —and in the village this meant something. Tom Black owned the most prosperous farm in the whole district, and had built himself a fine red brick house which was almost as large as the one belonging to Sir George Osgood; he owned and operated a brewery, and there was talk that he was doing some trade with merchants in the City of London. Tom Black was a man of means and authority, and Harry was his only son.

It followed that Jane was a very foolish girl to ignore Harry as she did. Tim Cooper went beyond that, accusing her of other and less creditable ambitions.

"It's bad blood!" Tim had raged at her last evening. "You'll turn out like that whore, your mother!"

"Hush! Tim, hush!" Sally said quickly. "What Anne Howard does is her own concern . . . and Jane's no need to account for it."

Tim bit at his pipe angrily. "You've high-blown notions, girl . . . notions that only belong with them as can afford them. Get yourself a dowry before you look beyond Harry Black." Exasperation seemed to choke him. "Why . . . why, who are you, when all's said and done? Nothing but a bit of a serving girl at an inn, and Harry could look much higher if he chose—and find a girl with a penny or two in her pocket, to boot!"

Stung and irritated by pressure which had been building over the last months, Jane became haughty. "Tom Black started as a com-

mon laborer, and I'm more than well enough born for the great
Mr. Black's son! My mother and father were gentlefolks!"

"Your mother's a whore . . . and your father died in prison! And
don't you forget it, miss!"

Jane writhed in the hay at the memory of it. They always spoke
of bad blood when her mother's name was mentioned. They used
the words with certainty, too, for the whole parish had known
Anne's history from the day she had arrived at The Feathers with
Jane to leave her in Sally's care. Anne had been twenty then, a
vivid young redhead whose clear beauty made strangers gasp. She
was the widow of Captain Tom Howard—"Merry" Tom Howard
they called him—who had died four months before in the Fleet
prison, where his creditors had finally put him. Two things were
plain: Anne hadn't been bred to work, and she had no money. A
young baby was obviously a hindrance in this situation, so Jane was
brought to The Feathers. She made no secret of where the money
came from for Jane's support: already she clung on the arm of the
first of her lovers, and she wore the silks and velvets she loved. There
were pearls about her throat.

Anne was as gay and exotic as some brilliantly plumaged foreign
bird; she was clever with cards and conversation—good-natured in
a careless fashion, and generous in a foolhardy, spendthrift way. No
one ever saw her wearied or subdued; late at night when others
were heavy with wine and sleep, her wit and spirits were as sharp
and pointed as over the noonday meal. Anne hated to waste time
in sleep; she was happiest to see in the dawn with cards and good
company.

Over the years she appeared occasionally at The Feathers, and
Jane came to look forward to her visits as she did to the coming of
spring at the end of a hard winter. She was dazzled by Anne's
beauty and vivacity, by the clothes she wore, the sound of her laughter; as she moved and talked she carried with her the breath of a
gay, cosmopolitan world. Anne was completely selfish, but that was
a failing Jane found easy to forgive. Hopefully each year Jane examined herself in the mirror to try to discover a closer resemblance
between them; when she remembered, she aped Anne's manners,
and the way she spoke. It was safe to imitate her; Anne had been
well born, and her air of breeding was unmistakable. What puzzled

and frustrated Jane was that Anne would never, even under pressure, speak of her family and background. It was the only aspect in which Anne ever disappointed her daughter.

Sally Cooper was disapproving of Anne's mode of living, and what she called her "giddyness," and yet she was quite as helpless as Jane under Anne's spell. They both left their tasks unattended to listen to Anne's lively chatter. The talk was of men, always different men. They came and went in Anne's life, rich and powerful men—some that were merely rich, and a few that attracted her for their own sakes, and were no profit to her at all. She could be prodigal of affection, as well as greedy and grasping for material returns. Men there were always about Anne—but none married her.

Sally would shake her head. "You're no businesswoman."

"But I'm lucky at cards," was Anne's reply.

When Anne fell in love finally she blossomed into a new and startling beauty, a mature beauty; even a stranger, watching her speak of John Hindsley would have known that she was in love. He was a viscount, and reputed to be one of the richest men in England. He paid Anne's debts, and gave her a small, elegant house in Albemarle Street; she wore exquisite jewels. She came, radiant, one day to The Feathers. One look at her face told Sally and Jane her news.

"Johnny and I are going to be married! Lord knows, I don't deserve to have him love me—but this is one time when I'm lucky in love as well as cards!"

The luck ended too soon. They read in a newspaper that Hindsley had been drowned in a river on his estate in Hampshire. There was no word from Anne, and she didn't appear at The Feathers; they felt her anguish in her silence. Then months later came a brief letter. Jane had never forgotten its opening lines.

Two weeks ago I gave birth to Johnny's son. I have called him William. Johnny was drowned two days before the day we had set for our marriage, so William doesn't inherit.

Sally looked at Jane with stricken eyes. "Hindsley's bastard! What will she do now, in Heaven's name!"

It was two years before Anne came back to The Feathers. Still beautiful, still with her restless vivacity, but there was a shadow of weariness in her laugh, and her eyes were not so warm. She did not

bring William with her, and when Jane asked about him, she replied
briefly, "He's a darling child—and too precious to be jolted about
in a carriage just yet." Jane, diffidently, asked if she might come to
London to take care of him. Anne gave a little smile and the
warmth returned fleetingly to her face. "You're too young to take
care of William—but soon you shall come to London to pay us
both a visit."

Jane lived through the next years in memory of that promise. She
applied herself with greater zest to the lessons that Anne paid for
her to have with old Simon Garfield, the retired schoolmaster.
Books and learning bored Jane somewhat; she could read and write
with fair ease, and add up the accounts at The Feathers. Beyond
this she had no accomplishments—but she paid rapt attention to
Simon because it had suddenly become vitally necessary that she
should be able to speak with the refined accents of the ladies who
stopped at the inn. Anne should not have cause to be ashamed of
her when the summons came to go to London. Simon, who disliked children, particularly girls, tolerated her, and taught her with
a certain efficiency, even trying to give her a smattering of Latin,
because he was well paid to do it. The lessons stopped when Jane
was fourteen, because by that time Simon was owed so much money
he refused to open a book again with Jane until settlement came
from her mother. Jane had almost stopped believing that Anne
would send for her.

About the same time one of the real delights of Jane's life vanished also. Years before, generous in a flush of prosperity, Anne
had sent a pony, Jasper, to The Feathers. Anne herself was passionately fond of horses, and rode superbly. It was the only accomplishment of her mother's Jane copied with ease. She was without
fear of horses, and sometimes in the early morning she rode, in
borrowed breeches, astride Jasper on the Heath. When the money
from Anne began to dwindle, Tim Cooper good-naturedly paid the
feed bills rather than curb Jane's pleasure; Jane attended herself
to Jasper's grooming. But in the end even Tim's patience ran out,
and Jasper had to be sold. For Jane there was nothing now but the
stolen joy of mounting, for only a few minutes, some of the horses
stabled for the night at The Feathers.

The money grew less and less, and finally stopped. Anne wrote that she had been ill, and that the doctor's fees were enormous. So as the months went on, Jane fell gradually into the role of a serving girl at The Feathers. She had learned from Sally how to cook, to sew, how to churn butter; now she learned how to sell and serve a good wine to a discriminating traveler, and to substitute an inferior one when she knew it didn't matter. She already knew how to groom and harness a horse, and from years of listening to it, she also had a fine command of stable language, which she was careful to keep hidden from Sally. She became, in a sense, a fourth daughter to Sally and Tim—sharing the hard-working routine of The Feathers, sharing the bed of the eldest girl, Mary, and sharing, also, the undemonstrative affection they each had for the others.

Anne wrote only rarely, always complaining of lack of money. Vaguely Jane still cherished the notion that some day she would be asked to come to London. Anne still lived in the house Hindsley had given her. There must be some way, Jane reasoned, in which she could be of help to Anne, even if it were to take the place of a servant. She read and reread the few books that were the relics of the days with Simon Garfield; she tried desperately not to let her voice slip into the broad accents of Sally and her daughters. She grew weary of the waiting, conscious of her developing body, conscious of the stares and the talk of the men she served at The Feathers, forever conscious of the time passing. She was always at hand to witness, with longing, the departure of the coaches for London.

The day after her eighteenth birthday she lay in the hay and thought that there must be something more for her than to marry and live and die without stirring outside this one village. There must be something more than Harry Black—but she didn't know what it was to be, or how it would come.

2

Motionless, Harry Black watched the door of the storeroom. His broad, heavy shoulders rested against the stable wall. His attitude suggested that it would have been an effort of will to straighten himself and move, but his mind was busy as it seldom was, flooding

with images which brought a flush to his fair skin, and made him
swallow jerkily.

He had glimpsed Jane as she entered the storeroom. Without
thinking he had started to follow her—and then retreated, cursing
his own hesitancy. He wiped his clammy hands against his breeches,
and swallowed again. Every instinct urged him to go to her, to take
advantage of her being alone to press the claims he had been making for these six months and more; he told himself that if he went
now he might be permitted to touch her, hold her body close to
him, might kiss her, might even wring from her a promise to marry
him. He thought of all this, and still he stood rooted to the spot.
He felt himself tremble, and wondered dully what had happened
to the strength which made him feared and respected by every man
and boy in the village. His determination and his strength both
seemed turned to water before this slight girl, whose glance held
only contempt for him.

Harry clenched his fists, and his wanting her was a slow pain
which burned through him. His mind never encompassed tenderness or love; he knew nothing of his feeling towards Jane except
that he wanted to possess her. He had no knowledge of her as a
person, for they had never talked together with any intimacy. All
he knew was the evidence of his senses. He knew the sensuous,
provocative lines of her body, the faint fragrance of her skin; for
many hours, as he had sat in the kitchen of The Feathers, his eyes
had followed her movements, rested on her shining red hair, her
soft young curves.

There were times when he hated Jane. She was making a fool
of him—he was Harry Black, the only son of a man who could have
bought up most of the village; he was strong, and he knew that
women called him handsome, and came easily to him. There were
plenty of girls in the village who were comely and were willing to
walk on the Heath at night with him—he was proud of the fine son
he had fathered a year ago by a girl over at Thornton. There were
even girls who could have brought him a little money in marriage,
and who were fitting matches for Tom Black's son. There were
many possibilities open, but like a fool he must turn his eyes on a
serving girl who had no possessions, who had not even the dignity
of being the innkeeper's daughter. Not a penny to her name, the

child of a high-class whore. But her lips were red and sweet, and
she walked like a queen. He knew she was conscious of no honor
in having his offer of marriage made to her. Her rebuffs filled him
with rage, and still she attracted him beyond his power to understand.

Voices in the stable close by reached him, and he jerked his head
round. He did not want the two young stable hands to come out
and find him. They would know why he was there; they laughed
at him behind their hands for letting a serving girl play him as if
she were a great lady. They knew his long hours of silent waiting
in the kitchen—and they knew that Jane didn't walk on the Heath
with him. It was almost as bad as the taunts his own father gave
him.

He straightened suddenly, and walked to the door of the storeroom.

Inside, the afternoon light was soft, and there was no movement
to tell him of Jane's presence. He shut the door with what was,
for him, unusual gentleness.

"Jane! . . . Jane!" His voice was hoarse as he called.

He hadn't expected an answer from her. His eyes flickered over
the accumulation of junk littering the floor, then he went quickly
to the ladder that reached to the hayloft. When he was halfway
up, her head appeared suddenly over the edge. She was lying close
to the opening; her greenish eyes stared at him hostilely.

"What are you doing here?"

"Damn you! I can come if I want to." He had forgotten that
he meant to be gentle with her. He climbed the last rungs, and
knelt there, for the moment speechless with anger and emotion.

"Why can't you leave me in peace!" she said irritably. "My head
aches, and my legs ache, and in two minutes I'll have to be in the
kitchen to help start the supper. . . ."

He looked at her, and his rage made him want to slap that scorn-
ful little face. He made a vague, ineffectual gesture towards her;
she behaved as if she didn't see it. Those strange green eyes of hers
under dark, upward-slanting brows, were fixed on him unmovingly.
She was a beauty—they said she looked just like her mother, who
had captivated one of the richest men in the country . . . like
mother, like daughter. He wondered again, as he had often done,

how she would be in bed. It was an image that stirred perpetually
and pleasurably in his mind, and to see her there in the hay evoked
it strongly. It was always said that the red-headed ones were fierce.
He hoped it was so.

Jane watched him carefully, watched his tongue flick over his lips.
His blond, good-looking face was flushed; she could even see the
pulse at the base of his heavy throat leaping. She had seen his gesture, and now he shook his head quickly from side to side, as if to
thrust away her words.

"Jane . . ."

She hated the harsh sound of his breathing. She put her hands
on the floor and pushed herself back a foot or two.

"Jane, they told me it was your birthday yesterday. I've brought
you . . ." He thrust his hand into his pocket. "Look what I've
brought you!"

In spite of herself she craned a little, but he kept his fist closed.
He saw her action at once, and some of the tension left him. This
sign of interest from her put him in the position of superiority he
should properly have held over her. He closed his fist more tightly.

"Do you want to see it, Jane—do you? Come here and I'll show
you."

She was immediately wary, and the look of indifference closed
down on her face again. "I don't care," she said shortly. "It's nothing to me."

"Isn't it?" Suddenly he opened his hand. In it lay a tiny locket
of a blue stone that Jane imagined must be turquoise. He began
to swing it on its fine gold chain.

"Pretty—isn't it pretty? Would you like it, Jane?"

She said nothing; her fascinated gaze rested enviously on the
locket. Her small wardrobe held nothing in the way of adornment,
and this was the first time in her life any had been offered to her.
She pictured herself wearing it, and treasuring it. With all her heart
she wanted to stretch out her hand and take it. Then she glanced
from it to Harry's face, and recognized his air of confidence.

"No—I wouldn't like it." She drew her knees up under her chin,
and turned her head away with a gesture of finality.

The action was a last goad to Harry; he flung the locket into
the hay. He felt that he hated her more than he had ever hated

any thing or person in his whole life—because she scorned him, because she looked untouched, and yet her body was a passionate,
living thing, and her hands and lips were strong and exciting. He
wanted to force himself on her, and then be finished with her; he
wanted to tear down, violate, use, even destroy.

"Slut . . . little bitch." Very deliberately he pronounced a string
of obscenities.

She looked back at him, her head darting round in a swift movement. For the first time she felt fear. Her lips puckered in an attempt at a smile; it was a grimace which showed her teeth.

"Harry . . . don't take on so!" She attempted to placate him.
"You shouldn't have bought the locket—your father will be angry. . . ." Her voice trailed off. He didn't even hear her words. She
watched him begin to crawl towards her—slowly as if he didn't care
how long it would take to reach her, because he was no longer
uncertain.

She looked around her, and there was no escape, because already
she was too close to the edge of the loft, and Harry was between
her and the ladder. The looming bulk of his body was full of menace; she knew she had made the mistake of treating him once too
often as a fool who could be laughed away. He came on towards
her with a kind of quiet purposefulness. At the last he moved
swiftly. He threw her back on the hay as if she were a featherweight
—angrily and cruelly.

The world seemed to slide towards darkness as she felt his great
weight press upon her—her whole vision was filled by him, the sunlight blotted out, the sweet scent of the hay no longer in her nostrils. She could smell the male smell of him; her lips tasted of his.
Then there was another taste; there was fresh blood in her mouth
from the wound his teeth inflicted. A helpless rage swept over her,
rage that she had so misjudged him, rage that all her foolish, im-
practical dreams had ended like this, and that she would be Harry's
wife, married with haste and resentment because of the fear of having his child—or even if there were to be no child, Harry would
only need to tell Tim Cooper what he had done to her and Tim
would see her wed as soon as was decent. She tried to cry out, but
only a harsh croak came past her lips; his weight made it nearly
impossible to breathe. She poked at his eyes, tugged savagely at

his hair, but he didn't seem even to notice. Clumsily he grasped
at the bodice of her gown, tearing it swiftly to expose her left breast;
she felt his lips urgently against it; his thigh moved and pushed
harder into hers. She fought to keep his hands from her skirts, but
he shook her away, all the time plucking at her petticoats and stockings. Then she felt his fingernails against her bare flesh, and there
was pain. Her breast also hurt, and she wondered if his teeth had
cut her. She closed her eyes, and imagined a whole lifetime of this
—pictured herself gradually learning to respond because there was
no satisfaction elsewhere, and because the future held nothing
different.

His weight pressed on her unbearably. She opened her eyes,
again and gave a last, desperate heave sideways. Her movement was
unexpected, and he rolled with it. For the space of a second or two
his great frame seemed to be poised. Then he started to grab at
her frantically; he lifted his arms, and grasped at her shoulders for
support. She sensed what was happening, and flung herself swiftly
backwards from the edge of the loft. His hands slipped off her. He
thrashed wildly in the hay, but he had no agility to maintain balance, and he was already more than halfway over. A flurry of hay
rose in the air as he disappeared, and she heard his body strike the
ground below.

For a moment she lay where she was, drawing in great mouthfuls
of air, feeling the sudden coolness of clammy sweat breaking all
over her. Then she rolled over and peered down.

Harry was directly beneath her. The fall seemed to have stunned
him; he had lifted his head a few inches from the ground, and was
moving it slowly from side to side. His eyes were open, but there
was no comprehension in them. He gazed about him stupidly; his
glance rested on Jane above him, but he gave no sign of recognizing
her. She dropped back in the hay and reveled in the wonderful
relief of knowing that he was moving, and alive. Then she heard
him moan.

By the time she climbed down the ladder, he had managed to
raise himself onto one elbow. He still looked dazed, but now his
face wore the tightness of pain.

"Harry—are you hurt? Are you?"

She squatted beside him, but he didn't take any notice of her.

With cautious fingers he was feeling the upper part of his right leg. Jane drew in her breath when his fingers touched his knee; then the agony was quite plain on his face. She was nearly sick when she heard the grating sound as he gingerly prodded his shinbone. In sudden panic he tried to move, and the fractured bone broke through the skin. They both stared at the blood which started rapidly to stain his stocking.

The sight of the blood seemed to unnerve him; he had not uttered a sound except for that single moan. Now he struggled and tried to pull himself to a kneeling position on his uninjured leg. His face blanched with the effort, and he collapsed again, the sweat standing out on his face and neck.

Jane put her hands on his shoulders to press him down.

"Be still, Harry—be still! I'll go and bring someone. . . ."

He turned his head, and seemed to be aware of her for the first time. His tight lips stretched back over his teeth.

"You!" he grabbed her arm savagely. "*You* did this!"

She tried to pull away. "I didn't!"

"Look at it!" His tone rose almost to a shout. "Look at my leg! I'll be a cripple . . . I'll be on crutches—*me!*"

"No, Harry! No!" She was panic-stricken, struggling to tear his fingers from her arm. "You won't be a cripple! Doctor Crosby'll mend it—he'll bind it up with two sticks, and it'll be straight."

"No one ever walked rightly again on a leg snapped in two— I'll be worse than the greatest weakling in the village. And it's your fault—you bitch!"

Suddenly he swung out with the back of his hand. She ducked, and the blow caught her fully across the left eye. Blinded, she stumbled back out of reach.

She squinted down at him. "I didn't do it—I didn't harm you, Harry!" Her voice rose in a wail of despair.

"You did, you bitch . . . and it'll be a long day before you forget it. There's more ways 'n one to skin a cat, and even if *I* can't give you what you deserve, you'll see what my father will do."

Jane didn't miss his meaning. Everyone knew that Harry's father had the ear of the local magistrate, Sir George Osgood. Suddenly she realized it was not Harry's rage alone that threatened her. He was only a young and dull-witted man; but his father yielded power

—and she was a serving girl at The Feathers, with only the doubtful protection of Tim Cooper, whom she suspected owed money to Tom Black, behind her. She looked fearfully at Harry's shattered knee, and the unnatural angle at which his leg lay. She had heard that the law could put you in jail or even transport you for breaking another person's nose—what was the punishment for crippling a man? In his furious threats she suddenly felt the menace of prison ships, and Botany Bay.

Harry was turning again, looking around him as if he were about to shout for help. Urgently she bent towards him.

"It wasn't my fault—I swear it wasn't! I didn't know we were so close to the edge. I swear to God I didn't!"

He looked at her with his face full of pain and rage. "If *I* must go dragging my leg about for the rest of my days, I'll see *you* don't go easy, either, curse you! I'll see that you don't forget Harry Black. You think you can throw back the present I bring you? I'll make you wish you'd crawled for it on your knees!" He stopped, exhausted with the pain and effort.

She backed away from him, numbed with fright. Her shaking fingers tugged clumsily at the latch. She tried to mouth words to soften him, but she could say nothing. The late sun washed over her again, and she looked at it, bewildered and unbelieving that it should still be there. She clutched her torn bodice and started to run across the yard. Before she reached the kitchen she heard Harry's shouts.

As Jane entered, Sally paused in her task of basting the poultry on the spit. A look of alarm crossed her face.

"Why, child—what is it? What under Heaven has happened to you?" Her gaze took in the torn bodice, Jane's dishevelment. As she put down the basting ladle the noises in the storeroom reached her.

"Jane—what's going on?"

Already the two stable boys had gone to answer his cries. Jane had a sense of pressures closing in about her; she felt the beginning of a frightening chain of events she had no way of stopping. Abruptly she seized Sally's plump hand and pulled her towards the pantry, then closed the door quickly behind them both.

"I have to tell you first. In a few minutes Harry will be in here screaming lies about me, and I want you to have the truth."

Sally's florid face grew still more flushed as she listened. She made little clicking noises with her tongue while Jane talked. At the finish she shook her head despairingly.

"I'm not saying he can set the magistrates on you, Jane—but I'm not saying he *can't*, either. Tom Black's a mean man when he's aroused, and there's no telling how he'll take it—Harry being his only son, and all. And there's no witnesses to say that you didn't entice him up to the hayloft . . . and that being the case, a man would be entitled to some—" A sharp look crossed her face. "You *didn't* entice him up, did you?"

Jane gave an exclamation of disgust.

Sally held up her hand. "All right, Miss High-and-Mighty. It might have been better for you if you had!"

Jane wrung her hands. "But what am I to do? That's the story he'll put about, for certain, and when he does—"

Sally cut her short. "There's only one thing to do. I'm not saying it's the right thing, but it's all I can think of."

"What is it?" Jane demanded.

Sally hesitated, her broad, rough hands outstretched for just an instant in an uncharacteristic gesture of indecision. It wasn't one thing she was thinking of, but many. The first of them was Jane's safety, and Sally hadn't lived here all her life without learning how far and how powerfully in this district Tom Black's influence could stretch. But there was another aspect of the matter that troubled her, and which she didn't try to put into words for Jane. From this point onwards she knew that Jane would have no use for The Feathers, and The Feathers no use for her. Whatever the outcome of Harry's threats, Jane's life would be a misery in the village, and The Feathers would be housing someone who had suddenly become hostile to those about her. In this final and savage rejection of Harry Black, Jane had placed herself beyond the sympathies of the people who had accepted her as part of their world; she had rejected The Feathers as well as Harry. She had, as plainly as if she had spoken, told this small world that she had outgrown it. The alternatives to The Feathers were uncertain, and they might hold a more distasteful future than Jane had even now. Sally knew

Jane thoroughly, knew her as willful, proud and, as yet, unchastened by life; she loved her also, perhaps even more than her own daughters because Jane demanded a different kind of love. Her heart ached at the thought of what she had to do.

"Come here with me." Sally flung open the pantry door. She strode across the kitchen, and reached for her shawl which always hung behind the door. "Where's yours? Well, never mind that now! Quickly, put this on! It'll cover you up a little for the time being—you're such an indecent sight, you'll have everyone on the highway stopping you."

"The highway?"

"You're terribly slow-witted, Jane, for someone who's in trouble." Sally was already reaching down from the tall dresser the copper jug where she kept a little money, out of Tim's sight and knowledge. She bundled it into her handkerchief and thrust it into Jane's hand.

"You must go to your mother, of course. She'll surely have friends who'll help you if Tom Black brings charges. And Master Black'll not be so quick to act if he thinks you've someone behind you, by the same rule."

"Oh, Sally! . . ."

"Quickly now, before Harry has the whole house listening to his woes. I want you out of the way before Tim starts arguing the whole thing."

A brief kiss on Sally's cheek, a briefer glance at the open door of the storeroom where she could dimly make out the figures of the stable boys bending over Harry; then she was on the village street, running and keeping the shawl wrapped well about her. The village was past—familiar houses she had known all her life. Then the open fields again, and the dip of the road southward.

She slowed her pace a little. She was on the road to London.

CHAPTER TWO

JANE SPENT THE NIGHT IN AN ABANDONED BARN, WHOSE FOURTH side was open to the skies, and to the piercing cold showers which fell before dawn. Sally's money was too precious to be spent on lodgings, and even at the humble inns along the road she would be a suspicious figure, arriving without baggage or decent clothes. There was always the possibility that Tom Black might have sent after her directly he had learned she was gone. With this in mind, she left the London road immediately she was past the village, cutting eastwards across the fields, and making wide detours of the hamlets, and even the isolated cottages. Just before dusk she judged that she was far enough beyond any immediate pursuit, and she turned south again along a narrow lane. She followed it until it merged with a broader road; there seemed to be a fair amount of traffic here for the time of year—carts laden with market produce, poultry and meat. There wasn't any doubt that they were making for the capital. She watched them for a time, and then went back along the lane to the empty barn she had noticed. The February night had turned raw and cold.

All night she lay in the dirty straw, miserably clutching her stomach, and listening to its empty rumblings; and the night seemed endless. She began to scratch at the lice which already crawled on her body and hair, ashamed to think that she would have to present herself to Anne tomorrow in this condition. She was frightened—frightened of many things . . . of Tom Black, of Anne, who very likely would not welcome her, frightened of the thought of arriving in London with only a few coins in her pocket. The only thing that seemed worse than her present condition was the vision of herself married to Harry Black, enduring his coarse love-making, his infidelities and his stupidity, with a dull, impotent hatred. All the same she was hungry and frightened enough to weep a little, and then to dry her eyes angrily because tears were so little help; so she just lay in the straw, sleeping fitfully, and waiting for the morning.

She was on the road early, walking briskly, and trying to stop thinking of how hungry she was. By sunrise she could already see the outskirts of the city lying before her, the morning still gray with mists, though the sun was breaking through and just tipping the chimney tops. The sight of it tore down the depression of the long night; she gazed at it with mingled satisfaction and wonder, smiling suddenly to herself, and enjoying the sensation of a new confidence and excitement.

She decided, then, firstly that she was a fool to go hungry when she had money in her pocket—and after she had filled her stomach, she would find someone to give her a lift. She was still several miles from Anne's doorstep, and the road was crowded with carts and wagons. Among all of them, one of the drivers was going to respond to a smile from her.

The tavern she chose was a poor place by comparison with The Feathers, and the clientele was shabby and hungry. But before its door stood a number of carts, so she walked boldly in, and asked for buttermilk and bread. Grudgingly she paid for it, and as she ate, began to take stock of the inhabitants of the smoky room. She wasn't conspicuously disheveled among them, she decided—and a great deal cleaner than most. Hurriedly she sifted them all—and finally fixed her gaze on a man whom she had seen tending an ancient equipage outside.

He responded almost right away; coming over confidently and dropping down beside her on the bench.

"That's a mighty fine eye y've got there, luv." He had a dark, gipsylike face, which looked as if it had been screwed up like a bit of old paper, and stuffed under the battered hat. "What 'appened? Did someone 'it you?"

Inwardly she cursed Harry, and at the same time forced a bright smile onto her lips.

"Looks as if I walked into the bedpost when the candle went out, doesn't it?" She grinned impudently at him, and winked with the good eye. He threw back his head and roared with laughter. Everyone in the room turned to look at the pair, and some of them laughed also. Suddenly Jane had a mental image of the sight she must present—almost in spite of herself she joined in the laughter.

She could feel the laughter down inside of her—deep in her throat and belly. After the miserable hours of the night it was a good feeling to be laughing again; she was grateful to the grimy little carter. She liked the twist of humor on his lips. Still laughing, she turned to him.

"Heading into the city?"

He nodded. "Aye, luv."

"Got room for me?" She thrust a foot forward, making sure to uncover and display her ankle. "My shoe rubs, and I've no mind to walk further."

He looked at the ankle, and then nudged her sharply in the ribs. "Always got room for a spot o' company—specially when it's red-'eaded!"

She gazed at him hoping she looked helpless, but not too demure. "Going anywhere near Albemarle Street? I mean . . . well, I've never been to London before, and I'm dead sure to get lost. . . ."

His brow wrinkled. "Well . . . I wasn't exactly going in that direction. Got a call to make on the Oxford road, and then I'm 'eadin' for Battersea. But seein' as yer foot 'urts . . ." Then he brightened up, and nudged her again. "Well . . . what the 'ell! The master'll not know it, and what's an 'our or so when it's t' oblige a lady?" He slapped his thigh in satisfaction. "What'd me ol' lady say if she could see me with a red'ead!"

So when Jane entered London at last, it was in the company of a ragged carter, and seated behind his skinny horse. His dark little eyes noted the wonder in hers as she gazed at the brightening spectacle of the city, stared at the tall, crowded buildings. With a gesture that indicated the jumble, he said:

"If yer the kind that takes t' city ways, then its the fairest place y' could wish t' see! They got everythin' 'ere—just everythin'! And all y' need is money. . . ." He turned and inclined his head towards her with a grotesquely gallant bow . . . "or a pretty face!"

They turned south off the Oxford road, and made their way through the great fashionable squares lined with the high, narrow houses. Servants with sleep still in their eyes polished the brass doorknobs and lanterns, and swept the refuse into the mud-filled streets.

In one of the crowded lanes between the squares, a pail of slops, thrown energetically from an upstairs window, caught the horse squarely across the back; he was too weary and too old to be startled by it. The hem of Jane's gown was soaked. She stared back indignantly at the window, but there was no one there.

The carter, whose name was Mick, grinned cheerfully.

"All in a day's work, luv. Y've just got t' mind where yer goin' in this man's town!"

The city was like a confused dream to her—so many faces and people, and noise such as she had never heard before. The noise was everywhere; it seemed to come from the ground and the roof-tops—raucous voices shouting at each other, tunes being whistled, and cries of anger as people stepped back out of the way of heavy coaches. The dirt was everywhere too—mud and refuse underfoot, the suffocating odors of rotting food, the smells from the fishmongers and the livery stables, the cloying smell of unwashed humanity, the smell of excrement.

Mick had spent a long time over his call in the Oxford road, and the city was getting into the stride of its day. The shutters were down from the shop fronts, and she feasted her eyes on the displays, the milliners, the gun-shops, the wine-shops—but it was still far too early for fashionable folk to be astir, Mick told her. But she saw carriages and coachmen waiting before the doors of some of the great houses, and the coffee shops were open, with the newspapers fresh on the racks.

Her senses drank in the excitement of it—the feeling that all the world was gathered here in this awakening city; here lived riches and fame and splendor. The sun had burned away the early mists; it lay on the slanting roofs and gave brilliance to the suits of livery she saw all about her, the gold and silver braid shining as if they were polished. The heavy, pungent odors drifting from the bake-shop made her realize that she was hungry again. She sniffed the London air—the stench and perfume—and her teeth chattered with indefinable excitement and dread.

They came to Albemarle Street at last—Jane suspected that Mick had taken her there by a roundabout way. She glimpsed the clock on St. James's Palace at the bottom of the slope on the other side of Piccadilly, just as Anne had described it to her; suddenly she knew that all of Anne's world was before her. They found Anne's house—elegant and in good repair, though Jane noticed the mud of several days caked on the doorstep.

Mick leapt down, and rapped on the knocker with his whip. He rapped twice again before the door opened; the sullen face of a young girl, bedraggled hair under an untidy cap, appeared. Her brows were knit sharply in a frown.

"Well? What do you want?" She looked critically at them both.

Jane drew herself up stiffly. "I wish to see Mistress Howard," she said, with her best imitation of Anne's voice.

"Mistress 'oward doesn't see anyone at this hour in the mornin'. Come back later."

Jane began to climb down off the cart. "I'll wait," she said shortly. She stepped up to the door.

The girl half-closed it with a threatening motion. "Look 'ere, you dirty baggage—you can't come in 'ere unless the mistress says so. So just you come back at a decent hour."

Mick waved his whip at her. "Y' mind yer tongue—y' nasty bitch! This 'ere young lady'll wait . . . an' I'm 'ere to see she does!"

Jane put her hand on the door. "Mistress Howard will see me. I'm her daughter."

The girl's mouth dropped open in disbelief. "G'on—don't give me none o' that. . . ."

Then she screwed up her eyes, looking closely at Jane. Her brow furrowed again; she put her head on one side, studying the other's face intently.

"Well . . . I must say you do *look* like the mistress—that red 'air an' all. . . ."

Mick lowered the whip slowly; he stared wonderingly at Jane. "Y' mean t' say yer mother's the *mistress* 'ere!" His eyes ran significantly over her dirty gown and Sally's old shawl. He pushed his hat to the back of his head. "Well—I dun' know. There's never any accountin' for 'ow folks'll act. Y'll be tellin' me next yer a bloody duchess!"

She shook her head. "I'm not! . . . more's the pity!"

He was already backing away; the game between them was ending and he clearly indicated that he didn't expect to have further dealings with folk who lived in Albemarle Street.

"Well, Duchess . . . thanks for yer company." The battered hat
came off in a flourish. He climbed into the cart, and sat waiting to
see her admitted.

Jane saluted him briefly. "I enjoyed the ride—thank you. You
saved my feet a lot of walking."

He nodded, and winked. "An' what use would yer pretty face
be t' y', if it couldn't save yer feet?" He touched his hat with the
whip. "Good day, t' y', Duchess—and good luck!"

Jane turned from him, and the girl opened the door reluctantly.
"I suppose it's all right t' let you in . . . though I ain't takin'
the blame if yer not supposed t' be 'ere."

She brushed past Jane, and started to walk towards the back of
the house, with a sullen, lumpish gait.

"Just a minute!" Jane's voice was firm. "Please tell Mistress
Howard that I'm here."

The girl spun round furiously. "Tell 'er yerself! I ain't takin' no
more orders in this 'ouse, believe me!"

"What do you mean?" Jane said. "You work here, don't you?"

"Not any more, I don't! Not a penny piece of wages 'ave I seen
in three months—'n' I'm packin' me bag this very moment, an' I'll
'ave the law on 'er if she don't pay up!"

Jane looked at her for a moment in silence. This was as bad as
anything she had imagined—and yet there was no time to sit and
lament about it now. She wasn't going to wait around down here,
feeling her confidence ebb away with every minute. She had to see
Anne now, while she could still use her tongue to convince her
mother that Sally's idea had been the right one. To confront Anne
now would give her the advantage; if she waited she would lose
courage, and become the frightened servant girl from The Feathers.

She stiffened her neck, and looked at the girl coldly. "Keep a
civil tongue in your head!" She gestured towards the staircase.
"Where is my mother—is she still abed? Where is her chamber?"

The girl shrugged indifferently. "You figerin' t' go up and see
'er . . . in that case you can announce yerself!" Then she hesitated,
and when she spoke again her tone was silky. "You'll find 'er abed,
all right. It's the big chamber two floors above this . . . above the
drawin' room." She indicated the way briefly, and then stood watching in silence while Jane moved past her to the staircase.

With the girl's hostile gaze still on her, Jane forced herself to assume a look of confidence as she mounted the stairs. Her hand trembled slightly on the balustrade. She caught a glimpse of the drawing room as she passed—pale green, and gold and white, with mirrors reflecting the brilliance of crystal. The stair well was paneled in light pine—the house was soft and feminine . . . Anne's house.

On the next floor she found the ante-room to Anne's bedroom —a prettily furnished apartment that made her more than ever conscious of her torn gown and matted hair, the lice on her body. She stiffened herself to approach the door and knock. With her hand poised, she heard Anne's voice—she had almost forgotten the peculiar beauty of that voice, its sweet, low pitch, and how it sounded forever on the edge of laughter. While she stood there Anne actually did laugh—that clear unabashed laugh, not now with the charm of long ago when Anne had been in love, but charming still.

It unnerved her a little to realize that her mother was not alone, but Jane was determined that she would not return to the hall and sit waiting meekly under the eyes of that sullen girl. She knocked firmly.

"Come in!" Anne's tone was indifferent, as if she had been expecting the knock.

The room had a warm, intimate kind of perfume which touched Jane's senses even before she fully took in the scene. She entered slowly, and had an instant impression of a frivolous kind of disorder, of luxurious things, of carelessness. There was a scatter of clothes about, and an embroidered glove lay foolishly in the center of the carpet. A caged bird was singing in the sunshine by the window.

Anne was naked, except for a shawl which lay across her shoulders, propped up against pillows on a tumbled bed. The bed was a huge one, with great carved legs, and hung with green silk. Anne's breasts were firm; like a young girl's. She displayed her body with a careless pride in its beauty.

Without turning she said, "Patrick . . . I rang hours ago! What's kept you?"

When she got no answer she glanced questioningly around. Her features froze in an instant of disbelief.

"Jane! Mercy upon us!" She half rose on the pillows, and dropped

back again, as if the breath had been knocked out of her. She gestured helplessly towards Jane, then looked immediately across at
the window seat.

A lean, dark-haired man, who sprawled there in shirt and dress-
ing-gown, straightened as he became aware of Jane's presence.
Then unhurriedly he rose to his feet.

Jane looked from one to the other, and her cheeks burned a dull
red. The rumpled bed and her mother's nakedness were clear
enough signs, even without the presence of the man; probably the
bed was still warm from his body. It was too late now to efface
herself; she must appear to them both like a naïve little fool, who
knew no better than to blunder into the room where Anne lay
with her lover. She knew now the full extent of the malice of the
servant girl in sending her here unannounced. She was furious at
her own stupidity.

Neither of them seemed perturbed. Anne had recovered herself,
and now she gestured imperiously.

"Jane! . . . what in the world are you doing here? Come here,
child . . . how you've grown! . . . what a sight you look!"

Jane went towards her. Anne's voice had been warm and surprised, but not angry. In the next second she felt her mother's arms
about her in a light hug, and her face brushed those firm breasts.
Anne smelled of scents and powder—a smell that Jane recalled from
a long time ago. There was another scent—the erotic scent of a
woman whose flesh is desired and loved.

Anne released her, and carelessly drew the shawl over her bosom.
For some seconds she gazed at her daughter's face in silence, then
she put out her hand and swung her in the direction of the window.

"Look, Ted, my daughter, Jane. Grown up—and looking like a
gipsy. Jane, this is Lord O'Neill."

He bowed. "I'm happy to know you, Miss Jane."

His accent was soft. She had heard this voice in gentlemen who
used the coaches to and from Liverpool—the Irish voices with music in them, and easy emotion. He spoke with polite gravity, as if
she were a great lady, and entitled to his consideration. As she
curtsied, she examined him more closely . . . a tall man, younger
than her mother, a graceful, slender-hipped body, a fine linen shirt
with costly lace ruffles. She saw this, and saw also, that with all the

gravity of his deportment he was laughing just a little at her. It wasn't unkind laughter—he was too lazy, and, at the moment, too content, to be unkind. He was merely amused.

She didn't like his being amused. With deliberate hauteur she looked away from him.

Anne had been studying her. "Jane, you've grown into a woman while my back was turned. How old you make me feel! . . . a hundred and two years, and toothless!"

Then she laughed, displaying for O'Neill's fascinated eyes her small, pretty teeth, and drawing her body up straight, so that her breasts pointed through the fine wool. O'Neill joined in the laughter, his gaze resting on her fondly.

Jane stood between them, feeling clumsy and gauche, feeling less than a woman because Anne was more of a woman than anyone she had ever laid eyes on. There were refinements in Anne's sensuality that she had never been conscious of before; it was easier now to see her as a man did. Like most other women placed beside her, Jane felt inadequate. She backed towards the door, preparing to excuse herself.

An agitated knocking halted her.

"Come in," Anne called.

The door was flung open.

"Oh, ma'am! It wouldn't have happened if I'd just been there. I slipped out for a second to give the butcher a piece o' me mind about the joints he's been sendin'—an' I get back an' what do I find but that stupid young piece has let a stranger in. An' upstairs, too, an' all . . ."

Jane stared in astonishment at the speaker, a young man whose dead-white face was topped by a great shock of lank-black hair. He was tall and angular, dressed in servant's clothes which fitted him, but seemed to hang limply on his thin frame. He couldn't have been more than thirty years old, judging by the way he moved, Jane thought, but he gave the impression of someone much older. His brow was furrowed with lines of worry, and his whole body seemed to be screwed up in a ferment of anxiety. He looked only at Anne; no one else mattered to him.

"Calm, Patrick! Be calm! There's nothing to get in a state about. . . ."

"Well, saints in Heaven, ma'am, I wouldn't have let anyone get past me. . . ."

Anne held up her hand for silence. "I know you wouldn't, Patrick, but this is one occasion when it's just as well you weren't there." She gestured towards Jane. "This is my daughter, Patrick."

He swung his head slowly.

"You remember," she prompted. "My daughter . . . who lives at Hampstead."

He gazed at her wonderingly, shaking his head. "Heaven help us! It can't be true! Why, ma'am, she's the spittin' image of y'. . . ." His face broadened into a kind of foolish grin. "Why . . . I would have known her anywhere . . . so like y' she is, ma'am."

"We're not as alike as all that, Patrick. . . ."

"Well, now . . ." O'Neill drawled. "I'm hardly telling the difference between you!"

Anne said firmly, "There *is* a difference, and you all know it, so stop flattering me." She looked across at Patrick. "Miss Jane will be staying here . . . for the time being. We'll need the small room upstairs made ready . . . and . . . oh, yes—it will be breakfast for three instead of two."

Patrick favored Jane with a low, untidy bow. " 'Twill be a pleasure to serve y' now, Miss Jane. An' forgive me, miss, for the disturbance . . . it's so strange to be seein' y', an' all, after hearin' about y' all these years, and not really thinkin' y'd come to life one o' these fine days. . . ."

Anne clapped her hands together. "Patrick, we're hungry. Talk to your heart's content when our bellies are full."

He made his strange ducking bow again. "To be sure, ma'am. At once! Right away!" He left the room swiftly.

Anne flung aside the covers. "Jane—reach me that gown, please."

Jane watched while Anne discarded the shawl, and put on the green velvet robe. She slipped out of the high bed, tying the gown at her waist. Her limbs were beautifully formed; she seemed no older than Jane herself.

She looked across at her daughter.

"Child, you should eat before you talk. I won't ask you yet what brings you." Then she gestured towards the end of the room. "You'll find water in the pitcher behind the screen—and soap and comb and things. Later Patrick will leave some in your own room."

Jane moved obediently towards the screen, wishing that Anne didn't have the effect of making her feel so coarse and dirty, wishing also that O'Neill didn't have to be present while she washed. She felt like a child being sent away in disgrace. And yet it wasn't, she decided, Anne's fault. There weren't any rules for dealing with a daughter who appeared from nowhere, looking like a bedraggled tramp—especially with a lover to witness the scene.

As she reached the screen, Anne's voice arrested her again. "Just one question, Jane—only one."

"Yes?"

"That black eye. How did you get it?"

Jane didn't answer at once. She stood looking at the toilet table, abstractedly noting its dainty appointments. With O'Neill looking on, she didn't know what to say to Anne. She shifted from one foot to the other, fidgeting with the heavy brush, twisting it in her hand. Then turning, she caught sight of herself in the mirror. The bruise under her eye was puffed and ugly; there was dried blood on her lip. She looked hideous, slatternly, like a brawling street woman.

Abruptly then, she turned back to face Anne and O'Neill.

"I've worse things than a bruised eye."

She let Sally's shawl drop to the floor. The torn gown and her bare bosom were fully visible to them now. On her left breast were the weals where Harry's teeth had bitten into her flesh.

"I got the black eye from the same man who tried to rape me. All *he* got for his pains was a broken leg."

Calmly she picked up the shawl again and threw it across the chair. "So that's why I'm here—I'm running away."

She stood there only long enough to see the expression change on both their faces. Anne had grown pale, and O'Neill looked as if he had suddenly seen a different person in the place of the one who had been there. It gave her a bleak kind of satisfaction to know that she had taken his attention from Anne.

Then she moved behind the screen, and one by one began to strip off her clothes until she was naked. As they dropped, each one, to the floor, she felt that she was shedding all of herself that belonged back at The Feathers. She washed every inch of her body, freely helping herself from all the toilet bottles to scent the water. Carefully she put on the dressing robe which Anne brought to her, an elegant, blue thing which was only a little worn at the wrists. Without tongs she couldn't achieve the fashionable curls she would have liked, but her hair combed down loosely on her shoulders looked even better, she thought.

A different and more calculating face stared out at her from the mirror. Whatever happened now, good or ill, she could never go back to being the girl who had climbed into the hayloft less than a full day ago to watch the London coach depart.

2

They ate breakfast in the ante-room. Jane knew that she had the full attention of both Anne and O'Neill, and she savored not only their attention, but the luxury of the room, the fine china, the silk gown she wore. More than that, she was not a stranger at Anne's table; she sipped her chocolate slowly, and a sense of intimacy and ease began to flow through her. Patrick had lit a small fire in the grate. The sun and the rosy firelight mingled on the faded carpet; Jane could feel the warmth and the peace as if they were things she could put her hands on.

Anne and O'Neill remained quiet to listen to her; as she relaxed she grew expansive, finding better and less clumsy phrases to explain her arrival, to tell of what had happened yesterday at The Feathers. It was important to her that they should feel the strength and the enraged despair of Harry Black; she sought words to tell them of the power and influence Harry's father wielded, of his arrogant pride in his own position and achievements. It was important to her own pride that they should know she hadn't come on any slight and foolish pretext.

She was also aware of the need to be brief, and not tearful. Anne was a woman of laughter, who wanted only to be amused; it would be fatal to make the mistake of boring her, or wearying her with a tale of trouble. Anne had always dismissed her woes with a shrug; Jane knew she must quickly learn to copy her.

O'Neill was full of noisy indignation. "Damn it, Anne, the fellow ought to be punished!"

Anne shook her head slowly. "No, Ted—it can't be that way. Jane did the best possible thing to cut her losses and run for it." She smiled wryly. "She's a pretty woman—and there's always, I hope, a little danger in being pretty." Then she spread her hands. "If Black doesn't pursue her, that's the best we can hope for. . . ."

"Nonsense!" O'Neill cut her short. "There isn't a chance that he'll do anything about it. I'll warrant the man's not such a fool as his son. He'll know that once Jane's come to you, he wouldn't stand a chance. I know that kind—big men in their own little field, but scared as the devil to chance themselves beyond it. If Jane had stayed around he'd have to bring charges to save his face—now he'll have every excuse not to."

"But if he should? . . ." Jane asked.

O'Neill looked at her, his gray eyes softening. "What are you thinking, my dear? Are you thinking that people go to the gallows or Botany Bay for less?" He shook his head. "Don't trouble yourself about it—you'll not see the gallows or a prison ship—not while I can help you. If you'd stayed at The Feathers it might have happened; here with Anne you're safe. Black would know well enough that her influence matches his. He'll leave it alone, you'll see."

Anne gave a short laugh, and shrugged. "Would to God that my money matched his! Then I'd go into court with the King himself and expect to win!"

They made it sound so easy, these two, Jane thought. They could joke, and shrug their shoulders, and the menace no longer existed. O'Neill could use the weight of a title, and a word spoken in the ear of a man belonging to his club, or with whom he passed the time in the coffee houses. Anne could probably use influence in certain places also, if she had to. It was no harder than that. They had made their decisions and cleared their minds of the problem. Now they wanted to put it aside, find something to laugh at, as Anne had done over Tom Black's money. If they were going to forget about it, Jane decided that she could forget too, almost as easily. It was pleasanter to revel in luxurious rooms and silk gowns than worry about what might possibly happen tomorrow.

Anne yawned delicately, like a cat, and fell to talking with O'Neill about a party which a woman called Myra Burke would give that evening. ". . . They say she's used most of the money old

Benson left her to decorate the new house. But just think—she has such frightful taste!" She gave a mournful little pout. "All that beautiful money going to waste on Myra Burke, when I could use it so much better."

O'Neill crumpled up his napkin. "Well, I don't care if the woman hangs her walls with tapestry or old bags so long as I win some money this evening. Blanchard took a load off me last night."

"Of course you'll get it back," Anne said quickly. "It always comes back somehow—if the luck's with you."

O'Neill turned to Jane. "Listen to her! There was never a woman courted luck so faithfully. I'll swear she bows to it three times before she goes out in the evening."

Anne shrugged. "What if I do? All the gods must have their offering. If I believe in luck hard enough—"

She glanced towards the door as it opened, and broke off her sentence. The half-defensive smile she had worn became tender and warm.

"And here's William come to bid us good morning," she said softly.

Jane turned her head slowly; she almost didn't want to look. It was impossible not to hear the love and protectiveness in Anne's voice; she hadn't realized before that she was jealous of William.

William was tall for his age, and he was every inch Anne's child —except that his eyes were dark and framed with heavier brows than hers. He had the same red hair, and features that were curiously strong and defined for a child; here also were Anne's graceful, easy movements. He wore a dark velvet jacket that made him look like a young prince. It was clear that he had known of Jane's arrival; he moved towards his mother immediately, but an inquisitive, eager smile had already started on his lips, and he looked directly towards Jane. He responded with a childish brevity to Anne's kiss.

"William—this is your sister, Jane. She's come down from Hampstead to stay with us."

He nodded. "Yes, I know. Patrick told me—he's in a bother about it. Betty packed her bags and went this morning—and he has no one to help him get the room ready."

Anne's brow darkened. "So Betty left! Well, there's one ungrateful baggage the less for us to trouble about."

"She says she'll be back, Mama—she wants her wages." William said it as if servants leaving with wages unpaid were nothing new to him. He moved around the table towards Jane. He held out his hand to her.

"I'm glad you've come," he said. "Patrick says you've come from Hampstead. Is that a long way?"

"Quite a long way," Anne said, a trifle irritably. "It's a long pull for the horses up to Hampstead." It was the first time she had made even the vaguest reference to the distance as a reason for her long absence from The Feathers. Jane knew that Anne would never make more of an excuse than this.

Jane held William's hand briefly. She felt no warmth towards him, only a jealous suspicion. This good-looking little boy had no business to be so self-possessed, so sure of Anne and of everything about him. He spoke with Anne's clear tones, and her inflections —he was everything that contact with Anne had made him. She fiercely envied him the years he had spent in this house, and the confidence they had bred in him. She was tongue-tied beside him, and angry because he had destroyed the mood of intimacy she had reveled in.

"How do you do?" she said formally, and let his hand drop.

He wasn't to be put off. "I want to show you General."

He went back to the door quickly, and emerged again, pulling on the collar of a large black dog. The dog came with just enough reluctance to assert himself; he went to Jane with almost as much curiosity as William displayed.

"I've had General for two years. Mama gave him to me on my birthday, and so General and I always have our birthdays together."

Jane ran her hand over the curling black coat. "He's very handsome," she said lamely. She couldn't find anything else to say, and yet it seemed to be expected, because Anne and O'Neill were staring at her, and waiting on her words as much as William was. She felt herself flush, and there were tears of annoyance and frustration pricking the back of her eyes. She had been doing so well, almost feeling that she belonged with Anne and her titled lover, sipping chocolate daintily and feeling at home in a silk gown. But William was obviously so much more at home here; by comparison she must seem once again the country girl, full of clumsiness and unease.

Even the dog gave William an added advantage—standing beside him William looked like a portrait child, straight and elegant, his hand resting possessively on the collar. She wanted to shake him; he was bred in the fashion of all the spoiled and favored children of the rich who had come to The Feathers—the ones who had given orders, and expected service from her as their due. And yet he was her half-brother; he had Anne's love, and so much besides.

O'Neill spoke at last. The pause had become too lengthy, and he was detached enough from the three to be able to sense Jane's feelings. There had been an instant sympathy in him for this girl with the bruised eye and marked breast who had, before his fascinated gaze, this morning slipped into a new world.

"Aren't they alike now, William—did you ever see two so alike?"

William considered for a moment, giving Jane a careful and unself-conscious scrutiny—just as if she were a stuffed dummy, Jane thought angrily, with no eyes and ears.

"Well—I don't know. . . . Patrick said that too. He said Jane was as pretty as Mama, but I don't know. I don't think she's *quite* as pretty."

"Indeed now—the pair of them would turn heads wherever they went. Indeed they would!" Suddenly O'Neill's face broke into a broad smile; he smacked his thigh appreciatively. "I've got it, Anne —by God, that would set the town talking!"

Anne looked at him quickly. "What are you talking about, Ted?"

"Why don't we take Jane to the reception this evening . . . you know, dress her up in one of your gowns, and let people think they were seeing your double. What a joke that'd be . . . why, it'd be around the town in no time."

Anne's face was troubled as she turned towards Jane.

"Jane . . . I . . ."

Jane knew suddenly that this was one time when she had to speak entirely from her own instinct—she must make a decision and override O'Neill, without fully understanding why this was so. To go to a fashionable party wearing one of Anne's lovely gowns had been part of the dream she'd carried. Now the chance had come, and it was hers only to say yes, and there would be the gown and the slippers, the headdress and the carriage. And yet she knew she wasn't going to accept. There was no reason she could put into words even now why she should refuse, but she did.

Anne's gaze was fixed on her anxiously as she spoke to O'Neill.

"Oh, come, Lord O'Neill! Would you have me at a party with an eye like the black end of a pot! Why, I'd no more look like my mother than I'd look like the Queen! The truth is, sir, my bones ache sorely from the hard ground last night, and I'm in need of a little rest."

She glanced across to Anne again—Anne who now cuddled William loosely in her arms as he leaned against her chair. In her eyes Jane read deep relief and satisfaction—and yet it was more than that, it was pleasure in her daughter, and commendation for a decision wisely made. She said nothing, but she nodded faintly, almost imperceptibly.

To Jane it was like a door being opened. William mattered now much less than he had two minutes before.

CHAPTER THREE

THE GOWNS LAY PILED ON THE FLOOR BEFORE JANE. SHE TOUCHED them with reverent and excited hands—the silk and velvet had the feel of enchantment beneath her fingers, and the colors spilled over the rose carpet in a mad and rich confusion. There were mostly greens—Anne looked best in green—with a blue and a cream and a white among them. There was a cloak with the trimming of fur, and a wide-brimmed hat. Anne had tossed them out of her wardrobe and bundled them carelessly together.

"They all need a stitch somewhere—and I'm useless with a needle. You're a trifle taller, I fancy, but there are hems. . . ." She examined the hems a little doubtfully, noticing the mud splashes from the London streets; then she tossed them aside with a shrug. "Well . . . do the best you can with them. I'm sorry there's no money at the moment to buy you new ones. Perhaps later . . . perhaps when my luck stops being so parsimonious!"

She had said this on her way out to an afternoon drive in the park with O'Neill. She had worn a fur wrap, and the brim of her hat dipped provocatively over one eye—but it was still possible to see that her eyes looked tired, and that when O'Neill or William weren't present, there was no zest in her voice. The soft perfume she wore lingered behind in the ante-room; Jane could smell it in the gowns piled on the floor.

One by one she tried them—startled to see, suddenly, how closely she resembled Anne. They were gowns meant to attract and hold attention; the low-cut necks that revealed her breasts were very deliberate. She would have to lace tighter to stay within the waists. They were the kind of clothes a woman like Anne would always wear.

The few hours she had been in Anne's household she had used to listen and observe, and as she sewed she tried to settle her jumbled impressions. From the unending contact with people at The Feathers she had learned enough to be able to sum up the situation here without much difficulty. Jane knew the feeling and atmosphere of a household deeply in debt—but here they lived only as the rich did. Here was recklessness and extravagance at its height. Anne needed money badly, and yet she lived at a rate that would have frightened most people, forever trusting that luck would bring the cards right, and that she would ride home with money in her pocket.

In a strange way Patrick was behind most of the façade of splendor. He sped about, his long body poking at awkward and ungainly angles, getting through the work of five servants. He ran the household, and even doubled as coachman; he supervised William through most of the day and made it unnecessary to employ a tutor for more than a few hours. Jane wondered, had Patrick been any kind of a scholar, if Anne wouldn't have pressed him even to that extra duty. The man had a nervous, agitated thinness, and his eyes were red-rimmed from lack of sleep; yet he never halted in his tasks, or seemed to notice the appalling burden of his work. He was devoted to Anne, worshiping her with his eyes and tongue, treating her with a mixture of grave paternalism, and the reverence he would have given to a queen.

Jane fingered the rich stuff of the gowns, and decided that possibly one of them would have paid for her keep at The Feathers for a whole year. But in Anne's life, new gowns were vastly important, and Hampstead was a long way off, and easily put out of mind. Here, where servants were clamoring for wages, and the butcher to have his bills settled, it would be easier to pay those on hand than worry about a daughter who never showed herself, and never asked for money. Jane tacked an edging of lace in position, and thought, with a wry smile, that her mistake had been in not coming to Anne much sooner. Anne would always take care of whatever problems forced themselves on her; the rest could wait or be forgotten. As long as she had been prepared to fend for herself at The Feathers, Anne had been prepared to let her do it. Now she was here, and Anne would bestir herself, and be as energetic on her behalf as she was on William's.

It didn't occur to her to feel angry over Anne's treatment; that was the way Anne lived, and nothing would ever alter her.

In a way, Jane thought, it explained why William had remained here, instead of being sent off to be nursed as she had been. Anne had been passionately in love with William's father, and his child was loved for his sake. By the time William was of an age to be troublesome to Anne, he had been a fixture in her household, and there would have been no thought of sending him away. Besides that, Anne, with the years slipping by her, had the need of love— and whatever men came or went, William was always with her, a perpetual reminder of the man she had loved unchangingly.

O'Neill's position, she felt, was impermanent. He would go when either he or Anne tired of the other. Jane guessed that he had no money; apart from Anne's complaints of the lack of it, O'Neill didn't have the air of a man who was contributing substantially to her support. There was no possessiveness about him. Rather, they appeared as two people who had come to an amicable arrangement which could be broken at any moment, whenever they desired. They were together because they needed company and amusement—and possibly, Jane thought, because there was no one better in sight for either of them. They were affectionate to each

other, but only the lightest kind of loyalty was involved. O'Neill
kept rooms in a tavern in Crab Tree Yard, Anne had told her; so
when the parting came there would be no sense of breaking up
Anne's household or her routine of life. They would part affection-
ately, but with a shrug of the shoulders.

Without Anne's presence about which to pivot, the house seemed
strangely quiet. Jane listened to the silence; she could no longer
hear Patrick's thick brogue shouting orders at the cook, or hear the
sounds of his feverish activity, the doors closing noisily, the dishes
clattering in the basement. There was peace here at last; the rooms
were dusted, the fires laid; upstairs William worked with his tutor.
The absence of noise was unfamiliar; Jane had always lived in the
midst of haste and bustle, and now, with tasks waiting to be done,
as she knew there were, it was difficult to grow accustomed to the
idea that she would not be asked, or expected, to help with them.
She decided that she liked the silence and peace of this house; she
liked sitting here with nothing more arduous to do than sew a few
ruffles, and lengthen some hems. She still wore Anne's silk robe,
and felt comfortable in it; the memory of the lice-ridden clothes
that Patrick had taken down to burn she put aside hastily. For the
moment there seemed nothing out of joint—except the sight of
her work-roughened hands against the rich material.

The door opened very quietly; it was only the sensation she had
that someone was staring at her which made her turn. William
stood shyly in the door, a hopeful, expectant smile on his face.

"Would I disturb you if I came in? Patrick said I must ask first."

She was tongue-tied and uneasy in William's presence, and she
certainly didn't want him; but there was no way of indicating that
without also letting him know her feelings. She had no alternative
but to motion him in. The black dog was with him—his head thrust
round the door just as William's was. They came in together, and
William drew up a footstool close to her. He seated himself where
he could watch what she was doing. The dog squatted beside him.

Jane glanced at him quickly, before bending over her work again.
He seemed different from this morning—to start with, his face was
streaked with jam, and his hair was wild-looking. He had changed
his jacket for an older one. He was still as self-possessed as before,
but now he almost resembled the young children who had played

in the village street at Hampstead. She felt herself warm a little
to him.

"I thought you were having lessons," she said quietly.

"Oh—they're finished," he said happily. "Mr. Taylor goes to give
lessons in mathematics to the daughters of Sir Sidney Stone at this
time."

"Math—mathematics? To girls?"

"Yes—it's funny, isn't it? But you see Sir Sidney is a sailor, and
Mr. Taylor says he makes the girls learn about mathematics and
astronomy just as if they'd been boys, and were going to sea."

"How strange," Jane said, wonderingly. Her own aptitude with
a column of figures was extremely sound, but she had once looked
in Simon Garfield's books of Euclid, and the strange drawings and
lines had seemed completely useless and bewildering. She began to
wonder how much William knew of the subject; she hoped it wasn't
very much.

"What lessons do you take—can you read and write?"

"Oh, yes!" he said quickly, as if it were an accomplishment to
be taken for granted. "And I have lessons in geography and history
and mathematics."

"Oh, do you?" She was vaguely envious of his knowledge, even
though at his age it couldn't be very great. "Is Mr. Taylor old?"
She had memories of Simon Garfield, crabby and impatient in his
old age.

"Oh, no—he's young. He's only been down from Oxford for a
year, and he's waiting now to go off on a botanical expedition to
the South Seas. He likes to talk more than teach."

"To talk? To you? What does he talk about?"

"Oh, all kinds of things. He talks about plants and birds. And
he talks about the Revolution in France. He's afraid if war breaks
out they won't fit up a ship for the South Seas." She nodded as
he spoke. There had been so much talk at The Feathers of the
Revolution and the chances of war; she had listened to the heated
discussions, and always agreed with the speaker of the moment.
She had never understood the aims of the Revolution, or what the
people of France expected to gain by it. Now she felt ashamed of
her ignorance. It was to be expected that London would buzz with
news of it. This was the city where people made and lost money

in wars and revolutions. Among the poor folk and the country people it was a matter of going away to fight in wars they didn't make,
and didn't understand—and in which, perhaps, they would die. She
nodded again at William. In the future she would have to listen,
and remember.

"Does—does he expect there'll be war?"

William nodded emphatically. "He says they're bound to find an
excuse to execute the King sooner or later, and England will surely
come into the war. Parliament talks about it all the time—and a
Jacobin hardly dares to open his mouth in this country."

"What else does he say?"

"That the brothers of the King of France are causing trouble
wherever they can—saying that everyone ought to go to war with
France. Mr. Taylor says that they don't care what becomes of the
royal family. With the King and the Dauphin dead all of them
would be nearer to the crown themselves."

"Can't they leave France? I've heard that a great many French
people have." It was all she knew about the present crisis, and she
repeated it rather desperately.

William's eyes opened wide. "Don't you know? The King and
Queen Marie Antoinette and their children are shut up in a palace
in Paris. They tried to escape and were sent back."

Jane applied herself to her work again. William was only repeating parrot-fashion what he had heard, but still he made a better
showing of knowledge than she could. But somehow she didn't dislike him for being better informed than she; it was simpler to accept the fact that William was a town child, brought up in the
society of adults. If he repeated what he heard it was useless to resent it.

He watched her in silence for a time, his hands clasped over his
knees as he squatted on the low stool. Occasionally he put out his
hand to pat the dog, to pull gently at the long, black, curling ears.
Then, rather shyly, he touched the silk of the dress.

"This is my mother's gown," he said. "Are you going to wear it
now?"

She nodded. "Yes—I'll wear it."

"You'll look pretty in it," he said matter-of-factly. Then his eyebrows shot up, as if he had just remembered something of impor-

tance. "This morning—" he began quickly—"you remember this morning when I said you were not as pretty as Mama?"

She took her eyes away from the green silk. His expression was serious. "Yes, I remember."

"Well, I didn't mean it. I think you're just as pretty. But I had to say that because Mama worries over how she looks. I see her staring in the looking glass, and it seems to make her sad. But I knew that *you* knew you were pretty, so it wouldn't matter, my saying that for once."

Jane nodded. She didn't know what to answer; if William had already begun to notice Anne's concern over her looks, then he was not going to be fooled by any denial she would make. She began to feel vaguely sorry for William; to her way of thinking it was an unnatural life for a child. He was cut off from the companionship she had known in Hampstead, the sharing in the village activities—but here in London, Anne's way of living would automatically cut him off from the society of the children of conventional families. Probably he knew this well enough; he was a lonely child who played with his dog—who talked to Patrick of household matters and the gossip of the street, and to his tutor of wars and revolutions. And he came in daily to greet Anne at breakfast with her lover. Suddenly she knew the richness of what she had shared with Pru and Lottie and Mary in the kitchen of The Feathers, things she had had which William would never know. He had Anne's love and attention, but it had created a prison for him. The picture of the envied child in the velvet coat faded for Jane, and it was never to return again.

Then she also put out her hand and stroked the dog's head, and played with his ears as William was doing; the child glowed with pleasure.

"He's nice, isn't he? Feel how soft it is here—look, just in this underneath part of his ears.

Jane's fingers followed his; the dog's skin had almost the texture of the fabric in her lap. "Why do you call him General?"

"He's called General after Great-great-grandfather Blake."

"Great-great-grandfather Blake? . . . Was he a general?"

William's fine eyebrows shot up. "Why yes! Didn't you know that? I would have thought that Mama would have told you!"

"But *who* was he?" Jane demanded impatiently.

"Why . . . he was a general, and he fought under the Duke of Marlborough. He fought with him at Blenheim . . . he's in all the old books about the wars. Mr. Taylor has read some of them to me." His smooth child's brow wrinkled in astonishment. "Do you suppose Mama *forgot* to tell you about him?"

"I expect so," Jane answered dryly. Whatever Anne's motive for not telling her about the Blake background she didn't imagine it was forgetfulness. But she didn't want to waste thought any longer over Anne's motives; she wanted to revel in the knowledge of what was, suddenly, and incredibly, hers. It gave her an awareness of identity to hear William group her with a family which had existed before she was born; she wasn't accustomed to the idea of belonging to someone. Always there had been just Anne, and, beyond her, a blank. William had peopled that blankness and made it alive; there had been a great-great-grandfather and he had been a general—there were even history books to prove it.

Jane touched William's arm. "What do you know about him? Tell me!"

He shrugged. "I don't remember all of it. Blenheim's somewhere over in the Low Countries, isn't it?"

Jane didn't know, but she nodded encouragingly. "Yes—I think so."

"Well, they won a great victory there, and Great-great-grandfather Blake was there with Marlborough all through it. Mama said he brought back a lot of booty from the wars . . . gold and tapestries . . . silver plate . . . things like that."

Jane stared at him wide-eyed. "What else?"

William cast back in his memory in an effort to satisfy her. "Well . . . I can't remember much else. Except . . . except I remember Mama telling me that Great-great-grandfather was all set to be made a lord—or something of the sort—and he offended Marlborough's wife, the Duchess, Sarah. The Duchess was the Queen's greatest friend, so of course he didn't get the title."

Jane gave a little gasp. "Is this true?"

William looked pained. "Why yes—it says so, right in the books. All except the part about the Duchess. I told Mr. Taylor, and he believes it. He says it's the only reason he could understand why Great-great-grandfather wouldn't have had a title."

"Well, imagine that!" Jane's tone was dreamy; she was wrapped already in the wonder of discovering a part for herself, a past in which great and famous names jostled one another. There had been money as well—gold, William had said, and silver plate and jewels, probably—and a family of whose blood she was. They had been people of position and prominence—all dead now, and vanished, but it explained why Anne moved and talked with that faint arrogance and authority. It explained many things—why William was brushed with the same dignity, why she herself had gropingly sought something beyond Harry Black. She knew that her hunger over these years at The Feathers had not been only a longing to be with Anne; she had wanted identity, had wanted to know that there were people and a place from which she was sprung. Her thoughts now were confused and excited; she reached out greedily for all that William could give her.

"What else do you know . . . about *them?*"

"Them?"

"Yes—the family!"

"There isn't a family."

"What? *None?*" In the few minutes William had been talking she had brought to life a host of personalities centering round the General—a wife, children, a house and all its accoutrements . . . grandchildren, and their children, who would be cousins to William and herself. She had fashioned them in her mind because she wanted them. Now William had wiped them away.

"Only Grandfather—that's all."

"You mean Mama's father—no one else?" She was sadly disappointed; the phantom world narrowed down to only one man, and he, she thought, would be an old man.

"Mama never spoke of anyone else—she had no sisters or brothers. She told me about a cousin, a little boy, who lived with them for a while. But he went away—to France, Mama said."

"Where did they live?—where does Mama's father live?"

William was becoming wearied by this questioning game. Anne's family had never troubled his thoughts greatly, except that he had had a child's pleasure in seeing the General's name in the history books. But there was too much happening all about him to leave time for speculation about people who were dead. He was puzzled by Jane's eagerness, and worried because she expected him to know so much.

"Some place in Kent, near the sea, I think. Mama says they used to have sheep—I would have liked to see the lambs," he added regretfully.

"What was the name of the place?"

William screwed up his face wearily, pushing his memory to one last effort. "I don't . . ." Then his expression lightened. "Why, yes —I do remember! They lived on the Romney Marsh, by the sea, in Kent. The house where Mama grew up is called Blake's Reach. Yes—that's it! Blake's Reach!"

She was almost satisfied. She had enough for the present to think about, to savor. Quietly she took up the silk again, and began making her minute stitches in the edging of the fichu. Blake's Reach . . . near the sea; a place called the Romney Marsh, where there were sheep. She turned the few details over in her mind lovingly; they belonged to her now, as much a part of her, and belonging as much to her, as they did to William. She looked at the child's head, with its untidy red locks bent towards the dog. They shared something in common now—something neither of them had ever seen.

They were together only a few minutes more before Anne returned. Below they could hear the carriage stop, and the bustle that surrounded her entry. She called instructions to Patrick over her shoulder as she came into the room; her lovely face looked a little drawn and pale above the dark fur wrap, but her eyes glowed softly with pleasure as she saw Jane in the big chair, and William on the stool close to her knee.

"Well, my loves!"

She held out her arms to William, but her glance included Jane. Again Jane was made acutely aware of the smell of her perfume, the rustle of many silk petticoats as she bent over her son. Anne's presence always seemed identified for Jane as much by smell and the rhythm of her movements, as by the sound of her voice.

She threw off her wrap and settled herself in the chair opposite

Jane. William came forward with a stool to put under her feet. He dragged his own stool midway between the two women.

"Ah . . . William! You have two women now to fuss about. Have you been watching Jane sew?"

He nodded briefly, negligently stirring with his foot the pile of gowns on the floor. "Jane sews so fast—like this!" He gave a comically swooping imitation of the needle flying in and out of the fabric.

Anne smiled; she bent down and examined one of the dresses closely, her fingers running critically over the hem, and a darn in the lace.

"How exquisitely you sew," she said quietly. Her eyes met Jane's over William's head. "I've rarely seen anything to equal this."

Jane nodded. "Sally was a beautiful needlewoman—when she had time away from the kitchen."

"I suppose she taught you to cook as well?"

"Why, yes . . . You couldn't help learning . . . seeing it day after day. I've not such a light hand as Sally with pastry, but my sauces are good."

Anne looked at her for a moment in silence. "Well . . ." she said at last, "you've learned things you'd never have glimpsed if you'd been living here." She fingered the lace again. "It's no mean accomplishment—Sally's taught you more than I know."

Jane wanted to say that Sally hadn't taught her to move across a room gracefully, hadn't been able to teach her how to fill awkward moments with light chatter, how to sit in a chair with perfect stillness. These were Anne's gifts, precious things that Jane hungered for. Bending her head, she scowled a little at the sewing in her lap.

"Oh, it's well enough, I suppose," she said dully.

William was picking through the gowns on the floor. "You wore that to a ball once, didn't you, Mama?" he said, poking the cream silk.

She nodded. "That was the last time I wore it—some fool spilt wine there on the side. Jane will have to take out that panel. That blue should look well on you, Jane." She sighed a little. "I thought it was a shade too bright for me last time I wore it." With an almost unconscious gesture she passed her hand over her cheek, as if she felt the lines of age gathering there. She got to her feet, restlessly walked to the window to look out at nothing, then came back and looked over Jane's shoulder at her work. Jane had seen her hurried, nervous glance towards the mirror as she passed. Her white hands looked transparent as they gripped the chair-back.

Suddenly there was a little exclamation from William. He looked quickly and guiltily towards Anne. In his hand he held the wide-brimmed velvet hat; in the other hand, forlornly, lay the velvet rose that had trimmed it.

"Look . . . look what I've done!"

Before Anne could speak Jane reached out and took the rose and the hat from him. "It's nothing, William! Just a stitch here . . . and one here . . . Looks better than it did in the beginning, doesn't it!"

Anne shrugged her shoulders helplessly. "You see, William . . . we have someone now who can mend things. Jane's clever with her fingers . . . very clever. Much more than any woman we've ever had in to sew." She paused. "I wonder . . ."

Jane sensed the request that was coming; she guessed the pieces of mending waiting, the things that the maids who were never paid had refused to do, the underwear rolled in the drawers laid aside for the stitch they never got, the fraying cuffs on William's coat. Everyone who loved Anne served her; it was natural for her to ask it, and to expect an acceptance.

The request didn't come because Patrick interrupted them. His long neck poked around the door urgently.

"Ma'am, Lord O'Neill has just sent word that you're to dine an hour earlier—with Mr. Richard Burgess."

"Dick—why, Dick's back in town!" Anne's face was pleased and animated. "Why, I wager he'll clean out Myra Burke's tables. Dick's always lucky—it's lucky just to be with him. I'll win tonight, my loves! I feel it in my bones that I'm going to win!"

Patrick had advanced into the room; he held a candle in his hand. "An' is it so poor we are that we can't afford to have a little light now? Sure 'tis wearin' yer eyes down to the sockets y'll be, Miss Jane."

As he spoke he lit two candles on the table, and hastened to draw the long curtains. Jane was surprised to see how the dusk had gathered, how little shreds of mist had collected under the eaves of the houses opposite. Without noticing it, she had been leaning towards the firelight to see her work.

Now Patrick had gone into the bedroom—setting a taper to the fire laid there, lighting the candles. Jane saw the colors of the room leap into life, the soft green of the bed hangings, the sheen of rosewood.

"Isn't it time now, ma'am, for y' to be gettin' ready? Lord O'Neill sent word that he'd be round on the stroke of the half hour, an' here y' are without yer hair curled, an' not even a gown laid out . . ." He clicked his tongue. "An' bad cess to that lump of a girl walkin' out this mornin' without even a word to a soul . . ."

As he talked he was busy about the room, taking out and arranging bottles on the toilet table, folding Anne's wrap, laying her hat away. He talked without self-consciousness, as if it were a habit of long standing; he knew Anne heard him, but he never expected an answer. His talk was a privilege that his devotion had earned for him. He enjoyed his monologue enormously.

"An' will you be wearin' this white one again, ma'am? . . . sure, y' look like a queen in it, an' there's many who'll be there this evenin' that I'd like to be gettin' an eyeful o' y'. . . ."

Anne moved into the bedroom. "Yes, Patrick, that one . . . though Heaven knows I'm tired enough of it. I saw a lovely thing —green—at Seiker's today. They wanted a young fortune for it, and I owe so much there already . . ." She wandered to the toilet table.

Patrick came close to her. "An' it's yerself that's not lookin' too well, ma'am," he said, peering solicitously at her reflection in the mirror. "Yer not strong . . . I keep tellin' y' yer not strong, an' ye don't get enough rest, an' there's all this comin' an' goin' . . ."

Still clicking his tongue disapprovingly, he bent over Anne. As a matter of long habit, he began to loosen the hooks of her gown.

Patrick and William had gone, and Jane sat hunched on a stool watching Anne dress her hair. She was skillful, her hands moved swiftly, arranging, patting, pressing. The smell of the hot tongs invaded the room.

"Just as well I've learned to do it myself," Anne said, looking at Jane in the mirror. "So many of these wretched girls are careless and stupid—and before you know what's happened, they've burned a piece off. I don't let anyone touch it now."

Jane nodded. "You're very quick."

"You learn in time . . . it takes patience in the beginning." She opened the drawer of the toilet table. "I have a pair of tongs here I don't use. You can take them up to your room."

"I don't know . . ." Jane began. Then she stopped, unable to voice her thoughts.

Anne laid down the tongs. "You don't know what?"

Jane gestured helplessly. "So many things . . . my hair—that's just a beginning. How do I wear a hat like the one you wore this afternoon? How do I learn to say the right things . . ." She clapped her hand over her left eye. "Why, look at me—I'm not even presentable!"

"Hush!" Anne said, soothingly. "There's much you don't know, but you're not a fool, and you'll learn. You'll learn very quickly, I promise you that."

"How?"

"Soon—soon enough," Anne said. "Almost before you know what's happened. Or before I know . . ."

Jane straightened herself. "I won't be round your neck long . . . you know that!"

"What are you talking about?"

Jane looked at her without wavering. "I'm strong, you know. I haven't been bred like you . . . to all this." Her hand indicated the room, the litter of the toilet table. "I know how to work. That's all I know."

Anne shook her head. "Too late for that, Jane. Too late, my dear. You've gone past that now—very suddenly. If you had chosen to stay behind and marry Harry Black, you would have stayed within what you know. You would have been safe there—your future settled, nothing more expected of you. But you went beyond that. You asked for something more. We don't know yet what that will be—better or worse than Harry Black. We've got to think, Jane— we've got to think about what's going to happen to you."

Jane shook her head, bewildered. "I get frightened when you talk like that. What is there for me? What can I do? There's no money for me to stay on here . . . I can't earn a living as a governess or anything like that. There's nothing—unless I'm a nursemaid."

"There has to be something! You'll have to marry!" She flung down the comb. "But where . . . where? And how? If I let you out as Ted wanted, you'd be as much of a sensation as he believed. You'd have men flocking about you, the fools! But would there be one to marry you? I don't think so, somehow. That's something I've learned from all these years. Only it would be harder for you. In two days the whole town would have named you your mother's daughter. Do you see that, Jane? Do you know what I'm talking about? If you had said 'yes' when Ted asked you to go to the party this evening, it would have been the end for you. In a few weeks you'd have offers—in a few weeks you'd be the mistress of some man, probably the one who could best afford you. It would go on like that—and men never seem to marry their mistresses."

"It happened once," Jane said. "Viscount Hindsley . . . surely you . . ."

Anne gave a little shrug of resignation. "But it didn't happen. In the end it was just as if Johnny had never been . . . as if I'd had no right to him. He was so madly in love with me he was blind to everything else, but when he was drowned I felt it was because he'd gone against the rules. It's perfectly natural to have a mistress—but she isn't married and allowed to bear children who succeed to the title and fortune. And it doesn't do William any good to reflect that he might have been the heir of a rich man." Anne gave a little shudder; her face in the mirror looked haggard.

"I know . . . I know . . ." Jane said.

There was silence between them, and Anne began slowly to draw the bottles and jars towards her. Carefully, patiently, she began to apply the cosmetics, the orris root powder, the rouge, the burnt cork for the eyelids. Jane's gaze never left her.

"It's money!" Anne said suddenly. "It's always money. Don't let anyone ever tell you it doesn't matter. It always matters!" She met her daughter's eyes firmly. "It wouldn't have made Johnny come to life for me—no matter how badly I wanted him—but it would have made things different for me after he was dead. It's always easier to bear sorrow when there are not bills waiting to be paid." She gave a short, nervous laugh. "Well, at least it's more dignified!"

She shrugged again. "Well," she added, "I suppose I've had my time, all the good years when it came to my hand whenever I wanted it. That was the time when I couldn't go wrong at the gaming tables—I just couldn't go wrong! And the men were generous in those days . . . and always the right ones seemed to come along when I needed them. I was younger, of course. Men are always more ready to open their purses to a young face. Well . . . well, I suppose mine isn't young any more."

She paused in her task, and craned to look into the mirror more closely. She turned from side to side, her fingers stroking her white throat.

"I'm glad now when it comes time to light the candles. I've grown afraid of the strong light. I don't want the sun to shine too brightly because it will show the lines." She sighed. "I used to love the strong sunshine."

She leaned back, away from the mirror. "I'm thirty-eight years old. That's not very old, Jane—but it's too old to find yourself without money, or any prospect of it. And without a husband to find money for you.

"I wonder if I've become foolish with age," she added. "I don't even seem to have the judgment about men I used to have. Once I used to pick and choose . . . I was cautious enough to make certain that he was worth choosing. When it came to parting we did it amiably. My bills were paid, and there was a gift or two thrown in—a necklace or a brooch. I used my head then . . . and planned. The pity of it is that I didn't use it enough to save a little of what I had in plenty. When you're young you think you can never stop being young.

"It's a sorry thing to see a woman being a fool . . . and when you know it's your own self being foolish, then it's worse. I've watched myself making mistakes, and go on making the same ones again. I've picked the wrong men—or haven't even picked—just let them happen along. A charming smile and a dash of wit were enough. All I needed at times was someone to make me laugh. A woman in business ought to know that she can't afford luxuries like laughter. *I* can't afford it.

"Look at Ted O'Neill. He's another mistake. He's good company —he's gay, and has spirit. And he has no money! He's here in London trying to sell the last of the few acres of bog he's got left somewhere off in Ireland. And he's barely got the price to take me to supper or to Vauxhall.

"And yet I keep him round . . . fool that I am! I don't know what else to do—I couldn't stand not having a man around me somewhere."

She stood up. She was clever with her hands, and the artifice of the cosmetics looked almost natural. What she had said about the candlelight was true; now she looked no different from the woman who had come to The Feathers when Jane was a baby. She stepped into the white gown; her breasts, pushed up by the high tight corset, were almost completely revealed. It was the costume of the fashionable woman of the town, and she wore it to perfection. There was a sensation of anticipation in her movements, a little color in her cheeks now that the day was finished, and the evening was come again—she would laugh and be gay over supper, and afterwards there was the beckoning prospect of the gaming tables.

Below they caught the sounds of O'Neill's arrival, Patrick's footsteps on the stairs hurrying to announce him. Jane watched the slight half-smile of pleasure widen on Anne's lips. Everything she had said of herself was true—she couldn't stand not to have a man about her.

2

Anne's household settled down to sleep. In the basement, the cook slept heavily in the arms of the stable hand who worked at the tavern four doors down the street; the room reeked of the gin they had drunk together. Above, in his narrow slit of a room that had once been a pantry, Patrick slumbered slightly, his ears ready to catch the first sound of Anne's return. William lay with his legs curled up to make room for General, who slept on the end of his bed.

Jane, with her hair washed and brushed, and wearing a nightgown of Anne's, sat before her fire struggling with a letter to Sally Cooper. The room was cozy against the chill of the night—not a luxurious room like Anne's; plain curtains and a single rug before the hearth. But she found it oppressed her less than the costly and delicate beauty below—she enjoyed the linen sheets and the good china wash set without being frightened by them. Most of all she enjoyed the sense of space and privacy—but all this was impossible to convey to Sally. She sharpened the quill again, and wrote a few more lines on the heavy, expensive paper Anne had given her. The words, written in her open, childish hand, looked stupid and ineffectual, she thought.

Earlier Patrick had brought her a toddy—hot and strongly spiced with rum. She fought against her closing eyelids, and wrote steadily on. It had been Patrick's last chore of the day—unless of course, Anne called for anything when she returned; he would then be ready, in nightshirt and tasseled cap, to do what she asked. But when he brought Jane's drink, he had a pleasant feeling of relaxation, and a need to talk. His homely face lightened with pleasure at the sight of Jane.

"Well, is it writin' y' are, now? That's grand—that's grand! Master William, now, he's a great hand with a pen too. Sure, learnin's a wonderful thing, for them that has it!"

He set the toddy before Jane, and backed reluctantly towards the door. "Is there anythin' else y'll be needin', Miss Jane? Sure y'll not hesitate to call upon me, now, will y'?"

Jane smiled faintly at his anxious and eager expression. "Thank you, Patrick. I have everything I want." She gestured towards the room. "You've made me very comfortable here."

"Sure, 'tis a pleasure, Miss Jane. 'Tis wonderful that y're here now. Master William, he's a mite lonely from time to time, poor wee soul. It's grand that y'll be company for him. An' the mistress, too . . . maybe you could . . ."

"Maybe *what*, Patrick?"

"Well . . . she's not strong, Miss Jane, as y'll have noticed. So thin she is, an' she'll take no rest at all. An' as for eatin' . . . why the sparrows do better! If y' could just persuade her now an' then to take a little more nourishment, to sleep a little longer—maybe in the afternoons . . ."

"I'll try, Patrick . . . I don't know. My mother's not a woman who can be told to do things."

"An' don't I know it, Miss Jane." He sighed, with the look of one whose patience has been tried beyond the point of speech. "I don't expect her to listen to an ignorant fella like myself, but I thought if y' just spoke to her, tactful-like . . ." He spoke with a kind of agonized concern.

"You worry about her a great deal, Patrick. . . ." Jane said gently.

"An' sure, who wouldn't . . . the precious soul that she is." He looked at her solemnly. "I don't need to tell y', Miss Jane, that yer mother's the greatest an' the kindest lady 'twill ever be me privilege to know. She has the goodness of an angel."

Jane looked at him silently, her eyes urging him to go on.

"I have reason enough to remember her goodness . . . she took me in when I was dyin', Miss Jane. I came over from Ireland one terrible bad winter . . . the harvest had been worse than nothin', an' there was terrible hunger through the land. There were too many of us already for the farm to feed, so I took the few shillin' I'd got, an' came to try me luck in London. Well, there was I, a raw Irish lad, green from the farm, an' it wasn't long before me money was taken from me, an' I was walkin' the streets hungry, like any other beggar. There was a terrible lot o' beggars on the streets that winter, Miss Jane. An' I was ill, too—a lung fever that came on so quick I didn't know what hit me. The mistress found me on her doorstep, half dead, one mornin' when she was returnin' from a party. Nothin' would do her but that I must be taken into the house, an' a doctor called—in the middle of the night, Miss Jane! For a poor fella like meself! I tell y', that woman's an angel! The best foods I had until I was better—an' me so weak I couldn't stand on me two feet for long after that night. I swear to y', Miss Jane, that I would have been dead by mornin' if she hadn't taken me in. I was past knowin' what was happenin' to me then, but I knew it later, believe me."

"And you've stayed with her since?"

"Could I think of leavin' her—'specially now when she needs me? I've been with her thirteen years—good years an' bad ones. I was with her when Lord Hindsley was drowned, an' when Master William was born. Oh, her grief over his Lordship's death was somethin' terrible. If I could have given me life to bring him back I would have done it, Miss Jane. The other servants—they've come an' gone, but I've stayed because she needs me."

"You haven't wanted to marry, Patrick—to have your own life? . . ."

He looked at her in wonderment. "Sure, where among all the dirty trollops about here could there be anyone even a little like the mistress? Sure, it would sicken me stomach to have to look at another woman about me who wasn't like her—she's such a lovely lady, Miss Jane."

"Yes . . ." she said softly. "Yes, Patrick, she is."

He left then, happy and complete because he had been permitted to talk about Anne. Jane went back to her letter thoughtfully. There were so many things to try to tell Sally apart from the bare fact that she was here, with Anne. There was this new side of Anne which Patrick had revealed, the compassionate woman behind the frivolity, the tender mother to William . . . there was this strange household itself, running on debt and the whim of the cards. There was also the new knowledge of Blake's Reach, of the existence of a family in Anne's past. There was too much to tell. In the end she wrote to Sally a self-conscious letter, telling her the details of the trip. And begging for news of Harry Black. She was dissatisfied and unhappy with it as she pressed down the wax with Anne's seal.

She fell asleep conscious that she was under Anne's roof. Patrick's toddy did its work even against the current of excitement which made her restless and wakeful. But she dreamed as she slept, and her dreams were not only of Anne, but of William also. She saw them both, walking by the sea, wrapped in the mists of the dream, and they entered together the house that William had called Blake's Reach. She herself stood by the gateway, and watched them enter; they didn't see or notice her, and she knew that she was an observer in the dream, and not part of it.

The gray dawn was breaking over the housetops when she woke briefly to hear Anne's subdued voice, and the deeper one which belonged to Lord O'Neill. Then she turned over and slept again, quietly this time, and dreamlessly. The noise of London's early morning began to stir about her.

CHAPTER FOUR

JANE HAD TO LIFT HER SKIRTS HIGH ABOVE THE MUD. JEROME Taylor had tried to insist on her staying in the carriage until they reached the other side of the square where the arcade was; but, of the London she had so far seen, Covent Garden remained Jane's favorite place, and she had overridden his objections and dismissed the hackney carriage, determined this time to walk among the stalls herself. It was her third visit here, and she looked about her, pleased by her growing sense of familiarity. Jerome held her anxiously by the elbow; William walked on her other side, his face bright in the midday sun. She found herself studying with interest and some affection the porticoed entrance to the great church which dominated the square. It was a fine thing to be able to recognize a London landmark.

"Do you like it, Miss Jane?" Jerome Taylor murmured close by her ear. "It was built by Inigo Jones."

Jane had never heard of Inigo Jones, but obviously his work was something to admire, so she craned to look at the building through the almost solid masses of people and traffic, of carriages, carts and wagons. Strangely, it did not seem at all aloof from the teeming activity surrounding it. She thought it joined with nice harmony into the arcaded shops that formed the side of the square. In the center of the Garden were the wooden stalls of the vegetable-sellers, the fruit-sellers, the herb-sellers—and overhead the pigeons wheeled and circled in endless monotony, their raucous cries mingled with the rapid voices of the humans who jammed the narrow alleys between the stalls. There was din and confusion—there were more people than Jane had ever seen together at one time. There was the strong odor of rotting food, and sweaty, unwashed bodies, of decaying clothes and grease. There was also the occasional whiff of scented hair pomade as some young man of fashion strolled by; there was the smell of London grit.

Jerome gripped her elbow more firmly as they stepped out into the stream of traffic to cross to the arcade; William also reached up, with an air of protectiveness, to take her other arm. Gradually they worked their way across. The ringing curses of hackney drivers, and the derisive laughter of the barefoot street urchins who dashed almost under their wheels were all about them. Underfoot, the cobbles were slimy with squashed, rotting vegetables and manure. In the arcade were the coffee houses, the music and print shops, the open doorways where the prostitutes lounged, waiting for clients. Above almost every shop were the bagnios where a couple could remain undisturbed for an afternoon or a night. At the back of the arcade were the crowded lanes and alleys where the brothels and bawdy houses flourished. It was an evil and noisy place, a hub for the city's teeming life. Jane's senses explored it wonderingly.

A tattered woman whose face was both young and old beneath its filthy cap, thrust a bunch of sweet-smelling herbs towards her; a peddler tried to sell her a brilliant blue bird in a cage; the bird was huddled miserably on the perch, shivering. William suddenly pulled his hand free and ran back to the woman. He fumbled in his pocket for a penny, and the woman favored him with a grin which showed her broken teeth.

"Gor blessya, luv!" Her breath reeked of gin.

William gave the herbs to Jane, pleased that he, and not Jerome, had thought of buying them.

They entered the Bedford Coffee House. It was dark inside; and they felt rather than saw the sawdust under their feet. The day's newspapers were spread on the table they were given. Jane blinked rapidly in the dimness; there was almost as much noise here as in the Garden. Men argued furiously, and in the same breath called amiable greetings to acquaintances across the room. The waiters sped about in dirty aprons. Jane wrinkled her nose a little, thinking of how Sally Cooper would have disapproved of the musty atmosphere. But when the chocolate was served it was delicious— sweet, hot, and as thick as syrup. They sipped it contentedly, making some cohesion now out of the din. At the table next to them a thin, middle-aged man sat writing at a steady pace, taking no notice at all of the traffic and the talk surrounding him.

Jerome leaned towards her. "It's probably a scandal sheet, Miss Jane. They sit in places like this and collect their information."

There were only two other women in the room. It was too early for the fashionable women of the town. The Covent Garden coffee houses were the last calls on the long way home to bed. When the more respectable places had closed their doors, the arcade and streets of this district sprang into dubious life. Often liveried coachmen and the carters bringing the early produce to market crossed angry words in the gray dawn. The Bedford was one of the most famous of the shops—the wife of the proprietor ran the largest bawdy house in the town. Jane knew that Anne came here sometimes to listen to the newest piece of scandal, lingering to read the latest pamphlets which thundered against the Jacobins until the light grew strong over the steeple of St. Peter's. Jane remembered how often Anne had spoken of the Bedford in the past; it was the place where high life and vice rubbed shoulders with the greatest ease.

Jane turned from her scrutiny of the man at the next table, and began to examine the room again; a low red fire burned in the great hearth. Over the years the smoke from it had blackened the paneled walls, and dimmed the vivid colors of the lewd painting that hung over the mantel. Jane studied the picture; in Hampstead there had never been a painting like this one exhibited in public view. She turned and found Jerome's eyes on her. He reddened, and looked down at his cup.

She had been in Anne's house for over four weeks, and March had passed into April. From the first day, the ease and softness of life in Anne's household fitted to Jane like the gowns she had made over for herself. She learned that it was possible to sleep after the sun came up, to expect hot water waiting when she did rise; she put goose grease on her rough hands and watched them grow soft and white, the bruise around her eye had vanished. Jane knew she enjoyed this sense of ease, but it never became wholly real to her; daily she expected it to end.

Jerome Taylor was a part of the new life. From the first day, when they had passed each other on the stairs, he had invented every kind of excuse to be in her company. She grew used to seeing his eyes follow her, but, without knowing the reason why, he irritated her vaguely. Perhaps it was because she had always imagined a scholar would have no thoughts to spare for women. But he was handsome in a quiet way, and had pleasing manners—and quite obviously he spared time to think of her. She needed friends in this new world, so she smiled on him, and accepted his stammered compliments. In return he gave her a gentle devotion.

The days passed and inevitably she began to grow restless. There was not enough occupation for her energies in the house—the gowns Anne had given her were all renovated, and she had finished all the mending that had piled up. With Patrick's help, she turned out cupboards all over the house, settling order into their chaos, and at the same time earning the hatred of Anne's slatternly cook. The time began to pass heavily, because life at The Feathers had never trained her to sit in the white and gold drawing room with a tapestry frame. Anne's round of activities was ceaseless; she was happy and lighthearted because the luck seemed to be with her and she gaily attributed this change to Jane's presence. She paid a few of the most pressing debts to get rid of the dunners, and ordered the gown she had admired from Seiker's—also one for Jane. Jane was pleased by Anne's good humor, but a sense of guilt gnawed at her. There was no sign that Harry Black was going to make charges, and she worried less about the danger from that direction. With this gone, the days stretched before her idly.

At last, a little desperate, she went to Anne and suggested that she must find some employment. It would have to be somewhere away from London—Anne's reputation and her methods of getting money would make a situation in London nearly impossible. Her fine gowns and her hands that grew always softer were no help either. Anne shrugged her shoulders.

"Child, enjoy yourself while you're able! When the money's gone will be time enough to think about what you must do. Enjoy yourself. . . ."

But where . . . with whom? There were only William and Jerome Taylor; the whole teeming world of London waited beyond Anne's silk-curtained windows, and her only companions were the child and his tutor. She began to slip into the classroom, and listened to Jerome's pleasant voice as he read history with William; with faint wonder she studied the maps that recorded Captain Cook's voyages in the Pacific, and heard accounts of the settlement at Botany Bay in New South Wales. Jerome Taylor responded instantly to her need and loneliness. He went to Anne and asked if Miss Jane shouldn't be taken to see the sights of the town. William, of course, would go with them.

Anne had lain back in her bed chuckling over it when Jane entered the bedroom one morning.

"Oh, Jane, that poor young man! He's dazzled! And I was just about to forget to pay his salary this month—now I'll have to find it somewhere. I couldn't have it on my conscience!"

And she told it to Lord O'Neill with great relish.

Jerome's devotion made Jane uncomfortable. She wasn't used to being treated as if she hadn't seen a mud puddle in her life before. But she learned to play the part he expected from her reasonably well, knowing that he had mixed with gentlewomen all his life, and was impressing her with the pattern. She stifled her impatience and high spirits, and tried to remember the things he talked about. She followed him quietly round the city's churches which Christopher Wren had built. She learned to draw him out. He would talk on happily, and nothing was beyond him—the Revolution in France, the War of Independence that had cost England her American colonies, the root system of the dandelion growing at their feet in the churchyard, the science of botany, and what he hoped to record on the voyage in the South Seas. She listened to it all, and tried to remember. He knew more than she had believed was contained in one mind. He loved music and painting too—as his confidence grew he began to talk of visits to the playhouses, occasions when William could not be present. She was eager for the experience of learning the city by night. These excursions to Covent Garden and the Bedford were a step in that direction, a faint brush with the world that Anne inhabited.

William's head turned and twisted endlessly; he sipped his chocolate and let nothing go by him. He had all of Anne's restless curiosity. These past days with Jane and Jerome Taylor had been blissfully happy ones for him—free from lessons of a formal sort, and mingling with the crowds and bustle he loved. He approved of the Bedford completely, approved of Jane because she drew the glances of the men, approved of the packed, suffocating odor. He liked the world as he saw it.

Then he spoke suddenly. "There's a man over there who keeps

staring. I've stared back at him, and frowned, and I've shaken my head at him. But he just goes on staring."

Jerome Taylor looked angry. "Who . . . where?"

"Over there, behind you." Jerome turned round quickly as William indicated the man—a youngish man, with the aged, timeless look of a sailor, the faded eyes and the weathered skin. He wore a sailor's jersey and a tasseled cap.

"Who—*that* fellow?" Jerome looked back at Jane. "Miss Jane, perhaps you would like to go. This is no place to have a scene. It would be all over the town in a day. . . ."

"Oh, hush!" Jane broke in. "Look—he's getting up! He's coming over here!" Jerome's eyes clouded, because she was visibly excited and expectant.

Without haste the sailor made his way through the crowd, never taking his eyes off the group, staring at them unblinkingly and without embarrassment. He bent over the table a little. Indignantly, Jerome half rose to his feet.

"Look here! . . ."

The sailor took no notice of him. "You'll be a Blake," he said to Jane.

"What?"

"You'll be a Blake," he repeated. "You'll be a child of Anne Blake, or I'm a dead man."

Jane looked at him with rounded, astonished eyes. "Yes . . . Yes, that's right! My name's Jane Howard. Anne Blake is my mother."

He nodded, a wide grin splitting his face. He pulled his cap off his head.

"I seen y' 'ere once before, an' I said t' meself soon as I clapped eyes on y' that y' were kin o' the Blake family . . . but this time I were sure." His eyes examined her face again carefully, wonderingly. "Well . . . so yer Miss Anne's an' Tom 'oward's child! Miss Anne—she were about yer age when I seen 'er last. She were much of an age with meself."

"You knew her when she was at Blake's Reach?" Jane said. It was strange to hear that name uttered like this to a man she had never seen before.

He nodded again. "It were like I said—she were much of an age with meself, an' she used t' come ridin' through Appledore most every day. Sometimes she'd stop by the cottage an' talk with me mother. Why, the whole Marsh knew Miss Anne. Blake's Reach weren't big enough t' 'old her. She were out in all weathers, an' she used t' talk t' every livin' soul she met on the road. The way she used t' act—folks used t' say the whole Marsh belonged t' 'er."

He warmed to his own memories. "Just you ask 'er if she don't remember ridin' into Appledore an' talkin' with Mary Thomas . . . an' young Adam 'angin' round t' catch a glimpse o' 'er. She were that pretty! There were so many Thomases around in them days y' couldn't 'ardly stir a step without y' fell over one o' them. Ask 'er if she remembers!"

"She remembers—I'm sure she remembers!" This was from William, who couldn't contain himself any longer. His face was flushed with excitement.

The sailor turned and regarded William carefully. "An' this will be another Blake—same 'air, same mouth."

"My half-brother," Jane said. After a slight hesitation, she added, "Won't you take a seat?"

Jerome Taylor's expression was thunderous as the man slipped easily into the seat by Jane; he was outraged and ruffled. But a glance from Jane forbade any objection; stiffly he acknowledged the introduction Jane made.

Adam Thomas was not at all disturbed by Jerome's scowl. He continued talking calmly. "We did 'ear, down on the Marsh, that Miss Anne 'ad a child—maybe two or three. Just scraps o' news, y' know—maybe picked up from one o' the folks from Rye, who'd been t' London. But I come up 'ere to London meself a few weeks back, an' I begin askin' about 'er. Was told she comes 'ere t' the Bedford once in a while. I've been keepin' an eye skinned for 'er— she always bein' so friendly-like, she'd never take offense at any of the Marsh folk speakin' to 'er. . . ."

He looked pointedly across at Jerome.

"Miss Anne ain't never been back t' the Marsh," Adam observed regretfully. "We always did 'ope that maybe someday she would make it up with the old man. But the Blakes—they always been 'igh-spirited an' proud people. Weren't no way, really, that Miss Anne could make amends, and the old man ain't the forgivin' type. Proud as peacocks, the Blakes are! Always 'igh and mighty they've been,

and there's some o' the gentry about as 'asn't liked it, but I say—
and there's many a one as says it with me—that it'll be a bad thing
when the Blakes go from the Marsh. An' the time's comin' pretty
soon, ma'am, when there'll be none on the Marsh who's a Blake,
either by birth or name. As long as the Marsh folk remember, there's
been a Blake. It'll seem wrong without them."

"Without them?" Jane echoed. "Why?"

Thomas shrugged. "Why, ma'am? Well, it's plain old Spencer
can 'ardly last the year—'e's drinkin' 'eavy, I do 'ear, and 'e's not
a young man any more. Seems like 'e don't care, neither . . . the
land's almost all gone, an' the 'ouse be fallin' down about 'is ears."

"The land's gone? Why?"

He shrugged again. "That's 'ardly my business, is it, Miss Jane?
What the gentry do is their affair—and it's not for the likes o' me t'
'ave anythin' to say about it. If Spencer Blake takes too much t'
drink when 'e settles down with the cards . . . well, a man's got
the right to gamble with 'is own property. But once y' start slicin'
up a fine property like that was—sellin' a bit 'ere, a bit there—
well, it don't amount t' much, now. The tenant farmers 'ave most
of it—an' old Spencer, 'e 'asn't troubled to improve the sheep, an'
they're a pretty run-down lot, not givin' anythin' like the yield o'
wool or mutton, or the fancy price the Blake's Reach stuff used t'
fetch. A pity like—that's what I say."

"The land's gone. . . ." Jane repeated it in a dazed fashion.

"Aye—it's gone, an' beggin' Miss Anne's pardon, there's no one
could really blame Spencer. There's the man all alone in the great
house, not kith or kin near 'im. 'Tain't any wonder 'e takes a drop.
It seems 'e don't care what 'appens t' 'im, or t' Blake's Reach.
There be no one t' leave it t' after 'e's gone—that is, no one who'll
live on the Marsh. After Miss Anne ran away with Tom 'oward,
'twas said 'e named the nephew, the dark little one who was half
French, in 'is will. But then 'e ran away back t' France. But it don't
matter whether Spencer left 'im in the will or cut 'im out, because
'e's dead."

"Dead?"

"Aye . . . 'is 'ead cut off in this Revolution that's goin' on. I
remember 'im almost as clear as Miss Anne—as dark as the devil, 'e
was, an' could ride a horse like I never seen before. Well, 'e's dead,

now—and 'tain't likely there'll ever be Blakes on the Marsh again. . . ."

"No . . . I expect not. . . ."

He scratched his head slowly. "Well—I was thinkin' that maybe I'd perhaps see Miss Anne about 'ere some place. I could'a told 'er about 'ow feeble old Spencer's gettin' . . . maybe she'd go and visit 'im. Guess even people as proud as the Blakes make it up sometimes. Would do the old man good if she went back and saw 'im—would kind o' lift 'im up if 'e saw 'is grandchildren. 'E's a touchy old devil, is Spencer—but there can't never be a man as won't feel like makin' friends when 'e's near t' dyin'."

Jane nodded. "I'll tell my mother what you've said—maybe some time she'll be here, and you must say it all again to her. How long will you be in London?"

He scratched his head again. "Can't rightly say. I get some work from time t' time. Was figerin' I'd get t'gether a few shillin's an' make me way t' Liverpool, and ship out from there." He grinned suddenly, and his face seemed full of an unholy glee. "'Ad a brush with the customs' men a few weeks back, so the Marsh ain't exactly 'ealthy for me right now. But I'll be back—someday I'll be back! The pickin's are too good t' lose. . . ."

He favored Jane with a broad wink, and another grin, as if she shared some fantastic plot with him. He rose to his feet then.

"I'll bid y' good day, Miss Jane—an' y'll please remember me kindly to Miss Anne. Just tell 'er what I've told you—an' say it come from Adam Thomas. That's all."

"Wouldn't you come and tell her yourself?"

He shook his head. "'Tain't for the likes o' me t' be callin' on Miss Anne. Just tell 'er the old man's slippin'—that's enough. No one tells Miss Anne what t' do—no one! An' this ain't none o' me business, see. Ain't none o' me business!"

He made a clumsy attempt at a bow, and strode out of the coffee house, disappearing into the crowd in the Garden. Jane watched his sailor's cap bobbing; when he was gone from sight she turned quickly to Jerome. Her face was pale; two brilliant spots of color burned in her cheeks.

"I must go back now. I must speak with my mother."

2

Anne sat once again before her mirror; she listened while Jane talked. Her face reflected in the pale oval, was thoughtful; she nodded quietly at Jane's words.

"So . . . Charlie's dead! And Father is dying! Well, that's the end of the Blakes!" Her voice was curiously hollow and lifeless.

"Don't you care?"

"Care?" Anne stirred a little. "I don't know—it's so long since I've seen Father I can hardly feel what it will be like to know that he's dead. And Charlie—he was a little boy when I left. He was my first cousin, the only child of Spencer's brother, who married a Frenchwoman. I can't think of him as a man who has lost his head. All I remember of Charlie was the way he used to ride across the Marsh as if he and the pony were one animal. He was so dark, Charlie was—and so silent. It's as if you told me a shadow was dead."

"But you don't care . . . about Blake's Reach?"

Now Anne's expression took form and meaning. "Care about Blake's Reach? You mean why don't I go and make it up with Father and he will leave Blake's Reach to me? Well, I'll tell you plainly. I hate Blake's Reach! And I'd rather die than have to go back to live there!"

"But the inheritance?"

"What inheritance?" Anne snapped. "Will it do me any good to inherit a crumbling pile of bricks, and a mountain of debts? I have enough debts of my own!"

"How do you know?" Jane persisted. "How can you be sure that Adam Thomas knows all the truth? Or that he knows any of it? He may be wrong."

"He's not wrong. The Marsh people always know everything that whispers or breathes on the Marsh. Adam Thomas' father was one of our shepherds, and his father before him. The mother worked in our dairy. Don't you think they know? Believe me, they know almost as much as Father does about Blake's Reach! Didn't he say the land was gone? Well, let me tell you—land is money. You need land for sheep, and sheep are all that matter on the Romney Marsh."

"But there must be something—*something* that's worth saving!" Jane's voice was anguished. She couldn't believe what her senses were telling her—that Anne meant to do nothing about Blake's Reach, that she wouldn't stir a finger to keep any part of it for herself, that she could let it all be submerged in a tide of indifference.

"There's nothing worth saving—nothing! There was almost nothing worth saving twenty years ago when I ran away with Tom. Father had a match all made for me with a man who could have put Blake's Reach back on its feet. Only he didn't take into account the fact that I didn't care enough for Blake's Reach to save it at the expense of myself." She gave an angry toss of her head, and her lovely voice grew a trifle shrill. "He pretended he loved me—worshiped me! But all it was was pride in the way I looked, and how I sat a horse. He gave me everything I wanted, but all it meant was that in the end I should be agreeable to marrying myself to Roger Pym, and living on that godforsaken Marsh for the rest of my days.

"Do you think," she demanded harshly, "that I care to go back now and drop on my knees to him, just so that I'll inherit the mess he chose to make of his life? I'm in a mess too—but at least it's one of my own making! Do you think I could go back there and live? You don't know what it's like, Jane. Just flat—all of it—and Blake's Reach standing on the cliff above the Marsh where the sea winds cut you to pieces, and the roads so bad in winter that you couldn't even travel the six miles to Rye for a little company and gaiety. There's nothing but flat miles of sheep, and beyond them, the sea. Just think of it! —sitting by the fire all winter long, and listening to the gales sweeping up the Channel . . . and knowing that there was nothing to do except struggle up the hill every third Sunday, to sit in the Blake pew in the church Great-grandfather Blake built with money he had stolen in the Marlborough wars. No news, no excitement—nothing except the whisper that runs round the Marsh when a big run of smugglers' goods have been safely landed. The only lights that show on the Marsh by night, Jane, are the beacons and the lanterns that light the smugglers' luggers into anchor. On the one hand you have murderers and cutthroats for company—on the other there's the country squires, with their dowdy wives and daughters."

"Murderers? What do you mean—*murderers?*"

Anne said quietly, "In all of England there's no district so favorable to the smuggling fraternity. They're born seamen, Jane—more brave and reckless than men have right to be. Tea and brandy and tobacco—the whole country uses smuggled goods without thinking that they break the law by not paying customs' duty on them. And it's the men along the coast from Kent to Cornwall who bring it in. The Romney Marsh has an edge on all the other counties because it has the wool that the Flemish weavers need. They take wool instead of gold to pay for the tea and brandy. They make fortunes, Jane—real fortunes! Don't you think men will murder for such money? I can tell you that the life of the man who informs isn't worth a penny piece on the Marsh. He had best say his prayers.

"That's what the Marsh means, Jane—smugglers, sheep and clottish squires. Could you expect me to want to go running there now to a father I have never cared for, and who has never cared for me? Could you see me *living* there, even if the land and the money weren't all gone. It's unthinkable!"

In those terms, it was unthinkable. Jane turned away slowly. "Yes, it is," she said.

Over by the window she stood for a long time pondering what Anne had said. It sounded bleak and somber—the long winters of Channel storms and the slow pace of country life. She thought of the old man who was dying there alone, who had quarreled with every living blood relation—and who, perhaps, was now regretting it. She thought of the long succession of Blakes who had been on the Marsh, the house and the family that Anne hated, but which symbolized part of the life of the Marsh itself to Adam Thomas. It seemed criminal to her that Anne should make no attempt to salvage some of it. The energies of a family for generations had gone into the making of this, the last one—and she was going to cast it aside like a gown out of fashion. The whole idea made Jane desperate and rebellious.

"The Blakes—they've been there a long time?" she asked. "Even hundreds of years?"

"Three or four hundred years for certain, Jane. They were there when the Marsh really *was* a marsh, with the tidewaters sweeping in when the Channel ran high. They helped dig the ditches and the innings that drained it, and made it one of the most fertile lands in England. They are part of the Marsh, almost as old as it is. They're a proud name there—even now, when the power's gone from it, it's a name that's remembered. They've held titles and positions—Lords Proprietors of the Romney Marsh, and Barons of the Cinque Ports with the right to carry the canopy of the Sovereign as he goes to Coronation.

"Oh, yes, it's an old and a proud name, Jane. But the Blakes are finished. Leave them in peace."

Then she rose from the toilet table, and went downstairs to the drawing room, her mouth folded in a bitter and angry line. The brisk rustle of her petticoat seemed crisp and determined. Soon the sound of her laughter floated up, the artficially gay laughter of a woman who was seething inside.

Jane stayed for a long time staring at nothing through the window.

"There has to be some way to convince her," she whispered to herself. "She has to go to Blake's Reach! *She has to go!*"

3

At The Theater Royal *The Beggar's Opera* was playing. Jerome Taylor had shyly stammered an invitation to Jane, and managed to ignore William's pleading eyes. Now he moved, tongue-tied with pride and happiness, beside Jane through the foyer of the theater. The first act was over, and the audience spilled out of the pit in a bewildering press, laughing, talking, humming airs from the opera which they had known all their lives. The people from the boxes came down to push their own way into the throng. The air was suffocating with the mingled smells of perfume and hair pomade.

Jane eyed the scene with delight, and Jerome with great contentment. He was quite certain that there was no other woman there to hold a candle to Jane. She wore a white gown, and Anne had loaned her a fur-trimmed wrap. He wondered how she managed to look like a woman of fashion well used to attending the theater, and still retain some of the freshness that had so attracted him when she had first come from Hampstead. Seeing her now as she slowly

swished her fan in an imitation of Anne's movements, it was an
effort to recall her bruised eye and frightened manner on that first
day. She had, he decided, used her five weeks in her mother's household to startling effect. It was only at this thought, and of the future,
that his brow clouded a little.

Jane had been happily silent beside him, watching the crowd and
storing up every detail against the time for recollection. Now she
suddenly stared and snapped her fan shut.

"Look, there's Lord O'Neill! Oh . . . he's seen us!"

Jerome turned and saw, and inwardly cursed. Lord O'Neill was
shouldering his way through the crowd, obviously making towards
them. He reached them, smiling good-humoredly at the crush,
bowed to Jane and kissed her hand.

"My dear Miss Jane—how beautiful you look!"

She thanked him with a smile, conscious that beside her Jerome
had greeted O'Neill in a tone that was barely civil. She broke in
quickly. "Is my mother here? I believed she was not feeling well
this evening. She said she would stay at home."

O'Neill shrugged. "That's what I was told—and she didn't appear to want my company, so I took myself off. . . ." He turned
his smile on Jerome now. "She told me, Mr. Taylor, that you had
accompanied Miss Jane to the theater, and I was wondering if I
could prevail upon you to allow a lonely man to take you both
to supper. It really would be a great kindness on your part. . . ."

Jerome stiffened, and his face grew red. "Why—I hardly
think . . ."

O'Neill turned appealingly to Jane. "You won't desert me, Miss
Jane? Think how lost I am without your mother's company. Perhaps you can persuade Mr. Taylor. . . ."

"I . . . well . . ." She wanted desperately to go with him, to
taste just once the sort of company that her mother knew night
after night. She wondered where they would dine, and whom she
might see there, what prominent figures from the political and social scene would be pointed out to her. Perhaps she might even be
introduced to one or two of them . . . Her thoughts ran on wildly.
She was wearing a gown that was fit for any occasion, any company;
just once she wanted to find out what it was like to dine with a
titled man who was a part of the fashionable world of London,

wanted to be treated as if she also belonged there. Only the thought
of Jerome made her hesitate. If she wished she could pretend not
to notice his discomfort; she knew he would submit to any decision
she made. But she had seen the look of disappointment that had
come over his face.

"Well, Miss Jane, what do you say? Will you come?"

She didn't have time to reply. O'Neill turned as he felt a hand
fall on his shoulder. His face brightened with pleasure as he recognized the two men standing behind him.

"Gerald! When did you come back to town? I didn't know you
were here!"

The other man, dark like O'Neill, and almost as tall, took his
outstretched hand. "Got back from the bogs today, Ted, and thank-
ing Providence I have! Ireland is no place to spend the winter. But
my good lady wife will present me with an heir in two months, and
is determined he shall be born on the estate. So I've left her to con-
template the bogs, and I've come to enjoy myself a little. . . ." He
was no longer interested in O'Neill, but was staring directly at Jane.

O'Neill turned. "Forgive me, Miss Jane. May I present my
cousin, Gerald Hickey . . ." His flourish indicated the second man.
"And my good friend, Sir Philip Guest. Miss Jane Howard." Then
he added hurriedly, "Oh . . . and this is Jerome Taylor."

Jane found her hand being kissed by both men, while appraising
eyes were run expertly over her.

The one O'Neill had called Philip Guest spoke now. "Charmed!
. . . and charming!" Then his brow wrinkled a little. "Howard!
Isn't that—"

"Anne's daughter," O'Neill said. "Miss Jane has come from the
country to visit her mother. Anne was indisposed tonight, and I
was fortunate enough to find Miss Jane here with Mr. Taylor. I
was just trying to persuade them both to keep me company at
supper."

"That's splendid!" Hickey spoke now; he was smiling broadly
at Jane, and still holding her hand. She had to give a little tug to
free it. "You'll allow us to join you, Ted?" He nodded to Jane.
"Your mother and I are friends of long standing . . . Sir Philip has
also known her for many years."

Then he clapped O'Neill again on the shoulder. "Where has

Anne kept her all this time? London has far too few redheads, and none so lovely as Miss Jane. Anne Howard's daughter . . . well . . ."

Guest broke in then. "Look here—do we have to stay to the end of this thing? Tony Cox is gathering some friends together at Drake's . . . why don't we all go there now? It would be an amusing evening . . . and Miss Jane would . . ."

Jane no longer hesitated. She laid her hand firmly on Jerome's arm. She smiled at them all demurely as she spoke. "I'll have to beg you to excuse me, gentlemen. I'm feeling a trifle unwell myself, and I was about to ask Mr. Taylor to take me home immediately."

As she curtsied she caught the wondering and puzzled exchange of glances between the three, the shrugs and the raised eyebrows. She knew that they were not at all deceived by her pretense. She hadn't intended them to be.

No words passed between herself and Jerome until they were settled finally in the hackney carriage, but she felt the reassuring pressure of his hand under her elbow. At last, in the darkness of the coach, she spoke to him.

"I'm sorry, Jerome. I'm sorry to spoil your evening. I had to leave —you know that!" And then: "I was getting beyond my depth."

"I understand, Miss Jane." There was more warmth than disappointment in his tone.

When they reached Albemarle Street she was still a little dazed by the shock of realizing how firmly she was labeled as Anne's daughter. Had she wished it, this evening could have been the beginning of a new episode, a whole career. It was there, ready and waiting for her; but if she were to repeat Anne's life, it would have to be because she chose to do it, not because it was expected of her. In those few moments she had felt her newly found identity threatened. In the minds of O'Neill and his friends she was not a person in her own right, but another Anne, and it was assumed that she would think and behave exactly as Anne did. She was discovering at last that she was not permitted to go into Anne's world on her own terms; the terms were already made for her.

Anne had heard them return, and she came out of the drawing room, and stood at the top of the stairs.

"Jane!" Her voice was shrill and unnaturally loud. "You're back

early!" And then as Jerome closed the door she added, questioningly, "Isn't Lord O'Neill with you?"

Jane shook her head. "I wasn't feeling well. I asked Jerome to
bring me back."

"Did you meet Ted? Was he there?"

"Yes, we met him. He was going to supper with his cousin,
Gerald Hickey, and Sir Philip Guest."

"Did he ask you to go?"

Jane hesitated, but Anne's eyes were on her firmly. "Yes," she
said.

"Why didn't you?"

Jane had had enough of it. "I thought I had already explained
that. I'm not feeling well." With great deliberation she turned her
back on Anne, and began to pull off her gloves. But the gesture
was wasted; Anne had already started up the stairs to her bedroom.

Later, when Jane was alone in her own room, she lay for a long
time, fully dressed, on the bed, staring at the ceiling. It was cracked,
and would soon need repair; she traced the line of cracks, her mind
busy with the new problem she had suddenly found tonight in this
house.

"I can't stay here," she whispered, twisting her face towards the
pillow. "I can't stay here!"

4

Jane knew that she had to go, and that it must be soon. But
there was no time to speak to Anne, or to try to disentangle the
currents of jealousy and resentment that had been so crudely revealed in that conversation on the stairs. What neither of them
knew was that, by the next day, time had almost finished for Anne.

It had been strangely humid for April, and when the rain started
in the early evening Jane and William watched it falling past the
window with a feeling of relief. They thought only momentarily of
Anne who had said casually that she might take a boat down to
Chelsea with O'Neill and some others. Jane and William were both
in bed when she returned, and so they didn't know that her gown
was still wet from the drenching she had had, or that even so soon
there was the dampness of fever on her skin.

It was Patrick who called Jane from the schoolroom in the middle of the morning, at the time he usually gave Anne her chocolate. His sharp face was made sharper by panic.

"It's the mistress, Miss Jane—she's ill!"

For four days they watched the struggle—it was only a slight struggle on Anne's part. Death waited on her almost from the beginning. She lay propped up against high pillows making a small effort to breathe; the flesh seemed to drop off her frame with terrifying swiftness. With frightened eyes Jane saw the bluish lips, heard the soft bubble of liquid in her lungs. When she coughed, the mucus was blood-streaked.

The doctor would give a despairing shrug of his shoulders. "Not strong enough to fight—she was worn out before it began."

In the end, it seemed as if she drowned in that engulfing liquid; her eyes looked out helplessly from a face sunken into age, and she paid no heed to Patrick's imploring voice and gestures. When she died, William was almost the first to know it. After Patrick's instinctive movement towards Anne, he gave one sharp shriek of terror, and flung himself into Jane's arms. O'Neill stood transfixed at the bottom of the bed, not moving or saying anything for a long time; his face had the look of confusion and unbelief. Patrick was weeping.

Jane bent and lifted William into her arms and carried him away from the sight of Anne. At the same moment she consciously recognized that she was taking up what remained of Anne's life.

It was Jane who made the choice of the place where Anne should be buried. Of all the churches Jerome Taylor had shown her, she remembered only one clearly.

"The one in Covent Garden," she said.

When it was over she knew that they all waited on her expectantly —O'Neill, Jerome, Patrick and William. They waited for her to speak as Anne had done, to make all the necessary plans and decisions. O'Neill knew that he had no place any longer in the household, but he waited still—waited for the woman he had seen buried in Covent Garden where the endless rumble of the wheels, and the nasal Cockney voices could reach her. He, like the others, hovered about Jane, because it seemed that in her Anne still lived.

She was completely Anne's daughter when she did make up her mind, prepared to face argument with stubbornness, and go ahead with her plans. She had lived with Anne for less than six weeks, but she knew all that Anne had been, and she knew what was expected of her. Even if she shed tears at night into her pillow, they weren't permitted to show next day on her face.

"We can't stay in London—William and I," she said.

"Where will you go?" O'Neill asked.

"We will go to Blake's Reach."

5

All of them had arguments against it—but none of them could suggest any other plan. Already the bill collectors were at the door, more persistent than ever because now Anne was dead.

"We can't stay in London, that's plain," Jane said firmly. "Wherever we go in this town they'll be dunning me for money, and there's nothing to pay them with. If I go to my grandfather perhaps . . . well, there's a chance he'll take us in. If he doesn't . . ." She shrugged her shoulders. "We won't be any worse off than we are now."

Patrick spoke up desperately. "Then I'll go with y', ma'am."

They looked at him, startled.

Jane shook her head slowly. "I can't pay your wages."

His face flushed painfully. "Do you think I'll take wages from y', Miss Anne's child? She clothed me an' fed me, an' that was all I required."

"I couldn't, Patrick . . . it isn't fair."

He set his lips stubbornly. "I'll be a grand help to y', ma'am. It'll give y' some standin' to arrive with a servant by y'. Y'll have me when y' need me."

He seemed to take it as settled, especially when O'Neill presented Jane with the beautiful pair of grays that drew Anne's carriage. The carriage was the one Viscount Hindsley had given her, and O'Neill had put his own pair of Irish thoroughbreds between the shafts. He made light of the gift.

"I always considered that they belonged to Anne," he said. "Besides, Patrick's right. The better impression you make, the bigger your chances. If you go cap in hand you'll get nothing, and no welcome." Then he shrugged. "Apart from that, those horses are worth money. You may need them."

Jane thought his graceful and lighthearted manner of giving was impressive when she remembered he was almost penniless himself.

Patrick then, was to go as coachman. A period of desperate and secret activity fell over the house. From the outside nothing must appear unusual, for while Jane remained, the bill collectors were confident of their money. So Patrick told them stories of Jane's being prostrate with grief, and unable to attend to business. At the same time the cook was given her wages and dismissed, so that her tongue would not wag about the preparations for leaving. In his market basket, Patrick took Anne's silver and sold it. The jewels Viscount Hindsley had given her were sold long ago—she had been wearing paste copies so that their absence wouldn't disturb her creditors. Jane shook her head regretfully over the few inexpensive trinkets that were left. The best of them Patrick took away to sell— she kept the rest, because by now she had entered completely into the idea that she must make the best impression possible. She packed boxes and hampers with Anne's gowns, her fingers busy half the night with alterations to them, and with the necessary repairs to William's clothes. She packed some of the finest linen, and the little soft, lace-edged pillows without which Anne had never traveled. The silver spoons and forks went into Patrick's basket. O'Neill told her that some of the figurines in the drawing room and the china were valuable; they also went. A fever of stripping and selling fell on them—Jane regretted that the crystal chandelier in the drawing room was too bulky to go into the market basket. O'Neill took a small painting to a dealer in Bond Street, and came back with fifty guineas. They ransacked cupboards to find more to sell.

Jerome didn't hold himself aloof from this. The hours he was supposed to give William lessons he spent helping Jane, his eyes anguished and already lonely. As, one by one, Anne's lovely things disappeared from walls and cupboards and tables his face grew sadder and more dismayed. Unlike O'Neill, he had no grief for Anne to bury in the bustle and hurry, so the dismantling of the house hurt him, because it made Jane's departure certain. But he was clever with William, keeping him so busy that there was hardly time for him to wander disconsolately into Anne's empty room. Sometimes at night he would sit with Jane as she waited, her hand in William's, for the child to fall asleep. They would talk very softly in the dimness.

"It can't be more than three or four months before the ship is fitted up, Miss Jane. We'll be in the South Seas for two years—I don't suppose . . . well, I don't suppose I'll ever see you again."

"Who can tell?" she murmured. "Much can happen in two years. My grandfather may be dead . . . I may have to come back to London. Anything can happen in two years. You'll enjoy the expedition . . . you've always said that. . . ."

"Yes," he agreed, but he said it distastefully.

The only unsalable item was the house itself. O'Neill advised Jane against doing anything with it at the present. "Once anyone finds out you want to sell, you'll never be allowed to leave here until every penny Anne owed has been paid up. You'll have lawyers' fees to prove you've the right to sell it—and agents' fees, and the Lord knows what. Besides, I know Anne mortgaged it . . . leave it until you see what way the wind lies with your grandfather. You may be glad to come back."

Jane looked around her and knew that she would never be coming back to this house. This represented Anne's extravagance and irresponsibility; to come back would be to admit that she would need men like O'Neill and Hindsley to pay for it.

She gave a short little laugh. "It's too late to give me notions of living in a house like this, Lord O'Neill! I'm not very handy at spending money I haven't got!"

He looked at her carefully, from her curled hair to the hem of the expensively simple gown she wore. "You could learn . . . learning to spend money isn't difficult. And you'd find better men than myself, Jane—ones who have money enough to satisfy every wish."

Jane bent over her sewing. "Anne made her mistakes—and she told me I didn't have to make them too."

O'Neill said nothing. He didn't think it was any notion of virtue that held Jane back—but rather a sense of thrift and good management. But it was a waste, all the same, he thought. He looked at her, and knew that she was made for a man's bed, and in this city she could have been highly paid for the privilege. Because she wasn't careless like Anne, she would make her choices better, and for her there wouldn't be Anne's career of debt and extravagance. He had observed her carefully since her arrival, and he knew that she took to ease and luxury with the eagerness of someone who has longed for it. And she could have had it—just by allowing herself to be seen about on his arm, by letting herself be displayed and examined, by giving up this ridiculous independence she had. Instead she had chosen to scrape together a few pounds, and set off for the wilderness of the Romney Marsh, and the doubtful welcome of an old man. And just for the hope of inheriting a ruin. It didn't make sense to him. He didn't want to think of all that beauty and excitement going to waste. It was worse than pouring gold into the Thames—he had thought she knew enough to know that.

He couldn't decide whether she was passing all this up because she hadn't fully realized the possibilities before her, or whether she was taking a bigger gamble in bidding for respectability, her family name, and the long chance of a good marriage. If that was the case, then he admired her courage and was doubtful of her chances. Above all, he hoped that she would have the good sense to show young Jerome Taylor the door, and that a moment of sentimentality wouldn't condemn her to a life of penny-pinching as the wife of an impecunious man of science. Besides that, Jerome deserved something softer and kinder than Jane—he didn't deserve to be ruined by a woman with ambition. They were wrong for each other, these two—totally wrong. But he guessed that Jane already knew it.

So he said nothing. He aided her with the preparations where he could, spent his time with her because he missed Anne so badly, and he continued to think his own thoughts—thoughts of the glittering success she could have been, of the jewels and money she could have had, the houses and the carriages, the notoriety. At the same time he was envious because she had the strength he didn't have to pass it all up.

The rush of preparation was finished, and they were ready to go. Patrick went to the livery stable, paid a little on account on the bill Anne owed there, and took the grays and the carriage. It remained outside the door until the streets were dark and quiet; Patrick carried the boxes out at intervals, and stowed them inside where they wouldn't attract attention. It was time for Jane and William to leave—O'Neill had agreed to stay in the house for some days so that the bill collectors should not realize it was empty.

Jerome was there to say good-bye. He watched as Jane leaned from the carriage window, and O'Neill stretched up and kissed her softly. Jerome hesitated a second, and as his hand clasped Jane's, with sudden desperate courage, he also sought her lips. It was a clumsy kiss, and full of heartbreak.

"I'll never forget you, Miss Jane. I'll think of you always. It's only two years . . . I'll come to Kent to see you as soon as I'm back."

She pressed his hand hard, and was astonished to find that there were tears in her eyes. Then Jerome stepped back and took his place beside O'Neill.

"As soon as I come back . . ." he repeated.

Jane waved, and the carriage moved forward. She and William strained from their seats to get the last glimpse of the pair. She held Jerome's words firmly in her mind against the terrible loneliness and panic which threatened to sweep over her. She tucked William's hand in her own.

"Did you hear that, William? Mr. Taylor is coming to see us as soon as he gets back from the expedition."

William stroked General's head, and said nothing. It was impossible to tell what he felt about leaving the house in Albemarle Street.

Jane didn't know, nor did Jerome, that war with France would be many months old when he returned, and that he would transfer immediately into His Majesty's Navy. He was to die under Nelson at the battle of the Nile; he was never to see Jane again.

But none of them knew it that chill April night in 1792 when Jane and William set out for Blake's Reach.

PART TWO

PART TWO

CHAPTER ONE

THE WIND DROVE IN HARD FROM THE SEA, PUSHING HEAVY GRAY clouds across the leaden Marsh sky. The ancient town of Rye was behind them on the hill—the sloping terraces of roofs, the square-towered church and the crumbling fortress walls. From Rye, they had been told, the road ran straight by the edge of the Marsh to Appledore. On the heights above the Marsh, a mile this side of Appledore, was Blake's Reach.

It had been a journey of fear and doubt and self-questioning. As they made their way over the weary, bone-shaking miles of bad roads from London, Jane had lived with a sense of unease and disquiet—made worse by Patrick and William's dependence and their faith in her. They never questioned, as she did, the wisdom of what they were doing; they accepted her decisions without thought, blindly believing that what she did could never be wrong. William and General often sat with Patrick on the box, and, alone, during those hours, Jane wrestled with doubts and misgivings. Viewed in a cold, sober light, it was expecting much of Spencer to hope that he would welcome them without reservation. They were trusting in the slender chance of his loneliness being greater than his pride, and greater, too, than an old man's desire for peace and unchanging habit. Every mile that brought them closer to Rye the words of the sailor, Adam Thomas, grew fainter, and Anne's forth-right rejection of Blake's Reach and its rundown inheritance louder and stronger. Anne had been a woman of the world—not a girl caught up in a romantic impulse. More than that, she had known Blake's Reach, and she had known Spencer Blake. Suppose Spencer Blake should shut the door on all three of them, should refuse to receive them even for a night? What then? William and Patrick would turn to her for the answer, and, as yet, she had none.

There had been too much time during the long, dragged-out days of fighting the mud and bogs of the spring roads, the delays of the tollhouses, the aggravating slowness of their progress, to wish that she had never seen William and Patrick, had never heard of

Blake's Reach. A few weeks ago she had been responsible only for herself, and for herself she had been able to provide with no other aid but that of her strong body and capable hands. Now her hands were soft and encased in soft gloves, and she traveled like a lady, and money flew from her purse into the eager palms of servants and lackeys. Now she had two mouths to feed besides her own, and shelter and security to find for them all. She sat in Anne's velvet-lined carriage as it bounced over ruts and potholes, and wondered if she had made a bad exchange.

Even the end of their journey was obscure. They knew only that they should go to the Romney Marsh in Kent, and that the ancient Cinque Port of Rye was their best goal. So they traveled slowly over the turnpikes, asking at all the tollhouses if they were heading in the direction of Rye. Most of the tollkeepers were as ignorant as themselves of what lay beyond the next ten miles of rutted road. They got lost several times, and there were delays which meant more nights spent in expensive inns—for it was obvious that a carriage and pair like this could not draw up before a modest tavern. Jane traveled with a purse containing some sovereigns and a pair of paste earrings close at her hand; this was in case they were held up by one of the highwaymen who haunted the turnpikes. The rest of the money was sewn into the lining of William's coat. Patrick lived with a pistol on the seat beside him, which he swore he could use. For all three of them there was fear—and for Jane there was fear and uncertainty, and self-blame.

Last night they had slept at Tenterden, and this morning about noon had reached Rye.

They entered the port through the great medieval gateway to the Old Town, and the grays had struggled to keep a footing on the steep, slippery cobbles. At Rye the air carried the tang of the sea— that's what Patrick had told them the smell was, for Jane and William had never seen the sea. The little silt-packed harbor lay below the town, and the Rother cut a sluggish course between mud banks to the sea a mile or more away. The host at the Mermaid Tavern, where they stopped for dinner, was talkative. He put Jane and William in a private room and pointed to the crest over the chimney-piece.

"The crest of the Cinque Ports, ma'am. Rye used to be the best and the greatest of them before they inned the Marsh, and the silt blocked up the harbor. This town used to stand on the cliffs overlookin' the sea—can you imagine that, ma'am?"

Jane didn't welcome his talk, or the curious glances he kept giving her when he came himself to serve their dinner; she paid no attention to his hinting at the strangeness of a young woman traveling with only a servant and a child. But when he asked her if she would accept a glass of brandy with his compliments, she was forced, out of politeness, to comment on its excellence. She tasted and approved it; Tim Cooper's cellar had held nothing so fine as this.

The landlord shrugged carelessly. "Oh—good brandy's one thing we have no lack of in these parts."

For an inn in a declining seaport, she thought, it was an absurd extravagance to offer brandy like this to its patrons free. But she sipped gratefully, for it helped to delay the moment of departure. It was almost time to face Spencer, and she was nervous. The landlord handed her into the carriage, and she could no longer avoid giving him the information he had wanted. She had to ask directions to Blake's Reach.

"Blake's Reach, is it?" His eyes narrowed. "Why, there ain't no one goes to Blake's Reach these days."

Then an expression of dawning comprehension appeared. "Why, you must be . . . Well, I was tryin' t' place you, and I should have known you for a Blake! I've lived sixty-six years in this town with Blakes comin' and goin', and I ought t' know a Blake face when I see one. But there ain't been none of them about these past years. . . ."

"If you please!" Jane said primly. "I am in a hurry!"

He made a half bow. "Why certainly, ma'am, certainly! You follow your nose t' the bottom of the hill here—the outskirts of the town it is, and you'll see the road forkin' to the right, sign-posted to Appledore. It runs along the edge of the Marsh. And on the left 'bout four-five miles, you'll see Blake's Reach. Can't miss it. A big, old house stuck up on the rise, where the cliffs used to be."

There was a flush of excitement on his pinkish, flabby face as he watched the carriage turn out of the courtyard. Without bothering to take off his apron he followed it to the end of Mermaid

Street. Then, at the best pace he could manage, he set off for Watchbell Street, gasping a little for breath, and heedless of the stares of his business friends in the town who hadn't seen Dick Randell move with such speed since the days when he had been a slim young ostler at the Mermaid.

But Randell was heading for Robert Turnbull's office in Watchbell Street. Of all the people, in Rye, Robert Turnbull would be the one most interested in the news that a carriage had set out along the Appledore road to Blake's Reach.

2

The rain had started to fall when they came to Blake's Reach. For five miles they had followed the road over the Marsh—on one side were the miles of flat pasture lands, interlaced with countless winding dykes and ditches and banks. The wind bent and swayed the new spring grass and the tall rushes; the young lambs huddled close by the ewes for shelter. On their left was the broken line of low, Kent hills—the cliff-face of past centuries—sweeping round in a wide arc to encircle the Marsh from east to west. Jane recalled the host at the Mermaid telling her that once the sea had lapped the base of those hills; now the wall held back the sea—a frail, man-made thing which the Marshmen watched and guarded ceaselessly against tide and wind and storm. In the gray light the Marsh seemed to Jane a faintly sinister place, fertile and yet desolate, unnatural-looking. The wild clouds came sweeping in from the sea. The farmhouses were tight and prosperous; they were also withdrawn and alone. Shut away from the rain and the wind in the snug carriage, she shivered momentarily, and could not have said why.

Suddenly William stirred and touched her hand. "Look—yonder! That's Blake's Reach!"

"Blake's Reach ahead, mistress!" Patrick called from the box.

She craned forward to look. It was on the left—as the innkeeper had said. The house stood halfway up a steep, sparsely wooded ridge which rose sharply from the level of the Marsh.

Through the rain and the gathering mist they could see only the outline of the house. There were two wings, one of mellow rosy brick, and the other, older and smaller, was a jumble of sloping roofs and blackened oak and plaster. A few poplars and elms gathered about it. An orchard straggled down the hill to meet the dyke at the bottom.

The carriage wheels rumbled on the bridge that spanned the dyke, and the horses started the pull up the steep hill. The tall gates of Blake's Reach stood open to the world—gates of massive rusted iron, and stone walls overgrown with ivy. Patrick took the difficult turning on the hill without pause, and swept along the short drive to the space formed by the L-shaped buildings.

Jane's hand moved convulsively. "Oh . . . oh, my lord!"

Against the racing clouds she saw the tall chimneys, and the cracked and broken chimney-pots. Over the porch were rose vines, grown to monstrous proportions and full of dead wood, like gnarled old trees; someone had tried to cut the vine away from the crest chiseled in the stonework over the door. Jane recognized some of the heraldings she had seen in the crest of the Cinque Ports. Ivy covered these walls too—some of it overgrown so that it sealed the casement windows. Nettles and weeds were high in the tangled lawn; shrubs fought halfheartedly with the vines that weighed them down. Midway down the slope was a broken stone wall which might once have sheltered a rose garden. The wind tore at the young buds on the vines, and spattered the rain against the dirty casements. The leaves of last autumn, and the winter's mud lay piled against the doorstep. There was an air of deadness over the whole place.

"There's no one here," Jane breathed, half to herself. "There's some mistake! This isn't Blake's Reach!"

But she uttered the words hopelessly, knowing that nothing she could say would make this spectacle of ruin disappear. This was Blake's Reach, without a doubt. This was the ruin to which Anne had refused to return, this was the decayed farm of Adam Thomas' description. A feeling of doom and hopeless fatality was here like a visible cloud.

Patrick jumped down from the box. He knocked loudly with the whip handle on the door. There was no sound at all from within. "Open up there! Open up!"

William got down beside him; General sniffed and pawed a little before the door, and then his ears cocked and he moved back down

the drive to the corner of the house. All three of them turned and
looked after him.

An old woman appeared there—an old woman wiping her hands
in her apron. She had thrown a shawl over her head against the
rain; gray wisps of hair had escaped it, and blew in the wind. She
stood and surveyed the group and the carriage warily.

"What do ye want? Who are ye?"

Jane got down from the carriage slowly. "This is Blake's Reach?"
she said.

"Aye . . ." The answer was choked off as the old woman's gaze
came to rest fully on Jane. Her features contracted sharply; her
wrinkled brow, knit in close lines. She began to walk purposefully
towards Jane, ignoring the others. She stood and peered up into
the girl's face.

"Mercy on us!" Wonderingly she shook her head. "Can it be?
Miss Anne's child? Is *that* who ye are?"

Jane nodded. "And William also." She touched the child's
shoulder.

The woman gazed from one face to the other. With a hand that
trembled slightly she reached out and touched William's red curls,
brushed them back off his forehead in a gesture that she seemed to
have been performing all her life.

"Mercy on us," she said again, more gently. "I never thought to
see this day!" Her eyes were bright with fierce, unshed tears. She
turned back to Jane. "You'll be her child by Captain Howard?"

"My name's Jane—Jane Howard."

The woman dropped a stiff, quick curtsey. "I'm Kate Reeve, mistress—an' I cared for Miss Anne from the day she was born, till
the day she went away with Tom Howard. She'll have talked of me,
perhaps?"

"Yes," Jane lied. "She talked of you."

The old woman nodded, gratified. "An' Miss Anne? . . ." she
hesitated. "She's livin'? . . ."

Jane shook her head. "My mother is dead."

Kate nodded, and there was no surprise or shock on her face.
"I never thought to see the day that would bring her to Blake's
Reach again. She went away with no love in her heart for Blake's
Reach and the Marsh. Glad to go, she were."

A fierce gust of wind whipped her skirts about her thin frame. She clutched the shawl tighter. "They do say, though, that blood be thicker than water." Again she reached out and touched William's curls. "You have come back—Miss Anne's children!"

"And my grandfather?" Jane prompted. "Is he here? Is he well enough to see us?"

Kate's jaw dropped. "Ye don't *know*?" she said in a thin whisper. "Know *what*?"

She looked at them solemnly. "Yer grandfather, Spencer Blake, has been dead this month an' more."

"Dead!"

Jane echoed the word, hearing it on her tongue, knowing the finality of it. Spencer Blake was dead. More than a month he had been dead, and she and William were his only living descendants. She didn't feel grief and shock at the idea that an old man whom she had never seen was dead. His death was safety for herself and William; there would be no one now to deny them entrance to Blake's Reach, no one who had the right to send them away. Blake's Reach was a slight inheritance—but it was a roof, and a place to be. It was a purpose for existence, an identity. She was a Blake, and William was a Blake, and this decaying house was a refuge for them for as long as they had a mind to stay. Her eyes swept over the building again, and now she felt some affection for the crumbling walls.

"Aye . . . he's dead," Kate said. "An' I thought 'twas the news of it had brought ye here. I thought Mr. Turnbull, the Blake solicitor in Rye, had found ye, and ye'd come to wait here with me for Charlie."

"Wait for Charlie? What do you mean, Kate? Who is Charlie?"

"Why, Charlie Blake! Yer mother's first cousin—the one that ran off to France. He be the one Spencer named in his will. He be the heir to Blake's Reach."

Jane gave a strangled gasp. "*Heir!* That isn't true! Charles Blake is dead!"

Kate shook her head. "That's what we first heard, but then the news came that it 'twer a mistake, an' he were still in prison in Paris. Robert Turnbull came out here to tell me about it. He told

me that I were to bide here, an' keep the house against the time
when Charlie should come back."

"Come back . . ." Jane echoed the words dully.

"Aye." Kate nodded. " 'Tain't a sure thing he'll ever come.
Mor'an likely he'll lose his head in Paris. But until he does, Blake's
Reach belongs to Charlie, and I must wait here for him."

She surveyed the house in much the way Jane had just done;
looked at the tall broken chimneys against the racing clouds, looked
at the garden desolate in the rain.

"Aye—I must wait here until Charlie either loses his head, or
comes to claim his own."

CHAPTER TWO

So THEY WERE ALL WAITING FOR CHARLIE. . . . THEY WERE WAIT-
ing for Charles Blake to come back and claim his inheritance.

Jane sat with slumped shoulders before the fire Kate Reeve had
lit hastily in the room that had been Spencer Blake's sitting room;
her stunned brain repeated the words over and over, trying to make
herself grapple with the fact of this new disaster. Somewhere in a
Paris prison Charlie Blake awaited trial, and if he should live, then
she and William were again homeless and rootless. Her mind
stirred sullenly in revolt at the thought; it seemed an overwhelming
injustice that Charles Blake, who had cared for Blake's Reach no
more than Anne, who had run away from it just as Anne had done,
should be named in Spencer's will. It wasn't just, and its injustice
spoke of Spencer's bitterness towards his daughter; the whip of an
old anger and hurt had been meant to reach out and touch Anne.
Jane shivered a little. If Spencer Blake had been alive when she
and William had presented themselves at his door she now believed
that he would have refused to see them.

Then, as she considered this chance, Jane shrugged her shoulders
with a grim kind of resignation. With Spencer dead, things were
difficult enough; had he been alive they might have been a great

deal worse. The thought took hold. They said possession was nine points of the law. She was here at Blake's Reach; Charles Blake was shut away in a prison in Paris. For the moment she was decidedly better off than he. And one could only live for a moment at a time; the future was anyone's guess.

But the present was with her now, and she would have to tackle it. Whatever happened to Charles Blake, she would still have to get herself and William through the next day, and the next week. The present crowded upon her; with growing interest she began to look about the room.

She knew without being told that Spencer had used no other room at Blake's Reach but this and his bedchamber. This room had a look of wear as well as neglect about it—books tumbled haphazardly on the shelves, papers still littered the tables, there were mugs and glasses on a battered oak sideboard, and many candles about, and the spatters of candle grease on the floor and furniture. She knew what had happened here; this was the orbit of a man who had withdrawn to live within one room, to eat his meals here, to doze here before the fire, to seat what little company came to Blake's Reach in the great high-backed chair facing his own. He had drunk his brandy here in solitude; she wondered if he had invited neighbors here to gamble, or if he had lost his acres and money in the taverns and inns at Rye and Tenterden and Dover. She saw the dust on the bookcases, the threadbare rug, the curtains whose silk had rotted and was faded to a dusty rose color. There were apathy and bitterness in this room; perhaps, before he died, Spencer had hated Blake's Reach as much as Anne. She suddenly became impatient with the Blakes. It didn't take much skill to be unhappy, and to hate; it was too easy. She was impatient with Spencer and Anne, and even the unknown Charles, because they had let themselves be defeated.

Now she looked about the room, and felt superior to the man who had lived here with his brandy and his hate.

There was a sound outside, and she stirred, and looked expectantly towards the window. But it had been a distant sound carried by the wind, and no one came. She was waiting now for Robert Turnbull, the Blakes' solicitor, and executor of Spencer's will. Kate had routed out a tow-headed youth—who was one of the only two hands left on the farm—to take a message immediately to Turnbull. It was more than five miles to Rye, the rain was coming down in torrents, and the boy's horse had been a miserable creature. It would be after dark before Turnbull could arrive. Kate had gone off towards the kitchen murmuring something about preparing food; Patrick and William were in the stable tending the grays. Jane moved her feet restlessly. She wanted to see beyond this room, and the dark paneled hall with the great staircase where her boxes were now piled. But it needed Robert Turnbull's arrival to sanction her presence here. It was too soon to go wandering towards the kitchen, or to open the heavy double doors that led off the hall. As curious as she was, she must wait.

The sounds of his arrival came much sooner than she expected. The dusk had come imperceptibly with a darkening in the rain clouds over the Marsh. The shriek of the wind was high and strong. She had grown accustomed to the absence of human sound in all that clamor, and it almost startled her to hear voices and the clopping of horses' hoofs on the weed-choked gravel. She had a quick glimpse of a man in a tall hat muffled in a heavy coat, followed by the tow-haired boy, before there came the sounds of his knocking. Instantly she rose, and was halfway to the window before she recovered her sense of dignity. She returned to her chair, and spread her skirts, taking deep breaths to calm the beating of her heart.

She knew why Robert Turnbull had come before time. There had been no need to send for him. She remembered the interest of the host at the Mermaid, and knew that in the towns that bordered the Marsh, a stranger did not inquire for Blake's Reach without arousing curiosity, especially if the stranger's hair and face called to mind too vividly the Anne Blake of twenty years ago.

She knew that Robert Turnbull had been told of the carriage and pair heading towards Blake's Reach; he had set out of his own accord without waiting for the summons. The tow-haired boy had met him on the road to Rye.

She sat stiffly and waited for him to enter.

2

A little more than an hour after Jane had driven over the Marsh road which led to Blake's Reach, Robert Turnbull also turned his horse right at the fork signposted to Appledore. He carried a strange, half-bitter ache in his heart.

For many years he had followed this road back and forth to Blake's Reach—ever since he had entered his father's law firm in Rye. Blake's Reach had always been important in the Turnbull firm, because none of them were able to forget that their prosperity dated from the time early in the century when John Blake, lately back from serving with Marlborough, had placed the legal affairs of Blake's Reach with the newly founded firm of Turnbull & Son. The prestige of the Blake name brought a flurry of business to the offices in Watchbell Street—smaller squires and farmers hastened to follow where the Blakes led, as well as the few more important men who trusted John's recommendation because he was their friend. It had been an easy matter to serve the Blakes when they were in the full flood of riches which John's loot from the wars had swollen; the rent roll was fat then, and the sheep from Blake's Reach fetched a high price in the market. John managed his farm with a soldier's precision, making every quarter acre yield its share; his wife had brought him a dowry of lands and money and at her death his manipulations had doubled them in value. Then with the extravagance which was lacking in none of the Blakes, he built and endowed a church on the hill above his house; it didn't matter to him that it was more than half a mile from the nearest village—he had wanted his church on the highest point above the Marsh and the inconvenience caused to the people in getting to the service held there every third Sunday only served to remind them that John Blake was a man not swayed by the wishes of any clergyman or bishop. John brought new luster to a name that had been a power on the Marsh for a long time; he built up a new fortune for his descendants, and his descendants betrayed him.

His only son, George, wasted and spent and mortgaged with a cheerful lavish hand; George's sons, Spencer and Richard, were bent in the same direction until Richard removed himself by marrying a French heiress and going off to mismanage her estate in

Normandy. Spencer continued to indulge his passion for gambling unchecked, believing that he was possessed of his grandfather's genius for investment, and that if he were patient there were fortunes to be made by the turn of the card, or from the tobacco plantation he had bought, sight unseen, in Virginia. He woke one day to the realization that his only child, Anne, was beautiful, and that in her, not himself, lay the hope of lifting Blake's Reach free of its debts.

The Turnbull firm had been with the Blakes through all the changes; the memory of what John Blake had accomplished for them by putting his business in their hands was sufficient to make it a tradition in the firm that the Blakes must be served, no matter for how many years the services of the firm went unpaid.

For young Robert Turnbull it was something much more personal than a tradition of service. He was only two years older than Anne, and he had watched the spoiled, imperious child grow into a woman of startling beauty. It was not simply a matter of knowing that he loved Anne, that she was a bright flash of brilliance and romance in his plodding existence. Along with loving her he must recognize that loving her was all he could do. The Turnbulls were servants to the Blakes, and Robert Turnbull was no more than the young man she consented to chat to while she waited impatiently for Spencer to be through with his business in the Watchbell Street offices. Not only was a marriage for a Blake with a Turnbull unthinkable, but Anne herself barely knew he existed. Robert knew very well what Anne's marriage was supposed to accomplish for Spencer and Blake's Reach; even in the unlikely circumstance of Anne's loving him there would have been no hope of marriage.

So Robert allowed himself only the indulgence of loving her, and inventing excuses for going to Blake's Reach. It was no surprise to him when the news came that Anne had got herself out of the marriage Spencer had arranged for her to Roger Pym by running away with Tom Howard. Tom Howard he knew only by sight—a gay, laughing captain of Dragoons without a penny to his name, and only average luck with cards. They went to London, Tom resigned his commission, and when Spencer tried to have the marriage annulled on grounds of Anne's being underage, she wrote that she was already pregnant with Tom's child.

That closed the matter. Anne's name was never again mentioned voluntarily by Spencer. His gambling continued, and now there were stories of his heavy drinking to add to it. His affairs grew more knotted and more complex for the Turnbulls to manage, with I.O.U.s written in a drunken scrawl turning up for payment, and lands being sold to meet them. The Virginia plantation hadn't shown a profit for many years. Spencer was drinking too much and refusing to listen to Robert's pleas to get rid of it. There was no reasoning with him; a kind of mad obstinacy had fallen on him now that Anne wasn't there to soften his moods.

Then two years after Anne had left, her cousin, Charles, who was then thirteen, also ran away. He was Spencer's nephew, and he had come unwillingly to England when his parents had died during an epidemic of typhoid fever in Paris. Richard's will had appointed Spencer as Charles' guardian. He had come to Blake's Reach when he was nine years old, and he had clearly detested the place. He managed to make his way to France, where his mother's family took him in. Spencer retaliated by keeping the money Charles' estate paid him for the boy's upbringing until Charles was of age to inherit. Spencer had never cared for the slim, dark-haired boy who had rarely spoken to him, but his going was a deadly insult. He was now quite alone at Blake's Reach.

As best he could, Robert Turnbull followed the events of Anne's life. He was not subtle about asking for news of her from the occasional inhabitant of the Marsh who happened to go to London. He heard about Tom Howard's death in the debtors' prison, and had flinched to hear the horrible derisive laughter of Spencer when he had been told. By one means and another Anne's career as the mistress of rich and fashionable men became known in Rye. The town buzzed comfortably with the scandal for years until it heard of Viscount Hindsley, whose prominence and wealth at once bathed Anne in respectability—which lasted only until he died. Anne never answered the letter Robert wrote her at that time, and the neglect hurt him more than he wanted to admit. It was then he gave up the struggle to make himself like some other woman well enough to marry.

It seemed to Robert that, even with the amount Spencer was drinking, it took him so long to die that he stood a good chance of gambling away the roof over his head before it could happen. Through the years Robert watched the Blake's Reach acres shrink, the land sold freehold to tenant farmers, and gone forever. The Blake barns leaked, and one wing of the stables was burned down. Spencer's farming methods were a laughingstock right across the Marsh. But the aging man, shut up in his sitting room with the brandy decanter, cared for nothing that was said about him. No one was bidden to tend the garden, or fix the broken windows; few people came now to Blake's Reach, and those few were at pains not to notice the disorder and neglect. Sometimes Spencer was to be seen walking on the Marsh itself, his shabby stained coat blowing in the wind. The farmers who met him raised their hats and hurried on.

Robert came to dislike and even dread his necessary visits to Blake's Reach, and to resent the tradition of service to the Blakes handed down to him since the days of his great-grandfather. He gritted his teeth and endured Spencer's sneers and bitter hatreds; he salvaged what he could of the wreck Spencer was bent on making of what remained to the family. Knowing that Anne had a legitimate child by Tom Howard he even ventured to protest Spencer's will which gave Blake's Reach to Charles. He had not been received at Blake's Reach for a year afterwards for his pains. Spencer, he knew, hated both Anne and Charles—it was a question of which one he hated more.

Now Spencer was dead at last, and Anne's child had come to Blake's Reach—a girl so like Anne that it had sent Dick Randell at the Mermaid scuttling along to tell him. Robert didn't know why the girl had come, but he sensed trouble, and he sensed that the complication of the Blake affairs had begun all over again.

But trouble or not, for the first time in almost twenty years he made the journey to Blake's Reach hopefully. Times and events were changing, he thought—the old things worn out and the new coming to take their place. A new and young Blake had come to the Marsh—maybe this time one with the blood of old John Blake, Marlborough's general, strong in her veins. Sometimes, just sometimes, miracles happened. The Blakes had need of a miracle now.

The wind blowing from the sea was like a knife in his back. Blake's Reach looked no different—slashed by the rain and showing its neglect painfully. Robert sighed. Anne's daughter would need all of old John's spirit and toughness.

When she rose to greet him, he knew that his premonition hadn't been wrong. He had seen the portrait of old John too many times not to know by what stick to measure his descendants. Here was old John's face in a feminine mold, the face of a young woman boldly drawn, with the familiar red hair curling crisply back, and greenish eyes that regarded him, not with apprehension, but a certain caution. She accepted his greeting with reserve.

He bowed. "Your servant, ma'am. My name is Robert Turnbull." She inclined her head. "I am Jane Howard."

He approved of her; not knowing whether he was friend or enemy, she didn't commit herself to any overtures. She met his stare firmly, not yielding an inch in confusion. She merely waited for him to speak.

"You're so like your mother," he said gently.

It wasn't exactly true—Dick Randell had told him she was as beautiful as Anne, but he, Robert Turnbull, who had memorized every expression of Anne's face with the eager diligence of a lover, knew that she was not as beautiful. Anne's had been a more delicate face, a gayer face. This girl had a certain toughness and directness Anne had never known. She was modishly dressed in a traveling costume of blue velvet which became her skin and hair wonderfully; it was tightly fitted to her pointed young bosom. Her body was provocative and arresting, and when she moved towards him she managed herself with an instinctive, undeniable grace.

He instantly liked and respected what he saw. The thought crossed his mind in those first few seconds that perhaps, after all, the Blakes were to have their miracle.

Their hands met briefly, and then Robert went to the chair Jane indicated on the other side of the fire. They studied each other carefully.

Jane saw a man of about her mother's age, with dark hair turned almost completely gray, and weathered skin that told her he spent much time in the sun and wind. He was not tall, but broadly and powerfully built, with strong hands covered thickly with hair; his eyes were remarkable, dark brown and deeply set, almost too sensitive in that rugged face. He did not dress as she imagined a country attorney would; his clothes were immaculate and of excellent cut, though the colors were discreet. If he had lived in London, she thought, he might have become a dandy. The only thing out of fashion about him was the absence of a wig. His might have been any one of those cosmopolitan faces she had glimpsed in the coffee houses or in Bond Street. It was a calm, intelligent face that looked at her now, and waited.

3

Kate came and served them wine in smeared glasses, carelessly set on a tarnished silver tray. Her old hands shook with excitement as she poured from the decanter; a smile played on her lips each time her gaze fell on Jane.

"This is a great day for Kate," Robert said when she had gone. "To her you are Anne come back again. You and William are young, and for the old, there is always hope in youth."

Jane's eyes regarded him gratefully over the rim of the glass.

William was brought in then to be presented. Patrick stood silently in the doorway watching as William made his bow to Turnbull. Then, tugging at General's collar, the child went to Jane's side quickly, and from that vantage point, viewed the stranger eagerly. He answered Turnbull's questions about his lessons, but he was watching to try to sense Jane's own reaction to the man before giving himself too readily. Patrick's anxious face softened a trifle; he glowed with pride as Jane described to Turnbull his years of service to Anne.

Then the servant took William back to the kitchen. As the door closed behind them, Robert spoke softly.

"A child of nine years is a burden for a young woman to take on . . . And Anne's servant . . ."

Jane shrugged. "What else was there to do? When Anne died, Patrick was as helpless as William. Over the years he had grown to expect Anne to decide everything for him. Without her he was lost. As for William . . . no one can turn out a child who's been gently reared to fend for himself. William's no baby, but he knows more about the fashionable life in London than he does about earning a shilling or two. . . ."

"And so you took them both?"

"I had no choice."

The formalities were completed between them; they moved on to the business of understanding each other.

It was less difficult than they had thought. Kate brought in supper; it was jugged hare, poorly cooked and served on chipped plates. With it she brought coarse, blackish bread and a large slice of stale cheddar cheese. It was many years since Robert had taken a meal at Blake's Reach, and he was appalled by what he saw. But the wine, brought up from Spencer's cellar, was excellent. When the dishes were cleared away they lingered over the wine, and they grew comfortable with each other. Their talk became easy and unfettered; Jane realized quickly that if she was to remain at Blake's Reach she needed Robert Turnbull; among all these strangers she had to trust someone, and she decided to trust him. It was obvious that he knew Anne's history in some detail, and when he pressed for more information, she decided that it was safer to tell him everything than to play with half-truths. As her ally he could be invaluable, and already he was almost that. Without holding back, then, she told him of the years at The Feathers, and how she had come to London in a wild flight and been absorbed into Anne's strange household. She told him of how Anne had died, and how Patrick, O'Neill, Jerome Taylor and herself had schemed to take whatever could be taken from the creditors. She told it matter-of-factly, and was startled to see the distress in his face.

"I hate to think of Anne . . . to die that way, in debt, troubled by creditors. . . ."

"Don't waste your pity, Mr. Turnbull. Creditors never troubled Anne. She never spared a moment's thought for them. She died in a comfortable bed, with people who loved her all around her. She had soft and pretty things all her life, and gaiety. I don't think she even minded dying because it spared her the pain of growing old."

"But leaving William to you and no provision made for him? . . ."

She shrugged. "I see it this way. Today I have a trunkful of beautiful gowns, a carriage and two fine grays, and I have some gold to jingle in my purse. When I left The Feathers I had Sally's old shawl and a few pennies." She spread her hands emphatically. "If I also have William, then that's only to be expected. Fair exchange, Mr. Turnbull!"

He smiled, half-reluctantly. "Most people wouldn't call it fair exchange, but I applaud your spirit."

"That's as you choose, Mr. Turnbull. I'd rather fight to make my own way, than sit and wait for things to happen. I almost waited too long at The Feathers. No more of that for me! From now on I take every chance that comes—*every* one!"

He nodded. "Then they'll come . . . or you will make your own chances."

"I will—if I can." She went on quickly. "Living at The Feathers has taught me things gently bred people don't know. You had to be sharp there, or you were taken in. An innkeeper on a busy road has to know more than two and two make four. I've learned things from him, and they've stuck with me." She added, with a touch of pride, "The idea of selling the things off quietly from Anne's house —that was mine."

"I heard that Hindsley had given Anne jewels," he said. "Wouldn't they have fetched something?"

"The jewels were sold long ago. Anne had paste imitations made, because it wouldn't have done for the people she borrowed from to know that the jewels were gone."

Again Robert gave a half-smile. "It's an inherited talent with the Blakes to conceal the state of their finances. In the old days Spencer also was cunning in hiding his difficulties from his neighbors." His face sharpened, suddenly. "He had a purpose, though. He had planned a good match for Anne from the time she was a child, and when she was fourteen he had the man picked out and ready. Roger Pym would have given half he possessed to marry Anne. He was a young man, just come into his father's estate, and he was more than ready to lend Spencer large sums on the understanding that Anne should marry him when she was eighteen. There wasn't any real wickedness in Roger Pym, I believe—but in Spencer's hands he was an inexperienced child, and he hadn't learned that his money couldn't buy everything he wanted."

"Anne wouldn't have him. . . ."

"Flatly refused to consider him! To marry Roger Pym would have meant burying herself in the country. It would have meant a life-

time of paying lip-service to all the past glories of the Blakes. She
was appalled at the thought of taking up the dull job of running
the estate, and giving a child to Roger every year. None of that
was for Anne. Tom Howard presented himself, and she ran off to
London with him."

"She couldn't have stayed? . . ." Jane said musingly.

He leaned towards her. "You must realize that Anne didn't give
a fig for position or family or almost anything else. She didn't care
in the least what the Blakes were then or had been. She was a creature of such gaiety—like a bright and improbable flame here among
all these solid country squires. She was too lovely and too spirited
to be tied down. . . ."

Jane knew the familiar tones the attorney used. Ever since she
could comprehend them, these were the tones the people who had
loved Anne had spoken in. It was clear that Turnbull had loved her
mother. She accepted the knowledge, not as something strange, but
as a fact that was decidedly to her own advantage. Having loved
Anne, Turnbull would feel nothing but warmth for a daughter who
resembled her. She fixed her attention firmly on him, encouraging
him with her eyes to continue talking.

"Spencer never recovered from the blow of her running away,"
Turnbull said. "She had hurt him financially, and she had wounded
his pride beyond bearing. He grew old very quickly . . . and bitter.
He didn't trouble any more to keep the Marsh from knowing what
was happening to Blake's Reach. He hated Anne, and I think he
took a fiendish delight in making sure that there should be nothing
left for her to inherit. He grew to a stage of bitterness when he
could laugh openly at Anne's misfortunes—Tom's death, and Viscount Hindsley's." Turnbull's voice was sour at the memory of it.

"Then," Jane said, "if he were alive yet, William and I would not
have been received at Blake's Reach? Strange how certain I was
that he would welcome us . . . Anne told me what to expect, but
I wanted to believe what that sailor, Adam Thomas, had told me."

"Most assuredly he would not have welcomed you," Turnbull
said dryly. "And as for Adam Thomas . . . well, people about here
feel for the Blake family. It's part of their tradition. They can't
think of the Marsh without a Blake. Adam Thomas was loyal—but
misguided."

She stirred suddenly in her chair. The firelight caught the red of her hair, burnished it like copper. Her face had grown sharper and whiter.

"And you—*you*, Mr. Turnbull—think that I was misguided to come here? Blake's Reach doesn't belong to me!"

"It's unfortunate," he answered, "that Spencer didn't know how good *you* would have been for Blake's Reach. The family have never needed one of the General's kind so badly. Spencer didn't know that you were one of the General's kind, Jane."

She said quickly, jealously, "And Charles? What will *he* do for Blake's Reach?"

"Ah, Charles . . . let me tell you about Charles."

She leaned back, her lips folded tightly.

"He was the only child of Richard, Spencer's brother—the one who married the Frenchwoman. Charles was born in France, and brought up there. For some strange reason, when his parents both died within days of each other from a fever, his father's wishes had been that he should come to Spencer to be cared for, instead of staying with his mother's family. She was related to the Poulac family, one of the oldest in France, and they were willing to have the child. Charles didn't want to go to England, but Spencer wasn't prepared to pamper a child's whim. Besides that, Spencer was to have an income from the French estate for Charles' education. He wasn't going to give that up! Charles came over to Blake's Reach— a very unwilling little boy, I recall. I fancy he was nine or ten years old then . . . about five years or so younger than Anne. . . ."

"Yes, yes!" Jane said impatiently. "But tell me *about* Charles. What sort of a person was he?"

"It's difficult to know. He spoke only French when he arrived . . . and I didn't quite know what to make of him. He was handsome, certainly—very handsome. And intelligent, too—quick to learn. After a time he spoke English very well. And I remember him on his pony. He could handle that, or even a horse, as well as a man. He was very dark . . . like his mother, they said. People thought he was sullen, but I think it was his shyness over the strange language in the beginning—and at the end because there was no one he cared to talk to."

"And what did Anne think of him?"

He waved her to silence. "I was coming to Anne. I think she was very important to Charles, but what she felt, I'm not sure. It was plain that he adored her. She must have seemed so light and gay among all these others—almost French, I suppose. She was kind to him when she remembered he was there . . . he was just a little boy, and she was growing into a young woman with thoughts and occupations of her own. But I remember they used to ride together on the Marsh. You'd see them in every kind of weather—he was such a splendid horseman, and he wanted her admiration so badly. He'd dare her to jumps she shouldn't have been allowed to take, just to show her how well he could manage them."

His tone grew reflective. "It must have been terrible for him when she ran away. Spencer had never taken much notice of Charles before, but when Anne left, the child was forgotten completely. Spencer used his money shamelessly . . . and Charles grew too tall for his coats and breeches, and he had holes in his stockings. In the end he settled the matter for himself by riding his pony to Dover, selling it, and paying for his passage to France. He went to his mother's family. Spencer clung on to the money from the estate until Charles was eighteen and could inherit. It was a bitter and vicious wrangle over the money. . . ."

They listened to the rain and the crackle of the fire, and Robert's thoughts were back in those years. Jane looked about the room, seeing it suddenly with the eyes of the little French boy whom Spencer had ignored—the boy in his jacket grown too short and worn at the elbows. This had been Spencer's room, and the boy must have watched him here with fear and loathing.

Suddenly Robert spoke. "I suppose he was the loneliest child I've ever known. . . . After Anne went he used to spend a great deal of his time in the tower of the church up there on the hill. On a clear day you can see the French coast from there. He was eating his heart out. . . ."

"And now he's eating his heart out in Paris—in prison!" she said.

He nodded slowly. "I suppose that's true. He's been in prison more than a year. I wonder if England seems a free and happy place to him now that he has seen France overrun by revolution—"

She interrupted sharply. "Over a year! When does he come to trial?"

He shrugged. "Who can say? We've already had one report of his trial and execution . . . and later found that it was false. I try by every possible means to get news of him. Some English interests are still functioning in Paris, but I've had no direct contact with him. I still am not sure that the letters I've bribed certain people to get to him have ever been received." He began to shake his head. "His cousin, the marquis, is dead, and other members of the family, so I'm told. If Charles ever comes to trial I have little hope for him. The excesses of the Revolution grow worse daily. . . ."

"What is his crime?"

"His connection by birth with a noble family—though I'm sure the Revolutionary courts will find some other name to call it by. I have very little hope," he repeated, "less and less as time goes on. I have a feeling that he will die."

He stopped speaking, and a deep silence hung between them. Jane began to wish, vainly, that she had not questioned Turnbull about the unknown Charles. Before, he had been a phantom with no substance, demanding nothing of her. His only reality had been given him by Anne when she had called him "Charlie." Now he was clothed in flesh and blood, he was a shy, dark-haired boy, growing out of his jackets and breeches; he was a lonely child gazing towards the coast of France from the old cliff-face. He was that child grown into a man, rotting in a Paris prison, waiting trial and almost certain death. Now he had become too real, a phantom no longer. Pity had stirred and awakened in her, and she could never be free again of the vision of Charles. By yielding to pity she had involved herself in him, in the question of whether he lived or died. Blake's Reach could be hers only by the death of Charles . . . and he was a stranger no more.

Turnbull spoke her thoughts. "So . . . you will likely inherit after all. . . ."

"He has no wife or child? No heir?"

He shook his head. "There is no one, I am told. The new French government has confiscated his estate; they would take Blake's Reach also if they could."

Jane gripped the arms of the chair. "And if I inherit . . . what is there for me? How much has escaped Spencer?"

"Very little. The inheritance is slight . . . almost nothing. Perhaps fifty acres, and some sheep. This house and the outbuildings . . . two horses and a few head of cattle."

"Is there a kitchen garden? Are there some hogs?"

He looked startled. "Why . . . yes, I believe so! But Kate is old and a poor gardener. There's been no one to care how things were done at Blake's Reach for so long. The hogs get swine fever, and Spencer couldn't keep a good shepherd, so at lambing time the flock has suffered. He hasn't bought a good ram for many years, and the quality of the sheep is poor—"

She cut him short. "Cows, hogs, chickens . . . a kitchen garden . . . I could live on that, Mr. Turnbull. To some people, that would be riches!"

"It's not riches to a Blake on the Romney Marsh."

"But it would do!" she said eagerly. "It would keep us going until I could build things up . . . until I could build up the flock, buy some rams. It would certainly do, Mr. Turnbull!" Her face was alight, and glowing.

He looked grave. "Those things aren't done in a week, or a year, Jane. And meanwhile the roofs leak, and the damp rots the wood . . . the mice take over all these unused rooms. Can you wait to build up a flock while the house tumbles about your ears? Do you want to give all your youth to a kitchen garden and a pigsty?"

The glow faded slowly, and was replaced by a look of stubbornness. "What else can I do? There's William to think of . . . neither of us can live on air."

He rose from his chair slowly, and went to stand before the fire. The moving light fell on his graying hair, and deepened the lines on his face. He stood there, with head bent, and hands clasped behind him for some minutes. Then he turned to her.

"If Charles dies, and you inherit Blake's Reach, Jane, there *is* something beyond the value of this house and land which will be yours."

"Something? . . . What?"

"There's a ring . . . a black pearl set in a ring. The Blakes have always called it the King's Pearl."

She gasped, and turned a little pale. "A black pearl! . . ."

"Yes . . ." he said. He spoke with faint reluctance. "It is reckoned to be worth a considerable sum of money."

"But why didn't you tell me! This could make such a difference!"
She drew in a long breath. "The ring could be sold, couldn't it,
Mr. Turnbull? It would fetch some money! . . . it could set things
right here!"

"I would not like to see you sell the King's Pearl if it were yours."

"Why not? There's so much needing here that it would
buy. . . ."

He pursed his lips. "What do you suppose kept Spencer from
selling it? Only a tradition stronger than his need for money, his
passion for gambling. Like all the Blakes he venerated it because
more than a hundred years ago it was the personal gift of a king."

Her face sobered. "What do you mean?"

"You've heard about the Great Rebellion—the time when Crom-
well took over and His Majesty, King Charles the First, was be-
headed?"

She nodded. "There were families in Hampstead who talked
about it as if it were yesterday, and they had all ridden with Crom-
well . . . or the King. They still hated each other for what happened all that time ago. . . ."

"A country in civil war isn't an easy thing to forget . . . some
gained by it, and some lost, Jane. The Blakes were Royalist, and
Henry Blake fought by the King's side. He almost went into cap-
tivity with him. One of the last acts His Majesty did was to take
from his finger the Black Pearl, and entrust it to Henry for safe
delivery to Queen Henrietta. Henry nearly lost his life attempting
to reach France with it, but eventually he put it in the Queen's
hands, and helped her find a buyer for it. The King's widow and
children were very short of money. . . ."

Jane was leaning forward. "And Henry? . . ."

"He went to Amsterdam, and worked for a Dutch merchant.
Blake's Reach and the estate were confiscated. His family fled into
exile with him. Like all the other Royalists they were very poor.
At the Restoration they came back, of course . . . and eventually
Blake's Reach was theirs again. King Charles the Second was a vain
and pleasure-loving man, Jane . . . but people do say that he never
forgot a kindness, and he was the most generous soul alive. He was
hard-pressed for money himself, and there were demands on all
sides, but Henry was eventually called to Whitehall, and another

Black Pearl was given him. Not as fine a one as the first, but still worth a good deal of money. Charles gave it to him as a remembrance of loyalty, and his service to the Queen. Henry cherished it above everything he owned, and the Blakes have always felt their luck rests in the Black Pearl. They feel that if it is sold, their luck will go."

He watched the struggle in her face between pride in the tradition, and the practicalities of her upbringing. At last she tossed her head.

"Luck! As if the Blakes' luck hadn't flown out the window long ago. Is it lucky to keep the King's Pearl, and lose Blake's Reach?"

"Well . . . and what would you do if you had the King's Pearl, Jane?"

"Sell it!" she said without hesitation. "The luck of the Blakes couldn't be any worse than it is at the moment—and perhaps Henry meant it to be kept for just such a time. I think he'd forgive me!"

"What would you do with the money?"

"I'd set this place back on its feet. I haven't lived among farm people all my life without learning a thing or two. I'd buy rams, and I'd grow enough feed to hand-feed the cattle through the winter, and they'd go fat to market. I'd get land wherever it was going hereabouts. I'd mend the roof and weed the drive. I'd plant new roses, and sit in a silk gown and wait for the gentry to come calling." She laughed as she spoke the last words.

"Wait for the gentry! . . . Why?"

She looked at him very pointedly. "Are there none about here to marry, Mr. Turnbull? Are there no eldest sons that haven't been snapped up? It's true I have no fortune, but I have the Blake name . . . and if it were mine, Blake's Reach itself would soon be no inconsiderable trifle."

"You mean . . . you mean you want to *marry* here? You want to marry some squire's son?" He looked at her in wonderment. "But you'd be like Anne—you'd die of boredom within a year!"

"I expect boredom, Mr. Turnbull—and it's not likely to kill me! You forget that I've lived as a servant, and I didn't care for that. I've also seen how Anne lived, and I could do without the excitement of the gambling table. If I have to die of boredom, it will be with a full stomach, and in peace and security."

Then she added, "What energies I have would be well spent on
Blake's Reach. Will I die of boredom if I have this? It would be a
game of patience to get back the acres Spencer lost. The man who
married me wouldn't be getting a bad bargain. I would be ambitious for his good as much as my own."

He considered her carefully. It was amazing how right she was
. . . it was a proposition as shrewd and calculating as anything he
had heard, and yet, he believed that she would be honest in her
bargain. She would give fair value—and more. He didn't believe
that she would cheat. The audacity of the plan was its strength
. . . she just might be lucky enough to pull it off. He looked at
her as dispassionately as he was able. She had beauty, and a certain
brash confidence which made it noticeable; he took in the rounded,
elegantly provocative figure, the modish clothes, and found himself
comparing her with the rather solid ladies of indifferent charm
whose families held the wealth of the Marsh. Beside most of them
she would have the sharpness of a new flavor. He knew she possessed none of the accomplishments ladies thought so desirable, and
which, in the end, bored men. The women, he thought, would see
through her quickly enough—but all the men were likely to see was
the graceful curve of her neck, and the way she moved her hips.
She was clever, more clever than Anne had been; she had prudence
and an eye to what side her bread was buttered on. It was possible
. . . mad as it seemed now, it was all possible. She might pull it off.

He looked at her and smiled. Suddenly he wanted to see it happen. He wanted Anne's child living here on the Marsh, doing suc-
cessfully what Anne had refused to do; he wanted to see a former
serving girl from The Feathers come and make fools of all the families who prided themselves on their birth and who said the Blakes
were finished. This was a descendant that old John Blake, Marlborough's general, would have delighted in—the best the family had
produced in nearly a hundred years. He savored and relished the
thought.

She was encouraged by his smile.

"Give me time! Give me a little money to begin with, and I'll
put Blake's Reach back where it should be. I could do it, Mr. Turnbull! *I could do it!*"

Now he smiled more broadly. "You could do it! Yes, I believe you could do it!"

He took a step towards her. "If Blake's Reach becomes yours, you shall have all the help I can give—in whatever way I can give it. And here's my hand on it!"

But even as his hand gripped hers he felt again the familiar sense of loss. For the second time in his life he was bidding good-bye to Anne Blake . . . the first time money and position had defeated him, and now, when he had accumulated money and when the Blakes could no longer bargain for titles or power, the years were against him. He studied the young face before him, and for a second wondered if, even now, it was too late.

She had reached eagerly for his outstretched hand, then abruptly the triumph and the glow was wiped from her face. Her hand dropped limply back into her lap.

"I'd forgotten," she said dully. "It isn't mine, is it? It isn't mine yet." She looked at him distractedly. "To wish a man dead—God save us, that's murder! But I *want* Blake's Reach, and before it's mine, Charlie must die!"

Unconsciously she had used her mother's name for him; she had called him Charlie.

4

The hired boy, Jed, had brought Robert's horse to the front door. The hinges creaked as it swung stiffly open. Kate put up her hand to shield the candle flame from the wind that ripped in from the sea, and flung itself against the house. Outside, the night was black; there was nothing to see, there was only the sensation of low thick clouds scudding across the sky. The rain had stopped.

Robert looked at Kate.

"Miss Jane will be staying here at Blake's Reach, Kate. She will be staying . . . until Master Charles comes back." He leaned nearer the old woman. "Care for her, Kate."

Then he went swiftly and mounted the horse. The boy backed away respectfully.

As she saw him mounted, and about to turn towards Rye, Jane had a terrifying sense of her aloneness. She was here, with this great echoing house behind her, and the vastness of the Marsh lost in the black night; she had spoken brave and defiant words, but now she felt small, and a little afraid. Impulsively she went to Turnbull's side, her hand gripping the saddle.

"You'll come again?" she said urgently.

He nodded. "I'll come this way from time to time. You'll find it strange at first, Jane. These are seafaring people, as well as farmers, and there are those with a touch of wildness. But many of them knew and loved Anne—they'll welcome you back. I have only this to say to you—"

He broke off, looking about him to see where Jed had gone. The boy had vanished into the darkness; Kate still stood by the door.

"Yes? . . ." Jane urged.

He leaned down, and spoke softly in her ear. "Take no notice of what seems strange to you in these parts, Jane. Close your eyes to what you had best not see. Those who mind their own affairs come to no harm."

She looked up at him, startled. "In Heaven's name, what are you saying?"

He answered her as quietly and calmly as before. "This is a seafaring race, Jane. These men have gone to sea for hundreds of years, and . . . well, times are hard, and a smuggler is paid a great deal for one night's work."

"Smu—!" She clamped her lips down before the word was fully out. She glanced back at Kate anxiously, but the old woman appeared to have heard nothing. The wind blew her hair into her eyes; she strained on tiptoe to be closer to Turnbull.

"Anne told me a little—I'd forgotten what she said. She hated it. She seemed to be afraid of it."

"Well—there have been foul crimes done in the name of smuggling . . . murder among them. But that happens only when folk get too talkative or too inquisitive of other folk's business. But mostly it flourishes without hindrance because there don't begin to be enough customs' men or ships to seriously check it. And the art of bribery is not subtle when practiced by determined men, Jane. Even when a known smuggler is caught the magistrates don't convict, either from fear for their own skins, or because there's no one can be got who will give evidence against them."

He straightened a little in the saddle. "This is their land, Jane —and never forget it! Deal, Dover, Rye—all along the coast as far as Cornwall they rule the roost. It would be safe to bet that there's hardly a fisherman along the coast that hasn't run a cargo in his time—when weather and moon is right. When it's done on a big scale, it can make men rich. And the rights and wrongs of it don't seem to matter against that. The Marsh is sheep country, and when the Government claps their stupid tax on the export of wool, and farmers are threatened with ruin, do you think they won't run their bales to Flanders, and be glad to take a contraband cargo in return? And for the laborers—they earn in one night what they'd get for six weeks work in the fields. So there isn't any use expecting them to see it in any other light but as bread in their children's mouths, and boots on their feet."

He looked towards Kate, who was staring at them curiously, her neck craned to try to catch the gist of that low-toned conversation. Then once again he bent closer to Jane's ear.

"Don't stand out against it, Jane. And don't talk of it—don't even see it! You'll find the whole countryside with the smugglers, and their hand against the excise men. And it isn't only the small people—there are rich and powerful men in these parts, Jane, who've grown fat on the profits they've had, who are always looking the other way when the customs man asks for help. And for the church—well, every parson within miles of the coast enjoys his contraband brandy and tea, and the only price he pays for it is silence, and a blind eye. At least that's what the wiser ones do. Otherwise there's trouble in the parish, and in turn trouble with the bishop. . . ."

She nodded quickly, her teeth beginning to chatter in the cold wind, and the nameless chill that Turnbull's words had brought out. Now the blackness of the Marsh was a hostile thing that screened what she must never see or talk of. She remembered Adam Thomas who openly said that he had left the Marsh to avoid the customs men; and there was Kate, standing there and perhaps guessing what it was they talked of so quietly. These people were your friends so long as you stood on their side, and closed your door to the riding officers. Between the two the line was clearly marked.

She drew back a little, and her hand slipped off the bridle. "I understand, Mr. Turnbull. I understand."

He raised his hat, and she stood and listened to the sound of the hooves growing fainter, and finally ceasing. Then she went back to where Kate stood waiting patiently.

The old woman looked at her with happy eyes as she shot the bolts in the heavy door. The candle flickered wildly for a second in the draught, and then grew still.

"It's a happy day for us that ye've come back, Miss Anne."

Jane glanced at her, startled, and then realized that Kate's memory had slipped, and that for the moment it seemed that it really was Anne who had come back to Blake's Reach.

She reached and took a second candle from the chest; lighting it from Kate's was a formal little ceremony.

"I'll light you to your chamber, mistress."

CHAPTER THREE

It wasn't, after all, Anne's room to which Kate led her.

"I've put Master William in the chamber beside yours, mistress, and you'll be sleepin' in Charlie's old chamber until I can get Miss Anne's room aired and ready. 'Tis smaller here, and the fire heats the place quicker than in that other great chamber." She opened the door and stood aside. "You'll be snug here, mistress, and little Charlie won't mind you havin' his bed these few nights."

Jane held the candle high, and looked about her. The room was still strewn with the things that Charles had left, his lesson books with the battered covers, the model ships he had sailed on the dykes, some dusty butterflies pinned to a sheet of paper, a riding whip with a broken handle. A row of sea shells were arranged carefully along the mantel. The four-poster bed took up most of the space; the bed curtains were limp and frayed. Charles' room was in the old part of the house, where the ceilings were lower, and laced with black oak beams. There was a knowledge of loneliness here, as if the walls had listened too frequently to a child's weeping, short cries that were choked back in shame and in fear that they might be heard.

Jane turned quickly to Kate. "I will do very well here, Kate, until my mother's chamber is ready. Good night!"

"Good night, mistress. Rest well."

She listened to the old woman's footsteps moving carefully down the passage. This room would not do very well for her; she would be out of it by tomorrow. She looked around again, shaking her head. Her lips were grim as she tentatively touched the bed Charles had slept on, and the table he had used for his lessons. She opened the great oak cupboard, and there were his clothes, painfully worn, and smelling of dampness and rot. With a stirring of pity she fingered them, picturing the long, thin wrists that had shot out from the cuffs. She didn't want to feel any more pity for Charles; she didn't want to think of him again. Almost certainly Charles would die. At this moment his life stood between her and her possession of Blake's Reach; she did not want to feel anything at all about him. Yet here the presence of the child he had been was a real thing—something she could touch as she now touched his coat. Nervous and angry suddenly, she slammed the door shut. She set down the candle, and began to undress with cold clumsy fingers.

Kate had laid her nightgown across the pillow. She felt the scratch of the rough bed linen against her, then her feet touched the hot bricks Kate had put there. Raised on her elbow, she blew out the flame.

The moving light of the fire filled the room—a warm, intimate light that played on the carved surfaces of the bedposts, and gave a ruddy beauty to a little mirror hanging crookedly on the wall.

Jane lay and watched the glow on the bed canopy. The room was peaceful. She turned her face wearily on the pillow, and then with a detached wonder, she heard herself murmur, *"Good night, Charlie! Good night!"*

2

The sound that woke Jane was almost lost in a sudden high shriek of the wind. She lay quietly, struggling against sleep, but becoming aware of the stillness and space in the room with her, and more certain that the sound had come from outside the house. She sat up, listening; there were red embers in the fireplace still, and she guessed that it couldn't be more than an hour since she had fallen asleep. It had begun raining again. She could hear no other noise, nothing to account for her waking, but she slipped from underneath the blankets, shivering as the chill of the night struck her. The casement was fastened tightly against the rain; she pressed her face against it, but could see nothing. There was no light from any of the windows below, nor in the wing of the house which jutted at right angles.

It came again—but this time a familiar and recognizable noise. It was the sound of horses' hooves on the driveway which led past the house and round the back to the stables. Quietly she opened the casement and leaned out; light needles of rain fell on her. In the blackness there was nothing to see, but the horses and their riders were now almost directly below her. She guessed that there were perhaps four of them. She waited for them to stop by the front door. But they swept straight on, moving at a quick trot. Then the sound diminished and changed as they rode through the gates, and started down the hill to the Marsh.

She gasped, and the explanation struck her coldly; it was their own horses that had been ridden away with such complete boldness—the horses belonging to Blake's Reach, and the two beautiful grays Lord O'Neill had given her.

The thieves were gone already—lost somewhere out there in that blackness.

Savagely she banged the casement behind her, and scrambled to find flint to light the candle. Then she flung a cloak about her shoulders, and thrust her feet into icy shoes. Outside in the corridor she paused, shielding the flame with her hand; the house was unfamiliar—the only thing she recognized was the head of the stair well in the new wing. In outraged haste she made for it.

"*Kate! Patrick!* Wake up! Someone's stolen the horses! Patrick —*wake up!*"

As she raced down the stairs she heard General barking—a frenzied sound in the otherwise still house. Now the strangeness of the house maddened her; in the hall downstairs she flung herself futilely against two locked doors in her search for the kitchen. She found it at last—a flagstone-paved room with a huge fireplace where the live embers still glowed. Leading directly from it was a twisting, narrow staircase. She stood at the bottom and called loudly, "*Patrick! Kate!* The horses—someone's taken the horses!"

It took her several minutes to light one of the lanterns she found ranged on the mantel, and more time went on struggling with the bolts on the kitchen door. Above her she could hear noises now—Kate and Patrick calling to her, and General still barking.

"*Mistress! . . . Wait!*"

Jane didn't wait. She ran across the rough paving to the stables, the rain pelting down into her face, making her gasp and twist to escape it. The wind struck cold right down to her bones. The stable door was latched, but not locked. She flashed the lantern quickly along the stalls; there was no answering movement of animals. The stalls were quite empty. In fury she banged the stable door again, and started back to the kitchen.

Her rage made her forget the cold. Angrily she faced Kate, who waited beside the door. Patrick was behind Kate, with his thick driving coat pulled over his nightshirt, and a long expanse of bony ankle showing above his shoes. By the light of the lantern he held, his pale face looked thinner than ever, and the hair blacker. At the doorway was William, barefoot and wild with excitement, straining on General's collar to hold him.

It was Kate who must bear the brunt of her wrath. "What sort of an idiot is Jed to go off and leave the stable unlocked! As if things aren't bad enough without losing the horses as well! Those grays—they were worth money! And the carriage . . . how can I use the carriage without horses?" Furiously she swept past Kate. "Oh, the fool! The blasted fool! Just wait until I lay my tongue about his ears—yes, and a whip about his stupid shoulders!"

"Hush, mistress! Hush ye now! There's no need to be frettin'."

"No need!" Jane's irritation increased. "Well, then, how are we to get them back? By morning they could be anywhere . . . day after tomorrow they could be sold, and gone forever!" Her voice quivered at the thought of it.

Kate shook her head; she closed the door firmly behind Jane, and reached out and took the lantern from the girl's tense fingers. Her wrinkled face was framed by two gray plaits hanging down across her shoulders.

"Easy, Miss Jane! They'll not be sold anywhere tomorrow, an ye'll find them back there, safe and snug. And more than likely there'll be a little present of tea or brandy to go with them."

Jane looked at her coldly, her anger dying in a second as the meaning of the words came to her.

"You mean, Kate," she said, "that this is the doing of the smugglers?"

"Yes, mistress."

"Why?"

With great deliberation Kate looked at Patrick. "Yer man, there —shouldn't he be takin' Master William back to his bed now, mistress."

Jane nodded slowly. "Yes . . . yes." Then to William she said, "You'll take your death of cold. Look, you have no shoes. . . ."

He grimaced. "But I want to go and look for the horses. Lord O'Neill wouldn't like to know that the horses are gone."

"We are not going to look for the horses now, William. I . . . made a mistake. They're not stolen."

He tugged irritably at General's collar. "We're *not* cold, and we're *not* tired," he said loudly as he turned away.

Patrick went with him, and as he was about to close the door, Jane motioned him. "Come back here—when William is settled."

Kate looked after them doubtfully. "Is it wise, mistress—yer man, can he be trusted to hold his tongue?"

"My mother died with Patrick by her bedside," Jane said sharply. "His devotion is to be trusted more than any soul I know."

When Patrick returned Kate had a brisk fire of kindling started. She had taken away Jane's wet cloak, and given her an old woollen shawl. The blackened kettle hanging on the fire crane had begun to steam. As Patrick eased his long body into the corner of the settle, Kate handed them mugs of strong, sweet tea.

"Take it now, against the cold," she urged. "I've put a drop o' brandy in to warm yer insides."

She settled herself in her own tall-backed chair, wrapping her soiled gray homespun shift about her thin flanks.

"Well, mistress," she said, "ye've lived inland until now, an' ye'd not be expected to know the ways of seagoin' folks. But where there's an easy bit o' money to be picked up, there are always men to be found to do it. The French coast is very handy-like to the Marsh, an' the tax on tea and brandy's high enough to make sure that a body would never get the taste of it."

Patrick moved indignantly. "That's all very well now—haven't we all been settlin' for contraband tea and stuff whenever we could get our hands on it. 'Tis only fools who pay the full price, whether they live inland or not. But look you, woman, this comes close to home—there's empty stables out there now, an' them two beautiful creatures that were the joy of Miss Anne's heart are gone. An' here's Miss Jane worryin' her head off about them. . . ."

She held up her hand for silence. "Will ye let me be? I've more to say, and I'll finish me piece in me own time."

"Go on, Kate," Jane urged.

The old woman swayed a little in her chair. "Ah, I know well that the whole country gladly takes what our gallant lads can get past the customs boys, an' I daresay the folks on the Marsh would go on runnin' the cargoes even if the other great injustice weren't here to ruin the farmers."

"Injustice?" Patrick's aggressiveness rose to the bait.

"Aye—a foolish an' cruel tax Parliament put on shippin' wool from the country. They say 'tis to help the weavers—an' the weavers pay as little as they like, an' it's ruin for the farmers. What could you expect men to do with the prices they offer for English wool across the Channel? What fools they be in London if they think a man will see himself ruined when all he has to do is run his wool across to Holland to fetch a fancy price.

"All along this coast, mistress—from here to Cornwall, the highest an' the lowest—there's hardly a family it doesn't touch in some way. Even the small people on the Marsh have a hand in it on their own account. The Dutch ships heave to off the shore, an' the folks row out an' buy the cargoes as free as you please. All it needs

is a dark night, an' some idea of where the revenue cutter is likely
to show up. And the revenue men—being paid as miserably as they
are, an' scared stiff, most o' them, to come up against the smugglers
—well, they're not always very slow to sell that kind of information.
In good weather yawls an' little sloops slip across to Jersey an'
Guernsey an' fill up with as much as they can hold. The Channel
Isles, mistress, are like big storehouses for everything the English
smuggler wants. 'Tis a profitable business, even when it's done in
a small way."

"We've all known that for a long time, woman," Patrick said.
"But in Heaven's sweet name will y' tell us where the horses are?"

"I'm gettin' to that," Kate said crossly. "I'm gettin' to that directly. Now—what I've been talkin' about's small stuff, a sideline,
you'd call it, for the smaller folk without much money. But for the
big men in the business it's a different thing. There are men on
the Marsh and hereabouts who've made themselves rich in a few
years on runnin' the tea and brandy. They're the ones who own
the big luggers—the Folkestone boat-builders make a fancy, handsome craft, with fore an' aft rig, that'll outsail anything the revenue
people put on the seas. All along the coast—places like Rye, Deal
an' Folkestone—they put out of harbor in the usual way, with a
small crew on, like as they was goin' fishin'. Then they heave to
off the coast somewheres, an' wait until the darkness. Then the
fisher folk and the village people come out in their rowin' boats,
an' leave a crew on the lugger of as many as forty to sixty men,
mistress, dependin' on the size of the lugger. Then they're off to
France or Holland, an' the people on that side be only too willin'
to give them the sort of cargoes they want—why, in places like
Flushing an' Roscoff, they leave a permanent man there to have
their stuff ready for loadin', just like a regular business."

She sipped her tea, nodding her head sagely at the thought of a
business well handled. "When it's all stowed, then back the lugger
comes, an' at night the boats come out again, unload the cargo an'
the extra men and run it in shore. That's where the horses come
in, Miss Jane. It needs a powerful lot of horses—maybe as much
as a hundred—to carry a cargo like that any distance from the sea
before dawn."

"And *that's* where our horses have gone!" Jane was shaken by the audacity and simplicity of it.

"Heaven help us!" Patrick said impiously. "To think of them two darlin's with a load on their beautiful backs—them that weren't built for it. I'll sit up wid them for the future—and see that it don't happen again."

Kate looked at him coldly. "'Twould be a foolish person who locked his stable when they thought their horses might be needed. Mor'an likely they'd find it burned down for their trouble. But if they're obligin'—why, there'll be a present, tea or a couple o' half-ankers o' brandy, nice as ye please, left back with the horses in the mornin'. Them fine gentlemen," she said slowly, "are easy to deal with as long as a body goes along with them. But it's a dangerous an' foolish thing to cross them. There've been bad tales o' murder an' beatin's. The smugglers are the law along the seacoast, an' there's none that dare stand against them. Informers have a bad time of it, I can tell ye. . . ."

Jane frowned. "But everyone must *know*. . . . A hundred horses can't pass along a road unnoticed."

Kate shrugged. "They do when everyone's particular to draw their curtains tight, an' close the shutters. An' in the mornin'—why, they've not heard a sound. It ain't healthy to have keen ears in these parts."

"Well!" Patrick said with satisfaction. "They'll not accomplish much on a night like this." He was still thinking sadly of the grays.

"Unless the wind drops they'll not land anything this night. It means that the lugger will put out to sea for the day, an' tomorrow night they'll try again. But it's a dangerous business, because by the second night the preventive officers may have got wind of it an' have called out the Folkestone Dragoons. There's often a drop o' blood spilled on nights like those, let me tell ye.

"The smugglers usually have a few different places they can drop the cargo a bit inland if they're pressed—'hides' they calls them. It depends on the information they get about the revenue people, which one they decide to use."

She put down her cup and leaned forward to stir the logs. The light played over the gaunt hollows of her face; the thin plaits of hair looked curiously childish now.

"In the past years, mistress, Blake's Reach has had a hand in that."

Jane stirred in alarm. From Patrick there was a frightened gasp. "Mother of God!" He looked expectantly round the dark kitchen. "You don't mean they leave the cargo here, Kate!"

"No, mistress! . . . No! They leave it at the church up on the old cliff-face there. Likely ye saw it as you came from Rye this afternoon? Aye . . . well that's John's church. One way an' another they do say he made a lot o' money—this is what I hear, mistress. It was all before my time. So he built this church that no one wanted in particular—St. Saviour's-by-the-Marsh, it's called. Ain't in any useful position, not for churchgoin' folks—stuck off by itself, away from the village, just because old John had a notion to build it where it looked right over the Marsh. He endowed it, an' there's a service there one Sunday in three, just for the sake of the vicar earnin' his keep, so to speak. Though he doesn't much like ridin' over from St. Giles. But he has to do it, like it or not. Not many of the villagers come to it, either—too far when the weather makes the roads mucky. As churches go, it ain't much use.

"It makes a good store, mistress, seein' as they have upwards of two weeks to move the stuff before the church is opened for the service. I expect the vicar knows—but he don't dare say nothin'. If truth be known, he's probably been paid to keep quiet. There's so much profit in a big run that any number of folks can be paid for services like that."

"Did Spencer know?"

Kate permitted herself a faint grin. "Why, bless ye, Miss Jane . . . there's a key to the church kept in this house, an' it's a privilege of the Blakes to walk in there whenever they've the notion! Yer grandfather was paid handsomely for forgettin' his privilege at times. Perhaps the smugglers might use the church only once in three or four months, but Spencer got his money regardless."

"Money!" There was an eager catch in Jane's voice. "Have they paid since he died?"

Kate shook her head. "Well, they've not paid *me*—that much I can tell you. O' course, I ain't important, but I knew what was goin' on because sometimes—well, yer grandfather wasn't up to seein' to things and he trusted me, mistress. I don't think Mr. Turnbull knows of it, so *he's* not got the money. Like as not they're glad to get out of payin'."

"Well, they *won't* get out of paying. Who else knows—Jed or Lucas?"

"No, mistress—or if they've found out they've kept their mouths shut, as it's prudent to do. They've no call to go to the church— or no call to poke their noses in where they're not wanted."

Jane looked firmly from Kate to Patrick as if daring a contradiction. "It's money that belongs to the Blakes . . . and for the time being it belongs to *me*. If Charlie ever comes back I'll settle my debts with him. Now—who do I see to get it?"

Patrick looked at the ceiling wordlessly, his melancholy face expressing his outraged feelings. Kate's horror was plain.

"Lord, Miss Jane, ye're not thinkin' of goin' after 'em. 'Tain't wise, I tell ye! Ye don't know these kind o' folks. Ye're new to the Marsh . . . an' the Marsh don't care for strangers pokin' into its business."

"I'm not a stranger," Jane said shortly. "I'm a Blake! Now tell me—what's the name of the man I must see."

Kate's voice wavered. "Oh . . . Miss Jane . . ."

"What's the matter, Kate? Are you afraid I'll inform? What sort of a fool do you take me for? All I'm interested in is the money for Blake's Reach. After that they can all drown or hang, and it's no concern of mine."

Kate shook her head. "Aye, but ye're young, mistress, to have words like those on yer lips."

"I have to have words and feelings like that or Blake's Reach will be sold over our heads. Now, tell me—what's the name of this man?"

"Mistress, I tell ye to stay clear of this business. Ye've no idea where it may lead ye. . . . Some bad things have happened. . . ."

"Kate, you'd better tell me. If you don't, I'll find other people to ask, and that could be worse."

Kate sighed and shrugged. "Then ye'd best be seein' Paul Fletcher, over at Old Romney. I doubt he's the man behind it all, but he's the man to see. He's not long back on the Marsh after leavin' the Navy. But, mistress dear," she added pleadingly, "you'll mind what you have to say to him? I don't trust none o' them what mixes in the business, an' Mr. Fletcher bein' a gentleman makes it harder to judge."

Jane felt a wave of anger and irritation sweep over her as she listened. She was tired, and the chill was beginning to creep into her bones. It seemed that everyone—Kate, Patrick, even Turnbull —was bent on putting only fear and frustration before her. At the same time they clung to her, and looked to her to provide the means and reason for existence—somehow. She wrapped her nightgown more closely about her ankles; it was wet and dirty where it had dragged in the mud of the stable yard. The wind had dropped while Kate talked, and she could no longer hear the sound of the rain. The smugglers would bring off the run, she thought, and someone—perhaps this Paul Fletcher—would be richer for it. She thought wearily and enviously of the gold that would be earned for this one night's work, and of the frightening way the golden sovereigns in her own purse had dwindled since they had left London—frightened when she considered all that was needing at Blake's Reach, and the demands that would be made on her. And the only salable possession left to her—the pair of grays—were out somewhere in the dark night, risking their precious hides to make someone else's gain. The thought enraged her; she felt young and ignorant, and the difficulties ahead were beyond counting.

She rose to her feet stiffly, gathering all the dignity and firmness that was left to her, because somehow, now, it mattered that Kate and Patrick should never sense her weakness.

"I've dealt with so-called gentlemen before, Kate. When the horses are rested, I'll drive over to Old Romney. Whatever sort of person Paul Fletcher is, he still must pay what he owes."

As she flung herself once again into Charles' bed she suddenly realized the implications of what she had said.

"God help me," she whispered, "I've thrown my hand in with smugglers."

She fell into an uneasy and dream-filled sleep, but when the sky over the Marsh was streaked green and faint purple in the dawn, she woke and heard them. She leaned far out over the open casement and listened as they went by. The grayness of the morning still hid them, but she knew the sounds well enough—the sounds of heavily laden horses climbing the hill slowly, the sounds of men's voices kept low and hushed. When they were past, she climbed back into Charles' bed and slept deeply and quietly.

She woke to a fair spring day, with the sun already high. When she went to the window the scene of the day before was gone. The Marsh was green and soft, the air as clear as polished glass, so that she could see the shipping in the Channel five miles away. Blossom was opening to its full in the tangled orchard; the warm air was alive with the hum of insects.

And then she remembered that it was hardly yet two months since she had left The Feathers.

CHAPTER FOUR

ALL OF THEM, KATE, JED AND LUCAS RECOGNIZED THAT THIS MORN-ing was different from others at Blake's Reach, and they hung around the kitchen waiting for Jane to appear. They expected orders from her, and she gave them as if she had been doing it all her life. A sense of urgency was upon her, and it made her shrewd and firm as she had never been before.

First of all she went with Lucas and Patrick to inspect the grays, to stroke their silken noses, and commend Lucas' grooming, to order the carriage washed and the stables swept. When that was done, Lucas would go to his usual duties of tending the sheep—there were new lambs in the flock, and she was sharply conscious of their worth. Grinning, Patrick helped Lucas move down to the cellar the two half-ankers of brandy, which had nestled innocently in the straw near the grays. Lucas' movements were eager and swift, as if, after the years of apathy at Blake's Reach, he welcomed the crispness of the orders. Before him, Jane made no comment over the brandy; if the acceptance of brandy and smugglers was part of the life of the Marsh, she meant to show how completely she belonged here.

Next Jed was dispatched, with a clip on the ear from Kate to hasten him, to the village—to Appledore, which was nearly a mile away. There he was to round up as many women as could leave their children and the cooking for a few hours, or to bring with them any children old enough to wield a mop or a rake. Jane was counting heavily on their curiosity to bring them, and, in the first flush of their enthusiasm, to get work from their tough, country-bred bodies that would lift the air of grim neglect from Blake's Reach. There was no money for carpenters and masons, but women and children were cheap to hire. For the present she would have to be content with clean windows and clipped hedges, and shut her eyes to the leaking roof and the crumbling plaster.

"Someday," she muttered, half under her breath, "I'll do the job properly!"

"What was that, mistress?" Kate asked.

"I said," she repeated distinctly, "that someday I'll do the job properly. Someday Blake's Reach will be the most respected house on the Marsh."

And they believed her. There was an immediate scurry to carry out her orders, as if they expected, magically, to see the old house dissolve and re-emerge before their eyes—just because she had said so. She noticed, with a touch of satisfaction, that this morning there was no talk of "Master Charlie."

"Jane!" She turned at a tug on her skirt. "Jane—what shall I do?" William's face looked up earnestly into hers.

"You? Why . . ." A gleam of mischief appeared in her eyes. "Why, William, you can be useful, too. Here! . . ." And for the first time in his life William found that his hands held a broom. "You can go and help Lucas sweep the stable."

He went without a word.

It was then, when the men were busy, that Kate led her to the drawing room.

"There was little a body could do to keep a great house like this in order, mistress, with no help," she said as she opened the door, "but 'twould have been a crime to let this go. I've done what I could. . . ."

She stepped inside, and Jane looked into the darkened room without much hope. Dust flew out of the curtains as the old woman drew them back. The spring sunlight came flooding in, revealing the long, finely paneled room, hung with portraits. She quickly took in the elaborately carved mantel and cornices, and the handsome high-backed chairs from which Kate was stripping the dust-sheets. Her eyes lit with excitement; she walked rapidly down the length of the room, lifting a cover from a marquetry table, bending to examine the exquisite work on the tapestry-covered chairs. She paused, and absently her hand cut a great swarth in the dust lying on a rosewood harpsichord.

"The master never used this room," Kate said laconically. "Too cold, he said. I think, myself, that he never fancied the company of his family on the walls."

Jane hardly heard what she was saying; she had begun pulling at a rolled-up carpet lying along one wall. Its color made her gasp— a brilliant gold and blue, with a texture like velvet.

"The Master said John Blake brought it back from Brussels when he was at the wars."

Jane was thinking that not even Anne's house in Albemarle Street had had anything as fine as this. She fingered it reverently, then looked around the room, and finally at Kate.

"We'll put it in order," she announced. "Some of the women who come must help you put it in order. We must have a room fit to receive guests in."

"Guests? To Blake's Reach? . . ."

"Certainly," Jane said tartly. "There will be guests here and we must receive them fittingly. Now, I want the floor waxed, the mirrors and windows cleaned, the curtains . . ."

Kate made a nodding acceptance of her instructions, believing by now that whatever Jane said would somehow be so. It was all too bewildering for her to take apart and question. The years since Anne Blake had run away from Blake's Reach had been dragging and weary ones, and her mind and her footsteps had slowed in acceptance of them. She had accepted the loneliness of this house, and the feeling of doom. She had expected to die knowing it that way. Now she was not fit to resist what Jane decreed, only knowing the joy of hearing a crisp young voice sounding in these rooms again, and the light, impatient tap of a woman's heels on the boards.

Jane moved from room to room this way, giving instructions, listening to explanations from Kate. On the way she discovered a chest of tarnished silver, and a stock of glasses begrimed with the dust of years. Patrick rubbed one in his apron, and held it to the light.

"From foreign parts, I'd say, Miss Jane. I've seen ones just such as these in Lord Ormby's house." His eyes gleamed over the silver. "Heavy as a bad conscience, mistress," he said, feeling it lovingly. "I'll warrant they'll fetch a good price. . . ."

She shook her head, and laid her hand restrainingly on his. "No more selling, Patrick, until we have no other choice. Clean it, and put it into use."

"It were too much for me to keep up with," Kate said in an aggrieved voice. "The master didn't care what he ate off . . . so I stacked it away here. . . ."

The talk and the small discoveries went on until they heard the voices in the yard. Jed was triumphant at the head of his band; there were eight women, and about as many children, three of them boys of almost thirteen, and strong and big enough for the work Jane wanted. They looked at her with expectant, excited faces, and she reminded herself that she must take the time to give them the gracious salute they considered customary. There were curtseys, and even small gifts—eggs and pots of honey and preserves; there were little speeches of greeting, and expressions of sympathy over her mother's death. They talked of Anne as if she had been at Blake's Reach only yesterday; Jane realized that a number of them would have been about Anne's age—perhaps had worked here in the kitchen or dairy, and grown up with her. Even her arrogance they had forgiven her, and had loved her for her generosity and high spirits; Anne's laughter had been a gift to this house, and to everyone who had come under its roof.

Then they proceeded to the real business of the morning, and they bargained a little over the price to be paid for their help. Everyone enjoyed it; it would have been a disappointment to them all if Jane had accepted their first price. But Sally Cooper had brought Jane up, and she was no one's fool. Finally the price was settled, and the mops and pails were brought out, the ancient gardening tools were oiled and scraped for rust.

Strange sounds which Blake's Reach had not heard in many years began to float out on the clear, bright morning—the sounds of mingled, good-humored voices, of stiff windows opening, the sounds of clippers in the overgrown hedges, and rakes crunching the gravel in the drive. Patrick was everywhere, shouting instructions, pulling ladders about, cleaning a window and then rushing to scrape the mud off the porch, to help a village child pluck weeds from the gravel. The acrid smell of soap and water meeting dust began to blend with the odors from the soup pot on the kitchen stove.

Clutching his broom, William ran about like a child in an excited dream, useless and unspeakably happy.

2

The morning was well on when Jane was free at last to get the key from Spencer's desk, and start up the hill towards the church. She was happier than she had been for many days, optimistic and confident. She kept twisting her face to get the sun fully on it. The stone church, St. Saviour's-by-the-Marsh, crowned the edge of the old cliff-face at its highest point. The sea that had once washed beneath the cliff was now the flat marsh land itself, rich and green, dotted with the grazing sheep, and the curving dykes. She turned off the road into the church lane, and then halted. The tracks left by the horses and men were quite distinct in the soft mud.

She stood thoughtfully, fingering the key in her pocket, gazing absently at the long waving grass in the graveyard, the motionless hands of the black-faced clock in the church tower. The light over the Marsh had a strange intense quality. She listened to the birds—plovers and a distant lark; there were two herons in the dyke at the bottom of the cliff. Below her the sloping roofs of Blake's Reach were touched with moss in places. It was a world suddenly familiar to her, and growing dear.

She turned and followed the path to the side door; the key slipped easily into the oiled lock, and she swung the door open, letting a broad beam of sunlight fall across the gray stone floor.

The damp and chill struck her instantly—and the strange, pervading smell. She caught her breath in a gasp of astonishment. The lovely, graceful church was piled high along each wall with bales of wool. The greasy smell of wool dominated that musty air, and with it was mingled faintly the woody smell of the brandy casks and the tea boxes. Everywhere—in the aisles, on the pews, in the carved choir stalls—were the bales and casks. She picked her way among them, collecting dust and fluff on her gown as she went. The delicate colonnade of three arches on each side of the nave was disfigured with this costly litter of contraband. She looked around with awe, trying to reckon what the cargo could be worth, and how many men had risked their skins and liberty to land it somewhere down on the Marsh shore during last night's storm.

The brandy casks were ranged in rows almost up to the altar itself. She stood at the bottom of the pulpit steps and tried to count them—and gave up. She glanced over her shoulder, the thought striking her suddenly that this was the first time she had ever been in a church quite alone before. On an impulse she mounted the steps, enjoying a sense of power as she stared down at the immovable, silent congregation of wool bales and brandy kegs.

She cleared her throat.

"John Blake built this church," she said loudly, sonorously. The echo, sounding back, startled her. "*John . . . this church . . .*"

She went on. "The smugglers own it now." "*The smugglers . . . the smugglers . . .*" it repeated mockingly.

The next words died in her throat. Horrified she listened to the sound of a key being fitted to the lock. She looked around wildly for a retreat from her absurd position, but there was only time to drop down behind the marble front of the pulpit before the door opened. A man's heavy tread sounded through the church. She counted the footsteps, purposeful, and growing nearer. About the center of the aisle he stopped.

At last he spoke, a calm, assured voice—unmistakably the voice of a gentleman.

"Well, preacher . . . Is your sermon finished already? You don't save much for latecomers!"

Scarlet with embarrassment and rage, Jane rose slowly to her feet. Standing below her, legs thrust apart and arms folded, was a tall, blond man, whose careless, unpowdered hair was dragged back into a short pigtail. He wore dusty breeches, and his faded, water-stained jacket had been part of a naval officer's uniform. The markings of rank and insignia had been removed.

He was smiling at her—a friendly, quizzical grin.

She returned his stare coldly. "Who are you?" she said, although she had already guessed his identity.

He dropped his arms and bowed.

"Paul Fletcher, at your service, ma'am." He raised his eyes to her again. "And you, of course, are the Blake of Blake's Reach."

"I have a name!" she snapped. "I'm Jane Howard!"

He shook his head. "It matters not, dear madam, what your name is. To the Marsh folk you are simply the Blake of Blake's Reach. And . . . while you look like Anne Blake come to life again, you can hardly expect to escape it."

"*You* knew my mother?"

"I knew her, of course. I was a child when she went away, but even to the young savage I was then, she was unforgettable."

Jane had nothing to say to this. The blue-eyed gaze of the man was disconcerting, and she was miserably conscious of all the things that were wrong with this meeting. She had had it planned—a carefully staged piece in which she would drive to visit Paul Fletcher in all her finery of silk and velvet, behind Lord O'Neill's grays. The advantage would have belonged entirely with her. Now he had caught her, disheveled from the morning's work, shouting to this empty church, and must surely think her half crazy. She had been made to look foolish—and with that had failed to uphold the prestige of the Blakes. She scowled at him.

"Would you please come down, Miss Howard?" he said politely. "I find it difficult to talk to a ghost in a pulpit."

She obeyed reluctantly. As she came towards him his eyes narrowed, and he cocked his head slightly.

"It's amazing," he said softly, as if he hardly meant her to hear. "The same walk even . . . almost the same voice!" He spoke louder. "You'll have to be patient with the stares you encounter, Miss Howard. Your mother was just about your age when we last saw her. No one here ever saw her grow fat, or her hair fade. . . ."

She shrugged. "Not you, or anyone else, Mr. Fletcher. She didn't grow fat or faded.

"However," she added, "it was not my appearance you came to discuss—or my mother's."

He was older than he had appeared from the pulpit. Now she could see the weathered lines in his face, and his eyes were alert and watchful—experienced; his body was strong and heavy-shouldered.

"I was on an errand at Appledore, and I learned that the Blake had come to Blake's Reach. I came to call, and bid you welcome."

"You came to call!" She ran her eyes over his shabby coat and the stained breeches. He was unperturbed. With equal coolness he surveyed her dusty gown, her hair carelessly drawn back off her forehead.

"The informality of my call was not meant as an offense, Miss Howard. As you can see—" he indicated the piles of contraband—"my business is pressing."

"Yes, indeed. So is mine."

He nodded. "Naturally, Miss Howard—there are many things to discuss." He gestured to the pew behind her. "Please sit down—this may take some time."

She sat down, perching herself on the edge of the pew. He dragged forward a brandy cask for his own seat.

"Of course, this isn't your rightful pew. The Blakes belong down there." He pointed towards the front of the church. "But it's already full."

She looked towards the altar, and noticed for the first time a large, boxed-in pew, on whose front panel was emblazoned the coat of arms which she remembered over the porch at Blake's Reach. It was set at right angles to the rest of the pews; on its faded blue velvet cushions were piled an assortment of odd-looking bundles, wrapped carefully in tarpaulin.

"Laces fit for a queen," Paul Fletcher said. "We're particular to put only the choicest merchandise there."

Swiftly she turned back to him. "Perhaps the Blakes are a laughing matter to you, Mr. Fletcher, but you'll hardly expect me to join the mirth. My family might have been fools, but I am one member of it who isn't going to be laughed out of what is rightfully their property. There's a question of some money to be settled between us."

He leaned towards her, both his hands resting on his knees. "Let us understand each other," he said carefully. "The smuggling fraternity is tightly knit, and we keep to our own rules. Certainly we make a living by not paying the King his revenue—but we *do* expect to pay for our privileges. Our business is highly organized, and it isn't run on debts. We use this church, and we pay for it."

"There's been no money paid since Spencer Blake died."

"Naturally not! Whom should we pay?"

With great deliberation she turned away from him and looked about her. She looked at the wool bales, the brandy casks, the tea boxes, and at the bundles of lace in the front pew.

"There's a great deal of money in this cargo, Mr. Fletcher."

She pointed to the bales stacked against the far wall. "You'll get a good price for that on the continent. The weavers in Holland pay well, I hear. Of course, there's a rub in handling so much—you need a good, large store, don't you? Somewhere not too close to the sea, and not too far inland."

"Yes?" he questioned.

"I mean," she said, turning back to him, "a store like this is a splendid one. You ought to be willing to pay handsomely for it."

"I'll pay what I paid your grandfather—ten sovereigns on the first of each month."

"Ten sovereigns . . ." She considered this carefully. "Ten sovereigns . . . But after all, that's only your word."

"There are no written contracts in our sort of business. Ten sovereigns was what we agreed upon."

She shrugged. "My grandfather's death ends all agreements and contracts he made. *I* have taken over now, and the new price is . . ." She paused, and considered. "The new price is fifteen guinea pieces, to be paid on the first day of each month."

He answered without hesitation. "I won't pay it!"

"And that, sir, will undoubtedly be your loss. This place suits you very well. The village is nearly a mile away, and the vicar a little further. A service is held only one Sunday in three, and the rest of the time everything's securely locked against preventive officers, who can't break into a church. It takes time—valuable time to you—for them to get permission to enter here. Oh, yes, all this is worth paying for."

"But not worth what you seem to think. Spencer Blake was paid that much money only out of deference to his position. 'Manorial rights' I suppose you'd call it. That sum of money doesn't bear any relation to the value of the store."

"Then if you're not prepared to pay what I ask, you must find some other place for your cargoes."

He leaned towards her again, and spoke quietly and sharply. "It distresses me to have to remind you of the fact, Miss Howard. But has it occurred to you that Blake's Reach can't afford to let go even the despised ten sovereigns?"

She shook her head. "You're very wrong, Mr. Fletcher. Blake's Reach needs money so badly that the miserable hundred and twenty pounds a year you offer is hardly worth thinking about." With the tip of her finger she began idly to trace the grooves in the carving on the pew. "Don't you see that once a certain stage of need is reached, a little money does practically nothing? Will a few extra pounds put a new roof on? Or buy a new flock? It wouldn't *save* Blake's Reach—it wouldn't even begin to patch it up!"

She was watching him carefully now, trying to feel how far she could go with the bluff. "It's really very simple if you look at it my way. I *can* afford to do without your money because it's such a small part of what I need."

His eyebrows had lifted a little—in amusement, Jane thought. "Then why press for more if this is a matter of indifference to you? Why not give it freely . . . let's say, as a generous gift of the manor? They say the poor are always the most gracious givers."

"It's a virtue I'm not very practised in," she retorted sharply. "I'm asking a higher price because I don't like to be undervalued."

He laughed outright. "Undervalued! I've never known a woman more conscious of her price!"

"Price isn't value, Mr. Fletcher."

His expression grew sober, and he shook his head. "I hope for your own sake, Jane Howard, that, in all you're getting yourself involved with here, you'll still be able to distinguish value from price. I mean, to know how much is worth . . . what!"

"I understand very well what you mean." She tapped her nail against the edge of the pew. "What I want to *know* is will you pay what I'm asking?"

He shrugged, losing his air of seriousness and concern, becoming flippant again.

"How can I say?" Reaching behind him he caught his coattails and spread them out for her inspection. "Do I look like the man who owns that cargo? You surely must know the difference between a prosperous smuggler and his hireling? It's not for me to settle what shall be paid. I'll carry your message, of course. . . ."

Jane pursed her lips. "I thought a man of your . . . talents, Mr. Fletcher, would hardly be content to labor for another man. I see you as a leader. . . ."

"Of course you do," he said, blandly ignoring her tone. "Talents I undoubtedly have, but it takes time to acquire your own lugger. I left the Navy ten months ago."

"The Navy regretted it?" Jane prompted.

"It would be idle to pretend they did—with a line of men ahead of me for promotion that would stretch from here to Rye. Too slow for me—too slow. What's the use of being made a vice admiral the year you die of old age?" He shook his head. "It was divorce by mutual consent. I can't really think the Navy grieves the loss of Lieutenant Paul Fletcher."

"So . . . you're not rich enough to own the cargo? Then who does?"

"I'm paid so that *that* gentleman doesn't have to soil his hands with the illegal business of smuggling. The dirty nights waiting for the boats are not for him—or the unpleasant thought that you might have to kill a preventive officer to save the cargo. No, that's not for him at all! One of the many nice things about being rich is that when you want to break the law, you pay someone to do it for you."

"You're not going to tell me his name?"

"I not only won't tell you—I'll even warn you it's not a question that's safely asked on the Marsh."

She felt the coldness of his words touch her like ice. She wished she needn't be constantly reminded that this was a world of suspicion and chase, of quick and savage revenge on the informer. It was all much better when smuggling was made to seem a fairly lighthearted business of keeping out of the way of the revenue men. She stirred restlessly, wanting to be free of the thought. All

she had wanted was a few extra pounds from this bounty in which
the whole seacoast appeared to share, but Paul Fletcher wanted her
to feel the darkest fears of any of the men who walked the roads
with contraband at night, or who sold information to the excise
men, and spent the gold with terror in their hearts.

"You make the Marsh an evil place," she said in a low tone.
"I'm afraid. . . ."

His features relaxed. He was almost tender when he spoke.

"There's no need to fear when you belong to the Marsh as the
Blakes do. They have been here as long as men have been recording
its history. They belong here—not like the Fletchers, who were
small farmers and newcomers hardly more than a hundred years
ago. The Blakes—"

He stood up abruptly. "Come with me!"

He held out his hand to her, and she took it without a thought,
caught up in his force and energy. He led her back to the door, and
stood aside to let her pass. They stepped out again into the sunlit
world, and the damp and smells of the church were gone. The light
was so brilliant and solid-seeming that Jane wanted to put out her
hands and feel it, like a living thing. The green miles of the Marsh
were there, the flat shores, the sea like a blinding mirror.

Impatiently he pulled her around to the other side of the church,
where the sweep of the view was much greater.

"Shade your eyes! Now look down there. That great dyke down
there—in the break between the hills towards Rye—that used to be
a tidal river, when the Marsh was still a marsh, and half-covered
with water in every high tide. And the smaller dyke branching from
it—do you see where it goes? It runs from there right along here
beside Blake's Reach!"

"Yes—I see." And then impatiently, "But what . . ."

"Wait! Try to think of a time, hundreds of years ago, when the
river found its way out to the sea through mud-flats, and this dyke
was a small creek flowing into it. A man called Blake came to settle
on a reach of this creek, and gave it its name. Not an important
man—just a very obscure cousin of a family who were prominent
ship-owners and merchants. In fact, they were Barons of the Cinque
Ports, and that was a title to be proud of in those days.

"*This* Blake," he said, nodding towards the dyke and the house, "had his chance when the Rother changed its course after a great storm—some time, they say, about the thirteenth century. Then this side of the Marsh was flooded only at exceptionally high tides. The reclaiming of the Marsh has been going on since the Romans came to England, and after the river changed its course, the time was right to start on this part. The Blakes began making their innings—reclaiming, ditching and draining, and the acres of pasture for their sheep grew with each generation."

He laughed suddenly, in amusement. "As your grandfather told the story, one day the Blakes stopped working for a moment to draw breath, and found themselves rich—and bearing the title of Lords Proprietors of the Romney Marsh, to boot! And they weren't humble folk any longer."

"That's a good story," she said with satisfaction. "I don't care if it isn't exactly true—it's still a good story. But what became of the other ones—the ship-owners?"

He shrugged. "I don't know. Died out, I suppose—or were lost in poverty. This used to be a great sea-trading area, but as the reclaiming of the Marsh went on, the harbors began to silt up. New Romney's a mile and a half from the sea now, and Rye harbor is a mile from the town itself. When the trade left the ports, I imagine the ship-owning Blakes went with it."

"It seems to me," she said coolly, "that you've too much information about the Blakes. How much of it have you made up?"

He laughed. "None! I swear to you—none! I've heard it from your grandfather when he wished to impress on me the inferiority of the Fletchers by comparison to the Blakes."

"You hated him, didn't you?"

"Hate him? Why should I? He was an old man, full of drink and despair. He was shamed, too, by the thought that he and his father had brought nothing but disaster to their family. At one time, he told me, the Blake land stretched to the great dyke in the south, and touched the fringe of Appledore."

"And now," Jane said, "there's only a few fields, and hardly enough sheep to keep them cropped. Don't tell me, Mr. Fletcher— I *know*."

"There are ways to get land," he said quietly. "When times are bad, small farmers grow less careful of their inheritance. It needs patience—"

She broke in roughly. "And money! Where do you think the money would come from?"

"The King's Pearl! Everyone knows that Spencer never sold the King's Pearl."

"The King's Pearl belongs to Charles." She pointed towards the house. "Down there we're all waiting for Charles to come back." Her voice shook with a scarcely controlled anger. "I've been here less than a day, and already I've fallen into the pattern. This hour, or maybe the next hour, he might come back." She looked away. "No—the King's Pearl is not mine to sell."

"Charlie Blake is as good as dead—if he's not dead already! You'll be mistress of Blake's Reach, and free to do what you please with the King's Pearl."

She stood silently, fighting hope and enthusiasm, not wanting Paul Fletcher to see them, but wanting to hear him say again that she would be mistress of Blake's Reach. Once again she wanted to hear that land could be won with money and patience. She struggled to keep the excitement from her face and eyes, and it wasn't possible. Paul Fletcher knew as well as she did what thoughts were hers, how the fate of an unknown man in a Paris prison could seem so little beside what lay under her hand. With a little money she could live with dignity and honor at Blake's Reach—so that by degrees she stepped completely and forever across the line that had separated her from this family, so that there would come a time on the Marsh when she and no one else would symbolize the Blake family, when the memory of old scandals would die. . . .

Paul Fletcher's voice, sure and firm, broke into her thoughts. "And I know what you'll do. You'll put every penny you can lay hands on into Blake's Reach—as careful and saving and industrious as any of the first Blakes who settled on this creek. You'll make a dull marriage to further your plans, and not to anyone who will take you from this place. You'll sacrifice everything to it—and it'll be wrong! It will take everything, too—your youth and all the good years there should be for you. It will take your beauty, Jane."

Vaguely she was aware that he had called her by her name, and she didn't turn to rebuke him. Nor did she attempt a denial of his words. "You don't like the Marsh, Paul Fletcher," was all she said.

"I'm unwilling to give my life to it! It's worked over—there's nothing but these eternal sheep and the blasted winds. Its society and people are stagnant, like all of England. I'll leave it behind when I can."

"Where will you go?"

"When I've gathered enough money from cheating the King's Revenue I'll go and trade more or less honestly in the West Indies. I'm a seaman. Not a porter of other men's brandy."

"Why the West Indies? —Why not one of the English ports?"

"Because I want to go where there's air to breathe, and sun on your bones, and rum for the asking. Money isn't so important. . . . I could live like a king there for what I'd earn on the profits from a single sloop. And if a man cares to exert himself, if he's got wits and guts, and will take a risk, then he can be rich. I said money wasn't important. Well, it is! To me it's important. I like money . . . and sunshine, and women who smile easily, and laugh. I'm sick in my belly of these stiff-necked dames who wouldn't unbend to pass the time of day with disreputable Paul Fletcher."

"Are you disreputable?"

"Never mind that," he answered shortly. "Ten years from now it won't matter."

Suddenly he touched her arm.

"Think of it! Ten years from now you'll still be living here—working and scrimping for the honor of a name. And I'll be free of it all, in a place where names don't count."

Her body stiffened, and she drew away from him. "Why do you talk like this? What can it matter to either of us what the other does?"

"Of course I talk out of turn—I always have! I'm saying this because I think you're making a mistake, and it's a damn shame! You've come here out of the blue, and now you've seen Blake's Reach, and you think you want to be part of it. You don't understand that it's finished, and that someone like you can't be walled up in a tomb for the sake of a tradition which seems dazzling in its fashion, but will drain the life from you."

She stirred, opened her mouth to speak, but he cut her short.

"Believe me, it isn't worth it, Jane," he said. "Get away before you're caught up in it all—before you forget there are such things as being young, and laughing whenever you feel like laughing. You're trading your youth and freedom for the empty game of playing a lady without a penny in your pocket. You don't know all the difficulties yet. But even in the few hours you've been here you must have felt doubts. . . . You're even breaking the law. You're throwing your hand in with a bunch of dirty smugglers. And what for? You're doing it for a crumbling old ruin and its debts that aren't worth a thought in a young girl's head. Get away from it, Jane!"

There was no response in her face—the obstinate, stubborn Blake face, immobile with anger and wounded vanity and pride. He felt saddened as he watched its unchanging stare.

"Since when, Paul Fletcher, have women been able to decide which way their lives will go? Do you think I have any choice? *You fool!* It's Blake's Reach, or nothing!"

She turned swiftly and walked away from him, the hem of her dusty blue gown swishing against the long grass. Her slight body was rigid, as if her anger and scorn were barely confined by good sense. When she reached the gravel path she looked back briefly.

"I'll expect you with the answer about the money tomorrow evening. *Without fail!*"

Only during his naval service had Paul Fletcher remained silent under a tone like this. He was moved to protest, and then dismissed the thought, shrugging. When a woman looked like Jane Howard you allowed her to say such things, especially when the sun was like fire in her red hair.

CHAPTER FIVE

JANE WALKED SWIFTLY DOWN THE ROAD TO BLAKE'S REACH, her mood savage and tinged with bitterness and disenchantment. She examined the house critically in the light of Paul Fletcher's words, and now she saw only the broken roof tiles, and the rusted iron

gates. Abruptly her plans became like a bright, romantic dream that
had fallen in pieces at her feet.

Her feelings softened instantly she turned into the drive, and
her shoes crunched on the raked, weedless gravel. The vines were
clipped away from the shining windows, now open to the April sun.
The boys had attacked the hedges too eagerly—they were cut un-
evenly and too low. The effect was drastic, but at least clean. The
nettles and dead leaves had been piled ready for burning. The tangled rose garden would be the next thing to set in order, she
thought. It seemed suddenly very desirable to grow a rose that
would be her own . . . roses were such beautiful, useless things.
She wondered if the orchard was past bearing fruit, and if it would
be possible to set out daffodils between the trees in time for next
spring's blooming. She knew nothing of growing flowers—at The
Feathers there had been a thriving vegetable garden, but nothing
so frivolous as a flower. Daffodils, she remembered, multiplied of
themselves, and five years from now . . . She checked her thoughts,
and turned to go indoors.

The whole place smelled of soap and fresh wax polish. From the
direction of the kitchen came the sound of many voices, and an
occasional burst of riotous laughter—she had no doubt that the
Appledore women appreciated Patrick's sallies, and his liberal hand
with the ale. There was also the smell of broth and new-baked
bread.

Patrick had already started in to clean what had been Spencer's
sitting room. It was still untidy, scattered with his books and the
piles of old papers she would have to read and sort through. But
the floor and windows shone; the curtains had been brushed and
shaken. Patrick had lighted a small fire in the clean-swept hearth.
The fire tools were polished. The table was set with two places—
clean silver and glasses laid on a fine damask cloth that had belonged to Anne. Patrick's sense of the dramatic had led him to
withdraw himself and his helpers, leaving the room ordered and
waiting for Jane's return.

Looking about her, Jane brushed aside finally Paul Fletcher's
warnings and prophecies; back here at Blake's Reach they lost their
power. Triumphantly, she reached out and pulled the bell cord.

William was as changed as the house. He sat beside her at the table, eating with those precise and assured manners that had startled her at first, but in every other respect he was different. He wore a coat too tight and short for him; at Patrick's bidding he had washed his hands impatiently, but the sweat marks showed clearly in the dirt on his face. The red curls on his forehead had caught a thin cobweb. Except for his greeting, he was quiet—for once too hungry to talk.

Patrick came to attend them at the meal, his swift, swooping movements like a fly. He accepted Jane's praises calmly, and waited for Kate's entry with the tray of food to start his attack.

"Sure, it's a real cook y'll have to be gettin', Miss Jane. Wouldn't this stuff be lyin' in yer belly like a lump o' lead, and y' comin' to an untimely death wid the indigestion. . . ."

Kate sniffed, and banged down the tray. "The Irish are naught but a bag o' wind, and so needn't be troublin' about their bellies."

"In good time, Patrick—in good time," Jane said. "Kate does very well for our needs at present . . . which, Heaven knows, have to be simple enough to match my purse. Time for a cook when we have a full pantry."

"Aye, mistress, aye," Kate muttered approvingly, casting a glance at Patrick's downcast face. She was delighted at this blow to his love of grandeur and ostentation. "Ye've wisdom far greater than yer mother, poor lady," she finished.

Jane held Kate back after Patrick had gone to supervise the vast meal spread in the kitchen. The old woman waited expectantly at the end of the table, her hands folded against her apron.

"I met Paul Fletcher this morning, Kate," Jane said quietly, spooning her broth which she thought was surprisingly good.

"Aye, mistress." The tone was careful.

Jane looked directly at her. "Tell me about him, Kate."

Her head jerked nervously. "What, in Heaven's good name, should I know about Paul Fletcher, mistress. It's not for the likes o' me to have anythin' to say of him."

Jane was impatient. "Oh, Kate, don't be foolish! I'm not asking you to tell me anything the whole Marsh doesn't know. Where does he come from . . . how long have the Fletchers lived here?"

"Oh . . ." Kate shrugged. "Is that the all of it, now? Well . . .

a bit of a wild one, is Mister Paul. He's one o' the Fletchers o'
Warefield. He's brother to Sir James Fletcher who lives at Warefield House over near Hythe. The family came to the Marsh some
ways back—about my grandfather's time, I'd say, and they've done
well out of it. Sir James is rich, mistress. They say he has a lot of
his money in some company 'way off in India—and that do make
him twice as rich as he used to be."

Jane raised her eyebrows. "Rich, is he? Well . . . Paul doesn't
look like a rich man's brother."

"It doesn't follow, mistress. Paul's the younger brother—and the
estate be fixed on the elder. He had some share o' his father's
money, though. Not a fortune, they say. But whatever it was, he
went off and bought a part of a plantation in the . . . West Indies,
wherever that might be."

Jane nodded. "The West Indies? . . . What happened to the
plantation?"

Kate shrugged. "I don't know the exact rights of it now, mistress.
Perhaps Paul hadn't much of a business head in those days. They
do say his partner tricked him, and then the fever wiped out all
the slaves. He lost whatever money he put into it."

"And so he came back?"

Kate nodded. "He came back and went into the Navy. He's a
good sailor—the people from this shore have always been rare fine
sailors—but he joined late, you understand. They say the Navy's a
slow place to rise in, and young Paul has too much of a will to enjoy bowin' and scrapin'. He stuck it for a couple o' years, and then
a year ago—more or less—he suddenly turned up on the Marsh
again. He took Jim Rogers' cottage at Old Romney, and I hear
he's makin' a book o' charts. . . ."

She added, looking first at William's head bent over his food,
and then at Jane, "O' course, what he does with the rest of his
time is his own business. He'll not make a fortune out of any old
book o' charts. He's quick and clever, mistress, but there are those
who must know what he's about—if you take my meanin'. . . ."
She glanced again at William. "They be waitin' to catch him. But
then—" with a shrug—"doubtless he'll get off lightly. He has influence, and he handles a pack o' men so big the magistrates be

mortally scared o' them. He's Sir James' brother, to boot—and Sir James is an important man on the Marsh."

"Yes . . ." Absently Jane fed General a piece of bread soaked in gravy.

"Though, mind you," Kate continued, "they say the pair o' them don't get on too well. Sir James is a solid man, and he's no love for anyone as wastes his money. Paul doesn't go often to Warefield House. His brother's lady wife, Alice, can't abide him. There be some old quarrel between them."

"Is Paul married?"

"Married? Not that the Marsh folks know of. With all them black women in the Indies he didn't need to have a regular wife, they tell me. He's a restless one, mistress. A handful for any woman."

William had finished eating, and he bent down and gave his plate to General to clean.

"I met Paul Fletcher this morning, too," he said.

Both women turned on him instantly. Kate gave a wail. "Master William, ye didn't go—"

Jane cut her short. "Where did you meet him? *How?*"

William looked indignant. "I didn't go *anywhere!* I was working there by the gate, and a man came up the hill leading his horse. He seemed to know about me—he knew that we'd come yesterday. He said his name was Paul Fletcher, and he promised to come back and bring me some white mice."

"*Then* what did he do?"

"Why—nothing! He just stood there for a while, watching all the people work. He just laughed a little, and shook his head, and went on straight up the hill. Do you suppose he'll really bring the mice? I'd like to have them."

"I wouldn't be at all surprised," Jane said, ungraciously. She pushed back her chair and rose. "I've no doubt he's plenty of time to collect white mice, as well as waste the morning standing laughing at other folks labor. . . ."

William looked at her in astonishment. Kate said nothing, merely started to clear up the dishes. Jane waited for her comment, and when there was none, she turned away, irritably brushing the dust off her gown.

William and Kate could hear her voice trailing off as she walked down the hall.

"They must be finished eating now. . . . I want them to understand I don't pay them to sit stuffing themselves. Patrick! Patrick!"

2

Paul Fletcher's cottage was at the lower end of the tree-lined lane that led to Old Romney Church. Every Sunday the bells tolled and the people walked and drove along this lane, and stared into this cottage, and shook their heads because he never showed himself at the church door. They said the wildness had got into him since he had sailed the Caribbean, and maybe—God save us—he had even brought back the taint of Popishness. Paul knew what they said, and didn't care.

He turned his eyes with relief away from the wearying distances of the Marsh, and fixed them on his own moss-touched roof. The landscape of the Marsh was oppressive to him—flat, dull, with the wind forever sighing in the elms and swishing the willow trees. It seemed to him that he had always hated the Marsh, but he knew that there must have been a time when he had loved it—perhaps long ago when he was a thin, sunburned boy hunting for birds' nests in the hedgerows, or being taught to sail by the Dymchurch fishermen. He knew the secret places of the Marsh, its twisting tracery of roads was etched on his memory; so often he had lain and watched the sky reflected in its thousand and one stretches of water. He might have loved it then, but it was a long time ago.

His horse headed down the lane towards the cottage, and the rooks in the trees over his head suddenly rose in a body, and filled the air with their unearthly screeching. His mind was closed against the sound because he could still hear the footsteps of the girl as she hurried away from him along the church path, with the sun on her wild red hair, and the dust on her blue gown. He smiled a little at the memory.

He unsaddled in the lean-to at the back of the timbered cottage. No smoke came from the chimney, and he knew as soon as he opened the kitchen door that this was yet another day on which Mary Bridges, the woman from the village who cooked for him, had neglected to show herself. Dishes from last night's supper and to-day's breakfast still littered the table. He had let the porridge burn again this morning, and its acrid smell lingered in the untidy room. Although he was hungry, he turned away from it in disgust.

His sitting room was a bare apartment, furnished for all his needs, and lacking any touch of warmth or ease. It was a functional room —a place to store his books and mariners' charts, his quadrant and compass; there were shelves for his wine and glasses, a peg on the door for his hat and coat. It was dusty; the red curtains were still drawn across the windows as he had left them last night. He jerked them back now, and the sunlight flooded in.

There were stiff, dead daffodils in a stone jar on the window sill. In a springtime burst of enthusiasm Mary Bridges had put them there a week ago.

He poured himself brandy from a decanter, and dropped wearily into a chair. He had had no sleep last night—and the rain had soaked through to his skin. He felt the brandy flow easily to remove the tenseness, and thought that six nights from now, if the weather held he would spend another night waiting in the darkness on the shore . . . another night waiting for the signal, waiting for the shape of the lugger to emerge from the blackness as they rowed with muf-fled oars towards the rendezvous . . . another night to listen to the tramp of the porters' heavy boots, with the armed batmen at the front and rear of the column. Another night . . . and another . . . until there was enough money to leave it all behind him. Enough money to leave the Marsh forever.

He was tired to death of the comfortless round of his existence —this dreary, sterile life that held none of the things he wanted, only risk and danger, and their accompanying terrors. But daring and courage of this sort commanded a high price. If the cargoes were good, and the runs successful, he wouldn't be here very long —not long enough to forget how to enjoy himself.

The sun beat warmly on the back of his neck. He closed his eyes; the uncomfortable, dusty room receded, and now he was crunching the sand of a soft-colored Caribbean beach under his boots, and the blue-green water beyond the surf line was strangely like the eyes of the girl who walked beside him. She laughed, and talked to him

lightly, and the breeze blew her wild hair. It was red hair, and the
blue gown she wore was faded by the fierce sun.

Paul fell asleep with the glass still clutched in his hand.

3

On the evening of the day after her meeting with Paul at the
church, Jane ordered a fire to be lighted in the drawing room at
Blake's Reach. She dressed herself in a gown that had been one of
Anne's favorites—a green silk with heavy cream lace—and settled
herself to wait for him. Responding to her lead, William also presented himself in the drawing room, wearing one of his velvet
jackets, and his hair darkened with water. With General beside him,
he sprawled on the blue and gold carpet before the fire, impatiently
thumbing his way through a book he had taken from Spencer's
shelves; he talked hopefully about the white mice Paul had promised, and kept looking at the clock on the mantel.

Jane stifled her own impatience; finally Patrick came and took
William, protesting, to bed. She added logs to the fire, and the
ticking of the clock went on in the stillness. The fire threw shadows
across the floor. In this light, Jane thought, the room looked handsome; the carved cornices and mantel took on depth and richness
—the frayed edge of the carpet over by the windows was lost in
the dimness. The Blake portraits, painted by provincial artists,
made them look calm, almost dull; people, with no history to speak
of. She could see her own reflection in the mirror on the far wall
—it should have pleased her because at this distance, the pointed
white face might have been Anne's own. But instead she sat, with
nervous hand plucking at the lace, wondering why she went to this
trouble to receive Paul Fletcher, and why it now seemed important
what he thought of Blake's Reach and herself. Yesterday she had
thought him a meddlesome and impudent stranger. She knew she
was looking at the clock as many times as William had done—and
she couldn't stop it.

At last she had to tell herself that he would not come that night.
She kicked the rug back from the hearth, and went slowly into the
hall. Patrick was there, dozing in a big chair, with the candle ready
to light her to bed.

During the day they had cleaned and aired Anne's old room. The fire was burning there, and her nightgown laid out. Patrick held the candle high.

"It doesn't look like Miss Anne's chamber," he said sadly. "I miss the pretty things she kept about her—like toys they were in her little hands. I just can't think now, that Miss Anne grew up in this gloomy old hole."

When he was gone, Jane crouched before the fire in her nightgown. The chamber was vast and chill; there was, as Patrick had said, none of the charm and warmth of Anne's London bedroom about it. Now, with Patrick gone, the silence was deep; she listened, remembering with faint regret the chatter of Mary in the small room they had shared at The Feathers, of the alert wakefulness of Lottie and Pru when Sally had imagined them asleep for hours. In this silence there was no companionship. Was this, she wondered, the solitude Paul had warned her of . . . was it possible that time and years could slip away in this quietness, as he said, and she would wake one day to find that she had missed too much? He had wanted her to leave Blake's Reach . . . perhaps he spoke from his own knowledge of the vast, empty bed, the unshared seat by the fire. She rested her head on her drawn-up knees, thinking of him standing below her in the church yesterday, making a joke of his poverty and his unkempt clothes. Yesterday he had had a feeling for her, a notion to help her, a thought for her future. Perhaps that was all yesterday with Paul; tonight she had waited, and he had not come.

4

Kate was scandalized when Jane took a hoe and set to work beside Patrick, Lucas and William in the neglected vegetable garden at the back of the stables. She worked with a frantic kind of energy, to try to rid herself of the fears of the night before, and she was still there, muddy and perspiring, when Kate came hurrying to tell her that there was a messenger from Robert Turnbull waiting for her in the stable yard.

He had sent her one of his own horses in the charge of a groom—a light roan mare whose coat had bronze tints as she moved. The note from Turnbull was brief, written in a quick, firm hand; its brevity gave Jane the feeling that he was writing to an intimate. "*I hope you will regard the mare as your own for the time you are with us here. Her name is Blonde Bess. You will find her willing and gentle, and her manners are excellent.*" It was signed simply, *Robert.*

In her pleasure and excitement Jane didn't stop to consider all the implications either of the message, or the loan of the mare. The manner of the action was, she imagined, typical of Robert Turnbull, offhand and understated; his motives she didn't trouble to question. She sent the groom from the livery stable back to Rye, and Lucas to the vegetable garden, but William and Patrick stayed with her to admire and touch, talking in soft voices to Blonde Bess, stroking her nose, fingering the fine leather of the harness. Jane helped Patrick lift William into the saddle, and, watching the sudden delight in the child's face, she was immediately saddened and angry at the thought that he did not have a pony of his own.

"She's beautiful . . . she's beautiful!" William chanted. Jane was struck by the sight of the red-headed child atop the red horse.

"Mr. Turnbull's a good an' generous gentleman, now," Patrick said with conviction.

Jane glanced at him sharply, sensing that his statement was not meant innocently. "Mr. Turnbull has been a valued friend to the Blakes for many years. He . . . he grew up with my mother!"

"Oh, to be sure," Patrick answered piously. "He will continue to be a valuable friend, I trust, Miss Jane. There's always somethin' to be said for a man that knows a good piece of horseflesh. . . ."

"Patrick! . . . Blonde Bess is a *loan!* Nothing more! And Mr. Turnbull intended nothing more! And you're not to gossip about what's not your concern!"

Patrick looked pained. "I swear to Heaven, Miss Jane, that there's never a word out o' me mouth. I was only meanin' that all I hear o' Mr. Turnbull is that he's a fine gentleman. . . ."

"Enough!" she said. "Enough talk now! There's the vegetable plot to see to—we're late already with the planting, and it could be we'll have no crop. William and I will stable Bess. . . ." Patrick bobbed his head in assent, but she checked him again as he turned away.

"Understand, Patrick—*Mr. Turnbull is not Lord O'Neill!*"

She gave her attention to William again, but he was no longer absorbed in the mare. A little open-mouthed, he was staring across the yard. She dropped her hand from the saddle, and turned around.

Paul Fletcher stood there, holding his horse's bridle. His hair was powdered and tied back carefully, he wore an immaculate frilled shirt, and sober, well-cut breeches and coat. He swept off his hat, and smiled, as if what he saw pleased him.

Jane took a faltering step towards him, her face coloring, and then the color as abruptly leaving it. She didn't properly understand why the sight of the tall blond man should affect her in this way; but she did know, despite his opposition to Blake's Reach, that it was a warming, comforting thing to see him standing there, smiling at her.

CHAPTER SIX

THEY HAD BEEN SO STILL THAT A FAMILY OF WILD DUCKS CLINGING to the shadow of the tall reeds had ceased to listen for them. Jane, lying on the grass, slowly raised her head, turning her face to catch the sun fully on it. On the other side of the dyke the willows trailed gently to the water; near the footbridge a wild apple tree was in full bloom. The warm breeze occasionally carried the scent and the falling petals towards them. Everything was quiet, save for the hum of the insects, and the faint plopping sound when one of the ducks broke the surface of the water.

"It's so peaceful," she said softly. "I haven't had such peace since . . . since I was a little girl."

"I used to think the Marsh was peaceful, too," he said. Then he glanced at her. "Did you know you've got petals in your hair? You look like . . ."

"And so have you—like snow." She twisted a little, resting her elbows on the grass and cupping her chin in her hands. "Such a day this is! Full of surprises and good things—I got more guineas than I asked for, and William got his white mice. And Blonde Bess there . . . Look at her, Paul! How lovely she is in the sunshine!"

"I can't think," he said lazily, "what possessed Turnbull to send you Blonde Bess, of all his horses. He loves horses—that I know—and he keeps a number of them at the stables in Rye. But Bess is the favorite, and the best of them."

She looked at him sideways. "Are you sure you can't think why he sent Bess? He was very fond of my mother. I think perhaps he was in love with her."

He shrugged, rolling over on his back and squinting up at the sun. "Turnbull . . . in love with Anne Blake. Well, why not? Stranger things have been. But I can never think of Turnbull allowing himself the luxury of such waywardness. Though, Heaven knows, Anne Blake was easy enough to fall in love with. When I think of her then . . ." He moved his head and looked at her. "Well, Jane, people will love you too, because of the memory of Anne." He chuckled, a quiet, derisive sound. "I can't think that it was anything but a romantic, sentimental memory that prompted my—my employer to increase the price on the hire of the church. I almost couldn't believe it when I was told. Twenty guineas instead of the fifteen you asked! Well, there are fools born every minute. I wouldn't have paid it!"

"I told you I didn't underrate what I had to sell."

"You did—somewhat! I sent a message saying you wanted more money, and the offer that came back was twenty guineas. I didn't mention what price you had put on it."

"Why didn't you go yourself? You knew I wanted the money quickly!"

"No use going," he said. "These things take time—I've more than a notion that the decision didn't rest completely with the man from whom I take my orders. There's another—or others. I'm sure of that."

"What does it matter," she said lightly, "so long as I get paid?" She turned to him suddenly. "I was angry with you last night for not coming. I thought you were trying to slight me."

"Slight you? Jane!—Jane! Do you think anything would have kept me away if it were possible to be there! This business I'm in

—we're in—isn't child's play. That's what I'm paid for. I must be ready to go where I'm bidden at a moment's notice—to London, to France, to Holland. It leaves no room or no time for the things that give life enjoyment or beauty. I wanted very much to come last night."

"If you're being honest, I'll be honest, too. I'll tell you something, Paul. Last night I put on the finest gown I have—green silk. I curled my hair, and had a fire laid in the drawing room. I think I wanted you to see how changed things were at Blake's Reach, how different it was all going to be from now on. And this morning you came and I had been digging the vegetable patch. . . ."

"You looked beautiful—even with mud on your face. I shall cherish the picture, even more than the imagined image of the girl in the green silk gown, with her hair curled."

"Why? That's not as a woman wants to be remembered."

He gestured helplessly. "How do I tell you? It is because I see you as something wild and free, wearing the look that courage wears. Even being here, as you are, with me now—riding out on the Marsh with me despite all they had to say against it at Blake's Reach—eating bread and cheese and ale with me in a tavern. And here you are, letting the sun freckle your white skin, and your hat has almost blown into the dyke, and you don't notice it. Oh, Jane —Jane, don't you see that it doesn't take much to sit by the fire in a green silk gown?"

"Hush! . . . Hush, now!" she said, laughing and not able to be angry with him. "Sitting by the fire was an accomplishment, too. Things have been done at Blake's Reach, Paul—and they're *my* doing. I'm responsible for the fact that the drawing room is fit to receive guests in . . . and carriages can drive to the door now and I've no need for shame."

"I know what you've done at Blake's Reach, Jane, even in these few days. At Appledore—and even further than Appledore—they think you're some kind of miracle. They expect to see old John Blake pacing the drive with you someday, passing on advice. No one can decide whether you've no more money than Spencer, or whether you've inherited a fortune from Anne, and know how to be economical with it."

Jane laughed outright at that; the sound was loud and unrestrained. The ducks fled to cover in the reeds; further along the dyke, two herons, startled, rose up quickly in lovely, graceful flight.

"Oh! . . ." She dabbed at the moisture in the corners of her eyes. "That's so funny—how Anne would have laughed! So Appledore thinks I'm an heiress. . . . Well, let them think it! None of them have to know that I've spent the last hour lying here wondering how I can spend the twenty guineas to get the best from it. Which, I wonder, of the leaking spots in the roof most needs attention? Or would it be better to spend it where it would show most? Should it go on the garden or the kitchen? You see, Paul, I'm being strictly honest—every penny shall go on Blake's Reach, none into my pocket."

"Well—I wish it were otherwise, Jane. I wish there was a shower of gold going into your pocket, and that there were green silk gowns without number."

She opened her mouth to make a teasing reply, and then closed it again; Paul's face wore a look of repressed irritation and annoyance.

"What is it? Why do you look like that? I was only joking. . . ."

"I wasn't joking! I'm disturbed because there *is* a way of sending a shower of gold into your pockets right at the moment, and I can't use it."

"Why not?"

"Because it takes money to make money—and I haven't got enough to start." He looked at her with inquiring eyes. "Not incidentally, it would send a shower of gold into my pockets as well. How much money have you got, Jane?"

"How much do you need?"

"Five hundred pounds—thereabouts."

"Well! You might as well look for five thousand from me! I haven't got that much, and if I did I don't think I'd want to risk all of it with—"

"Why? Because you've heard I once lost money you don't think I can be trusted. I tell you, Jane, this is as sure a thing as you'll ever hear of. It can't miss!"

"*What* can't miss?"

"It's this way." He rolled over on his elbows until he was facing her directly. "There's a man by the name of Wyatt in Folkestone

who's in trouble for money. He built a lugger to certain specifica-
tions—the chief of them being that it could outsail any revenue ship
on these seas. The man who ordered it has gone back on the order
—got into money troubles himself—and he's canceled. Wyatt is in
debt, and looking for a buyer."

"Are you suggesting we *buy* a smuggler's lugger?"

"Child! You couldn't buy a lugger for a few hundred pounds!
But Wyatt is desperate, and would be willing to take cash for the
hire of the craft. You see, it isn't just the matter of the lugger, Jane.
You've got to have enough in hand to buy the cargo, pay the
porters, a few pounds here and there as bribes . . . it adds up. But
the profits! Three hundred per cent isn't unusual! Even a few
months with the use of the lugger would pay us both handsomely.
On the very first cargo we'd make enough profit to buy the second."

She shrugged, unconvinced. "Well, suppose—just suppose—we
could hire the lugger. A few months wouldn't make us enough
profit to buy it outright. What would happen when Wyatt found
a buyer?"

"Well—" He gestured briefly. "We'd be back at the beginning,
wouldn't we—even if a little richer for our pains? Besides, many
things can happen in a few months. Fortunes change. . . ."

"What do you mean, 'Fortunes change'?"

"Exactly what I said. By the end of the summer news may have
reached you of Charles Blake. By the end of the summer you might
be able to sell the King's Pearl."

Her mouth dropped open slightly; she gave a short gasp. "Sell
the King's Pearl to buy a smuggler's lugger! You must be out of
your mind!"

"Some people wouldn't say I was—those who know the smuggling business. In a few seasons you could make the sort of money
you haven't dreamed of, Jane."

"Yes, and throw my hand in with a pack of murderers! It sounds
like a poor way to invest the King's Pearl. I don't think I want
any part of that side of it."

"You've listened to too many exaggerations, Jane. The smuggler's band is as good or as bad as its leader. There are some men
who'd think no more of murder than stealing a chicken from a
cottage garden. But I don't happen to be one of them. Don't for-

get, it suits them to keep up all the old tales of murder and violence. The more frightened the people are, the less interference there'll be. And don't pretend you aren't already a part of it, or that you can turn your head away from it. Every person who buys a half-pound of smuggled tea is part of it—which means about three-quarters of the whole of England."

She didn't contest the point, knowing the truth of it far too well. "All right—all right! But what's the use of talking? I haven't that much money, and the King's Pearl isn't mine. So there's an end of it."

"I wish it didn't have to be the end—there won't be another chance like this one. Couldn't you borrow? Couldn't you borrow it from Turnbull? Any man who lends you Blonde Bess could be persuaded to lend you more."

She sat up straight, two bright spots of color burning her cheeks. "I don't think I care to ask Robert Turnbull for money on *your* behalf. I don't want to have to hear him refuse. I don't want to guess what he thinks of me."

"Does it matter to you what he thinks, Jane?"

"Of course it does! He believes me, and he trusts me—he'd want to know how I'd use the money, and he wouldn't be fooled by the answers I could think up. No, not Robert Turnbull!"

"I didn't know you thought so highly of him," Paul said shortly.

She turned on him. "If you weren't so busy hating everything you see on the Marsh, you'd discover there *are* people here who know how to live. . . ."

"Hush! Jane—I didn't mean to rouse you!" he said lightly. "I should know better than to tease a Blake. They're famous for their lack of a sense of humor."

"Well! And I've known long ago that the salt water dried up your sense of . . . of . . ." She struggled helplessly for a word.

"Proportion?" he suggested.

"That will do as well as any—and I won't be badgered by you any more. Loans . . . money! I've only been four days on the Marsh, and you expect me to raise money! Why can't *you* do it— you must know enough people. They say your brother's a rich man. Ask him!"

Paul sighed. "Him last of all! I've just managed to pay off my

debts, and I'd need to match your five hundred with five hundred
of my own. It can't be done, Jane—hereabouts I'm reckoned to be
a bad risk."

" 'That wild Paul Fletcher'?" she said softly. "Do they expect
you to run off with it?"

He grinned. ". . . or spend it on women."

Suddenly she laughed. "What a couple of paupers we are! No
possessions—and no money!" She glanced over at him slyly. "Expensive clothes . . . fairly pleasing manners—but no money! What
can we do?"

Abruptly his face darkened; his eyes lost their amused, teasing
expression as completely as if he had pulled away a mask. He gazed
at her intently, his brow furrowing. Then he leaned over and
tugged at her arm, so that she collapsed on the grass; he pulled
himself nearer.

"We can use what we have, Jane—we can enjoy what we have."

He bent over and kissed her savagely, wildly—a frantic, searching
kiss that carried overtones of despair. He rubbed his face against
hers, cheek yielding to cheek, covering her face with soft, biting
kisses, that were passionate and yet protective. She murmured, and
he covered her mouth again with his. Gently he kissed her ears, and
her throat; his hand sought the swell of her breasts under the habit.
He could feel the tautening of her body as she responded.

"Oh, Jane . . . Jane," his voice was low and troubled. "You're
so lovely, Jane . . . and if I had everything the world could give
me, I'd still want you."

Their heads were close together, red and blond, in the sun. The
breeze stirred again, playing through the reeds where the wild ducks
hid, and lifting and scattering the blossoms over their two bodies,
lying so still on the green spring grass, and aching with their need
and longing.

They rode together on the Marsh until the approach of dusk—
disturbed and wondering, hardly speaking to each other, or looking
into the other's face—and yet there seemed no way to part that
would not be painful and violent to them both. Jane followed
Paul's lead on the winding roads mindlessly, without question, only
wanting above all things in the world that the closeness between

them should not be jarred or broken. She lent her body willingly
to the rhythm of Blonde Bess's movements, feeling the wind in
her face, hearing it thrust against the elms. Startled birds rose from
the hedgerows at their approach; plovers shrieked from their nests
in the fields. Jane looked about her and smiled, accepting the
subtle magic of the spring afternoon and the presence of Paul at
her side with equal sureness.

They rode westwards under the great sea wall at Dymchurch
where the level of the marsh was lower than the sea itself. Paul led
her off the road to paths among the sand dunes. They emerged
from the dunes finally, and halted.

To Jane the sea was part of the afternoon—no more or no less
strange and wonderful than everything that had preceded it. She
stared at it until her eyes ached; the wind brought tears to them,
and she saw the scene through a haze. It was a miracle of light and
movement, a heaving, crashing thing, that deafened, fascinated and
awed her. It was an immensity she was not able completely to
grasp.

Paul reached out and took her hand gently.

"Out there is France, Jane—someday you'll come with me and
see it. And over to the west there . . . that foreland is Dungeness.
It's nothing but a huge shingle bar the sea has thrown up over hundreds of years. It's a natural barrier against the sea on this side of
the Marsh, but it's helped, as much as anything else, to silt up Rye
harbor, and the mouth of the river."

The long miles of shingle Paul had called Dungeness were desolate save for the swooping gulls, but now, in the spring, it was
cloaked in patches with the wildflowers that somehow managed to
take root there—drifts of sea pinks and of broom, and starry stone-
crop . . . inhospitable, frightening, with the sea booming endlessly,
remorselessly against the rounded stones that formed its substance.
Jane struggled to repress a shudder.

Paul leaned towards her. "It frightens most people—those that
bother to come and see it. They say there's nothing like it anywhere
else in the world." He shook his head, gesturing briefly. "It'll be
even less inviting if we linger here, Jane. See those clouds coming
up along the coast? That means rain within a half hour, and we'd

best be away from here. This is the devil's own place to be caught in a storm—nothing to break the wind over all those miles."

He dropped her hand, and turned his horse swiftly. "Come, there's nowhere hereabouts to shelter, and you'll be soaked."

With a last look backwards to that desolate foreland, they turned their horses. Before they were clear of the sand dunes, the rain was falling lightly, the clouds racing ahead of them eastwards across the Marsh. It was the cold, cheerless rain of spring. Jane turned up the collar of her habit. They rode another mile, and the rain was heavier; it had started to drip from the brim of her hat.

Paul leaned towards her. "We'll have to shelter at my cottage—it's not much further on."

She nodded, looking at the darkening sky, and thinking without relish of the miles between her and Blake's Reach. When they entered the street of Old Romney it was deserted—not even a dog huddled in the shelter of a doorway. Smoke curled from the chimneys, and they heard the sounds of many voices from the ale house. Through the uncurtained window of a cottage Jane caught the bright gleam of a fire, and suddenly she felt the chill of the rain in her bones, and was conscious of the long miles in the saddle.

"I'm stiff," she said to Paul. "I'm hungry, too—and I think that Blonde Bess is almost too much for me. It's been a long time since I've ridden so far."

"We're almost there," he answered. "It's over yonder, in that belt of elms."

At the end of the village the road forked—a left turn to the church, which stood, oddly, by itself, and was reached by the lane that followed the curve of a dyke. Sheep grazed in an open field between the village and the church. Paul's cottage stood midway along the lane.

The rooks rose from the elms at their approach, their harsh cawing deadened a little by the steadily falling rain. Together Jane and Paul went to the lean-to stable at the back. Paul dismounted, and reached up to help Jane; she rested in his arms briefly, her cheek brushing his wet coat. Then she raised her eyes to look at him deliberately, questioningly, and she found an answer there. They knew, both of them, as surely as if it had been put into solid-sounding words, that, whether the rain had come or not, they would still have taken the fork leading down to Paul's cottage.

2

Jane pulled off her wet jacket and skirt, huddling gratefully into the warmth of the shabby padded dressing robe Paul had given her. Her boots and hat and gloves lay in a pile over by the door of the sitting room. Paul had built a fire, lighted candles and drawn the curtains against the gathering darkness. He was out in the stable now, tending the horses; faintly she could hear him whistle as he moved about. She stripped off a petticoat whose hem was heavy with mud and wet, and flung it with the other garments, shivering a little as she loosened her hair, and bent towards the fire. The wind had risen, and moaned fitfully in the elms by the gate.

Paul came back, and she watched him silently as he busied himself with rum and some spice jars ranged on the shelf. He had taken off his jacket, and his body, revealed by the fitted waistcoat, was lithe and strong. The day in the wind and sun had done its worst with his carefully powdered hair. It was hard to remember him as he had stood in the yard at Blake's Reach that morning. As he blended the spices, muttering softly to himself, she knew that she would always prefer him as the unkempt figure she had seen for the first time in the Blake church.

"It's a mixture used in the West Indies," he explained to her. He had heated a poker in the fire, and he plunged it now into the liquid. It hissed furiously and he thrust it under her nose. The fumes brought tears to her eyes.

"Good, isn't it?" he demanded. "Here, taste it! Best thing I know to drink when the rain gets down into your bones."

The liquor slipped down easily, and the warmth started to spread through her. He knelt on the hearth rug beside her, and instinctively she moved closer to him, wanting the reassurance of nearness and contact. Gently he put up his hand and stroked her hair.

"It's strange, Jane, what you have made happen to this unlovely place. An hour ago it was simply a roof over my head, uncomfortable and lonely. Now there is a red-headed girl sitting before my fire. . . ."

"Hush!" she said. "It's I, Jane Howard! Remember it's the girl you quarreled with two days ago! I'm no different . . . though I believe you've mixed a little spell with your brew, because I think I've almost forgotten what it was we quarreled over."

"Nothing that matters . . . nothing at all," he said softly. "If I could, I'd remove you from everything that has a taint of smuggling. Part of me doesn't want you here, sharing my rum and my vaguely shadowed reputation. But I couldn't deny myself the delight of your coming to share even so little . . . and most of it not good."

"Paul . . . I wanted to come!" She spoke with difficulty, looking towards the fire. "It's been lonely . . . and I've been afraid! I've needed to talk with someone who . . . who is my own kind." She uttered the last words wonderingly, as if realizing the truth of them for the first time.

"Then you'll never be afraid any more as long as I am here—or lonely. Now you have Blonde Bess, and you know that my door is never locked. . . ."

With quiet movements he pushed the robe back off her shoulder, and plucked at the ribbons of her bodice. He gazed at her for a while, and then put aside his mug.

"You have such beautiful breasts, Jane. . . ." He touched her briefly, and then his hand dropped as she pulled away, flinching.

Instantly she recovered herself, her cheeks coloring hotly. She reached out and took his hand, and cradled it between her breasts.

"I'm sorry . . . sorry. For a minute I forgot it was you. . . ." Her voice was muffled and low.

He gathered her into his arms. "Someone hurt you, Jane? . . . and you still remember!" He rocked her gently, as if she were a child. "I said you were never to be afraid . . . and you need never fear me."

For answer she lifted her face to him, seeking his lips.

"I'm not afraid . . . and I want to be sure I'll never feel lonely again."

He laid her down tenderly on the rug. "You never shall . . . never."

3

The rain had gone when Jane and Paul rode back to Blake's Reach. The wind was fresh, and the dark clouds scudded swiftly across the Marsh, parting sometimes to show them a glimpse of the pale young moon. Sometimes they saw its reflection in the pools of water on the road, and then the wind would stir and distort the water, and all they saw was starry points of light. The Marsh was dark and secret, and at this hour there showed from the cottage windows only an occasional light or the glow of a dying fire. The beat of the horses' hooves were loud in the village streets; the clock struck the hour as they passed by the church at Appledore. In a cottage garden Jane could distinguish the ghostly outline of an apple tree in bloom. Briefly her senses were filled with the remembered fragrance of the hour they had spent by the dyke.

They spoke no words of farewell to each other as they rode up the hill and passed through the gates to Blake's Reach; they had all the confidence of time to spend together in the future. Gently, before he dismounted, Paul leaned across and touched her mouth with his lips.

"Remember, Jane . . . my door is never locked."

They were engulfed then by a flood of light from the kitchen door; Kate and Patrick came hurrying out, lanterns held high and grave disapproval plain in their faces. Jane cut short their inquiries.

"I'll have you understand that I am mistress here," she said. Her tone was very quiet. "And when I come and go is no one's concern but my own."

Then she gave her hand to Paul. He dropped a kiss on it, mounted without a word, and rode out of the yard. Patrick took Blonde Bess into the stable; Kate waited silently to light her to the kitchen.

"I'll make ye a toddy, mistress," Kate said. "A little somethin' to get the warmth back into yer bones. Folk do go down with terrible fever from ridin' the Marsh by night. It's the mists in the dykes, mistress."

"I'm not cold, Kate—but I'll have the toddy, if it will please you."

She sat in the settle by the fire, staring into the flames, and hearing nothing of Kate's vague mumblings in the background. Dimly she understood that Kate was making dark hints of sickness and death and worse for those who didn't stay safely within their own walls when darkness fell, but she heard her as if the voice came from another world. So much had changed from the moment she had ridden away from here, so much was different, and could never be the same again. Her body and her mind had been stirred to a depth she couldn't as yet comprehend; she had been touched and altered and reshaped, and a deep peace and gentleness lay on her like a covering. The facts and personalities of her small world had not yet broken through it, nor did she want them. She sipped the toddy, and thought of Paul.

Patrick came back from tending to Bess, and he stood for a long time with his arm crooked over the corner of the settle opposite, his white bony face with its shock of dark hair on the forehead, meditative and wondering. She finished the toddy, and raised her head to look at him.

"Heaven help us!" he said. ". . . an' here she is wid eyes in her head as bright as stars!"

She rose to her feet, picking up her hat and gloves.

"Patrick, do you remember what my mother looked like when she was in love?"

She took the lighted candle from Kate's hand, and left the kitchen. Patrick straightened, shaking his head. The old woman clasped her hands nervously; her face, when she turned to Patrick, was gray and strained.

"May Heaven help us, indeed! When a Blake falls in love there's no tellin' what things may come upon us. And here she's fastened her heart on a wild one, an' it'll bring ruin to us all."

As Jane reached the head of the stairs she saw the light from William's candle under the edge of the door. She stood quite still, listening; she could hear his thin child's voice running on and on, softly, like a trickle of water. In the empty silence of the house, the sound was eerie and disembodied. She went to the door and opened it.

The dog, General, raised his head, and William glanced up at the same moment. He sat propped up against the pillows, and the candle behind his rumpled hair gave it a fiery aura.

He grinned, and patted the edge of the narrow cot in invitation.

"William—you should have been asleep long hours ago." It was beyond her ability then to make her voice stern. He sensed her mood and took advantage of it.

"I want to show you George and Washington."

"George and Washington?" she said vaguely.

"Yes—you remember!" he said, hurt by her forgetfulness. "Mr. Fletcher brought them this morning. I thought they might get tired being shut up in their cage—you know—cramped."

Jane sat down where he indicated. There was a tiny movement among the folds of the blanket, and William suddenly pounced with his right hand, and then his left. Each of his hands was pressed firmly against the mattress, and between the thumb and first finger of each, Jane could see the whiskers and small bright eyes of a white mouse. William looked at her expectantly.

"They're very handsome."

He nodded. "Yes, they are," he said complacently. He indicated the cage on the floor. "Would you pass that up? I'd better put them in—they're frightened of strangers, and they might run away. They might go down the holes in the floor, and the other mice would kill them."

She opened the cage door, and watched him deposit the animals, and close it quickly. She took a crumb of cheese from his hand, and poked it through the bars.

"Why are they called George and Washington?"

"That's what Mr. Fletcher called them. We gave them their names when you were changing into your habit this morning. The one called Washington is named after an American hero of the Revolution—though Mr. Fletcher said it wasn't considered the right thing in England to say he's a hero. The other one is called George, after the King—though Washington's name is George, too." He frowned. "I can't remember exactly what he said . . . something about the times when they fought each other they were the King George and George Washington, but the rest of the times they were just George and Washington. Mr. Taylor once explained to me about the American War of Independence, but I don't remember it all. Do you know much about it, Jane?"

She shook her head. "No."

The information seemed to please him. He bent his face towards the cage eagerly, tapping against the bars to attract the attention of the mice.

"Aren't they pretty, Jane! So quick and neat! I wonder what my mother will say when she sees . . ." His voice faltered, and he gazed up at Jane with an agonized look of realization and loneliness. He drew his breath in quickly, and his whole body seemed to heave.

"Oh, Jane . . . I miss her so! *I miss her!* She always looked so pretty, and she smelled so . . ."

She caught him into her arms, and he buried his face against hers. At first his sobs were loud and violent, cries of outrage and fear; then they came more softly, tired and whimpering. He held himself close to her for the comfort and security of her living presence. She stroked his head, hearing herself murmuring words to him, saying things about Anne she had never known, but which she knew now he wanted to hear. He grew quiet in her arms, and finally he slept.

General lay at his feet on the bed; she placed the cage of white mice where William would see it when he woke. She rested her hand for a second on the dog's head; then she took the candle quietly and left.

CHAPTER SEVEN

EARLY THE NEXT MORNING JANE SENT JED TO RYE WITH A MESsage for Robert Turnbull, asking for him to come to Blake's Reach that afternoon. There was only one thought in her mind as she carefully penned the note—that Blake's Reach needed money desperately, and Paul's plan to hire and use the lugger at Folkestone for carrying contraband was the only way to get it. But to hire the lugger and buy the cargo too she must find five hundred pounds to match what Paul could put up. And Robert Turnbull was the only one who might lend her that much money; there was no one else.

It was a golden May day, and the sun fell across the mirror as Jane dressed for his visit. She nodded to her own reflection as she brushed her hair.

"You're about to be a smuggler, Jane Howard! Have you thought what's going to happen to you if you're caught?"

Then she scowled, slamming the brush down, and reaching for her gown that lay ready for her. She turned back to her image. "Breaking the law, am I? Well it's nothing more than thousands of other people are doing. And there'll be no violence—Paul promised me that! I'll get into it and out of it quickly. And then I'll forget it. Just as soon as I have some money to get things started here again, I'll pull out and I'll forget it."

She studied herself in the lilac gown, that had been chosen with Robert Turnbull in mind. It gave her a look of calm and gentleness.

"But what of Paul?" she said suddenly. "I love Paul, and I want him. I want him and Blake's Reach both. There's got to be some way I can have both . . . and Robert Turnbull's the first step."

She chose to wait for Robert by the broken wall at the bottom of the garden, where the climbing roses had made their own wilderness. She began cutting out the dead wood, as she had seen the cottagers do in Hampstead, clipping and tying back, working at a leisurely pace, until she saw him coming down the garden towards her. The stocky, expensively clad figure was a shade too eager, the brown eyes were expectant and waiting. She waved a greeting, and then bent and clipped the rosebud she had been saving for him.

She held it towards him. "Welcome! This is for you—the first bud! It's early, and I don't expect it will open . . . but I thought you might wear it for me."

He accepted it from her, smiling a little, and put it in his buttonhole.

"Save me the last one, also, Jane. I'll come in the autumn to collect it."

"But the autumn's a sad time in a rose garden," she said. "I don't want to think of the last bloom . . . it makes me afraid I'll be leaving Blake's Reach. . . ."

"You won't be leaving Blake's Reach. I'll be here to collect the first bud of next spring as well." He stepped back from her, head tilted a trifle, studying her.

"You know—I find it strange to see you here in the garden. Anne never cared to work in the garden. She said she had no understanding of flowers."

"She was made to look at flowers, not tend them," Jane replied, laying down the clippers. She smiled teasingly. "You really must stop looking for Anne in me. I'm a woman in my own right, you know."

He nodded. "And I do you a grave injustice if I suggest anything different. Forgive me, Jane—it's the face that tricks me."

"How well you remember her," Jane observed softly. "You remember everything about her—everything she did and said."

He shrugged. "Why not? Life is too slow in the country not to make a personality and a face like Anne's exciting. It isn't likely I'd forget."

"You never wanted to leave Rye—to go to London perhaps?"

He shook his head. "When I was young I saw no reason to—and then years later when I woke up to the fact that I was bored, the habit of prosperity and comfort had become ingrained. I chose to remain where I was bored, rather than risk the dubious excitement of starving. I like good horses, fine wine and rare books. . . . I'm a dull man, Jane, and I've grown reconciled to it."

"A dull man? Never that, Robert!" It was the first time she could recall speaking his name aloud. She bent down swiftly, and began piling the clippings and tall weeds into a flower basket; he stooped to help her, and their hands brushed, and then withdrew as if they had been stung. Jane smiled a little shakily, handing him the basket. At the same time she slipped her arm through his free one.

"I've really brought you out here to boast," she said lightly. They began walking back towards the house. "I wanted to show you what I'd done. It was such a bright, wonderful day, and I have no conscience about bringing you away from piles of legal papers."

"Nor I in coming. Besides, aren't the Blakes my clients? I'm here to serve them, and if it happens to be a beautiful spring day—all the better!"

She halted, pulling on his arm. "I suppose . . . it's just occurred to me that you must have been one of the people who suffered most with Spencer's gambling. How long is it since you've had a bill to the Blakes paid?"

"Hush!" he said, urging her forward again. "You don't know

what you're talking about. Old John Blake, the general, put my great-grandfather into business, and made him prosperous. I don't think the Blakes have seen a bill from us in nearly a hundred years."

"More fool you!" she said. "But if that's how you choose to do business . . ." She tugged at his arm quickly. "No not there . . . I want you to come round to the vegetable garden. William and Patrick and I have worked on it—and we'll eat from it before the summer's out." She gestured briefly. "And over there—by the wall— I thought I'd start an herb garden. Sally Cooper taught me a little about herbs . . . she used to make herb tea for anyone who was sick in the village."

"And you hope to do the same?"

She shook her head. "Don't tease me! I need the herbs for the kitchen. Besides, the village has grown so used to Blake's Reach in a state of beggary and ruin, I think they'd laugh to see me step out of a carriage bearing herb tea!"

They inspected the vegetable plot, and stopped to exchange greetings with Blonde Bess in her box. Robert spent ten minutes admiring the grays, discussing and praising their fine points; then Jane and Robert went through the kitchen, Kate curtseying and looking disapproving of Robert's presence there, Patrick bowing, with just the suggestion of a wink to Jane. She took Robert to see Spencer's sitting room, and then in triumph, to show him the drawing room. His pleasure in all the changes was real and outspoken.

"Jane . . ." he said, shaking his head. "Jane! it's incredible! The place hasn't looked like this since Anne— No, even before Anne left it was showing signs of Spencer's lack of money. He had got rid of most of the servants—the highest-paid ones. How have you done it?"

"I have Patrick," she said simply. "And Patrick is young—and I am young. We believe in ourselves, and we don't think Blake's Reach is in a hopeless situation. Of course, I don't know when Patrick sleeps—if he ever does. He gets through the work of three men."

Patrick had laid a tea tray, and she made the tea from a spirit kettle, counting the tea from a rosewood caddy which had a tiny lock. She glanced at it, and smiled.

"I can't think why anyone who lived on the Marsh should trouble to lock up their tea. It isn't much of a luxury in this part of the world."

"No it isn't—and there's many an old laborer's wife with an ache in her bones who thanks the Lord it isn't. If it weren't for the smugglers' runs most of the people in this fair kingdom would never taste tea."

She handed him the cup. "Are you feeling generous towards the smugglers today?"

"Not especially. I don't care what smugglers do as long as they keep out of my way. I enjoy cheap brandy and tea as much as anyone else."

"I hoped you were feeling soft about everything today." She faced him across the tea tray, across the shining silver and the delicate cloth that had come from Anne's house. "I hoped you were feeling soft because I have something to ask of you."

"What?" He fixed his gaze upon her firmly, his eyes were speculative.

"You've looked around here, Robert. You've seen what I'm doing. You've looked at the grays, and the carriage. There's some silver Spencer forgot about, and didn't sell. You've an idea how much it's all worth."

"Yes."

She drew a deep breath. "Then I'm going to ask you for a loan— with these things as security."

"How much?" His voice didn't betray either surprise or distaste. He was brisk—the legal and business man.

"Four or five hundred pounds. As much as I can get."

"What would you do with the money?"

"Well . . ." Again she drew a deep breath. "There's the farm first. The stock is badly run down, and we need new rams. And with good rams we'd need better fencing, so that the strain remains pure. There's a chance I might be able to buy back a field adjoining our land on the Appledore side—good grazing, they say it is. I want to buy feed for the sheep to carry them through the winter better. . . ."

"Do you really know what you're talking about, Jane—or is this just hearsay?"

"Mostly hearsay," she admitted. "But I was brought up in the country, you remember—and I've learned a great deal from listening to Lucas. He's been a shepherd—a 'looker,' I think he said they call him here—all his life, and I think he's not without some skill."

"It's true," Robert said. "Lucas could have had better positions, but he's preferred to stay at Blake's Reach. Lord knows why—it wasn't for love of Spencer. But let us go on, Jane. That's the sheep—what else?"

"The roof," she said. "I went up to the attic to look at it yesterday. Another winter's rain might be serious. There are windows to be replaced, and in the old wing the plaster is cracking badly, and starting to fall off. There are some rooms where the ceiling's not safe. . . ."

"Nothing for yourself, Jane? No gowns or hats?"

"They're the only things I *don't* need. I've trunks full of gowns that once made London goggle, and will certainly keep a country district talking for years." Then she shrugged. "But there's always curtains—every pair in the house is rotting on the windows. But they'll hang for a while yet. Frivolous things—well, I'd like them in plenty. But they can all wait."

They sat quite still, looking at each other. Robert's fingers drummed quietly on the arm of his chair; the sound made Jane nervous. She wondered if she had gone too far, if she had misjudged his feeling for Anne, and how far he was susceptible. Suddenly she felt a little afraid of him. He was not like other men; there was little one could guess for certain about Robert Turnbull's feelings. He lived a life whose inner core was known only to himself. His reserve was deep and close; she wondered if she had tried to make a friend of him too quickly, and now had blundered. He might despise her for the crudeness of her request. He might despise her, and still give her the money, disappointed in her, and unable to forgive her because she was not Anne. The silence dragged out. She held herself straight, determined not to show the nervousness that now swamped her. Everything she had said to Paul about Robert Turnbull seemed true. She had made clumsy excuses for borrowing the money, and he had seen through them. Had he been mocking her about the gowns and hats? She felt that she had been a fool, and she was about to apologize and take back her request, when he spoke at last.

"I can make you the loan, Jane—there's no trouble about that. But why do you risk your own possessions as security when the money would go into the farm and house? It should be a loan to the estate."

Her head jerked back. "Just suppose one fine day Charles Blake walks in here? What then? Have I got to tell him I've further mortgaged the place to try out a few ideas I have? I'd look a pretty fool."

She rose from her chair, and began to pace the room. Then she swung around and looked at him.

"Can't you see what it's like—forever living with the thought that he may come back? I work here, and I scheme and think until my body and my head aches from it. And if he should walk in here it will all have gone for nothing. If you lend the money to me, and not to the estate, I will have a share in Blake's Reach. If *he* comes back I'll have some right here!"

Her voice was shaky. Suddenly she put her hands up to her forehead. "If only I *knew!*"

"Knew what?"

"About Charles Blake—dead or alive!"

"Dead or alive doesn't matter, Jane. You shall have the money as soon as you want it. Only it pains me to see you expend yourself and your possessions like this. You're too young, Jane—there should be other things in life for you. Don't give *everything* to Blake's Reach. . . . Keep a little of your life for living!"

She took her hands down from her head. "Someone else said that!"

"Someone else? Who?" His tone was sharp.

She bit her lips, realizing that she had almost brought out Paul's name—and that Robert Turnbull would not have liked to hear it. "Who?" she repeated. "Oh . . . I don't remember. Perhaps Kate . . ."

He cut her short. "There's just one stipulation I make. I will give you the money, but I don't want to hear what you do with it. I don't want it to stand continually between us. They say you can never make friends between borrower and lender—I don't want that to happen to us. Do you understand, Jane? Once it is done we won't talk of it. I'll collect my debt in, say, five years. And that will be the end of it."

"Very well," she said slowly. "That's how it will be."

He stood up to take his leave. "And the interest on it will be a rose delivered each spring. Agreed?" He smiled, and fingered his buttonhole as he spoke.

"Yes! Agreed! A rose each spring."

Jane was uneasy as she gave Patrick the order to bring Robert's horse around; Robert Turnbull puzzled and disturbed her. He had an air of power and knowledge that went past the simple function of a country attorney; his ordered bachelor's life didn't fit with his lack of concern over lending her the money—even more so because he could give it to her without inquiries or stipulations, or seemingly without a man's desire to manage the affairs of a woman. They stood at the doorway waiting, talking aimlessly of the work she had had done in the garden. She shot a glance sideways at him. The quiet eyes were faintly amused, and she had no idea why.

As Patrick brought his horse, suddenly there was a commotion. William dashed round the side of the house, gave them a brief look, and fled down the slope of the garden to the orchard. General followed him closely.

Robert laughed. "Those are energetic playfellows William has conjured up for himself. I wonder if he fancies he's being pursued by smugglers—or is it the preventive officers?"

"He's never had so much space to do what he likes with," Jane said. "And no one has time to mind what he's at, either. After London it must be a paradise for him. In a few days he's grown into a little savage. He should have a tutor . . . or someone!"

Robert laid a restraining hand on her. "Time enough. Let him have the summer to run wild . . . let him get to know the Marsh. For a boy it's a wonderful place. He ought to feel the Marsh in his bones . . . he's a Blake, too."

William's red hair was lost among the budding leafiness of the trees. Turnbull swung himself up on his horse.

"The child should have a pony," he said suddenly. "It was stupid of me to overlook it. I'll see what I can find—" he broke off. "I think I may be able to suit him. There's a pony I have stabled at

Rye—belongs to the child of a friend who's had to go abroad.
William could borrow it—keep it exercised."

"He would be glad of it," Jane said. "I know he'd be glad of it."

Turnbull bent to make his farewell. "Take care of yourself, my
dear. Blake's Reach, I know, is in good hands . . . rather astonish-
ing hands." His eyes were no longer amused; his lips were tight and
firm, as if he were keeping a check on his words.

There was something in the look that touched Jane strangely—a
lost, hesitant look, the look of someone wanting to ask for something, and not daring.

She gave him her hand.

"One other favor," she said.

"Anything you want!"

"Invite me to supper!" she said firmly. "Invite me into Rye to eat
supper with you!"

His tight line of his lips slackened. "Would you do that, Jane?
Would you really do that?"

"Haven't I just invited myself? I'll come gladly if you'll have me."

"Bless you, Jane—I'll be honored. Tomorrow evening, then."

She watched him ride along the drive, and turn out of sight on
the road, his broad, square shoulders erect and jaunty. The clip-
clop of the horse's hooves were loud in the still afternoon air. She
leaned against the stone pillars, gazing after him, wondering about
this quiet, powerful man, wondering at herself for what she had
just done. In the space of an hour she had moved much closer to
Robert, and yet was more puzzled by him than before. He seemed
aloof, but yet she could not say he was lonely; a solitary man, but
not one to invite pity. There was a strength in him that seemed as if
it had not met its test. She frowned, and shook her head.

As she turned to go indoors, Patrick moved nearer.

"You'll excuse me, mistress— Did I hear Mr. Turnbull say he
stabled a pony for a friend that Master William could use?"

"Yes—what about it?"

"Well, now—isn't that the strange thing! Sure wasn't that fine
fella from the livery stables in Rye—the same that brought Blonde
Bess, mistress—wasn't he boastin' o' the string o' fine horses Mr.
Turnbull stables with them, and there was never a mention o' a

pony. Never a mention! Sure I'm thinkin' Mr. Turnbull has only to snap his fingers for a piece of fine horseflesh to appear."

She fixed her gaze on him coldly. "And if he does, Patrick, is that any concern of ours? We'll just be glad of what he's sent, and not ask questions about it."

"Yes, mistress," he concurred. "We'll do that."

2

Quite a large part of the people of Rye, drawn into the narrow, cobbled streets by the mildness of the spring evening, saw the carriage standing before Robert Turnbull's house at the top of Mermaid Street. The carriage was handsome enough to attract attention, and the pair of finely matched grays would have drawn a crowd anywhere. A small crowd did gather, in fact, and the two young boys who had been lavishly tipped to hold the horses' heads were puffed with pride. Patrick, decked in a coat of livery that dazzled the passers-by, leaned against the door, ready and willing to answer almost any question asked of him.

And so it was that one part of Rye's population learned that Anne Blake's daughter, Jane, was inside having supper with Robert Turnbull; and yet another part of the townspeople actually saw her when she came out on Turnbull's arm, and headed up the lane towards the church. It was a sight Rye would talk about for the next month.

They could see that she was tall, red-headed, and moved well, and those who could remember said she had more than a passing likeness to Anne Blake. But it was her costume that they would mostly talk of—the costume, the carriage and the horses. Which was just as Jane had planned it should be. She had thought out each detail of her dress, knowing well enough that she was overdressed for the occasion, but knowing also that perfect taste was always too subdued to call for comment. So her gown was cut low enough for the women to say it was indecent, and the men to ogle; she wore a small fur piece about her shoulders, and ostrich feathers on the wide brim of her hat. It would have been a fashionable costume for Vauxhall—and she had worn it as much for Robert Turnbull as for the townsfolk of Rye.

She had asked to see a little of the town before they ate supper, so with her hand in Robert's arm, she walked Rye's streets—passed the square-towered church to Rye's grim old fortress, the Ypres Tower, that had endured through five centuries of weather and attack from across the Channel. Robert pointed out his firm's offices in Watchbell Street, and took her to stand on Rye's cliff-face, looking across the Camber Sands to the ruined castle, and beyond it to the sea that washed over what had been the town of Old Winchelsea.

"Drowned, Jane," he said. "Drowned in one of the storms that silted up the harbors of the Cinque Ports, changed the course of the rivers, and helped make the Marsh as you see it now. . . .

"It used to be a great town," he said as they turned back. "One of the greatest in the kingdom. Queen Elizabeth came here once . . . and of course Rye sent its quota of ships against the Armada. The beginning of the Navy, back in the days of Edward the First, came from these Ports. Great sailors, these men were—great men with ships!"

"So they are even now," she said dryly. "They make the run to France pretty quickly."

He nodded. "Yes, and they take risks to do it. You've heard, I suppose, that smugglers taken prisoner aren't sent to jail? As sailors they're much too valuable to rot in prisons. They're impressed into the Navy, and a bosun counts himself lucky to get a Romney Marsh smuggler."

"Your mind turns on smugglers, doesn't it," she said, forcing herself to make the remark come lightly.

"So does the mind of everyone in these parts," he answered. "There isn't any escaping it."

She found sharing a meal with Robert a fascinating and unique experience. He lived in a compact little house with a walled garden, from whose windows she could see the Mermaid Inn. It was a house devoted entirely to the care and comfort of one man, and everything in it reflected taste, and a feeling for beauty. It was a man's world, richly but soberly furnished, smelling of expensive tobacco and old, fine leather. His housekeeper was a silent, neat creature long ago trained to anticipate Robert's wants; she lived at the lower end of the town, and had learned that Robert Turnbull was a man who enjoyed his own company. After serving her excellently cooked meal, she left discreetly; they heard the door snap after her, and her footsteps on the cobbled street.

The contrast between the house and Blake's Reach was great, and Jane found herself responding to the atmosphere. They seemed to laugh together a great deal; Robert's attention was flattering and respectful—the wine was good, and it was potent. It was a relief to talk to Robert, and to know that from him there were no secrets kept; she could talk at will about The Feathers, about Anne in London, about her visits to Hampstead—even about Lord O'Neill. On only one subject did she keep silent; she never mentioned Paul Fletcher's name. Robert sat opposite her, the candlelight keeping his face a little in shadow, and he looked like a man well content.

During the evening he had given her five hundred pounds in bank notes, and she had insisted upon a form of receipt and acknowledgment of the loan which she could sign. She felt the bulkiness of the money in her reticule as she gathered up her things and prepared to leave; suddenly she was uneasy, the enormity of what she was doing breaking upon her coldly.

As he came forward with her wrap, Robert paused. "Jane, what is it? What is the matter?"

She touched the reticule. "This money . . . It frightens me! Two months ago I wouldn't have known what to do with it. Am I like Anne, do you think? Or Spencer? Perhaps I'll do nothing more than add to the debts the Blakes have piled up."

Gently he laid the wrap about her shoulders. "Have courage, Jane. Nothing is won except by the daring. And even I—"

For a startled second she felt his fingers on her bare throat, a fleeting and sensitive caress, like the brush of a bird's wing against her. She turned around. Robert held her by the shoulders. He leaned towards her slightly, and she thought he was going to kiss her. Her body went rigid in her effort not to show surprise.

Abruptly he dropped his hands and straightened.

"No . . ." He shook his head. "No, nothing is won by those who venture nothing."

All the way back to Blake's Reach Jane clutched the reticule tightly to her, gritting her teeth against the jolts of the carriage and the pain that shot through her head. She had drunk too much wine; the world swam before her in a mist in which the lights of the cottages along the road were fiery blurs. But her anger and contempt for herself were living things within her, fiercer than the pain in her head, more real than the wad of money in her hands.

"Fool!" she told herself. "Fool! Fool! What a little country idiot you are that you don't know what can be done to a man. . . . Smile at him, listen to him, ask and take favors from him. Yes— even bare your breasts for his eyes. And then you're surprised when he wants to kiss you! You've made yourself into the image of the woman he loved, and you're surprised at his caress. . . . You thought you could play Anne's game, but you don't know even the first rule of it. Idiot! . . .

The tears of anger and humiliation started to stream down her face, falling unheeded, and spotting the bright silk. The carriage jolted cruelly in the ruts, and she shivered and wept through the miles to Blake's Reach.

3

When the first streak of dawn appeared across the eastern sky of the Marsh, Jane had saddled Blonde Bess and started towards Paul's cottage. The roads were lonely and unfriendly in the gray light; the flush of the rising sun was low and small on the horizon; but the mists of the night still lay over the dykes, and wrapped like gray moss upon the trees. She would have taken to the fields, but a countless number of dykes lay between her and Old Romney— some narrow and weed-choked, others wide enough to halt Blonde Bess. There were bridges, Paul had told her, but it needed years on the Marsh to remember all of them; to the stranger they were a nightmare maze. She hunched her shoulders to keep out a chill that was partly of her own imagining; it seemed to her that at this hour, between night and morning, the Marsh had slipped back to the times before its wastes had been reclaimed, when little boats carrying raiders from across the Channel had used its swampy creeks. It was eerie and silent, a land possessed of old secrets and old terrors.

She was shaking with nervous impatience by the time she slid down from Bess and hammered on Paul's kitchen door. The sounds echoed strangely through the house. For the first time she paused to wonder what she would do if he were not there. She tried the latch and it yielded.

Paul was still sleeping in the tumbled four-poster. She shook his bare shoulder violently.

"Paul! Wake up! Do you hear me? Wake up!"

His eyes flickered open, and closed immediately. Then they opened wide with an expression of startled surprise.

"Jane! What in the name of Heaven are you doing here?"

She drew back a little from the bed, frowning. "You said I could come any time. Wasn't that what you said?"

He propped himself up on his elbow; the movement seemed to pain him. Under the covers his body was naked. He rubbed his hand wearily across his eyes. "Of course I said it—and I meant it! But I didn't expect you today . . . now. What time is it?" He closed his eyes briefly. "My head feels as if it's still the middle of the night."

She shook him again impatiently. "It isn't the middle of the night for me! I've something to talk to you about—and I want you to pay attention. Here!"

She tossed the reticule onto the blanket. "Look at that! Five hundred pounds!" Her voice had an edge of triumph.

Abruptly he sat up; she watched his expression change. His features seemed to contract, and even darken under the rough sun-streaked hair. He didn't open the reticule; instead he poked at it, as if it were a strange and vicious animal.

"Where did you get this?" he demanded. "What have you been doing?"

Her eyes grew cold. "Where did I get it? I went to the only source I have. The one you told me to go to."

"Turnbull!" Suddenly he reached out and caught her arm in a tight ungentle grip, pulling her closer to the bed. "Turnbull! That's who gave it to you, isn't it? *Answer me!*" He jerked at her arm again.

"Of course it was! Who else!"

Now he caught her by the shoulders, and dragged her down close to him.

"Last night you got it, didn't you? Last night when you went to his house?"

"How did you know that?"

"How could anyone who was in Rye last night not know it? I watched you—I watched you from the windows of the Mermaid. It was quite a show! And don't think it wasn't appreciated. You were all the rage in the taproom of the Mermaid—and every other ale house in Rye, I'll wager! Every story they could remember about your mother was raked up—and some that never happened were thrown in for good measure. Oh, yes—I knew about you, and inside of a week half the county will know!"

She tried to pull away from him, and couldn't.

"And so you got drunk!" she said. "You were stupid enough to be jealous, and you got drunk!"

"Why shouldn't I be jealous? It was more than any man could stand to see. . . ."

"Oh, hush! Like every man you're a fool—and a sentimental fool, at that! Didn't you guess why I would go to Robert Turnbull?— didn't you *ask* me to find the money?"

"You didn't have to make a spectacle of yourself! You didn't have to make it look as if you were paying a call on a man who was in love with you."

"Perhaps he is in love with me! Does that matter to you? Didn't I bring the money, and isn't *that* all that matters to you?"

"Damn you! No! Four days ago perhaps it *was* all that mattered to me. Can't you see that things have changed since then. You must know . . ."

He released her shoulders, and she felt his broad hands cup her face. She could feel the calluses on his palms as he caressed her cheeks gently.

"Jane! Dear Jane! There is nothing now that matters except you —and Robert Turnbull can take his money back and go to hell! We don't want it, Jane."

"Why?" She frowned, trying to push herself back to read his expression. "Can't you get the lugger? Has something gone wrong?"

He sighed and dropped his hands. "I want to talk to you, Jane. Come and sit here, by me." He patted the blanket close to him. She obeyed with some reluctance, mistrusting the softness of his tone. He leaned back again on his elbow, one of his hands holding hers tightly.

"We don't want the money because I think we should clear out of this place."

"What are you talking about? Leave here and go . . . where?"

"The West Indies."

She stared at him unbelievingly, her mouth dropping open a trifle as the meaning of his words came fully to her. "Have you gone mad, Paul Fletcher? Do you think I'm going to leave Blake's Reach?"

"Leaving Blake's Reach you'd be leaving nothing! I've told you —you can't put life back into a dead thing. And Blake's Reach *is* dead!"

She tossed the idea aside with a gesture, unable to give it any importance. "I seem to remember you told me you hadn't got the money yet to set yourself up in the Indies. Has something happened to change that?"

"Nothing has happened except you! Nothing is changed—I still haven't the money to set myself up."

She shrugged. "Then why talk of it?"

"Because I must! Because this is an ugly and foul business you're about to get yourself into, and I'd rather a thousand times take you out of this than own the finest sloop in the Caribbean."

Her eyes narrowed. "But what would you do out there?"

"There are smaller ways to start. There are businesses I could manage, plantations that need overseers. . . ."

"No!" The sound came from her almost as a shriek. She tried to pull away from him.

"You expect to take me to that! To be someone's servant! I've had enough of it, I tell you. Enough of it! A few months ago I didn't know Blake's Reach existed, but now I've found it, and I have position and respect, and soon I will have money. Do you expect me to leave what I've got now . . . and everything I hope for in the future?"

Then her tone dropped, and grew gentle and pleading. "Please, Paul, try to understand." She touched the reticule briefly. "Neither of us can do anything without money. And this is the start of it. Why shouldn't we take it when everyone else does? Just a few runs, Paul—just a few cargoes to get us on our feet. This money belongs to Robert Turnbull, and I mean to pay it back. I can't if you won't help me."

"But you still believe that you can make something of Blake's Reach?"

She was cautious. "I can try. If I fail, that will be the only thing that convinces me."

"And me? What becomes of me? Must I wait round here while you conduct your experiment? Or am I of interest to you only because I can be of service?"

Her mouth grew a trifle grim. "I don't want you to say that!"

"I do say it because it may be true. I've seen better men than I wither in the clutch of an ambitious woman. I won't let it happen to me."

"Nothing will happen to you that you don't want to happen! What difference can a few months make in your life? I've known you a few days—and you ask me to say I'll give up something that's in my blood. If Blake's Reach is no good I'll find out soon enough. But give me time. . . ."

"And time for me to make enough contraband runs? That's the time you're thinking of, Jane, isn't it?"

She didn't answer him directly.

"Will you do it, Paul? Will you do it for both of us?"

A look of defeat and weariness settled on his face. He seemed to struggle against it for a few seconds, knowing that the struggle was useless. He put his hand to his forehead.

"My head hurts," he said. "As if the boom had swung round and hit me. Perhaps I have been hit, and I'm too dazed and stupid to know it."

Then he shrugged. "Yes, I'll do it."

She leaned towards him. "It won't be for long. Just a few months. That's all."

"Will you be satisfied with a few months—or will you grow greedy like all the others?"

She put her face close to his. "Do we have to fight? Do we have to talk of the Indies or Blake's Reach? Can't we just be happy with one another, and because of one another? Paul . . . I've wanted you so much."

"Wanted me? . . . do you love me, Jane?"

"Heaven help me! Yes . . . yes, I love you. And I've wanted you close to me, near me."

"Is this true?"

She put her arms about his bare body, resting her head against his shoulder.

"Why do we have to disbelieve? Let us just be happy as we know how to be. I want to forget all the other things . . . I just want you."

The memory of the journey across the Marsh last night, weeping in the darkness of the carriage, and of her swift, lonely ride to Old Romney in the dawn was strongly upon her. She felt the strength of Paul's arms, and then felt them tighten about her, and the memory and the fear grew fainter. He was real and living, his head bent close to hers, his breathing in rhythm with her own. She could draw determination and confidence from him, and energy and a zest for living. Because he had strength, she also was stronger.

"Why is it," she whispered, "that I can find peace only with you?"

"Stay with me then," he said. He pulled her backwards, and their heads were close together on the pillow.

CHAPTER EIGHT

ONCE PAUL HAD COMMITTED HIMSELF TO MAKING THE RUN, JANE'S part in the matter was finished. She ran against a hard wall of determination when she tried to enter into the arrangements and plans.

"Stay out of this, Jane," he said curtly. "This is not something for a woman to dabble in—it's dangerous and it's ugly. Stay out!"

So he went his own way, and kept his own counsel, as he had done before, and she had to contain her impatience and her desire to share his activities and his dangers in the only way she could. In the following weeks she settled to the day-to-day routine of Blake's Reach. The spring flush of the May days gave place to June; over the broad acres of the Marsh the lambs were growing fat, and

the June roses were blooming in the hedges. The land lay peace-
fully under the bright summer sun, but it was a false sense of peace.
Even to Blake's Reach, unconnected with the main highways to
London or the ports, came the news from Paris, news of the growing tension and the powerless position of the King, of the daily
executions. With each mention of the Revolution, Jane's heart
stilled for a second—a little intake of breath; there was always the
thought that the next packet to Dover might bring word of Charles
Blake . . . Charles, dead or alive. As time went on she found it
easier if she pretended that Charles Blake had never existed. That
way there could be no guilt, and no pity.

But the fishermen of Kent and Sussex had a closer contact with
the Revolution than the mere exchange of talk and gossip. France
was now at war with Austria, and as the excesses of the Revolution
grew, its victims grew more desperate; many of them crossed the
Channel in a smuggler's lugger, paying their last gold for the
privilege of sharing space with a contraband cargo, sometimes cow-
ering among the brandy casks as the lugger ran from the guns of
the revenue cruiser, and landing on a lonely beach, thankful that
the moon was hidden behind the clouds. For many of them their
first knowledge of England was the sight of lamplight gleaming
faintly on muskets and pistols.

At this stage of the Revolution, those who came were penniless.
They could be met on the Dover road, frightened, bewildered,
streaming towards London and the hope of help and shelter from
the people they had called friends in the secure days of the court
at Versailles. The fear in Jane's heart was that someday one of them
would start out from Dover across the Marsh on roads he had
known as a boy, moving with certainty towards Blake's Reach.

Robert Turnbull knew her fear, and he encouraged her to talk of
it, to try to ease the load.

"One of my business associates at Dover inquires constantly
among those who come across, Jane," he said. "I hear nothing fresh
—some remember him in prison and most think he's dead. But
they're frightened for themselves, and have no thought to spare for
a man they scarcely knew."

And her hand, passing the tea cup, or the wine glass, would tremble slightly, and her young face grew rigid and disciplined into an

expression of indifference. He watched the struggle between pity and self-preservation.

"There will be war," he would say. "There will be war with England sooner or later, Jane. They will find a reason to execute King Louis. . . ."

"War? . . . If there is war, will we ever have news of him? There will be no way to know . . . your contacts will be cut off from news."

He nodded. "It could happen that you would have to wait out the war here at Blake's Reach. . . ."

She shuddered. "Waiting . . . and never knowing. I don't think I could bear it. . . ."

But her faith in herself was stronger than her belief that Charles Blake was still alive. Deliberately she went on with her plans for Blake's Reach, stretching into a future where Charles had no place. She spent some of her hoarded money to make further repairs to the house, to renew some window glass, to scythe the long grass in the orchard. Money had to be spent where it would be most noticed because it had to serve as evidence to Robert that she was directing his loan where she had said it would go. There was no possibility of buying rams until after Paul had brought a cargo across, and some gold flowed back into her pockets; but accompanied by Lucas and Patrick, she made tours of inspection to the best farms in the district, and afterwards filled Robert's ears with knowledgeable talk she had picked up. In the habits fashioned by London's best tailor she was observed by many sharp-eyed farmers' wives, and occasionally the occupant of a carriage, passing Jane and the small entourage on the road, would bend forward to get a better view. Jane was comfortably aware that her presence was known and talked of in the houses of the gentry across the Marsh, and she waited for the day when the first of those carriages should turn in at the gates of Blake's Reach.

By now the vegetable garden was planted, and in immaculate order; Kate went each day to stand and stare admiringly at the sprouting crop; the beginnings of the herb garden were made. Two lads from Appledore came to the kitchen asking for odd jobs, and Jane used this cheap labor to whitewash the dairy and the old cow stalls; the vegetable plot was fenced in, and the poultry rigorously

kept away. Two carpenters from St. Mary's—the village to which
the Blake church officially belonged—came and did some work on
the stables, at the same time appraising the quality of the grays,
Blonde Bess, and the pony which Robert had sent for William. Patrick and Kate kept their mouths closed, and the report went round,
neither confirmed nor denied, that the new mistress of Blake's
Reach might not be a great heiress, but she was not a pauper. Jane
stitched away at the faint signs of wear in the table damask she had
brought from London, added lace to a selected few dresses whose
necks were too low for day wear, and kept her own counsel. She
sensed the change in Blake's Reach, and was happy because of it.
She saw Lucas and Jed and Kate take pride in the new dignity that
had come to them, saw them go to their work with will and energy,
comfortable because Blake's Reach and its occupant were no longer
a subject for laughter and scorn in the village. She was beginning to
taste the satisfaction of her accomplishment. The days went on,
and Charles Blake's name was heard less and less.

She rode on the Marsh often with only William beside her, discovering its variety and its sameness, struggling to memorize the
tricks of its winding roads and its bridges. William's face now wore
a heavy pattern of freckles, and his hair was bleached with the sun.
His clothes were often dirty, torn and mismatched; his hands and
fingernails were grimy from weeding in the vegetable patch. But
even in these few weeks his child's body and temperament had
taken on a certain toughness that made him unafraid to walk the
mile to Appledore, and join the village children in the rough-and-
tumble games they played. He came back one day bloody from a
fight with the boy who had called him "the Bastard." In a fashion
he understood that this would be his name always, but he would
accept it only from those he knew were his friends and had earned
the right to call him that with affection. The day after the fight
he returned to Appledore as usual to join the games, and among
the women watching from the cottage doors there were raised eyebrows, and the opinion in the ale house that evening was that the
young'un at Blake's Reach was tarred with the same brush as the
mistress. In the village there was a kind of inverted pride in William because he had been beaten, and had come back to the possibility of more.

The schoolbooks he had brought from London gathered dust, but he was learning other things. He developed an eye almost as sharp as Jane's for a bargain—telling her at which farm the eggs were cheapest, and whose honey was the best, and at what price. It was he who brought the news of the widow at Snargate who was selling out, and whose sow Jane bought cheaply. General was, as always, close by him wherever he moved, smelling of the stable and the saddle-soap and oil William handled constantly. Looking at them, Jane found it difficult to recall the first time she had seen these two —the child in the blue velvet coat, with the delicate features, the silken dog posed at his side. William seemed years older, and the London child was gone. He had the run of Blake's Reach, and beyond, from sunrise until he grudgingly gave up his struggle against weariness at night. He went out to meet his new world with the ardor of someone who has been, unknowingly, in prison. Never again did Jane hear him weep at night for Anne.

But Jane forced William to return to the blue velvet coat on the Sunday they decorously climbed the hill to attend services at the Blake church. Neither of them wanted to go: in Jane's life there had been little time for church services, and they were something quite new for William; but they both knew what was expected of them now. And so they took their places in the carved pew with the faded blue cushions, emptied now of the tarpaulin-wrapped bundles of lace, and the brandy kegs. The church, Jane noticed, still smelled strongly of tobacco and wool.

No Blake had occupied the family pew since Charles had come, a boy of thirteen, reluctant and alone, to sit shyly in its shadows. The village of St. Mary's had turned out almost in a body in the hope of Jane's and William's attending. No detail of their behavior or appearance was missed—not from the exquisite lace that filled the neck of Jane's rose-colored gown and the slippers made of green silk, to the fact that neither of them was familiar with the hymn-book. But it was conceded that they were a fine-looking pair, red-headed and spirited in the traditional fashion of the family. No one voiced the thought, but they would all have been disappointed if these new Blakes had lacked the touch of wildness that was expected.

For Jane this was remembered as the morning she discovered that she was proud of William. She was proud of the straight shoulders which now strained the seams of the blue coat, of the high intelligent forehead and his bright, quick eyes. Behind his back they might call him "the Bastard," but it was plain to anyone's eyes that he was the bastard of a nobleman—there was the evidence of good breeding in every line of his body. His clear young voice bellowed the words from the hymnbook with magnificent unconcern for the tune; during the long sermon he kept his hands still and his back straight. Jane knew that he entered with her into a sense of the occasion, and after the service they were like a pair of conspirators going through the ritual of handshaking and greeting, William executing his formal bow that could only have been learned in London drawing rooms. It was almost, Jane thought, too good a performance to be wasted on so small a parish as St. Mary's. Perhaps if they had gone to Rye . . .

But there were other things Jane had to learn, during those weeks of waiting, of the life of the Marsh and the lands on its borders. Some of the knowledge was bitter and unpalatable.

It was not enough, it seemed, to parade London-cut clothes, and a fine carriage and pair. Nor was it enough to put Blake's Reach into a semblance of order, and walk to church services up on the hill. Much more was needed before the first of those carriages bearing the wives of the local gentry would turn into the driveway. They had to make sure that she was not Anne Blake all over again—and on the Marsh it took years to make sure.

Anne Blake's reputation, heightened and colored, had spread during the twenty years since she had left. In gossip she had been the mistress of half the famous rakes in London, and her only husband had been a commonplace captain of Dragoons from the Folkestone station. True, she had borne a son to the scion of one of England's oldest and richest families, but since the child possessed neither his father's name nor money, where was the advantage in that? Nothing was known about Jane . . . but there was enough speculation. She might possess the family failing of a weakness towards gambling, and set up gaming tables at Blake's Reach —such as Anne was supposed to have done in London. Without having seen her they already knew how she was looked at by men— and the low-cut gowns and tightly corseted waist, apart from the famous Blake red hair, were altogether too much competition for marriageable daughters. So Jane waited vainly for the carriages, and gradually she began to understand why they did not come.

There were two which did come. The first brought Roger Pym to her door, and when Kate rushed upstairs to tell Jane of her visitor, her old eyes were bright with excitement and remembrance.

"He's the one yer mother was to marry . . . the one the old master had picked for her. . . ."

Roger Pym was some years older than Anne, a shy, gentle man, clumsy and tongue-tied, wearing expensive, dowdy clothes. His face wore a wistful expression as his gaze rested on Jane. He played nervously with the silver knob of his cane.

"You're so like her . . . your mother. She was very beautiful, too."

Jane thanked him with a smile, and looked away from his regretful eyes to engross herself deliberately with the tea tray Patrick had brought in. Pym was in an agony of embarrassment and shyness, and Jane had the impression that he had needed to gather considerable courage to make the visit. But he managed to talk a little of Anne, and even speaking her name was a relief to him. He said nothing more than any other person across the Marsh might have said of her, but his voice betrayed the years of hoping and disappointment.

"I have children too," he said. "Some of them round about your age . . . five daughters and two sons. . . ." Then he was overcome with embarrassment again as he realized that they would be Jane's natural companions in other circumstances. He could not offer the invitation which he knew should have been forthcoming. There had been too much talk at home about Anne Blake's daughter. . . .

"No doubt my wife and daughters will be calling shortly," he said unhappily. "They've been busy lately . . . summer is a busy time. . . ."

He went reluctantly, wanting to stay on and indulge the desire to talk about Anne, and yet uncomfortably aware that to stay longer might involve or commit his family. He stumbled off, a shy man with sad eyes, who for thirty minutes had lived blissfully in the past. He would probably never dare to come again, Jane thought.

The second visitor was Paul's brother, Sir James Fletcher. This time there was no carriage, but a thoroughbred horse which brought warm glances from Patrick. Jane quickly changed her gown before going down to greet him.

Immediately she sensed curiosity of a different kind from Roger Pym's. It was cold curiosity—cold and examining. He looked like Paul; he was older, with blond hair turning pepper-and-salt, bulkier in frame, a good body going a little to fat. In a rigid, controlled way he was handsome; his clothes were well cut, and looked as if they had come from London.

He never once mentioned Paul's name, behaving exactly as if he had come on an ordinary social call. And yet he made a few slips— let fall small pieces of information about her that could only have come from Paul. She began to dislike him, sensing patronage in his remarks about the work she had done at Blake's Reach, and he referred too openly for politeness to the poverty of the estate.

"You've opened this room, I see. . . . Well, it's about time. Haven't been in here for years. Spencer didn't like this room. . . ."

He crumbled, but did not eat Kate's plum cake, as if to point up its heaviness, which Jane already knew too well; he drank two cups of tea, put his cup down and started to pace the room. He paused deliberately on the frayed edge of the carpet, flicked at it with his polished boot as if it had tripped him. Then he looked across at John Blake's portrait. He looked at it as if he had seen it many times before, and it was an old enemy.

"Spencer used to wish he had the money the family spent to build and endow that church up there. . . . Well, I suppose nothing else was good enough for them after John had covered himself in glory at the wars. Strange, wasn't it, that he didn't get a title at the same time?"

He looked back at her quickly, seeming to realize now that his words had been insulting.

"I've always thought," she said evenly, "that titles only went to those who asked for them. John Blake would have been a viscount or an earl, but there's some story about him falling out with the Duchess of Marlborough. It takes courage of a kind not to care what happens to a title. . . . And—who knows?—perhaps he was right not to take it. After all, the Blakes are simple people, and this is a modest house. . . ."

She said this with full knowledge that he had been made a baronet only seven years ago; she knew she took a risk in snubbing him, but it was important that James Fletcher should never be allowed to think she was a spineless ninny, too overwhelmed by his aggressiveness to claim for the Blakes what was their due. She waited for his reaction.

It was as she hoped. He came back to his chair, and settled to talk, more respectful now, attending to her carefully when she chose to speak. He was arrogant and overbearing, but he was a rich and successful man, the owner of many acres on the Marsh itself, and several large farms around Warefield on its border, where he lived. On farming matters he was worth listening to. He told her where to buy stock and, when the time came, where to sell it, which dealers to go to, which farmers she could trust.

He rose to go. "You'll do all right," he said heavily. "Yes, you'll do all right. I'll confess I laughed when I heard a female had come back here to take over—specially a Blake, for they've not been noted for their common sense in the past. But you'll be all right because you know how to take advice. Now . . . you come to me when you want anything, you hear? I'll tell you what you want to know. Robert Turnbull's well enough in his way, but he doesn't know about farming. Just you send a message, and I'll come along and set you straight on things. . . ."

Walking with him to the door, Jane tried to hold her rage in check. He had patronized her, snubbed her, and not once mentioned his wife, Lady Alice, or said that he expected to see Jane at Warefield House. He accepted Patrick's assistance in mounting without thanks. He fixed his eyes on Jane thoughtfully.

"You know," he said, "Paul didn't tell me the half of all this . . . you . . . the house . . . No, not even the half of it!" He raised his hat briefly. "I'll drop in from time to time . . . see how things are with you."

Jane watched him go, her expression angry and distasteful. "Pig!" she said. "You overdressed pig! . . . and I wish you didn't look so much like Paul!"

Her brows knitted together as she turned to go indoors. "And there's something here that's not right . . . he knows more about me than he should, and yet he and Paul pretend they hardly see each other. . . ."

The answer occurred to her suddenly, and her eyes widened with comprehension. The pieces fell into place with startling precision. She pondered the possibilities, and they carried too much weight to seem untrue. Was it, she wondered, James Fletcher who was putting up the money to finance Paul's smuggling runs, and that this was the reason Paul had come back to the Marsh? James Fletcher had known his whole financial situation, and when the plantation in the Indies had been lost, and the years in the Navy passed by without promotion, had he been the one to wave the money before Paul's eyes, and promise him enough of the spoils of the game to compel him back here even though he hated it? He knew Paul's seamanship, his ability to organize, and his crying need for money to start in trade again. Among the seafaring men of the Marsh, only Paul could appear at his brother's house without question or suspicion. He would be the perfect front for a man who had looked for a way to operate in the smuggling game on a large scale.

"It's possible," Jane said aloud. "It's possible . . . and it may be true. And that's why the money on the church was raised to twenty guineas without a fuss—he just couldn't miss the chance to patronize the Blakes! I wonder did he enjoy sitting here thinking that he was paying the wages of my servants . . . or the cake he didn't eat! Oh, damn him—the pig!"

She started to gather up the tea cups, rattling them irritably and then was annoyed to see that she had managed to chip one of them. She scowled at the Blake portraits on the wall, the calm, unanswering faces which belonged to her family; for the first time the sight of them gave her no pleasure.

2

She was not subtle when she took the story of his brother's visit to Paul. She questioned him bluntly about the things she had already half-guessed.

"So he talked too much, and you could fill in what he didn't say? Well . . . he always was a fool in dealing with people who weren't his inferiors, and I suppose coming to Blake's Reach was almost too much for him, and he had to talk. . . ."

"What do you mean?"

Paul shrugged. "It's an old story . . . some snub Spencer gave him long ago, and people got to know about it. James looked like a fool, and he's never forgotten. He's always disliked any mention of the Blake family—they've been here too long, they've held too many offices and posts, they've had time to become gentlefolk, and would have been aristocracy if they'd used their heads. Oh, yes, he thinks about it all, and it rankles. He's even jealous of that church, and the endowment, and the fact that the Blakes have the right of presenting a parson to the living there."

Jane smiled wryly. "How he must enjoy paying for it as a store-room for his contraband. . . ."

"Of course he does!" Paul snapped. "He wouldn't give it up if it cost twice the money . . . it's the kind of stupid joke he enjoys."

How easy it had been, she thought, to break this secret between James Fletcher and his brother once his vanity had been touched. The memory of that old snub of Spencer's had rankled, and had led James into an unwitting betrayal. Even shrewd men were fools when their emotions were touched, and he had allowed her to see through this elaborate system of operation he had built because he had wanted to feel his power over her.

"You dislike him very much, don't you?"

"I could hate him if he were worth sparing the thought and effort to. We've always been like this—he the elder son with the estate to inherit, and I the poor fool who had to earn his way. He didn't like it when I cleared off to the West Indies. . . ."

"But you came back . . . you came back to work for him!"

"Only a greater fool than James himself would have let his feel-ings stand in the way there. I was in debt, and James knew that. He believed that somehow if he could get me back here, working for him, no matter how much money I earned, I'd never keep it. He believed I'd always be in debt, and that I'd never be able to get back to the Indies. In his mind he saw me here forever—being paid by him, listening to his damn-fool instructions, tipping my hat to him and clicking my heels. The few times he's visited me here he can't believe his eyes . . . he doesn't know what happened to the old Paul, the one who spent money on fourteen silk waistcoats, and Brussels lace for his shirts. He suspects, of course, that I squan-der it on a fancy woman I keep somewhere—Dover, maybe.

"Most of the time I manage to ignore the fact that he's my brother. I try to think of him as the man who provides the money, and whose commission I take because I've earned it. In eleven months here I've paid off my debts, and I've put nearly six hundred pounds towards our cargo. Does that sound as if he's generous? Well, he's not! He knows what he has to pay in commission for my risking my freedom, and perhaps my neck five or six times in the month. He's bought the finest luggers, and he pays the top price for porters . . . and he makes a sweet profit. If I make two runs in a week he can land upwards of two thousand half-ankers of brandy, and seven or eight tons of tea. There's money in that, Jane—money for me, as well as him."

He ran his hand through his hair, pulling the loose ends from the pigtail. He looked worn and desperate as he talked, and his hands were tense.

"He doesn't know, of course, that I'll go as soon as there's enough money. It's a dirty, ugly business, and I've no mind to go on with it at another man's bidding—least of all my brother's!"

He threw his hands up suddenly. "Oh, Jane, you don't know what sweet relief it will be to be free of him, to breathe the air again knowing I'm my own master. I walk the decks of his ships, and I hate even the smell of them—I, who've loved the sea for longer years than I can remember. For me, there's an odor about my brother James and all his dealings that befouls even the ships he owns. . . ."

He brought his clenched fist down into his palm. "I'll be free, Jane! . . . Just wait a little longer and I'll kick myself free of this bog he has me in! There's a whole world out there in the Indies you don't know of yet—there's freedom for a man to be what he can make of himself, self-respect, gold if you've the skill to take it. . . . I mean to get back there if I have to land every one of my brother's blasted brandy kegs with my own hands!"

3

The daily round of Jane's life was open for the whole Marsh to see, for Appledore and St. Mary's to gossip about over their ale-pots. The other side of it, secret and hidden, concealed from cu-

rious eyes, was known only to herself and Paul Fletcher. It was
known also to Patrick—and it was guessed at by Kate Reeve.

Before dawn broke she would leave the house silently, saddle
Blonde Bess, and take the now-familiar route to Old Romney, the
route which Paul had shown her, across the fields and dykes, away
from the roads and cottages and farms, away from the chance of
gossip or speculation. The meetings with Paul were violent with an
ecstasy that was heightened because they were brief and stolen.
Here she entered a world completely apart from the planned routine of Blake's Reach; this was a world of love and pleasure and
pain, to be lived only in the racing moments between dawn and
the time when the Marsh folk began to stir abroad.

The rides were lonely, and sometimes dangerous as she set off
in the half-dark. But it seemed to Jane that only for the space of
time she spent in Paul's arms did she escape from the sense of loneliness and struggle; his presence banished consciousness of fear or
time or danger. The memory of being with him sustained her
through each succeeding hour of the day.

At first Paul made an effort to keep her away—and found that
he was weak and powerless to forbid her to come. Long before
dawn he was awake and listening for her. The days she did not
come he counted as lost. He raged against the furtiveness of their
meetings, and yet he knew there was no other way he might see her.
Too many people suspected him of involvement in some way in
smuggling—his solitary existence, the irregularity of his comings
and goings, and above all his knowledge of the Channel and its
ports, of ships and seafaring, of the Marsh itself, were suspect. He
knew there was danger to Jane in an open friendship with him. He
dared to do no more than stand in the stable yard at Blake's Reach
from time to time, ostensibly talking to William and Patrick, or to
bow formally if he and Jane happened to meet in the streets of Rye.
He tried to deny himself the sight of her, and was not able. She
had become an obsession, and he could not discipline himself to
stay away from her; he was swept towards her with a fierceness of
passion that gave him no peace. Jane was not peace or finality to
him; she was pleasure and joy and torment. She was love and she
was also despair. She was a volatile, elusive creature, whose body
was given to him, whom he did not yet possess; his rival was a crum-

bling house on the edge of the Marsh, and a worn tradition in which he had no faith. They quarreled and they loved with equal violence; for neither of them was there victory or defeat.

She came to know that chart-strewn room at Paul's cottage as if it were a territory mapped in her own soul; she knew its dust and untidiness, the books stacked upon its shelves. She watched Paul spin the globe and his fingers trace the names of the Caribbean islands, while his excited words spun a dream for her of blue-green seas, and lush vegetation. Paul's clothes carried the smell of salt water; there was sand in all his pockets, and in the cuffs of his sleeves. She rested her face against his shoulder and heard him talk of trade in the Indies, of fortunes won in trade, and how they could be won, and lost again. She smelled the sea water on his coat, and wanted fiercely to make him look at her, and to forget his dream. For a space of time she could succeed, and he was bound to her closely and strongly; the bright dream faded, and she possessed him and Blake's Reach as well.

But there was bitterness in knowing that she could hold him only with her body; she would cradle his head against her breasts, feel his roughened seaman's hands caress her flat belly and firm thighs, and she knew with all this that he was hers only for these moments —a short time of forgetfulness when his will was bent to hers, and that time was limited, and gradually he would awaken and become aware. And in awareness he would draw back from her, resenting the hold she had taken on him, resenting her domination.

"Stay with me," she would whisper when they were close together, spent and still, a little at peace. "Stay with me here. . . . Together we could do so much . . . so much, Paul."

She could feel the tension of his limbs, and his fingers would bite her flesh with his rejection. "With you I could build a kingdom . . . anywhere but here!"

And they would draw apart, angry with each other, wanting to deny their love, and yet sick at the thought of a parting. Bitterness and desire grew swiftly for them both, and the strange knowledge that beyond desire there was love.

4

"She's called the *Dolphin*, Jane, and as sweet a craft as I've ever laid eyes on . . . trim and smooth, and as fast as a bird."

Paul smiled at the recollection; his tone was soft and honeyed, as if he spoke of a woman. They were drinking tea before the fire in Paul's sitting room; the kettle was steaming gently on the fire crane. They both knew that in a short time Jane would have to leave, and they were pretending to ignore the fact.

"You've sailed in her?"

He nodded. "I've put her to sea under Andy Smith. She's on legitimate fishing business, and the revenue men can board and search her any time they like. All the better if they do, because I've put her out in the Channel to establish an identity as a fishing craft. Let the revenue men get used to the sight of her . . . but if it ever comes to a chase, she's faster than anything on these seas."

"I want to see her, Paul!"

He frowned, taking her hand in his and rubbing it gently. "You know how I feel about that, Jane. You must have no part in all this . . . it's bad enough that you even come to this cottage."

"But there must be some way to see the *Dolphin*—she must come into port somewhere."

"Folkestone's her port—and anywhere else along this coast that the revenue cutters aren't." He shrugged. "I don't see why you couldn't get a look at her . . . somewhere hereabouts. I'll think about it. . . ."

"If she's at sea, why are you waiting?" Jane demanded. "Why don't you bring a cargo over now?"

"Easy!" he cautioned. "Easy . . . these things take time. There have to be contacts, a whole new organization. I'm using a different agent in Flushing, different men as porters here—and have to arrange other landing places and hides for the cargo. The bribes have to be passed out with some discretion. There are a hundred details, and this time I can't afford a slip. This time it's my own money. . . ."

"You mean your brother doesn't know?" Her eyebrows shot up. "You're not using the same men . . . not buying from the same agent? . . ."

"He'll smell it out, sooner or later, but I'll keep it from him as long as it's possible. I'll go on doing his work for him, taking the commission until my own operations are big enough so that I can throw his orders back in his face." He grinned a little. "Of course, I won't get much sleep between the two operations, but what's sleep compared to money?"

The time had come for her to go; she rose slowly. "Why does it matter if he knows? What can he do?"

"He will try to buy out the lugger—demand a slice in the cargo. James is as eager for money as I am, and if he lays eyes on the *Dolphin*—especially if he knows I'm running her—then he will have her. Even for the pleasure of taking her away from me he would have her. He's greedy, is my brother James—and different from the way you and I are greedy, my love."

She squinted in the cracked and spotted mirror to adjust her hat. Then she turned to him.

"Paul, I want to come with you!"

"Where?"

"When the *Dolphin* makes the run—when they bring the cargo in."

His face darkened. "Have you gone mad, Jane? That's no place for you!"

"I've as much right to my place there as you! I want to help— I could act as a lookout . . . or hold a lamp. . . ."

He whistled through his teeth. "You little fool! Do you realize you'd be recognized by the men? If anything went wrong you'd be caught and charged as a common smuggler. This is the most dangerous time of the year, when the twilight is long, and the dawn comes early. It's madness even to think of it."

"You suppose I'd let myself get caught? Not with Blonde Bess! Your men wouldn't recognize me. I'll borrow Patrick's clothes, and ride astride. . . ."

"No, Jane!" He caught her roughly by the arm, and hustled her out to the stable; she struggled irritably to shake him off, but he held her, his fingers pinching her skin through the cloth of her habit. He helped her to mount, and then looked up into her angry face.

"Don't forget that I'm master of this operation—and my orders are obeyed! Just don't forget it, Jane!"

He gave Blonde Bess a smack on the rump, and the chestnut moved off smartly. He stood and watched as Jane, all sense of caution and discretion gone, dug her heels in and headed for the fence. In full view of anyone who might have been looking from the village in the direction of Paul's cottage, she put Blonde Bess over the jump. It should have been scrambled and ill-prepared, but somehow it managed not to be. Bess took it with confidence and grace.

"Well," Paul muttered, looking after her, "if you don't get yourself hung as a smuggler, you'll surely *break* your neck! You little fool!" He slammed the kitchen door behind him.

"And, sweet Heaven, why did I have to love you!"

She made no attempt to hold Blonde Bess in check after the first jump; the animal became the expression of her rage against Paul. Speed and movement were needed. She wanted to leave behind the memory of his dictates, wanted to tire herself and exhaust the emotion that she knew was childish and dangerous, and which she could not yet control. She put Bess recklessly over fences and dikes she could never attempt before, feeling the mare respond instantly to her touch, rejoicing in the way she gathered herself up for each obstacle, and took it without a change of rhythm.

Robert Turnbull was waiting where the road forked to Blake's Reach. He was riding his bay, Roger, a powerful horse, sixteen hands high, and broad in the chest. Robert sat astride him calmly; it was impossible to guess how long he might have been waiting.

He raised his hat.

"You jump well, Jane," he said as she came up beside him.

She was breathing heavily, not pleased to see him and trying to hide it. "Bess likes it," she said shortly. "I have to hold her in. . . ."

He smiled. "Well . . . she's young, too."

Jane jerked her head abruptly. "Will you come and have breakfast? It's only a mile from here." She tried to make her tone gracious, and didn't succeed.

"I'd be delighted to," he said. It wasn't the answer she expected, and she almost betrayed her surprise.

"We'd better hurry, then," she said. "Kate's food is bad enough at the best of times, but uneatable when it gets cold." She urged Bess forward.

He turned Roger and hurried to catch up with her. "I would ride with you some morning if I knew where you were," he said. "Do you come by here often?"

She spurred Bess to a canter. "I'm here often enough . . . you can ride with me if you can find me," she called back over her shoulder.

With a stifled curse, Robert followed her.

It wasn't the first time they had met on the Marsh early in the morning. She knew it had been Robert's habit for many years to ride before he started the day's business in Watchbell Street. At first she had encountered him in places she expected he would be— generally on a road that led directly to Rye. Then it seemed as if he had started a game of hide and seek with her, appearing in places he would never normally go. And now, today, here he was well past Blake's Reach and on this little-used road that led directly from the house to Old Romney. She was suddenly fearful, dreading to feel these brilliant dark eyes fixed on hers again, fearful of reading in them what he knew.

Robert Turnbull, without appearing to ask for information, seemed to know what went on behind every closed door across the Marsh. It was very possible, she thought, that he also knew she went to see Paul at Old Romney. There was no getting away from the man. Wherever she turned, there he was . . . polite, helpful, kindly. And he seemed to know the thoughts in her head before she had time to form them.

Patrick brewed the chocolate that morning, and it was good. Kate's bread was still warm from the oven, and not yet lumpy. Jane piled honey on it, and her mood began to soften. Robert had been talking of nothing in particular, and her suspicion and tension left her.

Then suddenly he put his cup down; the action, unnecessarily sharp, made her look at him questioningly.

"There's been a great deal of activity on the coast lately . . . and it's late in the season for it."

"You mean shipping?" she said carefully. "I thought summer was the best time. . . ."

"No, my dear, I mean smuggling. It tapers off, you know, during the summer. These calm clear nights with long twilights give the captains very little time to make their rendezvous on the coast and land the cargo before they're sighted by revenue cruisers. The revenue cruisers grow a little more daring, too, with the shorter nights, and besides, there's less excuse for them to lay up in port for bad weather or repairs."

"Oh . . ." she said faintly, nodding, and striving to hold down the wave of apprehension that swept through her.

"Yes . . ." He gestured to her for permission to use his pipe. Then he began to fill it, deliberately concentrating on it, and looking away from her. "Yes . . ." he repeated, "and the Dragoons become more co-operative with the riding officers during this season. On a winter's night they don't enjoy the discomforts of chasing smugglers they're not sure are there at all. But of course, if they capture a cargo they share the proceeds, and it's not a bad sport for a summer's night. They'd be a great deal more use to the revenue men if only those poor fools would realize that it's in their own interest to make sure the Dragoons always got their fair share of the spoils. There's discontent over that question . . . which, of course, is an aid to the smugglers."

He looked at her from behind the light haze of smoke.

"Do you see much of Paul Fletcher, Jane?" It was lightly spoken.

She shrugged, not so much afraid now that the question had come into the open, but she wondered how much Robert knew, and how much he should be answered.

"Oh . . ." she said, "I see him now and then. He has rather an attachment to William. He brought him some white mice when we first came. When he's passing he sometimes comes into the stable. He tried to give me advice on the vegetable plot. . . ." She added quickly, "I told you, I think, that Sir James Fletcher came here. . . ."

He waved the last aside. "Sir James' being here isn't important. Whatever he is or isn't behind that bombast, he's a respected man in these parts—I should know, because I handle his affairs. But Paul—that's another matter. . . ."

She drummed the table with her finger tips. "Yes? . . ."

"Let's look at it as people like myself see it, Jane. Paul Fletcher lost money in the Indies, and comes back here, penniless and in debt, to a place that he's known to dislike. He gave it out that he was making charts of the Caribbean. . . . Well and good, except that we know he can't make any money from that."

"So? . . ."

"So he has all the qualities needed to make an extremely successful smuggler! He's learned organization and discipline from the Navy, he's intelligent and—I imagine—brave. He's a good sailor, and knows every inch of this coast. And from a small boy he's been a leader . . . he's made even his brother seem slow and a trifle dull . . . for which, of course, Sir James hasn't forgiven him."

"So . . ." she measured her words carefully. ". . . so you think Paul Fletcher is responsible for the increased smuggling this season?"

He shrugged. "A guess, my dear . . . only a guess, but I've shown you the reasons why I think as I do. He's daring . . . not reckless, but daring . . . and I'm afraid he'll be caught."

"And do you tell this to everyone?" she said sharply. "Do you tell enough people so that however lazy or frightened the preventive officers are they'll have to make some effort to catch him? Is that what you do, Robert?"

He shook his head. "My thoughts and deductions are only for you, Jane. You're so new here . . . and rumor and gossip take little account of the truth, as Anne learned. I would not like to see the Blake name involved. . . ."

She stood up. "Are you the conscience of this family? Are you its guardian . . . or are you waiting to see the final end of it?"

"Jane!"

"Do I understand you? Are you saying that Sir James, who's a bully and a braggart, may come into my drawing room, but that Paul may not stand in the stable yard for fear the sacred Blake name might be contaminated?"

He rose also, shrugging again. "Make of it what you will! There's nothing more for me to say!"

They looked at each other, silently. There was a challenge now between them, and even this, strangely, drew them closer.

5

Behind them Jane and Paul could hear the horses pulling at the
sparse grass that grew on the sand dunes; compact gray clouds had
closed in overhead and the Channel was flecked with whitecaps.
They crouched in the shelter of a steep bank, and Jane reached out
to take the glass from Paul.

"There she is, Jane—the *Dolphin!* And as pretty a thing as I've
seen. . . ."

Jane swung the heavy glass, and could see nothing but the suddenly magnified gray swell; then there was the horizon and the
darkening sky. She dropped it briefly, sighted the distant lugger
again, then put it back to her eye. Suddenly the light, graceful lines
of the vessel sprang up to meet her. She watched the slow plunge
and dip; the sails seemed curiously white against the gray back-
drop. Her hull was painted black, and the long bowsprit was red.
She tried to count the gunports, then the glass tilted and focused
on the name lettered in gold—*Dolphin.*

She gave a short gasp of excitement.

"One hundred and thirteen tons' burthen," Paul said. "Twelve
guns, not counting the swivels, and thirty hands. I'll take on thirty
or forty more men for the passage to Flushing. That should be
enough to handle the cargo quickly, and with good weather the
Dolphin will be back here in two—maybe three—days."

"Where will the extra men come from?" she said, flexing her
arms to ease the weight of the glass.

"Swing over landwards to the right. That village there—got it?
That's Barham-in-the-Marsh. Most of the extra men will come from
there, and that's where I'll unload the cargo . . . unless the preventive officers are waiting for it too."

She moved the glass over it carefully. It was a village of gray
stone, gray slate roofs touched in places with moss, whitewashed
doors, and nets the color of seaweed spread to dry. It lay in a
crescent around a shallow indent, and upturned fishing boats
were drawn in on the shingle. Wooden breakwaters ran downwards
from high-water mark across the shingle and disappeared into the
surf. Broad-winged gulls wheeled over the rooftops and around the
gray square-towered church. The cottages, the church walls, the

cobblestoned street had been pitted by a thousand storms sweeping in from the Channel. Here no trees could survive the winds; over to the west she saw the finger of the Dungeness foreland poking out into the sea.

"I've got laborers coming from some of the farms round Lydd—over there to the west. They'll help unload the small boats and lead the horses. The hide is over by Ivychurch, or if that road isn't safe, we'll make for a place just this side of Hythe."

"The *Dolphin's* been fishing this water now for a couple of days," he added. "There shouldn't be anything new for the revenue cruisers in the sight of her hove-to off this shore."

"How close in will she come?"

"I can't risk her closer than a half mile offshore. She draws too much to make it safe. The shingle bars build up around here, and keep shifting."

"How many boats from the village will you use?"

"All of them. Practically the whole village will help—even the women. We'll signal the *Dolphin* from the church tower."

She put down the glass, turning to him. "Aren't you afraid someone will inform? If the whole village knows? . . ."

He looked at her sideways, faintly amused. "There are hundreds of villages along this coastline that support themselves on smuggling, and an informer has a pretty sorry time. Those among them who don't like it, take care to keep their windows shut tight and the blankets over their ears."

He laughed then, at the concern in her face. "Don't worry, Jane —it's a discreet little village. It's been handling contraband cargoes for as long as it's stood there."

He got to his feet, and put out his hand to help her.

"You must be on your way now. I'll guide you back to the road, but I won't come further than that. There's no sense in us being seen riding together—besides, I should turn back to Barham. There are one or two people I must see again before the *Dolphin* leaves for Flushing."

Jane rose reluctantly, handing back the telescope. "Will she leave soon?"

He scanned the sea and the heavy gray sky. "Just pray that this weather holds on—as dark as it can. It's any time now, Jane. As soon as I have news of the plans of the revenue cruisers the *Dolphin* will be on her way."

She turned back to look once more at the small spread of canvas, which was all she could now see of the *Dolphin*. She gestured briefly with her hand, half wave, half salute.

"There goes my luck and my fortune—well may she ride!"

CHAPTER NINE

THE STREETS OF FOLKESTONE WERE BEGINNING TO EMPTY, AND THE long shadows were reaching across the cobblestones. People were hurrying now, where they had strolled an hour earlier. Most of them were making towards home and supper, and those who weren't, like herself, had an idle, purposeless air. Reluctantly Jane turned away from the display of discreetly trimmed hats in a milliner's window; Patrick would be waiting with the carriage at the Wool Pack, and there was no further excuse to keep her in the town.

Sheer restlessness had drawn her away from Blake's Reach this afternoon to visit this port, where the shipping packed into the harbor and the bright coats of the Dragoons flecked the crowd. She could see the line of mastheads down by the harbor, with the gulls wheeling above them; the smell of fish and salt water was strong. Mingling with the crowds had stifled her restlessness for a time, as she responded to the noise and the movement about her. But her few purchases had been made long ago; the sun was dropping behind the chimneys and the tempo had slowed. Now the shops were emptying, and the ale houses came into their own, their windows lighted, their doors open to the summer twilight and the passers-by.

It was four days since she had been on the sand dunes near Barham-in-the-Marsh with Paul—and she had not seen him since then. Twice in the early morning she had gone to Old Romney, to wait hopefully until the sun was high and full before returning to Blake's Reach. She reasoned that Paul's increased activity could

mean only one thing—that the *Dolphin* had at last turned and
headed for Flushing, and that almost at any hour now she could
be expected back off the English coast. The full meaning of Paul's
refusal to allow her any active part in the run came home to her
now; it was hard to bear the knowledge of her own helplessness,
to realize how little she mattered now to success or failure. She
faced the thought unwillingly, and Kate and Patrick had had to
bear the brunt of her displeasure. Even William sensed her mood
and kept out of the way—making a vague excuse when she suggested driving into Folkestone. She had gone by herself—aloof and
lonely in the carriage, missing William's talk, and haughtily refusing
to let Patrick come with her as she made her tour of the town.
She was slightly ashamed and ill at ease now as she made her way
back to the Wool Pack, and obsessed with the feeling that every
other person but herself had somewhere to go. Her footsteps lagged,
although she kept her head held stiffly and erect.

It was a relief to see Robert Turnbull standing beside the carriage outside the Wool Pack. He was chatting amiably with Patrick, and he broke off as he saw her.

"My dear Jane! . . ." Now he was smiling broadly. "It was such
a pleasant surprise when I recognized the carriage. . . ."

"Yes, I had some shopping. . . ." The sight of him had never
been so welcome before. She found herself smiling unrestrainedly
back at him.

"I was going to have supper here before starting back to Rye,"
he said. "Could you stay and share it with me? The food here is
good. . . ."

"Why, yes!" she said at once, beaming at him. "There's nothing
I'd like more." And it was true—except for the fact that she wanted
to know above anything what was happening to the *Dolphin*. A
grin immediately appeared on Patrick's face; it pleased him to know
he would have a few more hours of ale and gossip in the taproom;
but for him the best thing was to see the smile return to Jane's
face.

The inn was crowded. But Robert Turnbull was well known
there, and he hailed the innkeeper confidently. The man shook his
head apologetically as he explained there were no private rooms
left. With lips pursed in annoyance, Robert took Jane's arm and

was about to turn away. It was unthinkable to him that Jane would eat in a public room.

"Your pardon, sir!"

Robert halted. "Well, what is it?"

"There is a small dining room, Mr. Turnbull, that has only one other party in it. I'm sorry I can't offer you better, sir—but the other party is very quiet. All ladies and gentlemen, they are."

"Oh, well . . . in that case." Robert turned to Jane, who nodded quickly. Not for good reason would she be cheated now of dining at the inn with the sound of people's voices pleasantly about her, and a blessed escape from Kate's cooking. She urged him forward firmly.

"It will do very well," she said crisply.

The innkeeper seated them at a table that gave a view of the crowded masts of the harbor; the sun was rosy on the still waters. But their attention went immediately to the group who sat about the table before the fireplace. Even though they had fallen silent, there was no mistaking the foreignness of those faces; they were wary and strained, but in every gesture as they ate they proclaimed that they were not English. Robert bowed to them formally before pouring wine for Jane. But his eyes flickered over to them many times as he sipped his first glass.

The innkeeper came himself to carve the duck and a side of mutton. Jane's lips twitched hungrily as she smelled the apple sauce and the mint jelly; she held her glass towards Robert again, preparing to enjoy the wine and food, pleasantly aware that the *Dolphin* and Paul were slipping to the back of her mind.

It was annoying then, to hear Robert softly question the innkeeper about the strange group, six of them, who sat at the second table.

"Frenchies, sir!" the innkeeper said, pausing with the carvers held high. Then he leaned closer to them. "*Émigrés*," he added in a whisper that was too loud. "Just got in. Making for London by tomorrow's coach."

At this single word uttered in their own tongue, the heads of all six immediately turned. They regarded Jane and Robert firmly, their faces showing a mixture of apprehension and fear. Robert set down his wine and rose, bowing again.

"Mesdames . . . messieurs."

In response the men of the party, four of them, also rose, executing bows that for nicety and precision were wildly out of place in
that simply furnished room of an English seaport inn. Jane caught
her breath sharply, and she was aware of sudden pain in her chest.
With hostile eyes she examined in turn those foreign faces that were
even now dissolving into smiles as they listened to Robert Turnbull.
She looked at each of them minutely, carefully, as if daring one of
them to assume the recognizable features of a Blake.

When she was satisfied she turned her attention, with growing
wonder, to Robert. Not for the first time she was surprised by the
extent of his knowledge. The phrases that came quite readily to
his tongue were French. She didn't know that the people opposite
shuddered privately at the horrors of their language as spoken by
an Englishman; once again she was filled with the sense that the
full extent of Robert Turnbull's personality, the quiet and modest
country attorney of Rye, would never be known to her.

Now the strangers were talking, breaking in upon each other in
their eagerness. From their sighs and despairingly raised eyebrows,
their elaborate shrugs, Jane knew that they were describing their
experiences—though it wasn't clear to her whether they were complaining of seasickness or imprisonment. She inclined her head
frigidly as Robert presented her, ". . . *Madame la Comtesse* . . .
Madame de . . . Monsieur de . . ." acknowledging the introduction to each in turn, conscious as she did so that the eyes of the two
women rested on her gown and hat with frank curiosity. She was
irritated with Robert for continuing the talk—she didn't want to
hear, even in a tongue she didn't understand, of revolution and
flight and death. Then at last she heard the words her ears had
been straining for. Robert spoke Charles Blake's name.

Now her eyes darted from one to the other frantically, waiting
for an expression to change, a look of recognition to come. One by
one they shook their heads. She breathed easily again.

Then one of the women suddenly broke into animated talk, her
sallow, handsome face wrinkled with an effort of concentration.

"*Lentement, madame . . .*" Robert gestured for her to slow her
pace to allow him to follow. Jane lived the next moments in an
agony of suspense. Charles Blake's name was used many times.

Then came the last expressive shrug, the final shake of the head.

Jane tugged at Robert's sleeve imploringly. "Tell me! . . ."

He looked at her, and now he also shook his head. "Nothing . . . nothing we didn't know before. They don't remember him at Court, but they knew his kinsman, the Marquis. The lady who spoke—the Countess—recalls him in prison. She says she remembers that he had an English name. She was in Paris in prison at the same time."

"What's she doing here?"

"She was released—over a year ago, I think she said. It is difficult for me to follow exactly. She went south to the château of her friend, Madame de Marney, and posed as her child's nurse until they learned that the de Marneys were about to be denounced and imprisoned. Then they had to flee with whatever they could carry with them . . . the child died on the journey."

"And the others? . . ." Jane said.

"Émigrés they met up with in Dunkirk."

"Do they know what has happened to Charles?"

Again he shook his head. "More than a year since she's heard of him—and even there he was one among many. She described him, though—dark and tall, as I fancy he must be now. Handsome, she said. . . ." Then Robert smiled a trifle. "She says he does not look like an Englishman."

The conversation seemed to be exhausted; Robert turned his attention back to Jane. In subdued voices the other group began to talk among themselves. Jane picked through her food dully, and drank the wine with complete indifference; the sound of those French voices across the room unnerved her. She was aware of nothing except that Charles seemed very near—a stranger full of menace.

Then one single word of Robert's penetrated her daze. "What?" she said suddenly, lifting her head. "What was that?"

"The Dragoons, my dear," he said patiently. "I was speaking about the Dragoons."

"Yes? . . . What about them?"

"Their commander, Leslie, is a good friend of mine. He's a man from these parts—I have handled some affairs for his family . . .

and so, whenever we meet we generally take time to share a glass of wine or ale."

"Yes . . . yes," she said impatiently.

Turnbull shrugged. "Nothing of importance, my dear . . . I was just talking so that you might remember that I'm here."

"I'm sorry . . . it's those people. . . ."

He smiled, and went on. "Leslie was grumbling because he'd have to turn out tonight. They're expecting trouble . . . smuggling trouble, I would guess, from the sound of it. Of course Leslie didn't say exactly . . . even he could hardly be so indiscreet. But I judge from his lack of enthusiasm that he's expecting an all-night affair, and the Dragoons have never looked on chasing smugglers with much enthusiasm. The revenue people frequently find it convenient not to pay them their split of the cargo when it's captured. After a time the Dragoons don't make very willing helpers."

"But it *is* tonight?" she insisted.

He set down his glass. "Yes . . . why?"

She shrugged weakly, the corner of her mouth twitching even with her effort at control.

"Oh . . . nothing. I must remember to draw my curtains tight, and not hear anything on the road."

He said lightly, "If the Dragoons are out, I wouldn't advise you to ride too early on the Marsh tomorrow morning. You may meet the stragglers—from either side." From then onwards it seemed that the meal dragged to an interminable length.

2

Robert even insisted upon riding back to Blake's Reach with her, although the sea road to Rye was much shorter than circling the Marsh as he would have to do. He barely listened to her protests— just hitched Roger to the back of the carriage, and then joined her inside.

"It's purely selfish, Jane," he said as he settled himself. "The fact that the Dragoons anticipate trouble tonight gives me the pleasure of riding with you, and at the same time imagining that I'm protecting you." He laughed as he spoke.

"Protecting me!" Jane shrugged. "These days I have so much protection I hardly know what to do with it. It's not like the old days at The Feathers—nobody fussed much about me then, but I never came to any harm."

He nodded. Lights from the open windows they passed fell across his face briefly, highlighting the firm, broad bones; now it was a sardonic and amused face.

"You'll forgive me speaking so, Jane—but these are some of the disadvantages of being a lady. She's expected to be as delicate as air, and yet strong enough to bear the pain of childbirth, to manage and run a house with skill and economy, but not intelligent enough to bother her husband—and she has to ride in a stuffy carriage on a summer's night flanked by men putting irksome restrictions on her, when her feet may be itching to get out and walk. . . ."

"She can also lie abed on a winter's morning," Jane broke in. "And she needn't soil her hands from one day to the next."

"And what about yours, Jane—don't they get stiff with the dirt of the vegetable plot, and scratched with the rose thorns?"

"And they'll be scratched for as long as they have to be," she answered shortly. "Blake's Reach can't afford a lady yet."

He did not reply, and they rode in silence for some time. The summer's night was fine, with a light wind blowing that whispered in the trees and the hedgerows. They left the lights of Folkestone behind; there was a faint moon, a waning moon which deepened the shadows. Low on the horizon was a mass of clouds, and Jane watched them carefully as they rode. There seemed no movement there, no sign that they would slip forward to hide the moon. If the *Dolphin* were to land tonight there was danger in that pale light. She was thankful for the silence and the darkness within the carriage, which made it unnecessary to keep the anxiety from her face and voice. She leaned farther back into the shadows and hoped that Robert would have nothing more to say.

Their peace was shattered on the outskirts of Hythe. Here the roads divided—one led on to Appledore, the other cut across the Marsh to the coast. Outside the first ale house in Hythe's main street they were hailed.

"Hold there! Hold in the name of His Majesty!"

Robert muttered something under his breath, and lowered the

window. They could hear Patrick curse, and his voice rose loudly in complaint. ". . . nothin' but a bloody edjit to be lepin' out at the horses this way. . . ."

Robert cut in. "Who is it? What does this mean?"

Two men came forward, the first of them carrying a lantern which he raised above his head to examine the occupants of the carriage.

"His Majesty's customs." Then the lamp was held near to Robert's face. "Why, it's Mr. Turnbull! Jack, it's Mr. Turnbull!"

"I can see that," the other man growled. "An' you'd best let me handle the lamp in future if you don't want us both run down."

Robert looked from one to the other. "What's the trouble?"

"Nothin's the trouble, sir . . . leastways not yet."

"Well, then? . . ." he prompted.

"Well, Mr. Turnbull, we were stoppin' the carriage to ask if you'd seen any movement on the road out of Folkestone. The Dragoons, I mean, sir."

"No . . . none. Are you waiting for them?"

The man swore softly. "All of three hours, sir . . . with it gettin' darker by the minute." He swayed a little as he spoke, and clutched the arm of his companion. "We're stuck here and darsant move for fear we'll miss the soldiers, and they'll go to the wrong place."

Robert's manner became more relaxed. He opened the door of the carriage, and leaned out. He gave the first man a light tap on the shoulder. "Now look, George . . . I've known you long enough to know that you think strange things with a drop inside you. Are you sure the Dragoons were meeting you here? I was speaking earlier to Major Leslie—"

The man broke in with protests of injured dignity. "This *is* the place, sir, and we can't go on by ourselves because the landin' place's been changed . . . leastways we've picked up information which makes us think it has. We heard of a cargo comin' in at Barham, and now we think it's been changed to Langley, this side of Dymchurch. . . ."

"Is it really tonight, George . . . are you sure that's not a mistake, also? From what I hear there's a cargo run in most nights of the week along here."

George spat on the ground in disgust. "Not this time o' year, there ain't. This one's in a hurry—an' it's a big cargo. An' if those perishin' fools wat call themselves soldiers don't show up, we'll miss the lot." His voice took on a tone of wailing complaint. "There's only two of us . . . and I reckon there could be mor'an a hundred owlers. We darsant go near 'em if the Dragoons don't show."

"They'll be along in due course," Robert said. "They're not likely to set out so early as to give the lugger and the captain warning and a chance to clear off." He closed the door again. "Just you stay out of the ale house until they come. After all, you can't expect a landing for a few hours yet."

"Tide'll turn early enough, sir—if she's a big lugger she'll need to keep it with her."

Turnbull shrugged. "Well, these are things I've no experience of. I'll bid you good night now, and advise you to be more cautious with that lantern. You might have frightened the horses badly."

They shifted about apologetically. "We didn't recognize the carriage or pair, sir. 'Tain't usual to see a strange carriage hereabouts travelin' as late as this. . . ."

"This carriage belongs to Miss Howard," Turnbull said briefly. "Miss Howard is the granddaughter of Spencer Blake, and is now living at Blake's Reach. I'm sure you'll recognize it in future and give Miss Howard any assistance she may need."

The lantern went high again. Two hats were pulled off sheepishly, as they ducked in awkward semblance of bows. "To be sure, Miss Howard . . . Welcome to the Marsh, mistress . . . I remember your mother. Most folk on the Marsh remember her."

As they drove on again, Jane could hear Robert's tongue click disapprovingly; he shook his head.

"No wonder smuggling has such an easy time of it when they're the sort who go into the revenue service. The pay's wretched, and most of the time they know they're against hopeless odds. I imagine in their place I'd stick to the ale house, too."

"Do you think the Dragoons will come?" she said faintly.

"In time, I suppose. Then they'll argue and finally decide where they'll go and look for the lugger. And by this time everyone in the ale house knows their plans, and I'm certain the smugglers do as well."

"You think so?"

"Almost certain—most people on the Marsh would rather hinder a revenue man than help him, and they can pass the word along with greater speed than you'd believe. This game is hundreds of years old, Jane, and so far the smugglers have managed to stay ahead of the revenue men."

She licked her lips, feeling the sweat break all over her body. She thought of Paul gathering his men quietly to await the lugger, watching and cursing the moon. She imagined the forms of men stumbling in the darkness under the weight of brandy casks, and then the faint jingle of harness as the soldiers rode, with the moon striking on their muskets. Robert was certain that the word had been passed along—but had it been passed? If the cargo was captured she was not only penniless, but in debt, condemned to fighting a hopeless battle against the ruin of Blake's Reach, and with it, herself. And for Paul it was the end of the dream of escape. Did he know that? *Did he know?*

She looked across at Robert. "How do you know so much of what goes on on the Marsh—those revenue men, you knew them, didn't you? And the Major . . . and everyone else, I think."

He shrugged. "I have time to know them, Jane. I've been here for many years, and many people have come to me in trouble. But it's not only those who sit in my office I know. I like to ride, and a man alone out here on the Marsh observes a great deal, and makes many acquaintances—some of them strange ones. I see a laborer's wife with a swollen belly, and pretty soon I can lean over the garden gate and admire the new baby—and maybe I have some toy for it to play with. I travel constantly between these towns all over the fringe of the Marsh, and I eat where my fancy takes me—I don't care whether it's the Wool Pack with Johnson's best wine, or bread and cheese at an ale house. People know that a man without wife or child of his own can spare time for them and their problems. They know there's nothing waiting for me in Rye but a housekeeper who daren't open her mouth against the irregular hours I keep. And if the dinner she cooks is spoiled, then it's spoiled—and as long as I pay for it, I'm the one who'll say how it's to be disposed of."

"A free man. . . ." Jane murmured.

He shrugged. "As free as man can be . . . and as empty."

After that they sat through the miles to Blake's Reach and did not speak, each completely wrapped in thoughts that were his own, and not to be shared. The heavy clouds crept slowly on the horizon; sometimes a light wisp darkened the moon. The willows along the dykes swayed and sighed. Out on the Marsh somewhere a dog howled. At Appledore the elms were stiff against the moon; the scents of summer were in the air, the heavy smell of flowers, and sweat, and dry crops in the fields. For Jane, the scene was touched with melancholy, a strange static feeling of deadness before some momentous action. She found herself at times holding her breath; it would have been a comfort, she thought, to reach out and touch Robert's hand, but she did not. Mostly she thought about Paul. If the lugger they talked of was the *Dolphin*, Paul was a few miles from here, and in danger. Perhaps it was danger he knew of, and had deliberately counted and calculated the risk. She considered all the other nights he had been in danger, and realized that only this one seemed real to her; always before it had been an anonymous, unknown danger in which she could not share. Now she had seen the *Dolphin*, lovely and built for a purpose; she had seen the village where the boats would land. Danger now had a shape, an identity, and a place.

She was frightened, badly frightened—and, for the moment, quite helpless. The carriage turned up the hill to Blake's Reach.

Robert lingered to share a glass of wine with her. They sat in Spencer's sitting room—altered now, somewhat, neater, but still his room, a frowning place. It was while she sat twisting the glass, drinking little, that the idea came to her. She wondered why she had not thought of it before, and then knew how strongly Paul's wishes had rested on her. The feel of life began to flow through her again, a tingling in her veins, a heightened sense of time passing.

She shifted impatiently in her seat.

Robert looked at her, and then rose. "Yes, Jane—I'll go now. I'm quite well aware that for the past five minutes I've not been here at all as far as you knew or cared."

Then suddenly he leaned over and kissed her fully on the mouth, a firm, hard kiss with no tenderness in it.

"I can kiss you now because it doesn't matter to you. When you slip off into your own thoughts, Jane, don't forget that I'm a man, and you are a very desirable woman."

Then he turned and left her.

3

When Robert left her, Jane sat for some moments, even though each minute was important to her. She pressed her fingers to her lips feeling Robert's hard, angry kiss again. There wasn't time to think of all he had meant to convey in the kiss and his words, but she felt ashamed, and sad that he should have had to say these things to her. Then she rose, trying to pull her wits about her, and called to Patrick.

"Is Kate in bed?"

"Ay, she is—an' snorin' fit to shake the rafters."

"Good! Then—" She broke off. "Patrick, pay attention to everything I have to say, and remember it! First of all, I think the revenue men have caught up with Paul Fletcher. They've got wind of a cargo coming in tonight, and I'm certain Paul is landing it. I have to warn him. I have to go to him."

A look of horror froze on Patrick's features. "Blessed saints, y' might get caught yerself!"

"Not with Blonde Bess." She moved closer to him. "I have to go! I've put five hundred pounds of Robert Turnbull's money in that cargo, and I've no thought to see the man I love dragged off to prison." She gripped his arm. "Patrick, this night is everything for us—you, as well as myself. If it comes off we stay at Blake's Reach, we start to live, with real gold jingling in our pockets, and no bills unpaid. If we lose, we're worse off than we've ever been, and I've no skill at a card table."

"Mistress, dear," he said in a low tone, "I'll not have y' expose yourself like this. I'll go, mistress—I'll take the message."

She shook her head. "You don't know the Marsh well enough— you'd be lost, and might be captured. You don't know the place where they're bringing the cargo ashore. It would be madness, and a waste for you to go. Now, quickly, saddle up Blonde Bess!"

A pleading frown came to his face. "Mistress, just stop a little. If y' go there—to wherever the landin' is—y'll be in danger y' haven't looked to yet. Y'll be seen by more than Mr. Fletcher. Some of the men will see y', even dark as it is. There aren't many ladies hereabouts that ride alone on the Marsh, an' they'll start to guess. Would y' have it known among a gang of smugglers that y' were one of them?"

"I *am* one of them," she said soberly, "and tonight I'll earn my place there—but they won't know it! I'm going to wear your breeches and shirt, Patrick, and bind my hair up. With any luck they'll never see me in the light, and they'll never know who the strange boy was."

He shook his head. "An' if the dawn comes, mistress—what then?"

"I'll plan for that when the time comes. If I'm not back here when the house starts stirring, you're to tell Kate I'm indisposed, and lying abed, and be sure you leave a window open for me at the front of the house. . . ." She ran her hand distractedly across her forehead. "Heaven help me, there's a hundred details . . . you'll have to think your way around them if anything goes wrong." Then she gripped his arm. "Wish me luck, Patrick—and I'll be lying safe abed by the time the sun touches our roof."

He saddled Blonde Bess, and watched her go, cold and sick with fear for her. She had looked surprisingly slight in his old breeches and stockings, and the shirt with the sleeves rolled to the elbows. Her hair was bound up in a cloth in the way sailors wore it, and she had darkened her face and hands with soot from the chimney. Over all that she had wrapped the ragged cloak Kate wore outdoors in the yard in bad weather. Only the tips of her boots showed beneath it. When she was finished she looked a fearful sight; she didn't in any way, he thought, resemble her mother now. Now she looked like some sexless spawn of the London gutter, an evil and desperate creature for whom he could feel no love. Miserably he saw her disappear into the darkness.

She headed towards Barham-in-the-Marsh riding astride on Jed's saddle. It was a relief to feel the strong rhythm of Blonde Bess's frame under her, to know the time of inaction was past. She wasn't sure that she would find Paul or the *Dolphin* at Barham, but it was nearer than Langley. At the back of her mind was the question of what she would do if Barham was deserted—Langley lay somewhere over beyond Dymchurch; she had never seen it, and never been there. There was also the thought that Langley was much nearer to Folkestone, and that perhaps the Dragoons were already there. She touched her heels smartly to Bess's sides.

She rode with head bent, making the best pace she dared on those roads. The clouds had moved up from the horizon; heavy drifts blotted out the moon intermittently.

"Paul will welcome it," she muttered, watching the faint light on the road ahead fade as a cloud with a heavy underside of rain moved across it. "But it could mean a broken neck for me!"

She pushed on, surprised to feel her body cold, although the wind did not seem strong. The road that forked to Rye was left behind, and vaguely, in short spells of moonlight, she could see the tower of Lydd church ahead.

"Move, Bess! . . . Move, sweetheart!" she whispered, leaning low to the mare's ear.

Lydd was silent and shuttered, the church dark behind the screen of elms. She listened fearfully to the clatter Bess's hooves made against the cobbles; she urged Bess to greater speed to carry them away from the menace of those still houses. They were free of the town at last, and Barham lay ahead. Soon she caught the smell of the sea, the smell and tang that conveyed a sense and a memory of Paul to her; soon she would hear it—and hearing it remember that for Paul it was the sound of freedom. As her straining ears caught the vague, distant murmur, a new thought came. Abruptly she slowed Bess to a walk.

If the *Dolphin* lay off Barham and Paul intended to unload it here, there would be lookouts posted. It was possible that there would be a road-barrier, or if warning of the Dragoons had reached Paul, there might even be a trip wire stretched across the road. The thought of what it could do to Bess's legs frightened her; she slipped down and took the bridle to lead the mare.

The deep quiet remained unbroken; there were no lights and nothing seemed to move in the town ahead. The thickening clouds parted for a moment. She scrambled up on a stony dune to get a vantage point from which she might catch a glimpse of the *Dolphin*. Briefly she saw the empty expanse of the moonlit Channel, before the clouds closed up once more. It was then she heard the sound she had been waiting for—the crunch of heavy boots against the hard ground.

Except for that one sound they were silent—and speedy. Bess's reins were pulled from her hand at the same moment that a strong pair of arms pinioned her own. Her short cry was stifled by a hand clapped over her mouth—a hand that had the ageless smell of the sea worn into it. She could feel them looming above her in the darkness; there were two of them, and a third who held Bess. She knew then the first moment of true fear that night. There seemed nothing that would stop the blow that would knock her unconscious so that they could bind her wrists and ankles with ease and speed.

She took the only way of saving herself. Wriggling desperately, she half-turned so that the free hand of the man who held her encountered the full roundness of her breasts under Patrick's thin shirt. He paused in only an instant's hesitation; then he ripped the shirt open to the waist and she felt the calloused palms explore her bare skin.

She heard his swift intake of breath. "Fer Christ's sake! . . . Hold it, Tim! Bring the lantern!"

The man who held Bess brought out a lantern from the folds of his cloak. Three sides of the glass were blackened, so that the light could be cut off by holding the fourth side against his body.

" 'Ere! You feel this 'ere, Tim!" And then another hand was on her, a hand that after a second of surprise began to fondle her with rough eagerness, so that even in her fear she felt her nipples rise and harden.

" 'Old the lantern up! No!—turn it away from the sea, y' fool!"

They lifted the lantern cautiously, and she felt the cloth pulled off her head. Her hair fell heavily about her shoulders.

"A girl! Fer Christ's sake, a girl!"

"Well, watdidya think, with them two pointin' at yer. Or mebby y' was thinkin' t' look further. Mebby down here. . . ." He put his hand on the belt Jane had hitched around Patrick's trousers.

"Cut it out, y' fool. This ain't no whorehouse—this 'ere's business."

"I wouldn't mind doin' a bit o' business with this one right now.

I'll be bound she wouldn't be unwillin' too long. Not from wot I felt . . . and these redheads get wild."

"Shut yer mouth! We don't even know 'oo she is—or wat she's doin' 'ere."

"Well, ask 'er! Take yer big paw away, an' ask 'er!"

He removed his hand from her mouth, though he still held both her arms tightly behind her back.

"Com'on, now. Spit it out! Whyarya 'ere?"

She took a deep breath and pitched her voice to the slower sing-song tone heard in the kitchen of The Feathers.

"Take yer filthy big mitts off o' me, and take me to Paul Fletcher. I'll 'ave a thing or two t' say about the way the men he hires do their jobs, y' no-good bunch o' slobs. . . ." She followed it with a string of obscenities that the stable hands at The Feathers would have admired.

"'Ere! Y' shut yer mouth, y' filthy little bitch. 'Oo says we can take y' to Paul Fletcher! 'E ain't 'ereabouts!"

"Aw, come orf it," she said. "I know 'e's 'ere, an' I've got a message t' deliver to 'im!"

"'Oo sent y'?"

She had her answer ready. "Adam Thomas—y' know Adam Thomas, of Appledore!"

"Then y' ain't speakin' the truth! Adam Thomas ain't been in these parts fer months past."

"D'ya think I don't know that! I'm a cousin o' his—Liza Thomas's me name. I live beyond the Marsh, up towards Tenterden a bit, and when 'e cleared out a few months back, I took a notion t' go with 'im. We been in London—together. An' now Adam's all fixed to slip across the Channel to Roscoff as an agent for a gentleman as I won't mention now. 'E and me, we're goin' together. An' 'e picked up this information, and I'm carryin' it t' Paul Fletcher. An' y'll kindly get out o' me way, or Mr. Fletcher'll likely pin yer ears back when 'e knows what I've t' tell 'im."

She looked at them challengingly, daring them to defy her confidence. They looked uncertainly from one to the other, then she felt the grip on her arms slacken.

"There! That's more like it!" she said, looking at the circle of wary faces. She drew the shirt back across her bosom, fumbling for the missing buttons.

"An' y' can just lower that lantern now, because y've all looked yer fill. That sight's only for those as 'as gold to jingle in their pockets. An' if y'll just lead me now to Mr. Fletcher, I'll say nothin' more about what y' done t' me."

They exchanged glances. "Well, can't do no 'arm—an' she's better under our eye than lettin' 'er go. . . ."

"Seems fishy t' me. Ain't never 'eard of Adam Thomas an' Paul Fletcher gettin' together. . . ."

"An' why should y'?" she retorted. "Since when 'as Mr. Paul Fletcher taken to discussin' his affairs with the likes o' you three?" She wrapped her cloak about her. "Come now—git movin'. I'm not a patient woman, as y'll find out if y' delay me any longer."

Mistrustful, sullen, they yielded then. "Well, com'on, then! Tim, y'd best stay to keep lookout, and we'll take the girl and the 'orse along."

They moved in single file. The man with the lantern was first; it was held low, and its beam carefully directed away from the sea. Jane was next, and the second man followed her closely, leading Bess. Without a word they entered the outskirts of the village, past the small, shuttered cottages, and the single inn. The white shingle was in sight now, gleaming faintly as the small waves lapped it. She had expected that they would go straight towards the beach, but instead the leading man turned aside abruptly to follow a white pebble path that wound through tall grass. The high building that loomed suddenly in the darkness she recognized as the square-towered church Paul had pointed out from the sand dunes. They ignored the great main door, and followed the path to the side of the building. Then the man in the lead started down a flight of stone steps that led to the crypt. She guessed that it also led to the entrance to the tower.

4

The stair well to the tower was steep and dusty, and the light from the lantern was dim. Jane groped for handholds in the rough walls, then finally the density of the darkness lessened; they came through a trap door onto the roof of the square tower. The figure of a man, leaning against the parapet, turned swiftly.

"We found her 'eadin' this way on the Lydd road, Mr. Fletcher. Leadin' a 'orse."

"We've brought 'er to speak for 'erself. Says she's got a message for you . . . 'er name's Liza Thomas."

"Liza Thomas? . . ." His tone was speculative.

Jane stepped forward. "You ain't never 'eard o' me, Mr. Fletcher. I'm cousin t' Adam Thomas from Appledore. He sent me."

There was a perceptible stiffening of Paul's body, but he said nothing for a moment. For Jane it was a moment to wonder whether he would recognize her voice before she was forced to begin explanations in the presence of the other men.

He spoke quietly. "All right, Harry . . . John. You can leave her. Hitch the horse by the south door. I'll be down directly there's any sign of movement out there."

They waited in silence for the men to leave. Paul made a warning gesture towards her; he stood by the trap door watching the lantern light grow fainter. Then he stooped and closed it.

"Big ears!" he said softly.

She moved close to him, taking his arm. "Paul, I had to come—"

He shook off her hold impatiently. "Damn you, Jane! Don't you know the meaning of discipline? How do you think this organization is run? We're not here to play games! You've disobeyed orders!"

His tone, stern and unfriendly, stung her to retort. "Just wait before you have too much to say!"

He ignored her, sweeping on. ". . . and you've exposed yourself to these men. How long did you think you'd go unnoticed in that ridiculous costume? And riding Blonde Bess, I'll be bound!"

"Wait!" There was a period of cold silence between them. "I'll leave when I've said what I have to say. I'm aware we're not here to play games . . . and don't imagine it was a game for me to find my way here across the Marsh tonight. Or to have those men pawing me!"

"Did they touch you?"

"It took them overly long to decide by feel whether I was a boy

or a woman . . . they were ready for a little sport. It's a good thing
they're afraid of you, Paul."

"Well, what did you expect?" he said shortly. "These aren't gentlemen with pretty manners. They take a woman when they want
her, and in whatever circumstances they can get her. And a woman
wearing breeches is an open invitation. In their minds you were just
asking them to put you on the ground and have their sport. . . ."

He went on. "Two of those men were impressed into the Navy,
and served their term. You know what happens on the lower deck,
Jane, when the Navy's in home port? The men have three feet of
space to lie with their women. And those who want a woman take
her there with all the others, or go without. It doesn't make for
reticence or consideration of the woman they use. . . ."

"Oh, hush!" she said angrily. "I haven't come all this way to have
you preach to me about the wenching habits of sailors. That was
a risk I took . . . along with breaking my neck if Blonde Bess
stumbled. I've got five hundred pounds at stake tonight . . . and a
good deal more. If we lose the cargo tonight, I lose Blake's Reach."

"I didn't know it was yours to lose. . . ."

Her voice was tense and slow. "It is mine—make no mistake
about that! And unless you lose this cargo it has a chance of being
something I might be proud of. . . ."

"Lose the cargo?" he said. "I've never lost a cargo!"

"You could—tonight. The preventive officers know you'll try to
land it and the Dragoons have been called out."

He was silent for a time; she strained to see his face in the darkness but there was nothing to see. There was no movement of surprise or alarm; nothing but stillness and silence. She had never
imagined such coldness in Paul, and she began to know, suddenly,
his qualities as a leader.

"How did you hear this?"

She told him quickly of the meeting outside the ale house at
Hythe, repeating as well as she remembered everything the two excise men had said. Between them the hostility dropped away; she
had the feeling that Paul had forgotten her as a person, forgotten
his own anger with her. He was completely and impersonally absorbed in her words.

"So they'll go to Langley—it's as I hoped."

"Then you knew!"

"Yes, I knew. The word leaked out. Perhaps an informer—or perhaps carelessness. One of the women, maybe. Time enough to deal with that after we're through tonight's work."

"Couldn't you have stopped the *Dolphin*—sent her back?"

"If you want profits, Jane, there's no time to wait around on the movements of the customs men. *You* have to set the pace! The *Dolphin* could make another trip to Flushing for a cargo in the time we would have wasted letting her cool her heels outside the legal limit. Organizing a run costs money, and I've no money to waste. So I let the *Dolphin* come on, and let the word get back to the preventive men that we had learned they were planning a raid, and we'd switched the operation to Langley. It's near enough not to rouse suspicion, and if the *Dolphin*'s sighted out in the Channel, she could be making to either place."

"If she's sighted, won't they send a revenue cutter out?"

"They would, if they had one. The cutter, *Falcon*, whose station this is, suddenly developed a mysterious leak in Folkestone today, and she's unfit for duty."

"You did it?" she whispered.

"I arranged it—and it cost plenty. But I had to be sure the *Falcon* wouldn't interrupt the unloading tonight. She doesn't have the *Dolphin*'s speed, but she could either force us to pull out to sea, or to fight it out. At any cost I want to avoid doing either—the *Dolphin*'s loaded with a cargo that'd make your heart sing just to see it, Jane. I managed to borrow some more money, and this cargo's worth more than a little risk."

Suddenly he gripped her arm, the even control of his tone breaking. "For the first time, Jane, I'm not being paid to take a risk! This time it's for myself, and the profit's mine! Nothing's going to stop me making that landing tonight!"

"The Dragoons . . ."

"Ah! . . ." The sound was contemptuous. "I'll take my chances on the Dragoons. They've no liking for chasing smugglers, and no heart in it. If they're clever enough to come back here after drawing a blank at Langley, then we'll have warning of it and clear out. Just an hour or two's all I need, and I've planted false scents at Langley that should keep them busy for that length of time."

"Just an hour or two . . ." she said. "Then could I stay? Paul, let me stay!"

"Stay! Why?"

"Surely there's something I could do . . . you need to hurry, don't you? Then why shouldn't I be of some use, even if it's just staying with the horses. I'll reckon there's not an able-bodied woman in this village tonight that's not lending a hand somewhere." Her tone warmed and grew persuasive. "Don't you see, Paul—it's *my* cargo too that's coming in tonight. It's my luck that's riding on the *Dolphin*. I want to be here. . . . As soon as they start unloading they'll all be so busy they'll never notice me, or stop to wonder who I am. . . ."

Her voice trailed off indecisively, and she stood beside him at the parapet waiting for his answer. He said nothing. The minutes dragged out, and still he didn't stir or speak. The moon was gone, completely blanketed now by the clouds that had built up solidly in the west. In the silence and darkness there was only the sea, not seen, but heard in the lapping against the shingle bars, and felt in the sharp wet smell in her nostrils. Gently Paul's arm came about her shoulders; he held her lightly against him, almost absently, seeming to draw comfort from her presence, but not surrendering his watchfulness to her. At this moment she was a companion, nothing more. Her eyes strained in the darkness to catch the signal at the same moment that he would. She was calm, knowing fully the danger in which she stood, and also aware, with another part of her mind, of the strange joy of sharing it with Paul; of feeling each second go with a heightened sense of its passing. She knew that there might never have been another moment like this in her life again. Her senses were sharpened to perceive and to remember; there was sadness in knowing that the memory of this might have to serve many evenings of dozing by the fire. Her body grew taut with stillness, so that she hardly seemed to breathe.

It came at last. A blue light flashing twice from the Channel. Paul uncovered the lantern that stood at his feet, and flashed it above his head once—twice.

He spoke softly. "Down to the beach . . . quickly!"

Confident and surefooted now, she followed him down the winding staircase.

The beach was crowded with people who seemed to move with
ease by the dim light of the masked lanterns. Low voices were
heard, speaking briefly with a pitch of urgency; she caught the sound
of boats scraping against the shingle, the subdued splash of oars.
Her ears were assailed with all the unfamiliar sounds of the sea and
the people who lived by it. Occasionally there was a woman's voice,
not authoritative, just part of the background, because it was recognized that speed was needed, and that a woman was no more
than a strong back and a pair of hands. Jane could only vaguely
make out the forms of people moving among the boats, the outlines
of the boats themselves, the small swirl of foam where the water
broke against the shingle. There was a string of horses waiting—
some of them were harnessed to carts. The shingle made heavy
walking; the rounded stones rolling under her feet; several times
she half fell, and Paul didn't notice. Once again he seemed to have
forgotten her identity, and even her presence. She hurried after
him, and humbly kept silent, suddenly aware of her ignorance and
uselessness in the midst of this orderly speed.

He gave one or two swift commands in passing along the boats,
stopping a moment to watch one of the craft being pushed off. But
for the most part his orders were unnecessary. The people along
this seacoast had been going out to meet the smugglers' luggers for
many years and many generations.

But he assigned no duty to her, and gave her no order. She followed him closely, and in silence, trying to efface herself, and merge
into the bustle about her. Then the last of the boats was gone, and
a quiet fell on the group left behind. A soft murmur in a woman's
voice now and then was all she heard—that, and the stirring of the
horses, and the impatient stamp of their feet. She wondered why
Paul did not go with the boats, and then immediately answered the
question for herself by realizing that in a crisis the leader must be
on the shore. The skipper of the *Dolphin* and Paul were the only
two that night who counted for more than their ability to lift a keg
of brandy.

She grew nervous in the silence and the waiting. Around her,
some of the dark forms sat down on the shingle; she stayed close
by Paul's shoulder, wishing for the easing of tension that would
come when the boats returned. There was no sign of a break in the

clouds, and she realized that she would not get even a glimpse of the outline of the *Dolphin*. The monotonous slap of the tide on the shingle grew oppressive. She stood with her chin huddled into the collar of Kate's old cloak.

It seemed a small age of time before she heard again the faint swish of oars, and the first of the boats showed through the darkness. Suddenly Paul was by her side no longer; he moved first towards the string of waiting horses, giving orders in a low, tense voice, then he brushed past her hurriedly, wading out into the surf to meet the first boat.

After that there was no time to wonder where he was, or what he was doing. She found herself surrounded by people pressing forward to unload the cargo. A young woman moved beside her, and started to hitch up skirts and petticoats and move out into the water —a deep-bosomed young woman with the strong supple body of a hard worker. Jane followed her, feeling the shock of the cold water as it rose above her boots and swished about her legs. She found herself next to the young woman as they both grasped the gunwale of the boat, and started to drag it ashore. It scraped with unnatural loudness on the shingle. Jane was half soaked with water as the crew jumped out; for the first time in her life she tasted the salt spray on her lips. Suddenly she could feel herself laughing inside with excitement and nervous expectancy. She became one of the group; she fell into line beside the young woman, forming part of a chain that extended to the waiting horses. A large package was dumped into her arms, and she passed it to the next woman; from the feel of the oilskin she knew it was tea. Moving past them were the line of men carrying the tobacco bales. Out at the *Dolphin* she knew they would be loading the wool bales which the boats had brought out—the wool which would pay for their next cargo in Flushing or Roscoff. Her body fell into the rhythm of the movement; she began to glow with a sense of exhilaration and triumph. It was difficult to keep from laughing out loud now. Suddenly and incredibly she knew that she liked being here for the sake of the excitement alone; that she was also securing the future of Blake's Reach was a thing quite apart. She knew that she was consciously enjoying the swirl of the water about her legs, and the knowledge that a few miles along the coast the Dragoons were searching for them. She found herself grinning at the young woman, and receiving an answering grin as she turned to pass on the next bundle.

They finished unloading, and helped push the boat off again. Then they moved to the next boat; the line fell into place, and the movement was set up once more. After a while her arms and shoulders began to ache and twice she nearly lost her footing in the water when she leaned forward out of balance to take an oilskin package. But the sense of excitement did not leave her; she knew her nerves were at a pitch where she could have gone on working to the point of collapse. She knew that time was passing; her feet grew cold in the water; her arms and shoulders felt as if they were on fire.

Now the first boat carrying the brandy kegs had touched the shingle. She paused briefly to watch the ease with which the men slung the half-ankers on their shoulders, and waded out of the surf towards the horses. Then she felt a tug at her arm; the young woman beside her, gesturing towards the carts. Quickly she scrambled to catch up with the others. The women were waiting patiently, bundles in arms, to help load the carts and the pack-horses. Here Jane was more at ease, and she slipped round to hold the head of each horse as it was loaded; most of them were work horses, heavy and strong, but others were of lighter build, borrowed from the stables of the neighboring farms. The tea and tobacco were all loaded, and they had started tying the kegs in place when the alarm came.

"Light in New Romney tower, Mr. Fletcher!"

A sudden stillness descended on the whole group; action was frozen for a second—arms upraised with kegs, fingers buckling harness. A low, uneasy murmur rose in a few throats. Over to the east they could all see it—a light that blinked and disappeared, and blinked again. Someone was waving a lantern from the tower of New Romney church.

Then Paul's voice was heard, dry, matter-of-fact, carrying along the line of waiting men and animals.

"All right . . . you all know what you have to do! There's time yet. That light means they've only got to the edge of New Romney. The kegs still in the boats are to stay there. Row them out and drop them overside. We'll pick them up tomorrow. Get the stuff that's been landed into the carts—and move yourselves or you'll all have the privilege of serving in His Majesty's Navy."

He turned and called to the end of the line. "Jerry! Start the potato carts moving! You've plenty of time to get to the turn-off by Carter's place before they do. Smartly, now! *Move, boys!*"

He strode along the line, checking the loaded carts. The head of the procession was ready to move; at the end two carts detached themselves and started off in the direction of New Romney.

Jane plucked at Paul's arm as he passed. "What's happening?" she said softly.

"Came before their time, damn them!" He was poised, ready to move on. "I've two carts loaded with potatoes as a blind. They'll wait by the turn-off to Carter's farm, and when the Dragoons come up, they'll think they're part of the cargo making towards the hide. If Joe can lead them a bit of a chase, then it's extra time in our hands."

Then his tone dropped. "Now you get out of here! Do you understand me? Go and get Bess, and by the time the Dragoons touch Barham, you should be the other side of Lydd. I'd send a man with you but I'll need every hand for unloading at the other end."

"Where are you taking the cargo?"

"It's better if you don't know that. But it's not far from here, and we'll all be under cover before the Dragoons start nosing round."

He put his hand on her shoulder and spun her round. *"Now, go! Quickly!"*

Without a word she started moving down the line, heading in the direction of the church. She ducked in between two carts, and started helping with the loading on the off-side, out of Paul's sight. There was haste but no confusion; the loading went on in an orderly fashion. The boats had already pushed off from the shingle, and out further in the bay she heard the first splashes as the kegs started to go overside. Although she knew it was common practice to dump the kegs in an emergency, and retrieve them later, each separate splash was like a blow to her. Suddenly she was conscious of her water-logged boots, and the weight of the wet cloak pulling at her shoulders.

The loading was finished. The women stood by watching as

the men tightened the last ropes, and the head of the procession started to move. It was heading towards Lydd. The hide Paul had selected would be an emergency one; no one wanted to leave the cargo close to the coast or to the place where it came ashore. But there was no choice. Mounted Dragoons could easily overtake the cavalcade, and the cargo was rich enough for them to risk an armed clash with the smugglers. Paul had to get it hidden as soon as possible, and move it when he could.

They were dragging the boats up on the shingle now. Out in the darkness she knew the *Dolphin* would be preparing to stand out to sea. The women were withdrawing silently to the cottages. She remembered Paul's orders to get away from Barham, and she turned and marched with the procession until she came to the gate of the churchyard. She slipped inside and stood pressed against the rough stone pillars until the last of the carts had passed. Quiet fell on Barham then. Only a few sounds—retreating footsteps on the shingle and the cobbles, doors closing, low voices fading into nothing.

By the time the single street rang again with the beat of the Dragoons' horses, Barham-in-the-Marsh would present the appearance of a sleeping village.

To Jane the strange new quiet was suddenly sinister and she wanted to leave it behind. She hurried along the path to the great main door of the church, and past it around the corner to the crypt entrance.

"Bess!" she called softly. "Bess!" There was answering movement in the darkness as the mare stirred. Bess meant for Jane familiarity and a means of escape; a warm sense of relief flooded her, and she quickened her pace almost to a run. It was already too late to stop when she remembered the steps leading to the crypt. Poised on the edge of them, she clawed the air frantically for a second before she started falling.

She woke to full consciousness with a gasp as the cold, evil-smelling water hit her face. For some time she had a sensation of nothing beyond darkness and the pain, and then she became aware of a warm hand cradled under her head. She could hear a voice—a woman's voice, but the words ran together in a blur.

She sighed, and turned her head to try to shut out the voice; she

wanted to slip back into the ease of unconsciousness, where the
pain didn't trouble her.

"Com'on now! Com'on! Y'll 'ave t' wake up quick-like because
there ain't no time. . . ."

Jane, more awake now, remembered the voice. It belonged to
the young woman who had worked beside her unloading the boats.
She struggled to respond to the urgency in it now. She made an
effort to sit up, and found the other woman's strong arms support-
ing her back.

"There—that's right, now. Y'll be yerself in just a minute. . . ."

The gloom lightened a little as Jane's eyes grew accustomed to
it. She was sitting on the stone flagging at the bottom of the steps
leading to the crypt door. The woman knelt beside her. Jane put
her hand to her forehead, gingerly, feeling the grazed skin and the
blood slowly oozing through.

"I dunno wat 'appened," she said, slipping back into the broad
accent.

"Y' just forgot them steps were there," the woman said. "Gave
y' a nasty bump. Sorry I 'ad t' wake y' so sudden-like, but them
Dragoons are 'ere."

Jane started. "Already?"

"Y've been out t' it a long time. I 'ad t' get one o' them vases
orf a grave t' throw the water over y'. Stinks, don't it?"

"The Dragoons . . ." Jane repeated. "My God, we gotta get
outta 'ere."

"Y'r dead right!" the woman said laconically. "First thing y'
know they'll be bustin' in here lookin' t' see if we've put the cargo
'ere. If they find y' y're a dead duck—y' bein' a stranger. An' dressed
like that. . . ."

Leaning on the other woman, Jane got slowly to her feet. A terrible weakening pain shot through her ankle when she put her
weight on it, but she didn't say anything about it because there
was nothing either of them could do. They started up the steps,
Jane supported by the young woman.

By the time she got to the top, Jane was breathing heavily. Beads
of sweat stood out on her face and neck. But the light breeze blew
coldly on her. She discovered that she had lost her head scarf, and

her hair was soaking from the douche of stagnant water. It smelled vile.

"'Ow did y' find me?" she managed to say between pinched lips.

"That's easy! I followed y'."

"Why?"

"Why—because I'm the curious type, and yer a stranger. An' . . . an' because I never 'eard of Paul Fletcher takin' up with one o' the local girls. . . ."

"I ain't local!" Jane said curtly. "An' I ain't 'is girl, neither . . . more's the pity! T'morrow I'm crossin' to Roscoff, and I ain't never goin' t' see 'im again."

"Then wat are y' doin' 'ere?"

They had reached Bess's side, Jane hobbling painfully. The mare began to nuzzle her inquiringly, and Jane could have sobbed with relief to feel Bess's great, patient strength under her hands.

"I'm 'ere because I brought a message to 'im—and 'e don't like t' see a pair of 'ands go idle."

She put her uninjured foot in the stirrup and with a grim effort swung herself up, pushed and half lifted by her companion. Up there she felt safe—almost independent of help. She looked down.

"I been told the Marsh folk never asks questions—it ain't 'ealthy!" Then she added, "But I'm grateful t' y' . . . would 'ave lain there waitin' for the Dragoons t' pick me up if y' 'adn't been nosey. . . ."

"Ain't nothin'," the woman said briefly. "Glad t' 'elp . . . an' I didn't mean t'— Y' wouldn't tell Mr. Fletcher, would y'?" she said in alarm.

"Told y' I ain't never goin' t' see Mr. Fletcher again," Jane said. "But I'm obliged t' y' . . . much obliged. Wat's yer name?"

"Rose."

She put her hand down to the woman. "Thanks . . ." Then abruptly she stiffened. "Wot's that?"

"It's them—the Dragoons! Y' gotta go!" At the further end of the village they could hear the steady beat of horses' hooves, and rough irritable voices raised.

"Wot about yerself?" Jane said. "'Ow are y' goin' t' get 'ome?"

Rose broke in. "I'm all right. I'll cut along the fields 'ere and get in the back door. Y'd best go the same way."

"Can't!" Jane said. "I only know the road from Lydd, an' if they chase me into the fields and with all them dykes . . ."

"Yer right!" Rose agreed. "Well—get goin' then. Y'll stay ahead o' them if y' get movin' now!"

They were too close. She knew that as soon as she drew close to the village street. Down near the beach she could hear them, hammering on the cottage doors, shouting questions and orders to the villagers. The main body of the Dragoons was still down there, but only a few houses separated her from the head of the column. But there was equal danger in turning back and attempting to find her way through the maze of dykes where she could be cut off with ease. Better to trust to Bess's speed. She knew if she were caught there was no kind of explanation that would cover her presence here in these water-soaked clothes.

She leaned low to the mare's ear. "Bess! Sweetheart, it's up to you!"

Then she dug in her heels and Bess sprang forward. The sudden clatter of her iron-shod hooves on the cobbles seemed in Jane's ears like the thunder of a thousand tiles sliding off one of the cottage roofs. She turned Bess's head towards Lydd, praying that by this time Paul would have cleared the carts off the main road, and that she would not be leading her pursuers directly to him.

The shout went up immediately.

"Halt! Halt in the name of the King!"

She did not waste time turning back to look—it was still too dark to see anything clearly, and while it made the road ahead full of unseen potholes for Bess, at least it covered her identity. Bess was too well known on the Marsh to allow her to be seen in broad daylight. Grimly, Jane remembered her own red hair streaming behind her like a banner that anyone could read.

She had overlooked the possibility that the Dragoons would send one man to the Lydd end of the village to stop anyone leaving it while they searched. She couldn't see him, but he was there—mounted, and directly in her path.

"Halt! —In the name of His Majesty!"

She rode straight on, and the dark shape of the other horse seemed to spring like an apparition out of the darkness. She tugged at Bess's head sharply to avoid a collision. Startled, Bess reared, and

Jane was nearly thrown. She was too frightened and occupied trying to keep her seat—clinging wildly with her knees and thankful
that she was astride—to be able to do anything about the soldier.
He was reaching out to take the bridle when she slammed her heels
hard into Bess's side. The mare started forward with a jerk, and
carried her beyond the reach of the man's hand.

She had gone a few yards when she heard the sharp whine of the
bullet over her head.

She had reason then to be thankful for Robert Turnbull's love
of good horseflesh. Out on the open road Bess had her head. She
responded to Jane's touch with a burst of speed that made the wind
sing past Jane's ears, and left the sounds of the soldier's pursuit
behind. She bent low over Bess's neck, not demanding any more
of the mare, knowing that she now had as much as Bess could give.
The mare had endurance and courage far beyond her own, and
she needed no urging.

At the outskirts of Lydd she checked Bess's pace to listen. There
was no sound of anyone on the road behind her. At a more sober
pace she rode through Lydd, and turned on the Appledore road
towards Blake's Reach. She felt very much alone, and lonely. The
light grew rapidly.

By the time Blake's Reach came into sight it was full dawn. It
had been a journey of acute discomfort—the weight of her wet
clothes, and the chafing where they rubbed against the saddle, the
stiffness she was beginning to feel from riding astride. Apart from
that her head ached violently where she had hit it in her fall, and
her ankle was swelling inside her boot. She eased herself in the
saddle to try to take the weight off her ankle, but it was necessary
to keep Bess to a fair pace because the danger of her situation increased with the growing light. She gave a long sigh of relief and
weariness as she crossed the dyke and began to climb the hill to
Blake's Reach.

The gates stood open as always. The house looked gentle in the
dawn—and welcoming. She looked at it with satisfaction, remembering the rich cargo and what it would do for Blake's Reach. It was
hers—and safe.

Nothing seemed to be stirring, and nothing seemed amiss. She
began to wonder if Patrick had stayed awake, and if he would come

to meet her. Her ankle now pained her badly enough to make her want help to dismount.

But no one came, and she couldn't risk calling out. So with infinite effort she pulled herself out of the saddle and slid to the ground, almost crying out as her weight came on her ankle. She saw that Bess had water and oats before leaving her, and then braced herself for the walk across the yard to the kitchen.

But the door opened before she reached it. And it wasn't Patrick or Kate who stood there. Jane saw a tall, lean man, whose black hair was pulled roughly back with a ribbon, and whose dark eyes in his sallow, handsome face, regarded her with calm intentness. He wore an old, faded jacket, and his stockings were badly torn. His complexion had the pallor of prison upon it.

There was no mistaking his air of belonging here at Blake's Reach.

She felt the blood drain from her face.

"Charlie! You've come back!"

5

Afterwards she was to remember, through the shock and the fear, how he cut her boot away from her swollen ankle with gentle, almost tender hands. He spoke hardly at all, except to murmur swift instructions to Kate and Patrick to bring him water and clean cloths to tear into strips. They obeyed him in silence, too much in awe of his presence and his authority to offer suggestions or comments.

After her ankle was bound up, he took fresh water and started to bathe the dirt and blood from her face. He put his hand under her chin, and turned her face towards the candle as he worked.

"Smuggling?" he said, looking down at her.

She nodded.

"How did this happen?" He indicated her ankle and the cut forehead.

"The Dragoons were coming. I fell down the church steps. . . ."

"Everyone safe? Is the cargo safe?"

She nodded again.

"Good!"

He waited, silent, in the settle by the fire, while she drank the

toddy that Patrick had prepared. It was impossible any longer for
her to fight the weariness which swept over her; even the shock
of Charles' return was numbed. She couldn't hold her confused
thoughts in place—thoughts of Charles, and of Paul and the cargo,
and of what the future would be now that the heir had come back
to Blake's Reach. Her hands grasping the pewter mug began to
tremble.

Charles was on his feet instantly, and took the mug from her.
Then his tall frame bent over her, and she felt herself being lifted
bodily. The room swam dizzily before her eyes. Patrick sprang to
open the door, and go before them with a candle.

"Anne's chamber?" she heard Charles say.

And she was conscious of him, waiting beyond the drawn bed-
curtain while Kate struggled to get off her clothes. She waved Kate
away when the old woman brought her bed-gown.

"Can't! . . . not now!"

She closed her eyes and sank gratefully into the softness of the
down mattress. Someone had drawn the curtains and the room was
hushed, but still she could hear, as if far off, the sounds of the
summer morning—the birds and the harsh cries of the sheep. She
breathed in the peace and safety of it, the knowledge that she was
home.

Then the memory of Charles intruded. She opened her eyes heavily. He had pulled back the bed-curtains, and was standing quite
close, looking down at her; even in the dimness she could see his
dark straight brows knotted in a reflective frown.

"So you came," she said drowsily. "You came after all, Charles.
Well, I should have known that some day you'd come. I have no
luck. I always lose—like Anne. . . ."

"Anne was a good loser, Jane."

She turned abruptly on her side, away from him, wanting to sink
into sleep, and feeling only the sheer physical pleasure of stretching
her naked limbs, freed from the wet, chafing clothes, in the great
bed. The weight of her hair dragged on the pillow. Suddenly she
was aware of a question that she had struggled with, and which had
now formulated in her mind. She turned back to him, opening her
eyes and half-propping herself up on her elbow.

"But you were in prison," she said. "How did you get out? Did they set you free?"

He shook his head. "Some of the money Turnbull's been sending over found its place. I came out of La Force in a coffin, and the dead man is buried in the courtyard. I got to Dunkirk, and a lugger —a smuggler's lugger, Jane—took me to Rye. They were Rye townsmen, and they trusted my pledge of Robert Turnbull's name to pay them for the passage. He gave them the money—and gave me a meal and a horse to bring me here."

She dropped back on the pillow.

"And so you knew about me? You knew I was here? . . ."

"Robert Turnbull described you well—with great feeling—but he omitted some aspects."

"Or he doesn't know them," she said drowsily. "Perhaps even Robert didn't guess it all. But what does that matter? He'll know soon enough. We'll talk later, Charlie . . . later."

"Yes—later."

She fell asleep under his gaze. Standing motionless, he watched her for some time, watched her features relax as her sleep grew deeper, and her movements less wild. Almost involuntarily the name came to his lips as he bent to pull the blankets higher on her shoulders.

"Anne! . . ."

Then he drew the bed-curtains tightly, and left her to sleep.

PART THREE

CHAPTER ONE

IT WAS A FAIR DAY, WITH LIGHT, INCONSPICUOUS CLOUDS MOVING across the Marsh sky, and the warmth of the sun came pleasantly through Paul's coat as he rode. But he had no thoughts to spare for the leafy greenness of the countryside, or the brilliant colors of the wild fowl in the dykes that beat to cover at his approach. Since yesterday, Charles Blake had occupied the center of his thoughts.

He had dressed with unusual care for the meeting ahead of him, and at the same time despised himself for doing so. He had no patience with the niceties of fine dressing, and no aptitude for them, but he wore his best shirt, and he had tied his hair back with some care. Even with all this, he felt that, beside Charles Blake, he cut no very elegant figure.

Yesterday, Charles had dismounted at his door, and had taken a glass of brandy in his sitting room. With a dismay Paul tried to contain, he had heard the story of Charles' return to Blake's Reach the night before, and of Jane's arrival in the dawn with a wrenched ankle, and the bruises and dishevelment of the night still upon her. Paul felt his face grow hot with shame as he realized that, while he had got his cargo safely to the hide, Jane had been left behind, and had nearly been taken. For Paul it was bad enough that she should have been in danger, but the knowledge had an added sting that Charles Blake should know how completely he had failed to protect her.

Irritably he had gone to pour himself more brandy, conscious of the other man's dark eyes upon him in quiet appraisal. Charles still wore the thin faded coat in which he had arrived, and coarse stockings borrowed from Patrick, but he looked, and was, a man of great authority. Paul didn't like the French, and was reluctant to praise them; but this point he had to concede to Charles.

Charles had come with something to say, and Paul gave his full attention as the other talked. Jane, he heard, had wakened about noon, and Charles had sipped a glass of wine in her bed chamber

with her as she had hungrily eaten the food Kate had brought up.
Paul recognized that there had been no point in Jane's trying to
hold back any of the truth from Charles, when he had already seen
so much; Charles had been brought up on the Marsh, and he was
no fool. She had to trust him, whether she liked it or not—and
trust the fact that nine out of ten bystanders were sympathetic to
the smuggler rather than the King's import duties. So she had told
him about Paul, and about the *Dolphin*, and in the course of telling him that, much more was revealed. Charles had heard, grudgingly at first, and then with more ease, how she had borrowed
money from Turnbull, and why; he learned what she had struggled
to do at Blake's Reach since she had come there.

It was a story Charles had heard the night before from Robert
Turnbull, but on Jane's lips it had reality.

"An amazing woman!" he said to Paul as he finished the retelling.

"Yes . . . amazing," Paul echoed, and there was a twist of pain
in his heart to have to discuss Jane in this way with a man who,
fifteen minutes earlier, had been dead to him.

Charles accepted more brandy, and sniffed and rolled it on his
tongue appreciatively. He was silent for a little time, as if weighing
up the man in whose house he sat. He examined, with minute detail, everything he saw—the jumble of books, the charts spread in
seeming confusion, the mariner's instruments, and lastly, the work-
hardened hands of the man himself.

He put aside the glass. "So then," he said, "after Jane told me all
this, I rode into Rye to see Turnbull again." He paused, looking
carefully at Paul. "From him I came directly here."

"So? . . ." Paul said.

"So . . . you must guess why I've come. I want to join you and
Jane. I want a part of the *Dolphin*."

Paul's gathering resentment broke out then. He spoke quickly.
"And what the devil makes you think you can just walk in here out
of the blue and say, 'I want part of the *Dolphin*'? What makes you
think you've any chance of getting it?"

Charles waved him to silence. "I'm sorry if I offend you—but
my own need is urgent enough to force me to be blunt. It's quite
simple. The government of the Revolution has taken every sou I
owned, every hectare of land. I come here and find that my uncle,

Spencer Blake, didn't weaken with age in his determination to leave nothing of Blake's Reach for his heirs." He spread his hands. "What am I to do? I need money."

"And do you think you can join us without contributing your share?" Paul said coldly. "Or is that your price for allowing Jane to remain at Blake's Reach? If so, then she doesn't need to remain. There are other doors open to her. . . ."

"You go too fast, Mr. Fletcher. And too far." Charles quite deliberately waited to take a leisurely sip of his brandy before he picked up again.

"As I said, I need money. And I haven't forgotten that here the quickest way to make money is in smuggling. For that I'm prepared to do more than contribute my share. I want to buy the *Dolphin* outright."

"Buy it! I don't see—"

"Unlike Jane, Mr. Fletcher, I, being the heir, have the right to sell the King's Pearl."

It was true, of course, Paul thought. For the first time he stopped to wonder if his words to Charles had been too hasty, and spoken clumsily. Possession of the Pearl implied a great many things, among them the fact that if Charles had wanted to take the *Dolphin* from him, he need not be here talking about it. The boat-builder at Folkestone was ready to sell it to whoever came with the purchase price in his hand. Charles could have had it without consulting either himself or Jane. Even in the light of this thought Paul wasn't prepared to like the French any better, but now he reminded himself that Charles Blake was half English, and also that he had been brought up on the Marsh.

He tried to cover his apprehension with unconcern. He shrugged. "I see . . . then I'm in your hands, Mr. Blake . . . as far as the *Dolphin* is concerned."

"Quite the contrary!" Charles answered. "Do you think I could run this operation without you, or someone as skilled as you are? Do I look like a seaman to you? —Or do you imagine these people would follow me as they do you? It's obvious that I shall need your services and your help."

He smiled a little. "No less an authority than Robert Turnbull

assures me that for this job there's no better man on the whole
coast than Paul Fletcher."

"*Turnbull* assures you? How the hell does he know what kind
of a man I am?"

Charles' eyebrows shot up. "I assumed that you would know—"

"Know *what?*" He almost shouted the words.

"—That Turnbull has money invested with almost every smuggling operation of size between here and Dover!"

Afterwards Paul thought that he must have made some vague
reply to Charles' statement, but he had no recollection of it. He got
to his feet slowly, fumbling for the glass, and walked over to the
table where he had put the decanter. He poured brandy into his
empty glass, not because he wanted it, but because he suddenly
found himself standing there, and he needed to give his hands
something to do. Then he wandered to the window, and gazed
out without seeing anything. Turnbull involved in smuggling. . . .
The thought needed getting used to. . . . And not just involved in
it in a small way, as many people were, but up to his neck in it!
What shocked Paul was that he, who was so deeply in the smuggling
trade himself, had not guessed where it was that a country attorney
would get the money to live in such style, or what kind of clients
Turnbull had who kept him riding back and forth across the Marsh,
instead of sitting solidly at his desk in Watchbell Street. He played
with the picture of Robert Turnbull in this new role for a minute,
fitting together the pieces, seeing the advantages the attorney
would have. There were few people who had such a close knowledge
of this whole area, or who could talk privately with so many different types of people without the slightest suspicion resting on him.
He made friends easily, and he was trusted, and since an attorney's
business was always private, no one would question his comings
and goings. His alert mind would store information as he plied his
acquaintances with ale or wine, and what could be easier than to
pass it on to the quarter where it could be most helpful. A man without an enemy, was Robert Turnbull, and the whole Marsh tumbled
its problems and its gossip into his ready ear. The enigma now made
sense, and Paul was conscious of a dawning feeling of admiration
for Turnbull, who could play the role of the bystander with such

ease. It annoyed him to recall how many times he himself had been deceived—not so much deceived, as simply unaware. He began to feel foolish because he had never before seen or suspected what was now so plain; at the same time he could admire the discipline that had kept Turnbull firmly in the background. Few men could have been in his position of power, and never succumb to the urge to use it.

Or had he used it? Suddenly Paul remembered that Turnbull was his brother's attorney, and he remembered how James had always seemed unwilling to give direct answers to Paul's questions, had delayed giving instructions, had seemed to wait on the word and command of someone else. If James was connected with Turnbull in smuggling operations it explained many things . . . how James had got his contacts, how he had information about the movements of the revenue cruisers and preventive officers up and down the countryside, how he had had plans laid, and a ready-formed group of men to carry them out when Paul had come back to the Marsh. Turnbull had been, no doubt, the source of all this.

Abruptly he turned back to Charles. "And how long have *you* known about Turnbull?" he demanded roughly.

Charles seemed indifferent. "How can I remember? It's a very long time ago. It was Turnbull who first asked Spencer to agree to rent the church on the cliff as a hide . . . more than twenty years ago, that must be. Turnbull was a young man then."

"All that time—!" Paul shrugged again, trying to dismiss his irritation. "Then he's devilish clever!"

Then he added, quickly, "What I don't understand is why he gave Jane the loan of that money. . . . Of course, he must have guessed what she wanted to do with it. He must have known she would find out about the church, and not stop until she knew the rest of the story. He must also have known that, if our venture together was successful, I'd refuse to work for my brother any longer. He cut off one of his own sources of profit. Why?"

"Probably because a woman asked him, and that woman was Jane," Charles said. "Turnbull has given a lifetime of service to the Blakes, and for Anne or Jane I feel that he would give much more than service. Even for me, who during these years have grown almost a stranger to him, he did more than could possibly be expected of him. He was the only man I trusted when I lived here on the Marsh. . . . Did you know he has been sending money all the time I've been in prison to try and buy my freedom? Is it surprising that he should find himself unable to refuse Jane? —Even if it meant a loss to himself?"

He added, quietly, "So I've asked him if he will join us—if he would like to have a share in the cargoes of the *Dolphin*. Do you have any objections?"

"Objections?" Paul repeated dryly. "I'm not giving the orders any more. And it seems that I'm back working for my old employer. . . ." He leaned back in his chair, and looked at the ceiling, a quizzical, half-defensive grin on his face. "What luck I have! Just time for one cargo from the *Dolphin*, and already Jane has been in danger, the Dragoons have been at my heels, and now *you* land on the beach. It's a wonder we didn't have the good fortune to bring you over from France as well. Under the circumstances, that would have been entirely fitting."

Charles rose to his feet, laughing a little, and shaking his head. "Ah, my friend . . . I'm too lately delivered from prison to wish to put my foot on another man's neck. You'll be master of your ship, that I promise you. And as for Turnbull—he has long since learned the skills of remaining in the background, and, as you know, he can sometimes be of very great value. We each of us need the other . . . it's as well to bear that in mind."

He put out his hand to Paul. "Turnbull will come to Blake's Reach tomorrow afternoon. May I expect you then also? I thought it only fair to Jane that she should hear what final arrangements we make between us. You agree? . . ."

Paul nodded, taking the other's hand firmly. Then he stood by the cottage door and watched Charles ride away towards Blake's Reach, noting his relaxed air and his splendid seat on the horse. He was hatless, and his unpowdered black hair gave him a jaunty, nonchalant look, almost gipsylike if one did not see the face beneath it—the sensitive, rather weary face with the dark eyes that had stared at death for a long time. Paul had searched for qualities in this man that his talk with the French merchants and fishermen had led him to expect in the despised aristocrat of their description. As different as the French and English court and society were, so he had looked to find those differences in Charles Blake. He had looked for the airs and manners of the nobles who had gossiped and flirted the days away at Versailles, whose refinements and fopperies were imitated by Europe, and whose perversions gave scandal to the world.

As usual, Paul thought, rumor had been colored and exaggerated, or else Charles Blake had not been touched by the reeking stench of decay that had hung over all French institutions. Charles had been less than a day in England, and already he was firmly gathering up the threads of his inheritance, weaving the strands closer and stronger, making the best that he could of its texture. Even with the effects of prison and the voyage from France still on him, he had set about taking his affairs in hand with a firmness and confidence that Paul could not help but admire. There was boldness and purpose in Charles Blake; it remained to see whether there was also staying power.

After Charles had left him, he had gone, more from a sense of restlessness than for a real purpose, into Rye. There, as he had expected, the place buzzed with the news of Charles' return. He sat moodily over his brandy in the George and listened to the comments and speculations passed on every side of him. They ranged from predictions of final and complete ruin for Blake's Reach, to the rosiest dreams of future prosperity; almost in the same minute he heard opinions that the touch of Charles' effete aristocracy was all the estate needed to finish it, or that he would revive and restore it with the money he had inherited from his mother. The opinions varied according to whether or not the speaker had approved of Jane; now that she was deposed some were regretful, others were slyly glad. Silently Paul cursed their busy tongues, and wondered why he had come to hear what he knew quite certainly would be said.

And they were saying it. As the unspoken thoughts had formed in his heart, he heard the words uttered aloud. They said that Jane would have Blake's Reach in any case—that she had always meant to have it, and there was one sure way. Charles had come without a wife to Blake's Reach, and Jane would see he did not stay that way for long. She had a better head for business than her mother, and would never allow things to drift as Anne had done. Jane and William would never leave Blake's Reach.

Close to Paul, a man stretched out for his replenished tankard and said confidently, "It weren't no light-minded thing that redhead did—coming all the way from London to Blake's Reach and spending good money on it. She has her heart fixed on it, and she'll have it, one way or t'other."

Paul wanted to stand up and shout to the crowded room that it was not so, to deny it with all his strength—but that was impossible because he was himself unable to stifle the doubt that had come to occupy and possess his heart. She said she loved him, and he wanted to believe it; but there was no telling how strong her attachment to the ideal of family and tradition had become. To him it was a false ideal, but to Jane it was new and exciting, and there was a chance that it might prove stronger than whatever she felt for him. Now Charles had returned, the real and legitimate heir to Blake's Reach, and he was no weakling fool, but a man who appeared to have combined some of the best results of good birth and character, a sharp-witted man willing to take a risk, a man with no illusions, but a dangerous charm.

Not even the repeated brandies Paul drank, as the evening wore on, would still the doubt. He had to face the worst danger he had yet known—and he could take no action against a formless, untouchable enemy.

He still carried his fear and apprehension as he rode towards Blake's Reach to keep his appointment with Charles—that, and the faint headache the brandy had left him. He was afraid of what he would see that afternoon; he was afraid to have his fears confirmed.

As he turned up the hill towards the house he saw a horseman by the gates. It was Robert Turnbull, and he had dismounted and stood talking to William; the heads of William and the attorney were close together. At Paul's approach Turnbull straightened.

"Good afternoon," he said pleasantly. His lips were slightly smiling.

It was a shock for Paul to look closely at Turnbull and to realize that, unconsciously, he had been expecting a change in the man's appearance. It was strange to know suddenly some of the things that had been hidden beneath the façade of the busy, respectable legal business in Watchbell Street, and to see that Turnbull himself betrayed none of these things. He was discreet and affable, as always, dressed in his usual expensive, quiet clothes. The glance he turned on William was kindly and warm.

Paul began to feel that it would be easier to command smuggling operations for Turnbull directly, than to do it through the agency of his brother. His features relaxed. "Good afternoon," he replied. Then he looked at William. "How are you? How are George and Washington?"

"They're well," William said hastily. But his mind was on something more exciting. "My Cousin Charles has come back," he said. "He escaped from prison in a coffin. He escaped from the Frenchies."

"Yes—I know."

"And he's going to live here now," William went on. "He's going to live here with Jane and me. Jane said he really owns Blake's Reach . . . but we don't have to go! We can stay here . . . and Charles took me riding with him this morning. We went clear across to Saltwood Castle. I've never seen anyone ride as well as my Cousin Charles. . . ."

Paul felt the dismay rising in his heart again as he looked at the bright, eager face of the child.

2

Already Blake's Reach was different. Following Turnbull into Spencer's old sitting room, Paul felt the difference. Jane had cleaned and put this room into order, but she had never been able to dent the masculine stamp Spencer had put upon it. Now Charles had come, and he had made this room his own—in a subtle fashion, without changing it visibly. There was no doubt who would be master in this house.

Paul's eyes went immediately to Jane, who sat on a high-backed chair with her bandaged leg resting on a footstool. He examined her face carefully, and felt the difference there, too; Jane was not sure of herself. She was wary of Charles, and feeling her way. But, Paul noticed, she didn't appear to draw any sense of comfort or support either from his own presence. She smiled at him, but it was a brief smile. It was the first time he had seen her since they had stood together on the shingle at Barham, but there seemed to be no acknowledgment of that in the rather reserved look she gave him. She put up her hand uncertainly to toy with the curls that lay on her forehead. He realized she must have arranged them that way to hide the cut Charles had told him about; she was pale, and her body seemed tense. He moved to go and take a seat near her, but she had started to talk to Turnbull. Disheartened, he stood where he was.

Then Charles came in, and they looked at him expectantly. In a quiet voice he greeted them, and poured wine for Paul and Turnbull. Jane declined it, and he took none for himself. Paul found himself, even in Jane's presence, unable to take his eyes off the tall figure in the same threadbare coat of yesterday, who had taken his stance, legs astride, before the mantel. He came to the business of the afternoon without preliminaries.

Tomorrow, he said, he was going to London, and he would offer the King's Pearl as security against a loan. He would bargain for the highest price he could get, and trust to luck to pay it back before the Pearl should be forfeited.

"I agree with Jane," he said, looking from one face to the other, "that if the Pearl has to go; it has to go, because Blake's Reach has never stood in such need of what it can bring."

They discussed then the details of using the money. Paul was to negotiate the purchase of the *Dolphin* from the Folkestone boat-builder, but Charles was to be the outright owner. All four of them were to share equally in the costs of the cargo, but Charles, as owner, would take two-fifths of the profits.

Jane, who had been silent until then, spoke. "I will, of course, now start repaying Robert's loan—from my share of the cargoes. I imagine Charles will prefer to make improvements to Blake's Reach in his own time, and Robert's money needn't be used for that. . . ."

Turnbull cut in: "With the interest . . . you haven't forgotten the interest?"

Charles looked across at him, his eyebrows shooting up.

Jane gestured quickly. "It was a . . . a pleasantry! I was to give Robert the first rose from the garden here each spring until the loan was repaid." She didn't let her eyes go to Paul as she said this.

Now Charles smiled. "It's most certainly an interest I should insist on being paid were I in Robert's place."

Paul moved restlessly in his chair. "The *Dolphin* . . ." he said sharply.

"Yes? . . ." They had all turned towards him.

He drummed his fingers thoughtfully a moment, as if he had not been fully prepared to speak his mind, and the words had come too quickly. But they were waiting for him. He frowned. "It seems to me from all I've heard about the value of the Pearl, that it will fetch more than's needed to buy the *Dolphin*. And with us all sharing the cargo, the individual contribution is smaller, and the profits less." Now he looked directly at Charles. "Why not use the rest to buy or hire another vessel? You can't put Blake's Reach back to what it was overnight, and in the meantime the money could be earning you round about five times your investment."

Turnbull gave a little exclamation. "Fletcher's right! As long as you're going to borrow on the Pearl, you must get as much as you can and let it earn for you. . . ."

Charles waved them to silence. "I have plans for the rest of the money. At the moment they don't include spending much on Blake's Reach . . . and I'm not sure even in the end Blake's Reach will have anything spent on it."

"*Other* plans?" It was Jane who spoke, the words forced from her in a gasp. She hadn't wanted to question Charles, but his rejection of Blake's Reach had touched her rawly. Two spots of color flamed suddenly in her cheeks. Paul wanted to turn away from the sight of her distress.

Charles nodded. ". . . a private matter." But then he looked once more at Jane, and suddenly he threw up his hands. "Ah, *mon Dieu*, why should it be private from my friends? I keep forgetting that I am free—and in England. I know that I may speak to you, and you will respect my confidence."

They nodded in agreement, Jane with them, but her hands gripped the arms of the chair tensely as she waited for him to go on.

Charles clasped his hands behind his back.

"It takes less money to buy a strong man out of prison than a sick woman. I will need every penny I can lay hands on—gold to

buy the silence of many people, not just a few—gold to buy the
service and the help she will need to reach a port. She cannot walk
or run, or sleep in the open, as a man can. Nor can she ride out of
La Force in a coffin."

Jane was deadly pale. "Who . . . who is it?" she said in a whisper.

"Her name is Louise de Montignot. She is the widow of the man
who was my greatest friend, Philippe de Montignot, Comte de
Labrit. He died on the guillotine a year ago, and Louise has lately
been brought to La Force. If the guillotine does not have her, she
will cough her lungs out in La Force."

No one said anything; their eyes were fixed on Charles' face. It
had become hard and tight, the cheekbones prominent, and his
eyes bright with anger.

"Philippe was with me in La Force, and before he was murdered
he learned that Louise had also been charged and imprisoned. I
swore to him that while I lived I would not cease trying to aid
and comfort her. I cannot consider myself free of that promise. She
still lives, and I must send gold until there is enough to buy her
out."

"Is it possible?" Paul asked quietly.

"The concierge is human, and, like most humans, greedy. As in
my case, it is possible that, if the danger to himself is not too great,
he can be bought. But from there on the difficulty begins. A sick
woman cannot travel easily, or without attracting notice. She must
have places to rest on the way, and someone to travel with her. I
have friends still in Paris, but it takes time, and there is much danger . . . for Louise and for them."

"And if . . . when she escapes, what then?" Jane's lips were
pinched.

"Then?" Charles repeated. "Then she will come here—to Blake's
Reach."

3

It had been a relief to Jane that the talk between Charles, Paul
and Robert Turnbull had continued until the supper hour; hardly
listening, she had let it flow over her, and her own thoughts had

gone on, thoughts that spiraled forever round Charles' statement that he would bring Louise de Montignot to Blake's Reach.

The three men had eaten supper heartily, absorbed in ever more detailed planning for running cargoes on the *Dolphin*. There was to be more money available, so there could be richer cargoes, more porters, more batmen, larger bribes and better protection. An atmosphere of confidence grew up between them, each adding suggestions and a little argument, but in the end always deferring to Paul's opinion. To Jane's confused mind there seemed to be many toasts to their mutual success, in which she joined, and she repeated the words of the toasts automatically. For some reason Kate's food was better that evening; she had either been inspired by Charles' presence to make extraordinary efforts, or she had been frightened into accepting a few of the hints Patrick poured into her constantly. The best china and glass and silver were set out, and Anne's good linen was on the table. Patrick had even plucked some roses from the vine over the porch and placed them in a silver bowl in the center of the table. Looking at it, Jane paused to wonder how many years it was since Blake's Reach had known such a festive evening.

After supper they had gone to the drawing room where Patrick had lighted a small fire—more to brighten the hearth than for any other reason. Patrick also had responded to the occasion, sensing that whatever plans had put the three men into such fine good humor could hardly bode ill for Jane or William. He left brandy and glasses on the marquetry table. This time it was Paul who lifted Jane and carried her to a seat by the fire. Robert went before them with her footstool. The brandy glasses were filled, and there was yet another toast; Jane responded with stiff lips.

Charles had been in this room before, but only for a cursory glance. Now he wandered about, glass in hand, examining the portraits and the pieces of china displayed in the corner cabinet. He opened the harpsichord, and pressed a few keys lightly, wincing at the jangling sound they made. Then he came back to stand by the fire. Jane saw him looking at the carpet closely. He felt her gaze on him, for he turned to her.

"Aubusson," he murmured, nodding towards the carpet. "It's valuable . . . pity that end is so badly frayed."

"Could it be repaired?" she said.

He shrugged. "Probably . . . but I wonder if it's worth troubling."

She looked away, staring into the fire and sick inside at the implication of his words. She felt the tears prick her eyelids, and once again the thread of talk slipped away from her. This room was familiar to her now—she didn't have to turn to see the colors of beautiful wood surfaces lovingly polished back into life, or the richness of the gold leaf on the china, or the texture and depth of the carpet. She had made this room come to life again. But Charles did not seem to care whether it lived or stayed moldering under its dust. She leaned her head back wearily, and her eyes half closed. Suddenly she was very conscious of the throbbing of her ankle.

At last they went, Paul and Robert, bidding her good night with a briskness that was part of their high satisfaction. Paul's face had undergone a change during the evening—no longer unhappy and full of suspicion. He was once again firmly master of the *Dolphin,* and he, like Jane, had been strongly affected by the news that if Louise de Montignot reached England, Charles would bring her to Blake's Reach.

Jane didn't want to be left alone with Charles. She wanted her bed, and solitude. But she raised her eyes, and found Charles staring at her thoughtfully.

"Paul," he said quietly, "he is your lover?"

She nodded, not troubling to deny it. It began to seem that Charles knew or made a shrewd guess at everything that happened at Blake's Reach. "Yes, he's my lover," she said.

"Why aren't you married? He wants to marry you, doesn't he?"

"I—I don't know. We haven't talked about it."

"You mean you won't allow him to talk about it, Jane. I know a man in love when I see one. He has run away from women before now, but you he would marry tomorrow. You're partners in everything else—why not in this also?"

She shrugged. "Paul isn't a partner in Blake's Reach. He'll go back to the West Indies as soon as there's enough money."

"And he wants you to go with him?"

"Yes."

"And you—you prefer Blake's Reach, Jane. You want him here, don't you? You want him and Blake's Reach both. You have a dream of seeing it back as it used to be, and Paul at your feet, adoring you. Isn't that so?"

"I didn't say it was so. Why do you twist things? . . ."

He gestured back to the portraits. "You're the first real Blake they've had in a hundred years—strong enough and determined enough to do everything you think should be done for this house and this family. Of course . . . you may destroy yourself, but you don't think it would be destruction. You don't see it that way at all."

She was silent. He paced the length of the room, and swung round abruptly, speaking in a louder tone.

"But I came back, Jane, and now you think the dream is finished. I'm a usurper under this roof, aren't I? —Not as good for them—" he nodded back towards the portraits—"as you would have been. Well, I'm not as good, and it's unfortunate for Blake's Reach that I didn't die as I was meant to. You're thinking that, Jane—and it's true! And you've heard me say that I'll bring Louise here, and you're thinking that this house may not have two mistresses. . . ."

Suddenly he flung out his hands in a gesture of dismissal. "Well, Blake's Reach was intended for you, and I'm not sure in the end that it won't be yours, after all. But take care you don't lose your happiness, your youth, and Paul Fletcher to it!"

She could feel the room move around her crazily and there seemed no blood left in her body, no will to deny his words, or oppose him. She pressed her lips together, but she wasn't able to stop the tears that began to slide thinly down her face. But she still was too proud to put up her hands and brush them away.

CHAPTER TWO

CHARLES WAS GONE FROM BLAKE'S REACH ALMOST TWO WEEKS, but even with him away, life did not fall back into the pattern Jane had established. It was true that her orders were taken, and attended to as before, but a feeling of impending change hung over the place. Her rule was temporary, and it was coming to an end.

With her ankle still bandaged she sat in the garden through tedious, impatient hours, and her thoughts were uneasy and confused. The time hung upon her heavily; she longed for the relief from thought and speculation which riding the Marsh on Blonde Bess would have brought. The days grew warmer, and the countryside lost its fresh green. The bright red of the roses on the vine began to fade in the sun, while Jane twisted restlessly in her chair, her thoughts forever on Charles.

Robert Turnbull rode out to Blake's Reach several times during Charles' absence. Not once did he refer to the last time he and Jane had seen each other alone, the night they had dined together at the Wool Pack in Folkestone. He talked without any sign of constraint: their plans for the *Dolphin*, Charles' return, the details of Charles' escape—all in his usual calm manner, and Jane began to wonder if perhaps she had imagined his firm, passionate kiss as he left her that night. But other things recalled it, if not Robert's words. He had withdrawn a little from her, no longer so eager or spontaneous; she began to be conscious of the difference in their ages. Now when he talked to her, he was once again the man who had loved her mother and was kind to her, Jane, only for the sake of the memories he carried. She knew that he would never again kiss her.

But to Robert, at least, she could talk about Louise de Montignot, and find some relief in that. Endlessly she speculated about Charles' saying he would bring Louise to Blake's Reach, and she wondered aloud about what he had meant by the statement that, in the end, Blake's Reach might be hers. Robert had no answers for these questionings; Louise de Montignot was still in La Force, and it seemed probable to him that she would never come out.

Paul also came to Blake's Reach. He came at night, and discreetly, but he was full of good humor, and an aggressive jubilation. Firstly, he liked Charles' absence more than his presence at Blake's Reach, and he would have preferred it if Charles had stayed in London altogether. But apart from that, in these two weeks, the *Dolphin* had completed two trips to Flushing, and was already on her way back there. The runs had gone off without delay or danger, and the cargoes had been large and profitable. Because of the long twilights fewer vessels were making the runs from France and Holland, and there were more men available as crew and porters. The added danger of these runs did not seem to trouble Paul. On his second visit, he brought Jane two hundred guineas in gold pieces. They lay heavily in her lap as she sat and listened to him.

He paced the length of the room, his excitement and impatience revealed in every movement. "Do you see it, Jane?" he said, gesturing towards the leather pouch she held. "Do you see it? And that's just the beginning! From now on it will be profit . . . and more profit! A few more months like this and we'd have enough to go." Then he frowned. "At least we'd have enough if we didn't have to split the profits with Charles and Turnbull." He shrugged. "Well . . . the one good thing in this arrangement is that I know the *Dolphin* won't be lifted from under my nose. And my brother James can't get his hands on it either."

Then the excitement would die a little, and his voice grow softer. He would sit on the floor by her footstool, leaning back against her chair, taking her hand and pressing it gently against his lips and cheeks. He would talk then about the Indies, his tone filled with a longing and a regret; he would try to describe to her how the beaches looked in the dawn, and the strange violence of a tropical thunderstorm. Her fingers would stroke his face lightly. She heard not so much his words, as the recollection he had of some bright dream. She didn't need to understand the sense of what he said; she knew that Paul, in this mood, with this tone of voice could sway her heart as nothing else could. She wanted to gather him to her, but there was no physical hunger as there had been before; these were the peaceful moments of love.

In these weeks the news of Charles' return had gone far beyond Rye, and the near neighborhood of Blake's Reach. Robert and Paul both reported comments they had heard, and she guessed bitterly that what they neglected to tell her were the questions and the gossip they had listened to about the probable future of herself and William. She thought of all the women of the prominent families who had refused to call on her here; and she knew what they would be saying.

It was Robert who brought her the Dover newspaper which reported Charles' presence at the reception given by the Prince of

Wales. The Prince was not popular, but he was still royalty, and
would be Regent at any moment his father's madness took a turn
for the worse; the Dover newspaper lifted Charles' name from the
list of guests, and printed the item eagerly. Jane read it, and thought
of how the Marsh would enjoy this piece of news. Charles had been
in England only a few weeks, and already he rubbed shoulders
with the highest in the land. Jane flung the newspaper away from
her in savage humor. Now that Charles had come back, the Blake
family would return to the place it had held in the affairs of the
Marsh, and she, Jane, would remain the outsider.

2

When Charles returned from London the house awoke to a life
that was subtly different from the reawakening it had had on Jane's
arrival. He came, riding a new horse whose lines bespoke fine breeding, with clothes tailored by London's most expensive firm and with
gold in his saddlebags. The day after his return the carpenters and
plasterers were called in, and Blake's Reach rang with the sound of
hammers and saws, and men's voices. Two new men were hired, one
for the horses, one for the garden; a man came down from London
to tune the harpsichord. The household watched these changes, and
regarded Charles with awe and excitement. This was traditionally
how the Blakes should behave; this kind of behavior was understood and approved.

Charles did only one thing that met with protest, though no one
dared at first to voice it before him. In London he had hired a
Frenchman called Henri, and he announced to Patrick and Kate
that in future the preparation of the food would be solely Henri's
task, and his word within the kitchen was to be law. Patrick was to
wait on table as usual, and Kate to attend to the household; a young
girl was to be engaged in Appledore to help both her and Henri.
The arrival of Henri threw Patrick and Kate into a strange alliance;
they both cordially detested the small, energetic Frenchman. Henri
spoke almost no English, and the kitchen was constantly in a tur-
moil because of the misunderstandings which arose. When Patrick
at last complained, Charles brushed him aside.

"You must do the best you can. Mend your own quarrels in the kitchen, and see that Miss Jane and I are not disturbed by them."

"A cook could have been found. . . ." Jane said acidly. "Even if we had to have one from London. But this Henri . . ."

This also Charles brushed aside. "Why should I trust to the doubtful ministrations of an English cook when I can have one of the finest French chefs? I found Henri in London; he had just made his way over here, and had no money. He had been cook to the Comte de Barzac, and committed the crime of remaining loyal to his master. I was very lucky to find Henri—I have tasted his food many times. . . ."

And so a foreign despot came to rule in the kitchen at Blake's Reach, and there was no more peace for Patrick and Kate, but, Jane admitted, the food was delicious. So also, she reckoned, would the food bills be enormous. Several times a week Henri sent the farm cart as far even as Dover to get the choicest fish and meat and game for his cooking pots and oven. He looked with some scorn on Jane's vegetable and herb garden, and pronounced it totally inadequate. With a wave of his hand Charles sanctioned the planting of anything Henri demanded.

Robert Turnbull commented wryly on the changes. "You see what the King's Pearl can do, Jane? We shall yet see a miniature Versailles at Blake's Reach. I wonder, though," he added, "how much of this Charles has actually paid for? He may be more of a Blake than he seems."

Since Robert would not question Charles about money, Jane herself did not have the courage to do so. Charles merely said that the Pearl had brought a very good price. The details of the transaction seemed to bore him.

Jane had not been forgotten during the London visit. Or perhaps, she thought, it was merely that he regarded her as a part of Blake's Reach. The evening of his return he sent Patrick to his room for three specially wrapped boxes, which he put into Jane's arms—two pairs of fine kid gloves, a length of blue silk, and a wide hat elaborately trimmed. Jane put it on, and turned from the mirror anxiously for his inspection.

"No! No!" He jerked the hat impatiently to a deeper angle over her face. "There—now walk away, and come back to me."

Meekly she did as he told her. As she wheeled he was shaking his head. "Keep your back straight, and—*mon Dieu*—pull your chin in. You're a lady, not a soldier!"

She colored, snatching the hat off, and flinging it into a chair. "Why do you bother? Why do you try to make a lady of me? Does it matter how I wear the hat? And that—" she pointed at the yards of shimmering silk. "I have gowns aplenty, and what need have I of one more? Where am I to wear it? Who's to see it?"

"There'll be plenty to see it—and you also! I fancy we'll not lack company at Blake's Reach."

"No, I suppose not," she replied, with an edge to her voice. "Not since the Dover paper reported that you were at a reception given by the Prince of Wales."

He raised his eyebrows. "So they picked up that, did they? Well, it won't do my credit on the Marsh any harm."

"Tell me about it," she demanded. "How did you get there?"

"Can't you imagine? London is swarming with titled French *émigrés*, some of them cultured and talented men, whom the Prince admires. The Marquis d'Orbec presented me to the Prince. It was nothing very grand—quite informal."

She shrugged. "Whatever it was, it will satisfy the gentry hereabouts. Now that they know you're back, they'll come in flocks like silly sheep!"

He appeared not to have heard her; he was fingering the frayed edges of the gold curtains thoughtfully, and whistling half under his breath.

Jane's prediction was right; within a few days the first of the carriages came rolling along the freshly raked drive, and a liveried footman sprang down to open the door. Jane, watching from the window of her chamber, saw Roger Pym alight, and turn to help a woman whose face was hidden from Jane's view beneath a plumed hat. She caught the sound of high-pitched voices, and two younger, slighter women followed their mother.

A few minutes later came Kate's agitated knocking on her door. "The master bids you come down, Miss Jane," she said. "Mr. and Mrs. Roger Pym have come . . . and Miss Elizabeth and Miss Sarah."

"The fish to the bait!" she said softly. And then, "Oh, damn the Pyms!" But she changed into one of her most becoming gowns—

one which Anne had worn for afternoon drives in the park—and
brushed her hair smooth before going downstairs. She sucked in
her breath a little with nervousness as she entered the room. She
felt the sharp scrutiny of three pairs of feminine eyes, and of Roger
Pym's kindly ones. Then Charles rose from his seat and moved towards her.

"And here is my cousin, Jane. . . ." She hoped it was not her
imagination which made her fancy that in his eyes there was ap-
proval. She went through the exchange of greetings with stiff lips,
angry with herself because she cared that these people would call at
Blake's Reach for Charles' sake, but not for hers. Roger Pym she
favored with a particularly brilliant smile, at the same time swallow-
ing hard at the obstinate lump in her throat.

She had no way of judging what kind of impression she made
on the ladies of the Pym family, but this was, as she had guessed,
the first of many times she was called to the drawing room in the
weeks that followed.

After the Pyms came the rest . . . Lady Stockton from Saltwood
Castle, Sir Anthony Burroughs from Meade House, the Berkeleys
from Ham Street, and the Wests from Ebeney. Sir James Fletcher
also came; this time his wife, Lady Alice, was with him. Charles
treated them all with friendliness, but somehow remained aloof. He
refused completely to discuss the details of his escape. They went
away curious and disappointed.

Inevitably there were questions put to Jane about her plans for
the future, some of them mere insinuations, others completely
blunt. Always Charles spoke for her.

"There's much to be done here, and my Cousin Jane has kindly
consented to remain on to attend to the housekeeping for me. The
recent death of her mother . . . you understand we Blakes have
need of each other at present."

And after they had gone he chuckled lightly. "We can't prevent
them talking, Jane, so better we put the words into their mouths
than have them invent their own. Do you mind very much being
compromised by me? . . ."

White in the face she snapped at him. "If you want me to go,
I'll pack my boxes at once!"

A look of laughing bewilderment came into his face. "But why, Jane? This is your home! I'd be devastated if you went!"

And hearing the teasing quality of his voice, she turned and left the room.

In one matter he was prompt and ready with payment. Within three days of his return the lugger, *Dolphin*, was bought from Wyatt at Folkestone, and the papers passed into Charles' hands. From that moment onwards, Paul turned his energies with grim earnestness to the task of running cargoes and making profits as quickly as possible. After the transfer of the *Dolphin* to Charles, Paul came to dine at Blake's Reach. He was in high good humor. He raised his glass to Jane and Charles.

"Will you drink with me? This is the day of freedom! I have told my brother I am his servant no longer."

"Then we'll drink to freedom and prosperity," Charles said gravely, "for each of us!"

Paul's eyes, bright with hope and excitement, were on Jane. Her heart warmed as she responded to the emotion she read there; she echoed the toast eagerly.

"James was furious, of course," Paul added, "and half sick to think he hadn't got me to order about any more. I didn't, of course, tell him that Turnbull was still involved. Turnbull can keep his own counsel on that. He was mightily suspicious of you, Charles. He knows well enough I haven't the money to buy the lugger, and your return falls in too happily with my sudden prosperity. It only needs you to tell him he may no longer use the church, and he will be certain."

"I think, though," Charles said thoughtfully, "that I'll let him go on paying rent until he puts together another organization. It might be foolish to store Blake cargoes so near the house . . . we'll think on it a little."

After that night Jane saw Paul very rarely, and almost never alone. Three times she rode over to Old Romney, and each time he was absent. She learned that he was pushing the *Dolphin* to make more runs than ever before, finding extra men for the crews so that they could work in relays. The *Dolphin* was making use of the fair summer weather, and remained no longer in port than was strictly necessary. Paul took on some Dutchmen as crew from Flushing, registered the *Dolphin* in that port, and made arrangements to water and provision the lugger there, so as to remain out of the sight of the English port authorities.

Flushing was not her only port; she made trips to Guernsey and Roscoff, and slipped briefly into Le Havre and Dunkirk, though Paul said nothing of these visits to Charles or Jane. Whenever the *Dolphin* sighted a vessel flying the revenue stripes, she put on as much sail as she could carry and slipped away, herself flying the Dutch flag. Paul himself made the trip to Holland a number of times, not skippering the vessel himself, but in order to help expedite the buying of the cargoes at the other end. The times he was not aboard the *Dolphin* he spent riding between the various rendezvous picked to land the contraband along the Marsh shore. He ate carelessly, and seemed never to sleep; Jane saw that he grew thinner, and his eyes were weary, though they never lost their look of feverish excitement.

With Paul absent so often, the time began to hang heavily upon Jane's hands. She was unsure of her position at Blake's Reach, and there was no telling, from one day to the next, what plans Charles would make for work on the house or outbuildings—plans which he seemed to forget to tell her about until the workmen arrived to carry them out. She was confused and uncertain of what to do, conscious that her help was unnecessary now that so many people came from the villages about to do Charles' bidding. Blake's Reach began to wear a clean and fresh air; men were hammering on the roof, and stripping away paneling where the damp had rotted it, an upholsterer came from Dover to measure for new curtains for the drawing room. Charles also ordered a small army of village women in to clean the dining room which had not been used in the past twenty years; new curtains were made for there, as well. Jane thought its splendor, the first evening they dined there, was decidedly cold. The candles in shining silver candlesticks cast pools of light in the center of the long table; Charles seemed far away from her and the corners of the room were shadowy. Even Henri's food tasted different here; Patrick moved about silently on soft-soled shoes. Jane shivered a little, and wished they were back in Spencer's old room.

It should have pleased her to see Blake's Reach begin to re-emerge as the house of charm and beauty it had once been. But she looked at it with a sick heart, counting the gold it was costing to make these restorations, and knowing, that for all this spending, not a single acre of land, or an extra sheep was being bought. There were new horses in the stables, but no new cows were bought; there was a new gardener, but not a shepherd. She made a faint protest about the bill from the upholsterer for bed-hangings and curtains.

Charles looked at her coldly, with raised eyebrows. "I've lived in prison long enough to want these things about me." He appeared to have forgotten that once he had said he did not intend to spend money on Blake's Reach.

"But . . . but how to pay?" she faltered.

"Let the *Dolphin* pay for it all—it's well able to!"

She was filled with rage as she watched him go. He was driving Paul to almost superhuman efforts in order that all his whims could be indulged, so that his cellar should be well stocked, and his kitchen boast a French chef. Paul's long hours on the shore at night, and on the deck of the *Dolphin* were paying for the silk coat on Charles' back, and the gold-buckled shoes he wore, for the thoroughbred horse and the new dinner service of fine china. And beyond the orchard the Blake lands had not received a foot of new fencing, nor was there any labor expended on digging the weed-choked dykes, or replacing the rotting footbridges. The profits of Paul's work would go on trifles, and Blake's Reach would be just as impoverished as Spencer had left it.

"And what," she asked herself, "will Charles do when Paul has enough money to go?"

But during these weeks she wouldn't allow herself to examine too closely the change that was slowly being worked in Paul. Charles and Turnbull had turned the running of the operation completely over to him, with authority to buy and to sell where he pleased, to hire what men he wanted, to send the bribes where he thought they were needed. The steady flow of profit that came back was his justification. He was left alone to do what he pleased with the *Dolphin*, and he reveled in his freedom. Jane saw that he was beginning to enjoy his work; he came to Blake's Reach more often now, still discreetly arriving and leaving by night, and always in

the same exultant mood of success. He laughed as he spoke of the
brushes with the revenue cutters, and boasted of how easily the
Dolphin left them behind. Only once had they ever been near
enough to a revenue cutter to be challenged, and even then they
had simply ignored her signal to heave to, and had been out of gun
range within a few minutes.

Smacking his knee with satisfaction at the memory, he gestured
towards Charles. "We should have a sister ship to the *Dolphin*.
When we have half the purchase money I could get Wyatt to lay
the keel . . . I've an excellent man who'd do as skipper. . . ."

Charles nodded his agreement. "A good idea . . ."

Jane could have cried out in despair. Charles was chaining Paul
to him as James had never been able. He was intoxicated by his
mastery of the *Dolphin*, by the efficiency of his plans, and their
smooth, quick operation. He no longer talked of the ugly business
of smuggling, but found it, instead, a fascinating game.

Sometimes, as he laughed, he reminded her unpleasantly of his
brother, James.

So there was a murderous rage in her heart against Charles during the long hot days of August when there was so little rain, and
the dust rose chokingly from the Marsh roads and fields as the live-
stock moved across them. Charles insisted that she accompany him
to repay the calls on the neighboring gentry; she sat beside him
stiffly in the carriage, and just as stiffly in the drawing rooms of
Meade House, Ebeney and Warefield House. She did all the cor-
rect things, faithfully copying the customs and habits of the women-
folk, joined the dull conversations which were no more than local
gossip repeated and retold at each place they visited. She found
herself irritated and bored with it, and the image of Paul was with
her all the time—Paul, confident and boastful; Paul growing a little
greedy for the spoils of the game, and caring for them for their own
sake; Paul, who saw her now only at Blake's Reach, and for short
periods of time.

But, perversely, it seemed to her worst of all that these days Paul
talked very little of the Indies.

Jane performed the social round as Charles expected her to, without protest, and sat at the head of the table when he bade people
to dine with them. She found the business of entertaining grow

easier with each occasion, and once the challenge of learning and mastering the niceties of it was past, it also began to bore her. She had none of the accomplishments that were admired in the drawing room, and she soon began to accept the admiring attention of the men with the same calm as she took the icy politeness of the women. She recalled longingly the dawn rides to Old Romney, and the eager embrace of Paul's arms.

In spite of her hostility, Jane recognized that when Charles chose to exert himself, he was a charming and interesting companion. She learned many things from him in their daily contacts; his conversation was full of references to events and ideas she had never heard before, and when she found that he did not despise her ignorance, she learned also to question him, and then to listen. He held up to her a mirror of a culture she had not known existed. For the first time she heard the names of Rousseau and Voltaire, and the *Encyclopédie* and learned that the Revolution was not an idea brought into existence in a single day by the National Assembly. It was difficult to reconcile the fact that Charles, an aristocrat, knew and sympathized with the ideals of liberty and equality. Sometimes when they were alone together he would read to her. In the cool of the orchard he would lie on the grass and read to her from the treasonable Tom Paine's *Rights of Man,* and solemnly intone the clauses of the American Declaration of Independence. She gazed at him in awe and admiration, and would spend long hours staring unseeingly across the Marsh, puzzling the things he had said to her.

Paul, who because of his knowledge of Louise de Montignot in Paris, could afford to ignore the gossip that Charles would marry Jane, was still jealous of Charles' learning and scholarship.

"I'm a simple Englishman," he said bluntly to Jane, "and I don't pretend to be a match for some fancy French philosopher."

"I understand only simple Englishmen," Jane replied. "And I don't think Charles supposes himself a philosopher."

But it was one thing to hear Charles execute the graceful little minuets and gavottes on the harpsichord, and quite another to try to follow him as he put his horse to jump the dykes and fences of the Marsh. On a horse he was matchless, as if he and the animal had only one identity; William was lost in wonder and reverence of him. The three of them—Jane, Charles and William—became a familiar sight on the roads and in the hamlets across the Marsh. Wherever they went the laborers and the village women knew them, and acknowledged them with lifted caps and curtseys. A great many of them came forward to congratulate Charles on his escape; Jane was touched by the obvious sincerity of their words, and she also began to think of the escape as something miraculous. William began to identify himself closely with Charles, beaming with pleasure during these encounters, and taking the congratulations as being meant for him also. With the working people Charles unbent to a degree he never did in the drawing rooms of the gentry; he was kind and leisurely in his speech, and talked with the children as well as their parents. After a short time there was nowhere they could ride on the Marsh that some "looker" would not pause from his task of herding the sheep to wave to them, or the carpenter's apprentice look up from his tools to smile.

This Charles was familiar to her—a companion, almost a friend, a hero to William, a master for Blake's Reach, and someone to restore honor and dignity to the Blake name. The other side of Charles was known to her only by what she could observe and guess.

At least twice a week he rode to Dover, sometimes more frequently. On occasion he would bid Turnbull come with him, and once Jane dared to question Robert about these visits.

He shrugged, a weary gesture that already had the look of defeat about it. "Always the same object—Louise de Montignot. He is pouring gold into the pockets of anyone who has even half promised him some information or aid. But so far as we know she's still in La Force, and he's growing desperate. . . . The news from France is bad. . . ."

Jane knew well enough what the news from France was; the whole of Europe was watching, unbelievingly, the events in Paris where the Reign of Terror was gathering force. When the news reached them at Blake's Reach of the second storming of the Tuileries and the massacre of the Swiss Guard, Jane saw Charles come as close to desperation as he would ever be. In a frenzied need for action he saddled his horse and rode to Dover. When he returned next day it was with the news that the royal authority had been suspended, and the royal family imprisoned in the Temple.

His face was haggard, his eyes dull from lack of sleep; at night

Jane heard his ceaseless pacing in his chamber. He left his food almost untouched. The long August days moved on slowly, and they gave up talking of the awaited storm that would freshen the still air, and lay the dust. Jane found what tasks she could to occupy her, but there were never enough to absorb her energies. Charles' tortured face was always present to remind her of what hung in the balance across the Channel, and her own thoughts were never far from Louise de Montignot, and that strange, inexplicable statement of Charles' that perhaps, in the end, Blake's Reach would belong to her, Jane.

3

Charles nodded at Jane down the length of the dining table, and for a moment the look of tight weariness his face had worn all day lifted. His smile was cynically amused.

"I had a visit from the vicar of St. Mary's this afternoon. I believe you know him—the Reverend Sharpe who takes the service at St. Saviour's?"

"Yes? . . ."

His long fingers plucked at the grapes on his plate. "He thinks it's high time I proved to the parish that I've not succumbed to the wicked influence of my despised French relatives, and turned Papist."

She shrugged. "Laugh if you like, but to the people on the Marsh you are English, and you had best show yourself in an English church. The vicar's right about that. No one expects the Blakes to be religious people, but they expect them to do what all the other Blakes have done before them."

"How stern you are, Jane!" he mocked her. "And what a tyrant! You should be the mother of a large brood, and bring them all up to be good Blakes!"

She hated him when he laughed at her. She glanced at his dark, lean face almost lost in the wavering candlelight, and thought that, with his thin mouth and black hooked eyebrows, he had a devilish quality about him. But afterwards, in the drawing room, when he sat at the harpsichord and played the chorales he loved, his expression was peaceful and at rest. Jane's heart was touched when she thought of the long months in prison, and the horrors he had seen and did not speak of, and she was glad that sometimes he could be at peace. They would sit wordlessly there for an hour and more, with only the thin plucking sounds of the harpsichord between them.

On the next Sunday morning, wearing his finest coat and gold-buckled shoes, he walked up the hill to St. Saviour's-by-the-Marsh. Jane and William sat beside him in the Blake pew, stiff and conscious of every eye fixed upon them. The word had gone around that Charles would attend this morning's service, and apart from the villagers who packed the church, people from two parishes away had made excuses to visit cousins in St. Mary's, and had come to stare at the man who had escaped from the hands of those Frenchies, and, as they believed, the jaws of death. Robert Turnbull, who had been bidden to take dinner at Blake's Reach with them, had come early, and slipped into a pew at the back of the church.

At the appointed moment Charles rose and went to the pulpit, and in his beautiful, sensitive voice, read the Lesson; he was a splendid figure standing there in wig and silk coat, his hands resting on the Bible that bore the Blake crest on its leather binding. His demeanor was perfect; humble and yet dignified.

The vicar offered prayers of thanksgiving for Charles' deliverance from the anti-Christs across the Channel, making it seem as if the God he prayed to were also an Englishman. Then, before he began his sermon, he made the announcement that, in thanksgiving, Charles would present St. Saviour's with a rose window for the south transept.

For Jane it should have been a great moment, a moment of complete identification with a family and a way of life that had continued here for hundreds of years. Instead it was almost a moment of imprisonment; she felt the heaviness of those years upon her like a load. For an instant she caught a glimpse of her own self as she had been the first Sunday she had attended service here, saw the puppet she had been, playing the game that Charles now played. But he had gone much further. He would give a rose window to the church in thanksgiving for a return he felt no joy in. She glanced out over the approving congregation, and their red-cheeked country faces dissolved before her eyes. Instead she had a second's vision of

the congregation of wool bales and brandy casks she herself had
addressed from the pulpit. But now she saw the softly colored light
from Charles' new rose window streaming down on the smugglers'
congregation. She closed her eyes to shut out the vision.

After the service Charles lingered just as she had done, playing
out the ritual of the handshakes and the greetings, accepting the
congratulations. William was close by his side, enjoying the occasion, performing his same courtly little bow; Jane joined them, but
her smile was set as if she were a wax doll, and her hand resting
in the vicar's was like lead.

Robert Turnbull was with them as they set off down the hill.
After the meal he walked with Jane among the rose beds, where the
blooms were dusty and faded, turning brown at the edges.

Jane paused, and nodded up towards the church. She said bitterly, "Well, we'll yet see the King's Pearl spent on silk bed-hangings and a window for the church. Was it for this the Blakes have
kept it all these years?"

Robert shrugged. "I wonder how Charles intends to pay for it?
However—it was a nice gesture and it makes the people happy, even
if it never comes into being. Well . . ." here he glanced across at
Jane, "it was a great sight to see all three Blakes at service this morning. You're making the family respectable, Jane!"

"Respectable! . . ."

"Once," he went on, "they were full of adventure and spirit—
even perhaps, nobility. Now they're merely respectable! Not a
good change!"

Abruptly, to avoid replying, she bent and put her face close to
a crimson rose, breathing in the dusty fragrance, which meant the
end of the summer.

CHAPTER THREE

PAUL STOOD ON THE SHINGLE AT BARHAM ON A NIGHT EARLY IN
September, and blessed his good fortune. The night was calm, but
dark, so dark that although he could hear the creak of the rowlocks,

he could not see the boats that were pulling away from the *Dolphin's* side. The first of the cargo was coming ashore, and from all the information he had gathered, he knew that no preventive officers or Dragoons would bother him this night. The cargo was a rich one, the biggest he had so far brought across, and he had chosen Barham for the landing because of the speed with which the cargo could be handled here. He smiled to himself in the darkness; along with the contraband goods the *Dolphin* had also brought two passengers, who had not only paid handsomely for their passage, but, once they touched the shingle, would be no further responsibility of his. Refugees fleeing from the Terror in France were the best kind of cargo to carry; they gave no trouble and their passage money didn't need to be reported to Charles or Turnbull. They were always worth the risk involved in taking them aboard in a French port.

He heard the scrape as the first boat touched the shingle. With a swift order to the waiting cart-driver, and the eager crowd of women, he moved forward.

As he expected, the first boat carried, among the kegs and the oilskin packages, the two passengers. Paul wasn't in the least interested in their identities or their persons; the captain of the *Dolphin*, Joe Shore, would have collected their passage money before the vessel weighed anchor in Le Havre. All Paul wanted now was to get them on their way, so that their presence wouldn't hinder the loading party.

He watched them, two dark figures climbing stiffly from the boat, moving with the timid movements of people unaccustomed to the sea. When they reached the shingle they stood close together, staring about them in a kind of helpless bewilderment.

He spoke to them in clipped tones. "Messieurs! . . ." They turned expectantly. "I have a cart waiting to take you to Folkestone. From there you may easily arrange transportation to wherever you wish to go."

"*Merci . . . merci beaucoup!*" The words were spoken dully, as if the ordeal of escape and the sea voyage had left the speaker unnaturally submissive. The second man, however, gestured to hold Paul's attention.

"Monsieur! . . . I beg you . . ." His English was heavily accented, but understandable. "I have to reach a town called 'Rye.' The captain, he told me it is near here."

"It will be possible to arrange your journey from Folkestone to Rye tomorrow," Paul said coldly. "I have only one cart and it must take you both to the same place. Now if you will—"

"One moment, monsieur! It is of extreme urgency that I reach Rye as quickly as possible—a matter of life and death."

"Whom do you wish to see in Rye?" Paul said.

The man gestured violently. "From there I must seek a gentleman called Charles Blake . . . lately arrived here from France. I am instructed that he lives close by that town. I must reach him! I repeat, monsieur, it is a matter of life and death!"

Tonight the lights of Warefield House were visible far beyond the park that surrounded it. Of all nights this was the one on which Paul had least wanted to approach the house where he had been born. Tonight all the families of the gentry living in or on the fringes of the Marsh were gathering here to celebrate the coming-of-age of James Fletcher's eldest son and heir, Harry. From the bonfires that blazed in the grounds, and the smell of roasting pork and the garbled shouts that carried to him on the wind, Paul knew that James' tenants were also making the most of the occasion. There were precious few times, Paul thought, that his brother's tenants ever got a free glass of ale from their landlord.

But the very fact that this was a night of celebration had made it impossible to send anyone else. There was a message to be delivered to Charles Blake, and he was here, somewhere among the guests who thronged James' hall and drawing room, and spilled into the garden outside, and even went to mingle with the tenants round the roasting-pits. As little as he wanted to appear on James' estate tonight, where he was most certainly an uninvited guest, Paul could think of no one who could be less conspicuous here than himself. He knew the back passages and staircases of the house intimately, and two of the menservants here gave him occasional service as porters when there was a cargo coming in—this, of course, being regarded as none of Sir James' business. If he could find one of these men, it would be simple to get a message to Charles to meet him in an upstairs room. Paul knew that all the local magistrates and the military officers of the surrounding countryside would be among the guests; it would have been extreme folly to allow an emotional Frenchman, who had been robbed of all discretion by his anxiety and exhaustion, to appear in this assembly. There was no telling what the Frenchman would have blurted out, and perhaps not only the landing place and the name of the vessel he had come over on would be revealed, but Charles' name linked, even indirectly with the smuggling trade. And where Charles' name was linked, so inevitably, must Jane's.

As he approached the back of the house, Paul slipped from his horse, and stood waiting within the heavy shadow of the trees. For some minutes he studied the activity in the kitchens and servants' quarters, which were clearly visible through the lighted open windows. One by one he identified the servants, and watched their movements as they hurried back and forth between kitchen and dining room. He grimaced with distaste as he plotted how he would creep, like a thief, into his brother's house.

Down on the shingle at Barham he had struggled with himself before making the decision to come here. It would have been simple to pretend not to hear the urgency in the Frenchman's plea, and tell himself that tomorrow would have been soon enough for Charles to know what news had come for him from France. He would have to admit now to Charles that he had been bringing over refugees, and receiving payment for them without Charles' knowledge, and it would have been much easier to do this anywhere but here under these circumstances.

But the Frenchman had said "a matter of life and death," and the name he had whispered to Paul on the shingle at Barham had been that of Louise de Montignot.

2

The music and the laughter and the voices had been too much for Paul, and almost without a choice in the matter he found himself walking softly along the upstairs passage towards the gallery and the great staircase. He knew he was drawn here by only one thought; with good luck it was possible he might catch a glimpse of Jane.

Once the fireworks display had started on the terrace, entering the house had been easy enough. He had waylaid Shelby, the man-servant, in the stone passage between the kitchen and dining room, and had dispatched him to find Charles, and conduct him dis-creetly to one of the disused nursery rooms. But for Paul the wait in that bare, dusty room had been too long. When the fireworks were over, and still Charles had not come, he had succumbed to his own desires. One sight of Jane would be enough—just one, he told himself.

He crouched in the corner of the gallery where the shadows were deepest, and searched the lighted hall below. The guests were streaming back in from the terrace now; they made a moving mosaic of textures and colors—silks, velvets and satins in every color he could name. And there was Jane at last, in blue silk, with her bril-liant hair like a flame above it. He saw her white shoulders and bosom which the gown revealed, the sway of her body as she moved, and he knew that there were many other men down there who looked at her as he did. He pressed his face against the wooden balustrade, sick with his love and desire, sick with the frustration of being unable to walk down those stairs and claim her before this whole company. He tried to look away, tried not to hear her laugh or to see the movement of her hands as she opened her fan. On one side of her walked his nephew, Harry, on the other was a man he did not recognize, in the uniform of a captain of the Royal Navy.

He risked discovery when he stood up and leaned over the balustrade to watch her as she disappeared through the open doors into the drawing room.

Charles waited until the hall was almost deserted before coming upstairs. Wordlessly Paul motioned him to follow, as he led the way back to the nursery.

"What has happened?" Charles said as he closed the door be-hind him.

"You know a man called Pierre Latour?"

"Latour!" Charles exclaimed. "Pierre Latour was Philippe de Montignot's secretary. Is there news? . . ."

Paul nodded. "Not good news, Charles. Latour landed tonight

from Le Havre. He needed to see you urgently, but I could not let
him come here. . . ."

"Quickly . . . tell me! What has happened to Louise?"

"Still in Le Havre," Paul said. "Latour brought her down from
Paris by barge, and they lodged at the house of friends of Latour,
whom he swears are loyal. Then he looked around for a ship to take
them to England. They had to wait . . . you understand the
tension has been growing this past month, and everyone is suspicious. . . ."

"For God's sake, *tell me!*"

"He found Joe Shore, the skipper of the *Dolphin*, and arranged
passage for them both. But before he could get back to the Countess
he learned that he was under suspicion himself. He dared not go
back to the house where she was, because it would have led to a
search, and her description is circulated in every port in France.
She would have been recognized and taken. There was nothing to
do but slip back to the *Dolphin*, and bring the news to you. He
says someone else must be sent to get her."

Charles' thin lips tightened. "And Louise herself? . . . What did
he say of her?"

"She's very ill. How ill, he's not sure—they couldn't risk calling a
physician. He says . . . he says that even when he was making the
arrangements he doubted that she would have the strength to make
the journey across. . . ."

Charles was silent; he clasped his hands behind his back and
paced the length of the room. As he turned back Paul saw that his
face was drained of color, the skin pinched tightly on the high
cheekbones.

"She will die!" he said distractedly. "If she is left there, she will
die! *Mon Dieu*—think of it! She is there all alone. . . ."

Paul shook his head. "Latour assures me she is in good hands,
and that his friends will care for her. . . ."

Charles waved his words aside. "But she believes she is deserted!
—And she will die!"

A burst of laughter from the kitchen yard below seemed suddenly
to mock his words. Then there were drunken, ribald whistles, and a
girl's high-pitched voice, laughing also, and protesting. Someone

gave a faint cheer, and there was more laughter. James' tenants, Paul thought, were making good use of his free cider and ale.

"We will find someone to go over," Paul said. "There are plenty who will do that for payment . . . there are some I know in Folkestone and Dover who speak French tolerably, and may come and go without. . . ."

"It would take too much time," Charles cut him short. "We cannot afford the days—even the hours! It grows worse in France all the time. Since the royal authority has been suspended, and the King a prisoner in the Temple, every hour a royalist stays alive is an hour of grace—"

Abruptly he broke off, looking now directly at Paul. "You say the *Dolphin* brought Latour over?"

Paul stiffened, preparing now to face Charles' accusations of double-dealing. "Yes, it did. Joe Shore brings over anyone he can give passage to on my authority, and if you think I've no right—"

Charles gestured impatiently. "What does it matter! That's your affair. I want to know where the *Dolphin* is now."

"Lying off Barham. She's waiting for me to come back—I'm captaining her to Flushing this trip. . . ."

"Good!" Charles exclaimed. "Then ride to Barham and hold her there. Don't let her move! I'll join you as soon as I can break away from here."

"What do you mean, hold her? The *Dolphin* leaves for Flushing as soon as I go aboard!"

Charles laid his hand quietly on the other's sleeve. "Ah, no, my friend! The *Dolphin* will sail for Le Havre as soon as *I* go aboard!"

Paul's expression darkened. "I'm captain of the *Dolphin*, and I say she'll go to Flushing, as arranged. There's plenty in Dover who'll go for the Countess, and in the meantime she'll come to no harm. She'll be more rested, and better able to undertake the journey. . . ."

"Every day she stays in France the danger grows worse," Charles said calmly. "The *Dolphin* will sail tonight for Le Havre!"

"But I have a cargo of wool loading that's due in Flushing. . . ."

Charles' grip tightened on Paul's arm. "I'm not asking you for the *Dolphin*, Mr. Fletcher. I'm commandeering her!"

3

The group who waited in Joe Shore's cottage at Barham turned their heads expectantly as they caught the rumble of the carriage wheels on the cobbles at the end of the village street. Paul rose, took the candle and went quickly to the door; he had posted Joe's son, Matt, to watch for the coach and direct it to the cottage. It stopped before the door, but Paul waited, his hand on the latch, listening to the low-toned conversation outside. Then he heard Patrick's voice as he urged the grays forward again, and the carriage moved off towards Lydd. Shielding the candle with his body, Paul opened the door.

But it was not Charles who entered first. There was a tap of high-heeled slippers on the cobbles, and the brush of heavy silk against the door-frame. Startled, Paul fell back a step, and Jane moved past him; she was followed closely by Charles and Matt Shore. Matt dropped the latch into place, and leaned back against it.

"Jane!" Paul's tone was a shocked protest. "Why are you here? Why have you sent the carriage away?"

She turned back to him. The billowing silk seemed to fill all the space in the small room, and her perfume was heavy on the air.

"I'm coming to France with you," she said simply. Then she glanced to Charles for support before she went on. "I'm coming because the Countess is ill, and will need a woman on the journey back. . . ." Her voice faltered a little as she encountered Paul's thunderous scowl.

"This is madness!" he said. "Utter madness!" He turned furiously towards Charles. "Have you gone out of your mind to permit this? There's danger—you said yourself there's danger! If anything goes wrong there'll be no leniency for Jane."

He swung back to Jane appealingly. "Jane, have a thought before you do this! —I beg you, have a thought!"

"Why should there be danger for me? I'm not wanted in France."

"You'll be aiding the escape of a Royalist. . . ." He looked back at Charles. "Why don't you stop her, since you seem to be commanding this expedition!"

Charles shrugged. "I don't stop her because I don't believe she'll be in danger. And . . . and I was profoundly grateful to her for

offering her help. Louise may be dying, and a woman alone on this
sea voyage. . . ."

Paul threw out his hands. "Oh, this wretched Frenchwoman! So
long as she is served it doesn't count what danger Jane is exposed
to. . . ."

Charles held up his hand. "I think we've talked enough. I have
pointed out to Jane what risks she will run, and she is still willing
to come. Is that enough for you, Fletcher? The time is going, and
we stand here and make talk. . . ."

He looked carefully around the group—from Paul to Joe Shore,
the Dolphin's captain, to Matt, to a man he had never seen before,
sitting wearily hunched over the table, and finally to Pierre Latour.
He held out his hand.

"Latour! It's good to see you here in freedom!"

Emotion crossed the other man's face swiftly as he gripped
Charles' hand; he held on tightly for a moment, struggling for
control.

"I do not feel as if this is freedom, monsieur. I have saved myself
and failed my master, and Madame la Comtesse. . . ."

"You have not failed, Latour. She is out of La Force, and only
a few hours by ship from England. We shall have her safe here—"
He broke off, as the other shook his head.

"Monsieur . . . I fear for Madame's life. The time in prison has
weakened her greatly. We only made Le Havre because it was possible to come directly there from Paris down the Seine by barge.
And getting her out of La Force . . . I tell you, Monsieur, it was
genius! And it cost a fortune!" For an instant his melancholy face
lit up. "Such a beautiful plan, monsieur . . ."

"I'm sure it was, Latour, and you deserve great credit . . . your
skill and loyalty have earned Madame's unending gratitude, and
mine also. . . ." He broke off, and put his hand on the other man's
shoulder as he saw the tears well up in those tired, bloodshot eyes.

"Oh, Monsieur," Latour whispered, "go to her! She needs help
so badly, and she may be dying. So brave she has been, and so
helpless . . . and since Monsieur le Comte was so foully murdered
by those fiends she has no one but yourself. All the family dis-
persed, or dead . . . living in exile and poverty. Her son is dead,

and her brother—there is only you, Monsieur! You will take care
of her?"

Charles nodded. "I will take care of her."

Then he motioned the other to a chair, and he drew one up for
himself. "Now, Latour, you must remember every single detail we'll
need to know to reach her. . . ."

Their talk went into French then, rapid questions and explanations, and finally Latour produced a piece of paper on which he
had drawn a crude map. To this he added a name, and an address.
As he wrote, Charles looked up at Paul.

"Is everything ready to sail on the *Dolphin?*"

Paul nodded curtly. "Yes—I shall captain her myself. Joe here has
made six trips without a break, and, in any case, there's only one
cabin, and we shall need that for the Countess and Jane," he added
grimly.

Charles' gaze slowly turned on Jane. "My dear, I'm afraid to ask
you if you've reconsidered your decision. You heard what Latour
has said . . . Louise needs kindness, and a woman's care. . . ."

"I'm coming!" Jane said brusquely. "Let's have no more talk
about it!"

Charles nodded. "Very well—I'm glad to hear it." Then he gestured towards her gown. "Couldn't you find something—" he ap-
pealed to Joe Shore. "She'll be in more danger from that gown as
she goes up the side of the *Dolphin* than from the Frenchies."

Shore nodded. "That she will! There should be something about
the place to borrow." He moved towards the passage leading to the
back of the cottage. "I'll fetch my daughter—I sent her packin' t'
bed when I knew Mr. Fletcher an' the two others was comin'. . . ."

He opened a door at the end of the passage, and they could hear
a low murmur of voices. Then a woman's figure appeared, wearing
nightgown and wrapper. But by the smoothness of her lustrous dark
curls, and the fetching angle of her cap, it was plain she hadn't
been in bed. She held a candle, and it shone directly on her pretty,
lively face.

"Well, quite a company we have 'ere!" She gave a little gasp as
her eyes fell on Jane. "Didn't know the Queen o' France 'ad escaped."

Jane remembered the voice, the warm, rough voice in the Bar-

ham churchyard on the night of the run. She held out her hand.
"Rose!"

4

The hull of the *Dolphin* seemed to tower above Jane, the masts
and riggings lost in the blackness of the sky; she had crouched
stiffly in the boat as they were rowed towards the *Dolphin*, afraid
to move in this strange new world where everything was damp and
smelled of old fish, afraid of catching her feet in the tackle at the
bottom of the boat, afraid of losing her balance—afraid, most of all,
of earning a rebuke from Paul. She felt lost and forlorn, and she
had a moment to wonder if she had been in her right mind in
agreeing to go, before Paul motioned her to start on the ladder
up the side.

Matt Shore's shoes, which she had borrowed from Rose, were
too big for her, and she was clumsy. It seemed an incredible labor
to haul herself up the rope. The ladder was a treacherous thing—
giving and swaying with each movement from her. Her face was
wet with sweat when she drew level with the deck, and rough hands
pulled her the rest of the way. She found herself set on her feet
with less care than a bundle of cargo. Charles' head had appeared
at the top of the ladder, and soon he also was on the deck. She
took another hitch in the belt that held Matt's breeches loosely
about her waist, and waited for Paul. He was the only one reassuring thing in this bewildering scene, and she needed him.

But he would come to her only after he had given detailed orders
to the hands, and consulted in low tones with his mate. She stayed
away from Charles, feeling humble and unsure of herself, and not
wanting to betray it. As she stood there, questioning her own san-
ity for offering to make the journey, she tried to fix in her mind
Rose's words, and the expression on the girl's face as she had helped
Jane change into her brother's clothes.

"If Paul Fletcher was my man I'd go with 'im, too! I'd follow 'im
wherever 'e went."

She could hear the rattle of the cable as the anchor came up,
and the quick movements among the crew as an order from Paul
sent the hands aloft. She watched the mainsail unfurl, and the sight

as the breeze slowly filled it was one of new, unbelievable beauty
to her. A slight shudder ran through the *Dolphin* as the vessel
lifted to the breeze. Her bow swung slowly about, and she set course
on a tack that would take her clear of the tip of Dungeness.

Jane squeezed herself in against the bulwark, and hoped she
would get in no one's way until she was told what to do. The
breeze caught the ends of the cloth Rose had bound about her
hair, and they flipped across her face. She could feel the heave and
drop of the *Dolphin*, and the motion, not yet too strong, pleased
her. At her feet on the deck was the cloth bundle containing the
old gown and petticoats Rose had given her to wear in Le Havre.
In the box under Rose's bed lay her own blue silk ball gown.

At last Paul came to her; he stood beside her staring up at the
starless sky, listening, she thought, to the steady thrumming of the
wind in the rigging. He leaned back, his back and elbows against
the bulwark, feeling the rhythm of his ship.

"Well, Jane," he said. "Here you are, aboard the *Dolphin*, and
there's a woman lying over there in Le Havre, who'll take Blake's
Reach from you!"

In the darkness she moved and pressed herself close to him, standing on her toes and reaching up to put her arms about him, to put
her hands behind his neck and pull his face down to her.

"Forget that woman lying over there," she whispered. She opened
her lips to meet his kiss, and pushed her body firmly against his,
feeling her breasts hard against his body, feeling him tighten and
respond to her urging. They rocked together with the motion of the
vessel.

"Yes, I'm here aboard the *Dolphin*," she said softly. "And you
promised me that one day I would see France!"

5

Jane lay wakeful and restless in the narrow cot, huddling naked
under the thin blankets that smelled of sea water. She occupied
the tiny stern cabin, the only one on the lugger; at the end of the
companionway Charles had tried to stretch his length in a hammock
slung between two beams. She wondered if he also lay awake, listening to the creak of the timbers, the wind that now shrieked high

in the rigging. The weather had worsened steadily, and for more than an hour the *Dolphin* had been rolling in high seas. Sometimes the wind brought flurries of rain against the stern ports; Jane shivered and pulled the blankets higher about her shoulders, wishing that the morning would come, so that at least she might see how rough it was, instead of imagining mountains of water beating against the small vessel. She lay with her hands on her queasy stomach, and a kind of respect began to dawn in her for the men whose livelihood was the sea, for Paul, on deck now since they had left Dungeness, and for the hands who had swarmed up the rigging.

She sat up and fumbled in the darkness to find her shirt; after she had put it on she slid out of the cot, easing her way along the bulkhead until her groping hands encountered an oilskin she had seen hanging there. She brought this back and spread it over the cot, and once more crept down between the blankets, wishing she now had the biscuits Paul had offered, and which she had declined.

The *Dolphin* suddenly gave a much more violent pitch, and she grabbed the side of the cot to save herself from rolling out. The *Dolphin* might be a thing of beauty and joy to Paul, but to her it was damp and cold, and possessed of sly, ungracious little tricks to trap the unwary. The night seemed endless.

Still clutching the side of the cot, she closed her eyes, and kept them closed firmly; after a time she seemed to drift towards sleep. The *Dolphin* settled back to the steady pitch of the past hour.

She was brought to complete wakefulness by the boom of a cannon. The sound was close by, and loud, even in the wind. She sat bolt upright, frantically trying to make out some shape in the blackness beyond the stern ports.

Above she could hear orders being shouted; she distinguished Paul's voice, but could not hear the words. The orders were followed by the rush of horny, bare feet drumming on the deckhead above her cot. She could feel the swing as the *Dolphin* went about on a different tack. Then, for an instant, through the ports, she caught sight of the riding lights of a vessel. Then the *Dolphin* gathered way, and the lights fell astern.

She sat there, shivering and frightened, straining to try to hear what was going on about her. In the passage she heard a muttered curse in French as Charles struggled to find his shoes in the darkness. Then she heard his steps on the companion ladder. She wondered if she too should dress and go on deck; she remembered Paul's orders, and that crowded deck space where every inch seemed to be given over to equipment and gear. She slid down between the blankets once more, and decided that, unless a cannon shot came through the stern ports, she was better where she was.

There was no hope of sleep now. She listened, but she could hear nothing more. There was no further fire from the other vessel, and the *Dolphin* did not return the shot. She sensed the increased speed of the *Dolphin*, as if Paul had risked putting on more sail. There were no more shouted orders from the deck, and Charles did not return, either.

She lay there still, watching the ports for the first light of dawn, wondering how long it would be before the storm blew itself out. It was September already, she thought, and this was the first storm of autumn.

A watery sun rose, breaking through the racing gray clouds. Except where the sun touched it, the sea also was gray, with a heavy swell running. The *Dolphin* seemed to be all alone in the Channel; Jane lay and listened to the cries of the gulls who followed in the wake of the ship.

At last Paul came down to the cabin, his eyes dull-looking, the lines of fatigue set hard on his face. He wore a sou'wester, but no oilskins, and his clothes were wet. He dropped into the seat under the ports, flinging his arms and legs wide in a mighty stretch and a yawn.

"Lord, Jane, I'm tired! No sleep since . . . since days ago!" He closed his eyes for a moment, moving his head from side to side to stretch his neck. Then he looked at her again. "We'll be in Le Havre by afternoon. Got blown off course last night."

"Is that all you can say?" she asked. "Or didn't you notice the cannon shot?"

He grinned. "I wondered if it woke you!" Then the smile faded; he shrugged. "We came near to it, Jane! Lord, it got so dark when that weather blew up that you could hardly see your hand in front of you. Then suddenly I got a sight of the riding lights on this craft, and we went so close I could see she was flying the revenue stripes. We weren't flying anything at all, and I'm hoping she'll still be trying to guess who we were."

"But the shot? . . ."

"She fired a blank to signal us to heave to, but we weren't stopping for courtesies like that. We went about as quickly as we could make it, and got to hell away from her. The *Dolphin* was built to run, not to stay and fight. . . . Well, there wasn't a sight of them this morning."

"I was frightened," Jane said. "I was scared stiff!"

"That's the most sensible thing I've heard you say for a long time. Anyone but a fool would have been scared . . . we've got a load of wool aboard I was supposed to ship to Flushing, and we have no export license to show if we'd been searched."

"Charles went on deck," she said. "I heard him go up."

Paul nodded. "He stayed there right through it, and, for a landsman, he managed not to get too much in the way."

"He's still there?"

"Yes—stayed there all night. Hardly spoke a word, either. Didn't seem to be afraid—didn't even ask if we'd lost the revenue cruiser. Just stood all night on the deck, and didn't say a word! Wouldn't even go to the galley with me to get something to eat. He's still there . . . just looking at the empty sea."

Jane shivered. "I don't understand Charles."

"Nor do I! —Don't even understand myself for doing what he tells me to! This trip to Le Havre . . . it's madness! Even though he owns the *Dolphin,* I'm her master and I could have refused to do as he said. I tried to refuse, and then I shut up, and let him have his way. Why does he have to go himself? . . . he could have sent someone for this Frenchwoman, and he wouldn't have endangered his own life. To escape once is enough. . . . Doesn't he know he's asking too much of his luck to do it again? Doesn't he know that, Jane?"

"I think he knows it," she said soberly. "And perhaps that's why we do as he says, and go where he tells us. He has great courage, Paul, and somehow he carries you along with it. Look at me! I lie here and wonder why in Heaven's name I ever said I'd come along. I don't feel brave, and I don't love Louise de Montignot. But Charles has such courage and he's so direct and determined about what he has to do for that woman—and I found myself saying I'd go."

Paul rubbed his hand wearily across his eyelids. "You admire him, don't you, Jane?"

"I think he is brave," she said frowning, "but he is cold! It is almost as if he didn't know what it would feel like to be afraid. He looks at you with those cold, black eyes . . . and he drinks and he rides and he spends money—perhaps he even makes love—and I don't think his heart ever beats any faster for it! Can you think how he looks now? —As cold as the sea!"

She pulled the blankets close about her chin, and rolled on her side, facing Paul. "I wonder," she said musingly, "I wonder if he loves Louise? I wonder if it will make him happy to have her at Blake's Reach?" She looked at him questioningly, and yet did not expect an answer. "Or does he think of it only as a promise he gave, and must keep, no matter what he thinks or feels about Louise? . . ."

Paul's eyes had closed again; his lips looked thin and pinched.

"You're very tired, Paul," she said softly.

"Yes . . ."

"Could you sleep if you came in here with me? If I lay very still, could you sleep?"

His eyes flickered open. "Not even you could keep me awake now, Jane."

He sat on the edge of the cot, and she helped him strip off the sodden clothes. They lay in a pile on the deck; he kicked his boots aside and they slid across the deck and collapsed against the door. She squeezed herself against the bulkhead to make room for him in the cot, then she put her arm under his head, and covered his shoulders with the blanket.

He lay still for a few moments, breathing heavily; she began to think he was already asleep. Then suddenly he spoke, in a low, dull voice. "What will you do, Jane, when she takes Blake's Reach from you? Are you going to come with me?"

Softly she pressed a kiss on his temple. "Sweetheart, we'll talk about that when the time comes," she murmured.

Then she gathered his chilled, weary body close to her, holding him against her to give him warmth. He seemed to yield himself to her then, not protesting or making any further effort to talk. His wet blond hair had fallen down across his forehead. He slept, with his head cradled against her breasts, a heavy, exhausted sleep that lasted until the sun was high.

CHAPTER FOUR

ALL THROUGH THE HOURS OF THE AFTERNOON AND THE COMING OF dusk Jane and Charles waited for Paul to return. It had been a golden September day, warm, with only a hint of freshness in the breeze to carry the premonition of winter. And even that slight chill had gone once they passed the entry to the port of Le Havre, passed the round, battlemented tower that had dominated the fortifications since the days of Francis the First. Jane watched the gray granite walls of the quais slide by them, and tried to hold back the shiver that touched her, in spite of the sun warm on her back. Charles looked unconcerned, as if he were not aware that the menace of an enemy now lay all about them.

"That is La Citadelle," he said, gesturing over to the right of the entry. She turned and looked, and the sight of it was not reassuring. It was a high, square pile of masonry, facing both to the estuary and to the town itself, with fortified lookout towers at intervals along the walls. Not even the green of the trees within the enclosure softened its lines. Jane turned away quickly.

The Basin du Roi was more cheerful. The town clustered close about the shipping docked here; the bustle of people going about their everyday affairs had a normal look to Jane's eyes. It was a town not so very different from Folkestone, and she could almost persuade herself that this was England, peaceful and safe. And while she looked, her hands clutched the bulwark tightly to conceal from Charles their trembling.

The houses were of plaster and timber and tile, many different colors, whose top storeys overhung the cobbled streets. Washing was hanging from the windows, brightly colored clothes flapping in

the breeze like a great flock of birds on the move . . . or banners,
Jane thought, yes, banners for a celebration day. She wondered
why she thought these things, why she tried to persuade herself
that this was a happy place, that no danger for them existed here.
Behind one of those windows Louise de Montignot lay, and perhaps she even heard the harsh voices of the *blanchisseuses* Charles
pointed out to her, calling and gossiping to each other over their
wash tubs gathered about the fountain. The tubs were colored also
—blue and green.

During the afternoon the crew of the *Dolphin* had made an exaggerated show of discharging and consigning to a warehouse the
cargo Paul had carried aboard at Barham. The bales of English
wool had, after all, served their purpose in providing a pretext for
being in the port.

Paul memorized the map Latour had drawn; from where they
had dropped anchor in the Basin du Roi they could see the stream
of traffic moving along the Rue de Paris. In the Rue de Paris Paul
was to look for a wine-shop, which also sold bread; there he would
inquire for Albert Cornand.

Jane and Charles watched while Matt Shore rowed him to the
steps of the quai. Then he was lost from sight among the crowds.
They settled to wait.

Dusk came down slowly on the town. Jane had tried to sleep
down in the cabin, but without the wind of the open sea it was
stuffy and oppressive. Charles was still on deck when she came up,
and it seemed as if he had not moved from his position by the
bulwark. He turned as she paused beside him.

"A boat has just put off from the quai," he said briefly. "I think
it is Paul, but there are two other people with him. One of them
is a woman."

In the gathering darkness it was difficult to see the boat, but as
it drew nearer she recognized Paul in the stern. Matt Shore had
stationed himself by the steps of the quai throughout the afternoon; Paul had wanted to remain as inconspicuous as possible, and
had avoided using one of the small craft which waited there to
serve as a ferry. The boat pulled in to the *Dolphin's* side; it carried,
as Charles had said, two passengers beside Paul. The first, a man,

and a stranger to Jane, began to climb the ladder; Paul tried to
steady it as the other climbed. Timidly the woman followed.

It was not Louise de Montignot; Jane knew this as soon as the
woman stepped onto the deck. She was middle-aged, heavy with a
pasty fleshiness; she wore a gray gown with a fraying, dirty fichu
and a soiled cap on her gray hair. She looked weary and afraid, her
brown eyes regarding them suspiciously. Jane had had many different ideas of what Louise de Montignot would look like, but she
knew certainly that this was not she. Charles said nothing.

Paul joined them, and wordlessly motioned them all towards the
companion-ladder leading to the cabin. Jane opened her mouth to
speak to him, but his face was set with an anxious preoccupation
she knew she could not break with a casual word; she let her hand
rest in his for a moment as he helped her on the ladder and he
smiled in response, a smile that briefly warmed her, and let her
share his anxiety. Charles was the last to come down the stairs; he
stood by the open doorway while Jane, Paul, and the two strangers
tried to find space for themselves inside.

Paul gestured towards the pair, who had settled themselves side
by side on the seat under the ports. The man, Jane guessed, was near
sixty, with straggling, scant hair. His eyes looked out of his lined
face with a desperate appeal.

"Monsieur and Madame Duval," Paul said. "I found them in
hiding at Albert Cornand's shop, and they asked me for passage
from France."

"You will be going soon?" the man asked. "It is imperative, Monsieur, that we leave quickly." With a kind of shock Jane realized
that he was speaking English, and in passing she wondered how he
had learned it.

From the doorway Charles spoke. "We will leave Le Havre as
soon as our business here is completed—not before."

"Completed!" The woman spoke, a deep voice that carried the
tones of disgust and bitterness. "If it's the Comtesse you've come
for, then your business is completed. I know a dead woman when
I see one, and she's as good as dead."

Charles said coldly, "But she still lives?"

"She lives, yes. . . ." The woman shrugged. "But for how long?
A few hours, a day at the most!" She nudged her husband, and

nodded towards Paul savagely. "You've paid good money for this passage! You must demand that we leave immediately. I have no use for this waiting about for a dead woman!" She heaved her plump shoulders as she spoke. Beside her husband Jane noticed that she appeared strong and muscular, despite her fatigue; in her fierce way she was protective of him.

The man gestured apologetically to Charles. "Forgive her, monsieur! It is not usually Marie's way to be so—so harsh. But we have had an unfortunate experience trying to help a lady who was sought by the Commune . . . most unfortunate! I had a business in Paris, you understand. I am a violin-maker with a high reputation. . . ."

"Ah!" Marie Duval exclaimed contemptuously. "A sentimental fool, that's what he is! Involving himself with the escape of an old patroness of our firm—one who should have taken her chance of justice before the courts as all good citizens do! But no, he must meddle, and now we are ruined! Lucky to get out with our lives, and what gold we had in the house. We are ruined . . . ruined!"

"Then be thankful you're not dead!" Charles said, dismissing the Duvals, and turning now to Paul. "What news is there? What of Louise?"

"It is as they say," Paul answered. "I have seen her, and she still lives." Then he shook his head. "But as for getting her aboard the *Dolphin* . . ."

"You have spoken with her?" Charles said eagerly. "Have you told her I have come, and soon she will be in England?"

"I told her," Paul said, "and she was glad to know you were here. But when I told her you were coming, and that tonight we would take her aboard the *Dolphin*, she said nothing."

"Nothing?"

"She said only that she would be happy to see you, but nothing else."

Charles brushed his words aside. "It is only her weakness—she must have time to get used to the idea that we have come to take her away." He frowned as Paul began to shake his head. "What is wrong with you? Have you turned into a miserable coward like everyone else—like this pair here?" He indicated the Duvals. "Are you going to desert her when we are so close?"

"I think," Paul said quietly, "that the Countess hasn't the strength to reach the *Dolphin*."

"We will *make* her reach it! It can be done—a carriage or a sedan chair to the quai, and then we will carry her into the boat. Matt Shore must rig up some kind of sling to get her aboard. Damn you, why are you shaking your head? Are you defeated before we have begun?"

"Not defeated! Not yet! But things have been happening in France in the past few days that make even the short trip between Cornand's shop and the quai dangerous for a woman who must be helped every step of the way."

"What has happened?" he demanded impatiently.

"Has Monsieur not heard?" Duval said. "The news came from Paris this morning, and the town is in a fever."

"What are you talking about?"

"Since the affair at the Tuileries last month, when the Swiss Guard was overthrown and the royal family taken to the Temple. . . ."

"You mean when the Swiss Guard was murdered," Charles said tersely.

The man shrugged. "As you wish, Monsieur. Others have a different way of looking at it. Towards the end of August the citizens of Paris saw the funerals of the patriots which *they* claim were murdered by the aristocrats during the same attack on the Tuileries. All through the month the arrests have been countless, and the temper of the people so inflamed it was not safe to open one's mouth unless to denounce a neighbor or a brother to the Revolutionary Tribunal. It was necessary, you understand, to prove that one was a loyal patriot. It was then we fled. . . ."

"Yes—what more?"

"Terrible rumors have been spreading about Paris. . . . The Prussians were at the gates, the National Volunteers had gone to the front and Paris was unprotected. The word went around that the attack on the city was to be the signal for a counter-revolution. The prisons were to be thrown open, and the women and children would be at the mercy of the aristocrats and their paid assassins. I thank God we got away. . . ."

He shuddered, closing his eyes for a second. "Today the news reached here from Paris. An order was issued two days ago—September the second, that would have been—by the Commune that all the prisoners in L'Abbaye and La Force were to be tried immediately . . . it was an order for execution or release. At midday the same day an alarm gun was fired from the Pont-Neuf, and a black flag was flown at Hôtel de Ville. They say already hundreds have died, hacked to pieces by the mob who wait only the few minutes given to the mockery of a trial. It is the same for them all—criminals, priests, prostitutes, royalists. It is release or death! A massacre, monsieur!"

"And it continues?"

"So far as we know, monsieur. The news reached here today, with orders for a special watch to be set for persons attempting to escape, the Seine being one of the best ways to leave Paris. . . ."

"This morning we were nearly caught," Marie Duval said. "We left the house in which we spent the night but a few minutes before it was searched by the National Guard. You know now why we have no wish to wait here like sitting ducks until they decide to search all the vessels in the port. I tell you every citizen has suddenly two pairs of eyes—one for himself, and another for any action or word he thinks suspicious. It is a time when patriotism cannot be taken for granted. It must be proved!"

She looked fiercely at Charles. "And this Comtesse . . . the de Montignot woman . . . her description is circulated to every port and border town in France. If I had guessed she was lodged in Cornand's house I wouldn't have set foot in it! This town is not Paris, I tell you. This is a small place, and everyone knows the other's business. A strange, sick woman will not go long undiscovered, even hidden away in the back room!"

"Keep your tongue still!" Charles said roughly.

Her face reddened. "I'll not be quiet. We have paid good money for this passage, and we demand to leave immediately. There isn't a hope for that woman, and while we stay here the lives of all of us are in danger!"

"There are other foreign vessels in port," Charles said. "You are at perfect liberty to find a passage with any captain who will take you. Or else—" he paused—"or else get down on your knees and pray that Louise de Montignot lives to board this ship."

He turned slowly to Jane. "You have heard all this, and now the task is more difficult than we believed when we left England. Are you still willing to come ashore and help us with Louise?"

Jane nodded. "I'll come!"

Paul got to his feet, his face wearing a look of irritated resignation. "I've always believed that this whole venture was a piece of folly committed without thought. *You*," he said, looking at Charles, "should never have set foot in France while the present madness is on them, and you already know what I think about Jane being here." He gestured briefly. "However, we are here, and every hour we remain increases the danger, so let us go and be done with it."

Duval's delicate hands gripped his knees convulsively. "Monsieur . . . as things are at present, the National Guard is likely to search all ships in the port. I implore you, Monsieur. . . ."

"We will return as speedily as possible," Paul said.

The Duvals sat in grim, unwilling silence as the three left the cabin.

2

Matt Shore and another hand from the *Dolphin* rowed them to the quai. They already had their instructions from Paul; they were to wait by the steps of the quai until the next morning, if necessary, and if they were questioned they were to say the master of the *Dolphin* was ashore negotiating the purchase of a cargo. Nothing was to be said of the passengers who had gone aboard the *Dolphin*.

The evening was mild, and there was still a great deal of activity in the streets, with doors and windows flung open, and the sound of rapid voices everywhere. The stern lights of the ships riding at anchor in the basin made broad gleaming paths across the water; the tide was running high, and the stench from the rotting garbage and debris tossed into the basin was not so strong as it had been through the afternoon. The boat nosed the granite steps of the quai gently, and Paul stepped ashore, turning to give his hand to Jane. She found it was a miserable business trying to scramble from the boat to the slippery steps, hampered by her skirt and petticoats. As soon as Charles was ashore, Matt used his hands to pull

the boat along to a mooring ring on the dock wall; the oars were
shipped, and the two men settled themselves for their watch.

There was the usual number of idlers on the dock, sitting about
on the bales and crates, enjoying the warm evening, chewing tobacco and spitting with relish as they discussed the day's news from
Paris. Charles began to mount the steps first; Jane followed, with
her arm through Paul's; Charles was wearing the oldest coat he
could find among the crew of the *Dolphin*, and a battered, stained
hat. In his hand he held a lantern. Jane's eyes were on him as he
climbed to the level of the quai, and she wished that he would
carry himself with less pride. With his height and his head erect,
even in those deplorable clothes, he was a figure to turn and look
at. It was a mistake, she decided, and one that Paul had spoken
against from the beginning, to allow Charles to come ashore. Already two groups at the top of the steps had fallen silent, their
gazes fixed curiously on Charles. He stood very still, holding the
lantern low to light the steps.

Under his breath Paul muttered a restrained curse. "Why does
he have to look like that—even here?"

Jane was looking beyond Charles as she reached the quai, and
she sensed that what happened was not as accidental as it was made
to appear. A man detached himself from the group nearest Charles,
making some remark in French she could not understand. He
stepped backwards and cannoned into Charles with considerable
force. With an exclamation of annoyance, Charles spun round. Instantly his body went limp, and she saw him sway a little as he
stood. The lantern, she noticed, he held well down at his side.

They exchanged a few words; even in the unfamiliar tongue
Charles' voice was slurred and thickened, the stranger's apologetic.
The man, however, did not step away from Charles; he was shorter
than Charles, and he stared up intently into his face. Then Charles
turned, still swaying, and caught Jane's arm. He leaned on it heavily.
Quickly Paul reached over and took the lantern from his hand. Suddenly Jane felt herself caught roughly in Charles' arms; he tipped
her head back and the hood of her cloak slipped off. Then Charles'
lips were on her mouth, and he was kissing her. She stayed in his
arms obediently, numb with astonishment. She could feel his hands
in her hair, pulling it free of the cloak so that it spread about her

shoulders. He went on kissing her, and from one of the groups there came a little chorus of appreciative whistles and cries.

Charles said softly, his mouth still pressed against hers, "I'm drunk, and so are you! Understand?"

Then he pulled himself away from her a little and looked in the direction of the whistles. He held his arm about her shoulder, and sketched a grotesque, clumsy bow, swaying as he did so. He called something to the men in French, and there were some answering comments, and laughter, and someone shouted, *"Une Anglaise!"* Jane could feel the pressure of Charles' hand on her shoulder forcing her down in a rough curtsey. She smiled as she did it, and knew that Charles was laughing too. A small round of applause greeted her action; standing on tiptoe she managed to place a kiss on Charles' cheek, at the time reaching up to tweak his ear.

All this time the man who had cannoned into Charles stood silent, his eyes moving rapidly over the three of them. Suddenly he put out his hand to detain Charles. Paul stepped in beside Charles and brushed roughly against the stranger.

"Pardon, monsieur," he said amiably. He spoke with an exaggerated English accent. This seemed to amuse the men standing about; there was more laughter. By the time Paul had recovered from his stiff, foolish bow, and replaced his hat, Charles and Jane had already moved down the quai, Charles walking with the absurd erectness of a drunken man.

"Hey! Hey, wait for me!" Paul cried, starting to run after them. He waved his hand with a flourish to the men by the steps. When he joined the others he slipped an arm about Jane's waist. They walked as rapidly as they dared towards the Rue de Paris.

In the Rue de Paris there were more people, and more noise. There was also more light from the taverns and shops, as well as the upper storeys of the close-packed houses. The doors of the brothels were wide open, the half-naked prostitutes soliciting briskly among the seamen and townspeople who passed by. Charles pulled his hat forward on his head, tipping it at an angle so that it partly shadowed his face.

"Who was it?" Jane said in a low voice. She stopped by the doorway of a shop to poke at a great hoop of cheese displayed there.

Charles crumbled the edge of the cheese with his forefinger. "Has he followed us? Is he anywhere near?"

Paul glanced casually back. "I can't see him." He leaned closer to Charles.

"His name is Bouchet," Charles said. "He used to be a steward on Philippe de Montignot's estate. It was he who denounced Philippe and gave evidence against him at the trial. As a reward for his display of patriotism he was given a position serving the Commune. I imagine he's grown fat on bribes during the last year."

"What is he doing here?"

"I can think of only one reason. They must know in Paris that Louise is believed hiding here, and they have sent him to stir up the authorities, and to identify her. It must have been he who saw Pierre Latour, and hoped he would lead them back to Louise. He must have been waiting here in Le Havre hoping that she would be forced to show herself. Maybe he knew that Latour got away on the *Dolphin* and he is having a watch kept on all the quais in case the *Dolphin* should return. He must be certain that Louise did not escape with Latour, or he wouldn't still be in Le Havre."

"But *you* . . ." Jane said. "Did he recognize you?"

"I think he did," Charles answered. "He isn't quite certain—it was dark enough there to make him doubtful, and he's only seen me a very few times some years ago. Either he was confused by what we did there at the quai, and believes we're no more than smugglers taking a lady on an escapade to France, or else he knows that Latour left on the *Dolphin*, has recognized me, and now he waits for us to take him to Louise."

Then he suddenly shouted to the shopkeeper, and demanded that he come and cut some cheese immediately. Charles paid for it, counting the coins with drunken solemnity into the man's hand. Then he broke it in three, and handed a piece each to Jane and Paul. They nibbled it as they continued on down the street.

Paul began to hum softly, unmusically, waving his hand to match the rhythm of the beat; suddenly, to the air of *Greensleeves* Jane heard him sing: "*Cornand's shop is on the corner over there. . . . Cornand's shop . . .*" Jane nudged Charles. "*Cornand's . . . Cornand's . . .*"

They marked it with only the briefest glance; it was a triangular building, commanding a view of two streets, and it didn't seem to lack customers to sit at the tables in its dimly lighted interior. Paul had continued to hum, now he broke into a whistle. Under cover of it, Charles spoke.

"We'll go to a tavern where you're known, Paul," Charles said. "We'll have to find someone you can talk to about buying a cargo."

"I know only a few people in Le Havre," Paul answered. "It isn't one of my regular ports. . . . We could try the Three Brothers in the Rue d'Ingouville. Will Bouchet follow us?"

"Of course he will! That's why you've got to behave exactly as you would if you were here to get a cargo."

"We'll have to separate if we're to get rid of him. He can't follow each of us. The one he follows should go back to the *Dolphin* —that will keep him away from Cornand's."

"Supposing he has other people helping him?" Jane said.

"He hasn't had time to get help yet, and if we keep moving he won't dare let us out of sight. . . . We'll make the Three Brothers first, then move on before he has time to send a note or message to the Guard. . . ."

Les Trois Frères was a dim little shop, heavy with the odors of stale sweat and tobacco. It sold good brandy and was a recognized meeting place for seamen. The proprietor nodded to Paul with a half-familiar gesture, and came to serve them immediately. As he placed the glasses before them, Bouchet entered. He did it quite openly, without trying to efface himself. Charles had carefully seated himself with his back to the door. Paul spoke to the proprietor, using slow precise English, loud enough for Bouchet to hear.

"Have you seen Monsieur Bordillet this evening?"

"*Monsieur Bordillet? Ce soir? Non, Monsieur.*" He shook his head.

"Damn!" Paul said. "Swallow your drink, and let's move on. He'll be about somewhere." The shopkeeper shrugged uncomprehendingly, and pocketed the coin Paul gave him. Paul helped Jane to her feet; Charles caught her arm as before, and they walked out to the street. Behind they could hear the scrape of the chair as Bouchet stood up.

At four other taverns they did the same thing. At each Bouchet either entered boldly, or stayed within sight of the door. At the fifth one a large, moustached man suddenly rose as they entered, calling cheerfully to Paul.

"Oh—my friend! They tell me you've been inquiring for me!"

"Every blasted place in the town," Paul said. "Drinking too much of your bad French brandy."

"My friend, you cannot insult our brandy—they pay too much for it back in England. . . ."

He seated himself at their table, and called for brandy. Jane didn't even attempt to drink it when it came; she merely smiled in acknowledgment when Bordillet raised his glass to her. Suddenly she felt Charles' arm round her shoulder again; he spoke softly in her ear.

"Can't you do better than that? You're supposed to be gay!"

Obediently she reached for the glass, forcing it to her lips, turning to toast Charles smilingly. The brandy was like fire to her throat and her protesting stomach. It was a long time since the scrappy meal one of the hands had thrown together on the *Dolphin*, even a long time since that bit of cheese they had eaten in the Rue de Paris. She wondered how many more taverns there would be, and how many more glasses of brandy. The room was growing hazy before her eyes; in a little while she would be too stupid to be of any help to Charles. She looked appealingly towards Paul, but he didn't see her. He was engrossed in a drawn-out haggle with Bordillet over the price he would pay for tobacco. Their voices became loud and aggressive. This was one cargo Paul would never take aboard, but certainly Bordillet could not have guessed it, nor did she think could Bouchet, seated two tables away. She half-turned her head, and took a long look at Bouchet's intelligent, bitter face; he returned her stare unblinkingly. She hated the mocking falseness of this chase where pursuer and pursued remained only a few feet apart.

She leaned towards Charles, smiling at him for the benefit of Bouchet.

"How long do we go on this way?" she whispered. "We're no nearer to Louise!" Her hand tightened on his arm. "Why does he just follow you? Why doesn't he arrest you and be done with it?"

"This phase of our play is coming to an end now," he said. "It is important that Bouchet believe you and Paul are genuine, even if he suspects me. Now he has seen you here with Bordillet, I think he won't trouble you."

"But *you* . . ."

"He may not be sure that I'm the same person he knew as Charles Blake, who was a friend of Philippe de Montignot, though I'm sure he knows that Charles Blake was imprisoned and escaped. Prison changes a man's appearance, and it's some years since he's seen me."

"But he follows you, just the same."

"What else can he do? He has no other clue. When Latour escaped from Le Havre, Bouchet lost the trail to Louise, and now he is sticking with me because he hopes that I'll lead him to her."

"Why doesn't he have you arrested on suspicion?"

"What good would it do him? Even to prove that I was Charles Blake? He knows I wouldn't tell him where Louise is—and to the Commune, and for Bouchet's own future, she is a much more important capture than I. Besides, with luck, he might get us both!"

"So . . . what do we do?"

He drained his glass and set it down firmly. "I will leave here, and Bouchet will follow me. When you see that he is gone, take Paul and go to Cornand's shop. If necessary, you must take Louise to the *Dolphin* without my help."

"She will find more strength for the journey if you are there," Jane said slowly.

He nodded. "I know that, but if I can't shake off Bouchet, you and Paul must manage it alone."

"How long are we to wait?"

"No longer than an hour. The streets are quieter and it grows more dangerous." He dropped his hand onto hers, lying on the table. "At all costs you must get her to the *Dolphin*—and Paul is to sail as soon as he can make ready."

"To *sail!* But what about you?"

"Don't wait for me."

He pushed back his stool and prepared to stand up. "Don't wait for me, do you understand? If the *Dolphin* sails without me, I'll make my own way back to England."

"And if you don't? . . ."

"If I don't get back to England, Jane, then I know *you* will welcome Louise to Blake's Reach in my place, and care for her."

He stood up then and began to make amiable, careless farewells to Paul, calling the tavern-keeper to refill Bordillet's empty glass. Jane watched his stumbling exit, and watched Bouchet also rise and follow him to the door. She was startled to discover that it was not the brandy, but tears, that blurred her last sight of him.

CHAPTER FIVE

THE STREETS WERE EMPTYING, AS CHARLES HAD SAID, AND THEIR footsteps were too noisy on the cobbles. Jane had never before known the kind of fear that gripped her now—not even those moments when the Dragoons had entered Barham had been like these. This was a fear of something unknown, a betrayal, a false word, a moment of time lost, and the hope of safety with it. She held her cloak tightly to her body, and paced her steps to Paul's quick ones. The dark streets were no longer friendly.

Albert Cornand's shop in the Rue de Paris was locked and shuttered; it had a sad, deserted look—gray plaster peeling off the walls, and no lights visible anywhere. Paul's knock seemed thunderously loud, echoing in the canyon of those overhanging houses. To Jane it seemed as if everyone in the street must hear that knock, and come to stare at them, and to question.

"*Qui est la?*" The urgent whisper on the other side of the door startled her.

"Fletcher—Captain of the *Dolphin!*"

The bolts were pulled back softly, and the door swung open just enough to admit them.

"Quickly!" Then the door closed behind them, and they were in total darkness.

"For Heaven's sake bring a light!" Paul said. "What's the matter with you?"

"Pardon, Monsieur, but I did not want anyone who might be watching to see who it was came in."

"Is someone watching?"

"I don't know, Monsieur, but one can't be too careful." As he spoke a door at the other side of the room opened, and a woman stood there holding a candle. Jane glanced about her quickly, and recognized the room she had seen from the street earlier in the evening, the room that had been packed with Cornand's patrons. There was the smell of wine characteristic of each place they had visited while searching for Bordillet, but here there was also the smell of bread and sweet pastries.

The woman was tall, and had a frail appearance; it was hard to imagine her living with the sweet pastries and the wine.

"Monsieur Fletcher! Thank God you have come!" Her voice was a soft whisper as she moved towards them.

"What is wrong, Madame?"

"The Comtesse, she is going to die! We thought that you would not come back. . . ."

"How do you know she is going to die?"

"Ah, Monsieur! . . ." The light of the candle fell on Albert Cornand's worn face; he had the pallor of someone who spends his life indoors, but his body was stocky and well built. "She is worse!" he said, shaking his head. "I fear it is but a few hours now."

Madame Cornand spoke quietly. "What are we to do, Monsieur? She must leave here, or she will die on our hands—and how are we to explain the body of a dead woman? Before God we have been loyal, Monsieur, but this is asking too much!"

"Dying . . ." Paul looked at Jane. "All of this—and she will die, after all."

"Yes, Monsieur, she will die—and very likely we will die also for harboring an enemy of the People. It is cruel. . . ." Jane had the feeling that Madame Cornand had been brave for a long time, and now, at last, the control was beginning to slip.

"Courage, Cecile!" her husband whispered. "We are not taken yet, and perhaps Monsieur will devise some—" He broke off. They had all heard the quick footsteps in the street outside, and had paid no attention except to lower their voices still further. Now the footsteps had stopped outside. Someone rapped lightly on the door.

"*Qui est la?*"

"*Un ami—un ami de* Paul Fletcher!"

"It's Charles!" Paul said. "Quickly, open the door! Get him inside before he's seen!"

Charles slipped inside like a shadow. He was panting, and drops
of sweat stood out on his forehead. He leaned back against the
door.

"I got away from him! He followed me to the quai, so I went
into a wine-shop and had some brandy. Then I went into the
brothel next door. He didn't follow me there—he waited outside.
As long as you have enough gold they don't ask questions in those
places, and they helped me through a skylight, and showed me a
passage into the next street. I told them it was my brother-in-law.
They were most sympathetic."

He stood upright then, taking a deep breath. "Forgive me—I
stand here talking, while there's so much to be done." He looked
at Cecile Cornand. "Madame, is she up there?" he said, nodding
towards the stairs.

"A moment, Charles!" Paul said. "It's more serious than we
thought. The Countess is dying—Cornand says only a few hours
now."

Jane watched his face as he listened; instead of shock or grief
there seemed to be anger there. He was angry with Paul for speaking the words.

"I don't believe it!" he said. "I don't believe it! She can't die
now that she is so close to freedom! Louise has more courage than
that!"

"It isn't a question of courage, Monsieur," Cecile Cornand said
gently. "I think the Comtesse thought of herself as dead when she
knew Pierre Latour would not return. She is worn out—there is
nothing she can do for herself."

Charles scowled. "I don't believe this talk," he said. "Let me
see her." He motioned Madame Cornand towards the stairs. She
moved to go ahead of him with the candle, but on the bottom step
she paused, and turned back.

"Monsieur, you understand the position? If the Comtesse dies
here, Albert and I, we are lost! There is no way we can take her
body from here. . . ."

He cut her short. "She will leave here alive, and you will not be
troubled, Madame! Now—please take me to her!"

Jane climbed the stairs behind him, her eyes fixed on his erect shoulders and back. He was a strong man, and a courageous one, and she wondered if he had, perhaps, the strength to will Louise to live, if he could breathe into her his own spirit of defiance. He was so stubborn in his belief, and single-minded in his determination to get her to freedom that, for the moment, no other life but hers was of any importance. Paul and herself, Albert and Cecile Cornand, the Duvals waiting on the *Dolphin*, they were all helpless before him, like puppets doing what he bid them, bending before his formidable purpose. Perhaps Charles knew that with Louise it would be the same, and from him she would gather the strength to go with them. Whatever happened, they were all in Charles' hands, compelled to do as he instructed them.

Jane looked at the face of the woman in the bed, and she wondered how she could ever have feared her. Louise de Montignot could have been any age; her face was not wrinkled, but it was drawn and haggard, so that she appeared, at first, to be an old woman. Her hair, which might have been blond once, was almost white. But there were traces of beauty in the features—delicately fashioned chin and brows; her eyes were light blue. She wore a plain, coarse bed-gown; the clumsy material stood away from her thin bones. Her hands were blue-veined and transparent.

She had spoken to Charles briefly when he entered. Now she closed her eyes, and seemed to rest for a time, with long intervals between drawing each breath, as if she were trying to save her strength to speak again. Her eyelids flickered open heavily; she moved her hand in a slight gesture that motioned Jane closer to her bedside.

"Monsieur Fletcher told me you had come from England to be with me," she said slowly. "It is most generous—I am grateful. But you must go now, while there is yet time." Her hand touched Jane's briefly, then it fell back onto the bedcover. She closed her eyes again, and the difficult, slow rhythm of her breathing was resumed.

"Charles!" Paul called softly from the shadows over by the window. "Come here!"

Charles rose stiffly from his seat by Louise. Jane caught a glimpse of his face, rigid and sober, his lips folded in a tight line. Albert and Cecile Cornand stood by the open door, and as Paul spoke there was a slight movement from them, a stirring of alarm. Albert took a step further into the room, as if he meant to join them. But then he paused, shaking his head.

Cecile Cornand had hung blankets before the two windows to make sure none of the damp night air would reach Louise. While Charles had sat by the bedside, Paul had moved between the two windows, each on a different side of the triangular-shaped room, and parted the blankets cautiously, just enough to give him a view of the streets below. Now he stepped back and gave place to Charles.

"Down there!" he said.

Charles stood by the window, looking down into the Rue de Paris. The seconds slipped away, and an unspeakable suspense gripped the people in the room. It even communicated itself to Louise, through the isolation of her weakness. Her eyelids moved.

"What is it?" she whispered to Jane.

Jane touched her hand reassuringly. "Nothing—nothing at all." Louise didn't seem to hear her.

Charles stirred, and dropped the blanket back into place.

"It's he. . . ." he said wearily. "It's Bouchet—he has more cunning and more tenacity than I gave him credit for."

From Louise there was suddenly a sharp cry, a much louder and stronger tone than she had used before.

"Who is it? Have you been followed?"

Charles spun round. "Keep her quiet!" The words rang out harshly, cruelly.

Then, as he realized that it was Louise who had spoken, his face underwent a swift change. It had the stricken, contrite look of one who has sinned unforgivably. For the first time Jane saw self-accusation and dismay in Charles' face. He strode across the room to Louise's side, bending low over the bed. His hand groped wildly for hers; but his voice was very firm and strong when he spoke.

"Louise, I love you! I have always loved you!"

"I know."

The listeners barely heard her. The words were a whisper, a sigh. Charles straightened, and laid her hand gently back on the bed-cover. Then he motioned them all to follow him from the room;

they went without question, feeling that they ought never to have been there; and yet they knew that Charles didn't care that his words had belonged to them all. Nothing mattered to him but that Louise should hear them.

They grouped together on the landing at the head of the stairs. Charles closed the door softly, and then turned to meet their questioning gaze. He looked firmly at each face in turn, not shrinking from what he saw there.

"I am sorry," he said. "I regret I've brought this trouble on all of you. The man out there in the street is Bouchet, an agent of the Paris Commune."

Madame Cornand covered her face quickly, in a gesture of distress.

He went on. "I believed I had shaken him off. I came here only because I thought my presence would give the Comtesse better heart and strength for the journey."

He shrugged, but not casually, as was his custom; it was a gesture eloquent of the inevitability of fate, and his acceptance of it.

They had the feeling that he spoke the words because he had to, because it was owing to them that he should speak. But his thoughts and needs were back behind the closed door.

Slowly Madame Cornand's hand came down from her face. "Monsieur, we cannot blame you for mistakes made from compassion. But—" she tried to hold her voice steady—"but what are we to do?"

"Bouchet has only one concern," Charles said. "He has been sent to find Louise, and because he recognized me, he *has* found her. He has never heard the name Cornand, and the Commune expects no arrests of such people. Neither will he risk his quarry to follow you, Jane—or Paul. So long as this house is watched only by Bouchet, you are able to go. If you go immediately, Bouchet can do nothing. He is helpless. He has followed me here, and here he will stay until the National Guard can be called out to take the house, and whoever they should find inside it. When they come they must find only Louise and myself. She will not live to be moved from that room, and for myself . . . I may not leave her."

CHAPTER SIX

IT WAS ALL FINISHED; BY NOW LOUISE WAS DEAD, AND CHARLES taken.

All day, while the *Dolphin* beat her way against perverse winds towards the English coast, they had lived with the knowledge that this must happen. But while the day had been young, with the sun hot and strong on the white sails and reflected blindingly off the surface of the water, they had not quite believed it. They had heard Charles' words, and knew that he was committing himself to his own death, but they had clung to some light hope of his escape. They didn't speak of this to each other—none but the most necessary words passed between them—but they had kept the thought stubbornly. Then, as the shadows of the masts and the bulwarks grew long on the deck, and the white chalk cliffs came into view, they began to admit secretly the foolishness of this hope. There was no possible escape for Charles and he, better than anyone, had known it.

As if drawn by a common thought they had come together in one place at the bulwark, watching the coastline as the *Dolphin* slowly inched her way to Folkestone. Paul had taken on no cargo in Le Havre, and for once the *Dolphin* had no need to fear a revenue cruiser coming into sight. The sun lay gently and pleasantly on the low hills of Kent; to the watchers on board the *Dolphin* the land looked safe and peaceful.

Suddenly Albert Cornand spoke: "It will be all over by now— yes, by now it is all finished, and he is perhaps even on his way to Paris."

"He was a brave man," his wife said gently.

"He was a rash fool," Marie Duval commented.

Auguste Duval sighed. "He was a man in love." His tone was low, but for the first time since he had come aboard the *Dolphin* it seemed that he was prepared to hold to something on his own conviction.

"Never will I forget it," Cecile Cornand said. "I hope I never again have to live through minutes as long as those when we were getting to the quai. That man, Bouchet, staring at us . . . and not knowing if he'd let us go, or if there'd be a guard on the quai when we got there." Her voice trembled. All day she had been waiting to say these things, and she couldn't hold them any longer.

Marie Duval looked at her hostilely. "How do you think we felt? Trapped like rats on this ship, and waiting every second to hear the Guard come on board searching. And not knowing what had happened to those three . . . going off like that and leaving us . . . I tell you, Madame, *they* were long hours."

"Not so long as the time he spent waiting for them to come," Cornand said. "Though, for him and the Comtesse I suppose it was not slow. Strange to think of them alone there in our shop, Cecile. I wonder if she died before the Guard came. I hope so. . . . It must have been a very bad time for him. . . ."

Jane turned suddenly and faced them.

"Can't you stop talking about it?" she demanded fiercely. "He made his own choice . . . and if he wanted to be with the woman he loved, then he had what he wanted. There was no 'bad time' for Charles. There would only have been a bad time for him if she had died alone, before she knew that he had come for her. Don't you see—as long as she knew that, he didn't care!"

"It's well for the rich, who can afford to be romantic," Madame Duval said. "For us it is different . . . we are still alive, and have to go on living. And what with? And how? Everything we had is gone, Mademoiselle! We are ruined . . . ruined!"

"I've heard you say that before," Jane answered, "and I don't believe it. You have your lives, and you have a future. England is a strange country to you, but to make a living and to have a future is not any more difficult there than in Paris. People are much the same wherever you go—as greedy or as kind. There's love and there's hate. There are people who'll help you, and those who won't."

She nodded to Auguste Duval. "You take your talent with you, Monsieur, and your wife has shrewdness enough for six people."

Marie Duval shrugged. "You talk easily, Mademoiselle!"

Jane was not listening to her. Her gaze had shifted to the

Cornands, still leaning against the bulwark gazing at the land where they would be alone and without resources. What was there to say to them? she wondered. They had no talents, and no gold. They were ordinary people with only the virtue of the courage that had kept them loyal to the dead Royalist cause; now their courage would have to see them through loneliness and perhaps poverty. They might later decide it had been too high a price to pay. There was nothing to say to them, she decided—nothing they didn't already know, and they would not thank her for platitudes. They had each other, and they knew that also. Each counted on the courage and loyalty of the other. There was no need either to point out that to them. So there was nothing to say; they knew well enough what was ahead of them.

She slipped away from the group and moved aft, where Paul was taking his turn at the wheel.

She had spent no time alone with him since they had left Le Havre. She knew that he had been on deck most of the night, and this morning had flung himself into the hammock Albert Cornand had vacated to snatch a few hours of sleep. All through the day he had been preoccupied, as if he hardly knew she was there. But now he smiled at her, and his eyes came to life.

"A few hours and we'll berth in Folkestone, Jane. It seems wrong to be heading back this way in broad daylight, without a cargo and without a worry about a revenue cruiser."

She leaned back against the bulwark, slightly behind him. He had to look back over his shoulder to see her.

"That's not what you're really thinking, Paul."

"No," he admitted. "I'm thinking of him—and so are you."

"Yes . . ." she said. "I'm thinking of him."

Charles would stay with them all of their lives. They would never be able to forget Charles, not they, or the Cornands, or the Duvals. For her and Paul he was someone they would remember, not at intervals, with faint surprise that he had gone so long unthought of, but he would be with them constantly. Jane knew that he had had many things to teach her, and that she would not be finished realizing and learning them for a long time. She wondered if he had ever known or cared how much she would learn from him.

For one thing, she had learned that the tradition and pride of a family like the Blakes did not lie in such things as building and endowing a church, or presenting it with a rose window, but in loving, and giving one's life in proof of love. She would remember Charles as a self-centered man, proud and cold, indifferent to the feelings of those about him, and sacrificing everything, even to his life, for Louise. He had given his life carelessly to serve his own sense of honor, and it was in such gestures that the greatness of a family, as well as an individual, lay. Perhaps he had tried to tell her this when he had clothed Blake's Reach with the trappings of position and importance, when he had hung silk curtains and bidden his neighbors to eat with him in the chill splendor of the dining room. He had shown her a cold house, without love.

Now she looked at Paul, looked at his profile against the sky, the short blond ends of hair blowing in the wind. His strong hands were at ease on the wheel, and his feet planted on a familiar deck. Here was a man in his own element, a man she loved. And Charles had warned her not to lose him.

Suddenly she knew that it did not matter now that she owned the deck he stood on, that she owned the *Dolphin*, she owned the Pearl, and she owned Blake's Reach. She could not fully possess these things without the wisdom to use them in the right way, and the right way was not in fashioning them into a chain to bind Paul. He would always have more energy than discretion, more will to make money than skill in keeping it. But he had a dream, a vision, and his eyes were happily blinded by it. He wanted no fetters, and no burden of convention or tradition. She did not know if his dream of a kingdom to be won in the West Indies was something he would always keep, merely to carry before him as an eternal, unrealized hope, or whether he would attempt to turn it into a reality. Whatever he chose—to stay on the Marsh where he had been born, and to live out his life with her at Blake's Reach, or to seek the source of the dream in the West Indies—she would be with him. She had glimpsed the dream and the vision in Charles when he had elected to stay with Louise; it was this same shining thing she could never permit herself to destroy in Paul. If Blake's Reach had to be sacrificed to it, then it would be, and she would hold her peace.

And now she had to try to tell him this.

She called softly, "Paul . . ."

He looked back at her, wearing the slight, familiar smile that warmed her.

EPILOGUE

IN THE GRASS-GROWN GRAVEYARD OF ST. SAVIOUR'S-BY-THE-MARSH are the headstones that mark the graves of Jane and Paul Fletcher; the tall gray slabs, weathering in the rains that sweep across the Marsh from the Channel, record no more than the bare facts of their names and dates. Beside them are the graves of those of their children who, being born on the Marsh, chose to live out their lives there. In the church itself a plain tablet, not a rose window, records the name of Charles Blake.

For Charles there is no marked grave. His headless body lies in quick-lime, along with the others who perished during the Terror, in the cemetery of the Madeleine in Paris.

Nor is William's grave marked. He was lost when the *Raven*, largest vessel of the merchant fleet he had gathered together for trade between London and the West Indies, was wrecked off the island of Jamaica.